PAMELA HILL

Fire Opal

St. Martin's Press • New York

Library of Congress Cataloging in Publication Data

Hill, Pamela.
  Fire opal.

  I. Title.
PZ4.H648Fi   1980   [PR6058.I446]   823'.914   79-28424
ISBN 0-312-29111-6

Author's Note

I should particularly like to thank Commander Denis Conlan, R.N.. the authorities of Fort St. Elmo and of the National Library, Valetta; and Mr. Roger di Giorgio for making known to me certain evidence of the Great Siege which is seldom shown to the ordinary visitor.

P.H.

One

"Mr. Bainbridge is expecting you, Mr. Muntz."

The young man in the mourning-cravat, who carried a thick folder under his arm, noted several things in connection with this statement. The first was that, as he had assumed, he had not been kept waiting in the downstairs office where the clerks' heads, bent over their ledgers, had not raised themselves as he passed (soon, as he hoped, matters would be different); the second was that the speaker, as a Highlander, had almost said "iss expecting" with an intonation that in many ways resembled German, his own tongue. The third was that the stairs up which the usher led him were, like everything else in the building, swept and meticulously clean; and, lastly, this, he already knew, had been a house once. Its ceilings still had their mouldings and the gas-brackets jutted from the walls in places that had no relation to the men who came and went.

But all conclusions paled before the significance of meeting the Old Man, Timothy Bainbridge, himself. Even in Germany he had been spoken of as that; his fame as a shipbuilder, as an inventor and modifier of engines worked by steam, was international. His office looked over the river with its clustered cranes and huge half-completed hulls. The sounds of the shipyard came clearly, riveting and hammering and the murmur of men's voices. He was filled with a sense of excitement, of certainty that this interview would be a success.

"Mr. Bainbridge, it is Mr. Muntz." They did not say "sir" here on Clydeside.

From behind a huge mahogany desk, across a patterned expanse of red Turkey carpet, the legendary figure rose to its feet. Timothy Bainbridge was tall and lanky as a youth despite his seventy-three years; he wore a high cravat beneath his white side-whiskers, and above them was a long-lipped face. The blue

eyes—their colour had hardly faded with age—surveyed Anton
Muntz keenly. Then, gravely, the Old Man held out his hand.

"So you are Karl Muntz's son. I received his letter."

He bade the young man sit down, and Anton did so, feeling
the firmly upholstered horsehair support his thighs. The letter
referred to had been dictated by his father from the latter's
sick-bed. It conveyed the information that his only son Anton
had taken first-class degrees in chemistry and engineering and
had already perfected a secret alloy. Anton reflected on the
alloy, knowing that news of it accounted for his civil reception;
otherwise, he would have been only one more applicant jostling
for a place at Bainbridge's. He sat immobile, somewhat stiff, the
faint dusty sunlight shining on his black clothes. His hair was
dark brown, slightly curling about a high forehead. Otherwise
his features were not notable except for the eyes. His figure was
stocky and not very tall. His gaze met old Bainbridge's steadily.

"I was sorry to learn of your father's death," said Bainbridge
sincerely. "He and I, as you will know, worked together here in
the yards thirty years back. In those days I lived in this house,
and Karl married your mother from it." That, Timothy
Bainbridge was thinking, was where this young German got the
eyes; Highland grey like rain on slate, fringed with black lashes.
The mother had been a parlourmaid here, fresh from Glenur-
quhart. She had been a head taller than her German bridegroom. The young man took after his father physically. If he
were as dedicated, as efficient, as Karl Muntz, leaving aside the
matter of the alloy with its incredibly low coefficient of
expansion—

"Show me your drawings," he commanded. He lowered his
head as Anton Muntz rose; his fingers sought and turned the
brass inkstand on his desk. If his own heir, Julius, had proved
worthy of anything, there would have been no need to consider
this young foreigner or any but his, Timothy's, own son, with
Bainbridge blood running doubly in him. But why dwell on
disillusionment, when there might be a second chance?

The folder lay open on his desk. Young Muntz began to talk,
to ask and answer questions, while Timothy thumbed through
the carefully scaled plans with their slender greyhounds of
outlined hulls. For half an hour they talked, argued respectfully,
queried one another, pondered the replies. They talked, without
impertinence on the younger man's side, as equals. Anton

Muntz knew his worth. But there was one matter on which he was secretive; the alloy. He would reveal nothing of that, nothing, without a distinct promise to be taken into the firm, not yet as a director but with prospects. He could be of use in the Bainbridge yard; he was almost as strong as the Old Man who in his youth, they said, had been able to bend a bar of pig-iron. He glanced out of the window at the cranes tall and lacelike against the sky, and beyond the river; and clustering round, on either bank, his mother's city, adopted when she had left her home. Many Highlanders had had to come south to Glasgow to find work when the sheep took over the glens. He remembered her tales of the Highlands, and of here; she had died of cancer when Anton was fourteen. Through his boyhood she had seen to it that he knew English as well as German. The Gaelic she had kept to herself. She had been a woman of great character. His father had not married again. The two of them, man and boy, had been everything to one another after her death. Now, with Karl dead also, there was no reason for remaining in Germany when he could do better here. Since the Atlantic steam venture this was the most famous shipyard in the world, with even the Admiralty coming here for contracts from London. He did not expect to have to return to Hamburg.

As he resumed his seat he caught sight of a portrait on the wall, an enlarged daguerreotype of perhaps twenty years back. It showed the fine head and broad shoulders of a man with a great spade beard and brilliant eyes, staring out at the onlooker, the camera, the world. Anton knew who the man must be; David Bainbridge, his cousin's partner, whose fiery genius had blazed at the beginning of the firm's rise to power and who, after an invention of his had caused a boiler-room explosion and the deaths of many men, had taken his own life before he was fifty. Anton Muntz did not comment on the portrait. He bent his head deferentially to listen to the Old Man. Evidently Timothy liked the drawings. He began to sound Anton couthily, carefully. Both men knew the game they played. While fencing with his wits, Anton permitted certain thoughts to drift through the back of his mind, not paying full heed to them. David and Timothy Bainbridge had been close; Timothy had married David's sister, then David's only daughter had married the pair's son after ... had there not been some kind of scandal, an elopement? Anton shrugged mentally; such things did not concern him. He was pleased with his presentation of his work, and himself, to Timothy Bainbridge. The interview had taken place precisely as intended, and the offer ...

Timothy did not make it yet. He felt his mind like a bolt fitting exactly into the younger man's; precisely as couplings correctly aligned could convey power with the levering of a switch. But one must not put too many cards on the table ... yet.

"You must meet my family," he heard himself saying. "My wife and I live quietly nowadays down-river, but my son and his wife are in town." It must be a quiet occasion, as Anton was newly in mourning; but perhaps an informal supper, with a little music afterwards? "All of your nation love music, I know. My granddaughter plays the pianoforte well."

Anton Muntz had no objection to such a meeting. He inclined his head, smiling and murmuring thanks. One must lose no opportunity; and, besides, he would be glad enough of friends in this strange land.

Two

Agnes Bainbridge raised her large white hand to reach for the bell which would summon the maid to be instructed to bring in the tea-things. The carriage clock on the mantelpiece, with its revolving globes of brass, had just struck a quarter to the hour; that meant Julius would be on his way downstairs. A shade of apprehension crossed his wife's statuesque features for moments, and it almost seemed as if she would smooth her elaborate gown and her prematurely white, thick hair, neither of which needed attention. She looked as she always did, the gracious, handsome presiding effigy at Julius Bainbridge's tea-table. It was the most intimate occasion of the day, this lush and correct ceremony involving embossed silver, hot scones and tea-cakes in covered dishes, and the top of the milk in its Georgian jug. Yet for some reason, just as she should have come into her own, Agnes was nervous and apologetic. It was perhaps a measure of the apology she still felt, had incessantly been made to feel, for having jilted Julius in a time long ago to run off with an artist. To think of it now was incredible, and Agnes seldom did. She was, when all was said, Julius' wife now; having been graciously taken back after poor Edward died of pneumonia and Fiona's birth, like everything else about her, had been difficult. But the Bainbridges had received her into the fold again; after all, she was David Bainbridge's only daughter, still fit to breed Bainbridge heirs. At a decent interval after Fiona's birth she had been married to Julius, who had fathered upon her not a son, alas, but another daughter, now seated placidly embroidering within a frame. Juliana Bainbridge's honey-coloured hair shone from the daily application of a hundred brush-strokes and polishing with silk. Otherwise she was not handsome. To have failed Julius a second time had been almost worse than the first.

Agnes spoke, to down the crowding memories. "Dearest," she

said to Juliana, "I think you should put aside your fancywork; it is almost time for Papa to come in for his tea." Her tones were level, her accent that of the expensive school for young ladies at which her father, advised by Uncle Timothy and Aunt Isabella, had had her educated for Julius, ready to become his hostess and the mother of his sons, keeping Bainbridge blood, Bainbridge genius and the money it brought, within the family.

Juliana's soft lips smiled a little as she obediently secured her needle in its canvas. Dearest Mama said the same thing every day. In ways, it was agreeable that life was so orderly, so uneventful. Juliana had a peaceable nature and would have disliked storms and uncertainties such as were always happening about the person of poor Fiona, kept as a rule upstairs. To know that Papa would come in at four o'clock was pleasant; he was fond of her. But could one be blamed for wishing, at times, that things might vary themselves just a little? If one made a joke, for instance, Mama would not understand it; she would turn her heavy-lidded gaze on one mildly, exactly like—to be indelicate—a Jersey cow, and say "Yes, dearest," or "Very likely," without the least notion of what it was all about. Juliana nursed her sense of fun to herself, accordingly, for she knew that she was neither clever nor beautiful. Her skin was good, if a trifle pale; and provided she put ear-pads under her hair when it was dressed, it looked quite thick. But her figure needed padding also; it was too slender, almost childish, ridiculously so when one reflected that she was by now twenty years of age. Most of her schoolmates were married by this time, some rearing families; but Papa and Grandfather had discouraged any young men who might have looked in Juliana's direction; they were, she was told, after her fortune. It was pleasant to have a fortune, no doubt; but must she be an old maid because of it? The young minister who had been sent packing only last year had certainly had a mind above such things as money. No doubt Papa and Grandfather knew best; and it was so seldom they agreed with one another about anything that one must feel thankful when they did.

Precisely as the clock chimed the hour, Julius Bainbridge came into the drawing-room, pecked his wife drily on the cheek, and said to Juliana, as he always did, "A good afternoon to you, my dear."

"Good afternoon, Papa." Her mouth set once again in its firm, sweet line. Juliana had never been given the opportunity to show that she could be stubborn. Julius allowed his considering hazel eyes to dwell on her approvingly; the news he had received from his father today about the coming visit from the young German engineer was good. Julius' pallid fondness for his daughter was the only affection he now felt; since the day Agnes—his marble-cold, predictable, long-bespoken Agnes—ran off with the drawing-master, uncertainty had overtaken them both; he himself never missed the chance of some petty meanness, to punish Agnes still. She had long ceased to show any response, to that or to anything.

Julius permitted himself a flicker of interest as he noted the contents of the tea-table, while Agnes undertook her dignified pouring from the silver pot. His boyhood's wish—it did not accord with his cold nature to call it a passion—was to have been a surgeon. The positioning of nerves and arteries, their possible mending, would have sufficed instead of the steam and metal his father knew as gods. It had not been permitted to Julius to depart from the fold; how could a son of Timothy Bainbridge be anything but a shipbuilder? And so, outwardly unprotesting but loathing it, Julius had suffered himself to be put to work in the yards. Since that day he had had little human feeling; he did well enough, though not brilliantly, in the career chosen for him. His father's and his cousin David's passion for the great hulls and their engines had passed him by. He had compensations; he was an elder of the church, subscribed to a club, drank sparingly, and did not run after women. The men at the yard disliked him, a fact of which he was not aware. He was mean with money, and could inspire fear. Agnes watched him like a rabbit fascinated by a snake; his archaic pronunciation of certain words was never laughed at. Perhaps the reciprocal coldness, the fear between them had prevented the conception of a son.

Tea over, Agnes rang for the maid to clear away. Juliana said submissively "Papa, may I go upstairs now?" It was at this time of day that she liked to visit her half-sister, and admire the latter's drawings. Fiona was deaf and dumb and the drawings—

she must have inherited the talent from her father—made up most of her life.

Julius inclined his head and, as if it were an unusual happening, replied "If your mother permits it," and Agnes signified that she did so. The existence of Fiona was tolerated in Julius' house, but seldom spoken of. It was assumed to be sufficient cause for gratitude that Julius provided the outcast girl with a roof over her head, clothes, food to be eaten upstairs, and a companion. Agnes herself knew relief that because Fiona could not be taught table-manners she was obliged to remain mostly in her room. The one regrettable lapse in her own life was over; she never spoke of it and hardly ever thought of it, so that with the passing of the years it could almost seem that it had not happened. But in Fiona's presence, one was reminded that it had. Fortunately dear Juliana had an affection for her half-sister.

She did not watch Juliana as the latter went out, but waited for Julius to speak, perhaps to tell her some news of the yards which, as a female, she could of course not fully understand. But today it was different.

He spoke. "The father—" he always referred to Timothy so—"sent for me today and said that a young German is to join us. It will be proper, I think, if you were to invite him to, perhaps, a little supper. He has recently lost his father; it need not be elaborate." That was all Agnes need know; the fact that Anton's mother had been the parlourmaid was not spoken of. Agnes bowed her head. "Certainly," she said quietly. The little supper would take place. No one asked where Anton Muntz was staying; the father would know, as he knew everything.

Juliana had run upstairs as soon as she was out of her parents' sight, and arrived breathless at a white-painted door. She knocked as she always did, and a thin middle-aged woman in a plain gown and pince-nez opened it, her knitting still in her hand. Beyond, at the window, a red-haired girl sat painting, her slim shoulders hunched over the work. She did not turn her head.

Juliana moved gently to behind the wooden chair, allowing her own presence to be made known gradually. Presently Fiona Tilney flung down the brush and swivelled herself about, so that the eyes of the half-sisters met. Fiona's were arresting, oblique, and green as a cat's. Her face had high cheekbones and no colour, for she was kept mostly indoors; her skin was thick and creamy, her figure voluptuous, with full breasts that strained at her ugly grey gown. Her hands, stained with paint, were long and slender, alien in this setting; they should have been ringed with jewels in a Renaissance painting. She stared up at Juliana without smiling or showing pleasure. The younger girl—there were two years between them—looked down at the work the other had done. It resembled nothing she could understand, being a mere jumble of colour with, here and there, a line scratched in pencil. Juliana smiled, and turned to the woman in pince-nez, who had remained standing near the door.

"What is she painting today, Timpy? You know and I don't."

"I do not know either, Miss Juliana." Miss Mary Timpson had been the sisters' governess in childhood, though it had been impossible to teach Fiona anything except to keep quiet. After Juliana went to her school the woman had been kept on to have an eye to Fiona, as she was one of the few people who could control the girl. They shared the upstairs meals, and were infrequently seen in the lower part of the house; once daily, bonneted and shawled, they would descend for a walk if it was fine. Sometimes Juliana went with them.

"She gets pleasure out of it." Timpy's reply was not as servile as that of most governesses; by now she was something more, a privileged inmate, for the Bainbridges would have been hard put to it to do without her. Juliana smiled at her sister, who slowly returned the smile, close-lipped. Poor Fiona, her sister was thinking; she is so beautiful, when we are out walking it is to see her the gentlemen's heads turn, never me. Yet she can make no sound that is not ugly. If only she had been like other folk she would have been married well by this time, had a title, perhaps. But perhaps again she would not want that. It had been evident to Juliana for as long as she could remember that Fiona lived an inner life of her own, unlike the rest of them. Maybe she took after her father in other ways than being good at drawing. Juliana had heard very little concerning the late Edward Tilney, and did not dare to ask more. Had he possessed that bright hair, spiralling in bronze-gold ringlets about a white neck, and those eyes? If so, he must have been very handsome; no wonder poor Mama had found herself unable to resist his proposal of marriage.

After she had gone the silent girl returned to her work; it was as though the governess were not in the room at all, in her place again knitting. Fiona Tilney stared at the jumble of colours and tried to recapture their meaning. Once it had been clear; the mingling saffrons and reds and indigos of the girls' robes as they moved about the women's quarter in the palace of Dragut Rais, at Mehedia near Algiers. She had even known their names, Hafiza, Yaya, Gulbehar; and her own, which was Safieye of the Bright Hair. She had heard them calling her; Safieye, Safieye, the Mistress of Girls says you are to go to the Master, the Great Lord, in his garden pavilion at the place of the cypresses. And she had gone, and could remember a turbanned tall old man with piercing eyes and drooping moustaches still as black as jet. He had caressed her hair and said it was not yellow, like her mother's. Then the clouds had come down and now she sat in the strict upstairs room again, hearing no sound except for the crying in her head, knowing that the old woman with knitting sat behind her and would presently come over again to try to understand what she had been painting and point beyond the window to the rooftops, as though she ought to paint those. At first, when she was small, Fiona had used to put her hands over what she had done to hide it, but there was no need; neither Timpy nor Chuli could understand. She knew those names because Chuli often, when they were children, used to sit close by her and lay her cheek against Fiona's own and say slowly and distinctly, pointing to herself, "Chuli, Chuli," with lips pouted and then drawn back to show her little square teeth. Then she would say "Timpy" and point to the woman. In the end Fiona had learned the words. Chuli was a friend and wished no one ill, but Timpy had used to rap one's knuckles when one tried to speak apart from the names. "Quiet," everyone had said, "quiet," with finger to lips, and in this way Fiona learned that the sounds she made were harsh and useless and not to be permitted. When she was in a rage, however, she would make sounds; she screamed, and sometimes was whipped for it. It was not unlike the palace at

Mehedia where the Mistress of Girls had used to beat her on the soles of her feet for faults, lest the marks of the whip scar her skin so that she could never give pleasure to a man. All of the girls endured this, and other things, when they were disobedient; she herself had always been self-willed so that it happened often, both there and here.

She had always been thus, even at home; but there she had been happy. Earliest in her memory, held there by feeling rather than by sight, was the caress of water. She had learned to swim in the pools and inlets jutting below her mother's gaunt Scottish castle where she had been born. Beyond was the sea, to which she could not yet venture; at first, even at the pools, there had been hands holding her up; her father, whose hair was red like her own, his sea-blue eyes and long weather-beaten face laughing down at her, urging her on. He was proud of her prowess; she might have been a boy, without fear. Later he and she would swim together, in the summers when his ship lay at berth below the castle and they could dive over decks; the cold embrace of the water, the strong tides running out from the shore, challenged her. Only her mother had been afraid, waiting above on the rock with her fair hair blowing loose from her round hood, calling out to her lord to have a care with the child, for if she got cramp she would drown. Always her mother's arms had been waiting to envelop her fearfully, when she clambered at last out of the water, shaking the wet from her hair like a puppy, and laughing. "Why are you always afraid?" she said to her mother. "Only those who fear it drown in shallow water." They had let her grow pert, for she was an only child.

In winter there had been lessons, with a dominie from Edinburgh. Master George taught her Latin and Greek and some Arabic, for she was quick to learn when she troubled herself. His great beard stank a little, for he seldom washed, but he was a fine scholar; often he lamented her laziness and said that the young Queen Mary, who was the same age as herself, had outstripped her by far in French conversation and deportment and the writing of Latin. Master George would have had her whipped to make her learn faster; but again her mother was always at hand, sheltering her with white hands against a soft perfumed bosom laced into a green gown. The maidservant,

who was Portuguese and had been brought by Andrew Murray
from far parts to tire his wife's hair and lace her gown, would
cross herself often and say that to wear so much green was
unlucky; it was the fairy colour, and would make them angry.
The child herself thought her mother herself was like a fairy, so
beautiful, small and soft and white, with a scent like flowers as
she moved. That white, loving bosom had meant known and
secure things for so long that when everything changed
suddenly, and they were on board the ship making for Venice,
there was no need to trouble oneself greatly so long as in the
cabin, under a swinging lantern at night, her mother would still
bend over and say goodnight as she had always done in the Fife
castle.

"Why have we gone away?" she remembered saying, not to
her mother but to her father, who could be relied upon to
answer sensibly, as though she were not a child. They were on
the captain's deck and he, dressed in a leather sea-jack against
the wind, narrowed his eyes into the skyline and considered
before replying. She would always remember him so, blue eyes
thoughtful and narrowed as if her opinion mattered to him; it
was the last time they spoke alone together.

"We have gone because the Lords of the Congregation have
seized your mother's castle, and will hold it for use against the
Queen Regent's Grace. And as we are of the old faith and they
of the new, I am taking you and your mother to Venice for
safety, after which I shall go back and fight."

"Fight whom? The Lords of the Congregation?"

"Ay, the Protestants. There is civil war in Scotland. Now run
back to your mother and Manoela before it grows dark. I must
stay up here till the watch ends."

She had run obediently, leaving him; chattering French to a
deck-hand on the way, for like all high-born Scots children she
was bilingual. He tossed her up in his arms and cried the name
the Venetian sailors had for her, because of her flaming hair;
"Fiammetta! Fiammetta!"

Her mother and Manoela were telling their beads. Fiammetta did not join them. She was at that time little interested in
the faith; she preferred doing the things a boy would do, tying
knots in rope, rowing a boat, riding a pony, shooting with
arrows. Reading and sewing did not amuse her. "You will never
be a good wife to any man," said Manoela the servant.

"Then I will marry a sailor, like Sancio abovestairs. He can thread beads in little patterns to make purses."

But there was soon more to do on board than beadwork; and Sancio's voice was last heard, high with terror, above on deck.

"To arms! To arms! The Barbary corsairs!"

Then there was scurrying and noise over all the ship, then silence; then, soon enough, the clash of swords. And Sancio, who had made bead purses, was one of the first to die fighting by the side of his captain when Dragut's ship attacked the Scots vessel in the narrow seas south of Venice.

It was soon over. Fiammetta did not see the fighting; she was held close below with her mother, after the alarm, during the clangour and then the silence, the unfamiliar silence of death.

They waited, trembling. Fiammetta's mother strained her child fiercely in her arms until she did not even see, soon enough, the door-curtain stripped back and a tall mustachioed man in chain-armour stoop his head to enter the cabin Others crowded behind him, but he bade them stay with a curt order. On his finger was a bright ring, like fire. He had a drawn sword in his hand, still red with blood, and something in her mother's stillness told what would never be spoken of in words; that her father had died by that sword. She stayed there hidden against her mother, swallowing the bitter certainty like physic, forgotten as long as she kept still. The gnawing of horror in her mind set Dragut's image there forever as he was that day; tanned with the Mediterranean sun, tall and spare, and looking at her mother in a way no one had done, had dared to do, before. Something in the manner of it bade the child be still, be very still, and not cry out or weep. Her mother also was still as a dead woman; one dared not look up at her face.

"They will take you now to my ship," said Dragut gently. He spoke French, as though he knew they would both understand it. When they had been taken up on deck and dusk had fallen so that the lights of the Turkish ship shone out clearly nearby, Fiammetta looked along the decks to find the body of her father. But there were only heaped empty clothes and dark slippery stains on deck. She heard someone sobbing and then her mother, grown strangely remote and cold, silencing her as they descended the ropes at the ship's side. For instants

Fiammetta stood alone on the silent deck where she had once played, and heard the voice of Dragut addressing her. Always, she was to remember, he had treated her with adult courtesy. "Your father died bravely in battle, my child, and we have cast his body back into the sea. Who is to say that if a man fights bravely, whether he be an infidel or not, he will not gain Paradise?"

But then desolation had overcome Fiammetta, and she sobbed bitterly as they lifted her down to the waiting galley-deck.

She remembered little enough of that voyage, for where they were going she had not been told. Now and again, though no longer daily, she saw her mother. Fiammetta knew that she had changed in some way; when she asked the waiting-woman about it, she was told sharply to ask no questions and to tell her beads. "If they take them away from you, count the mysteries on your fingers; do not forget."

During part of each day they were allowed up on deck, to watch the sea passing. There was no land in sight; the many green islands, the inland lagoons of the coastline near Venice had vanished till there was only the empty sky. Sometimes the child would long for her mother. Where were they keeping her? What was to become of them when this voyage came to an end?

Down below decks were galley-slaves, chained fifteen to a bench and forced to row constantly, except when the boat should be in port. Fiammetta watched the overseer go down the ranks with their food sometimes, armed with his whip. She could not tear her eyes away from the cruelty, though it chilled her. Once a slave fell forward at his oar and was then flogged till his back was an open wound and he was dead and they flung him into the sea. Had her father looked like that, raw and lifeless at the end, all his laughter vanished? As time passed the remembrance of his living presence receded; he became someone who has always been dead.

One night her mother came to her. She no longer wore the stiff green gown but a loose white garment which covered her body and head. She knelt down by Fiammetta where she was lying in her bunk and laid her hand on the child's shoulder, saying nothing, Fiammetta kept still, sensing that something had happened which she did not understand; otherwise it would

have been as it had used to be, and she would have been
enveloped in the demanding softness of her mother's embrace.
Now it was as though her mother was herself a child, asking for
comfort. "What has happened?" she said timidly. A lock of her
mother's bright fair hair, spiralling down, answered her; that at
least was unchanged behind the strange concealing veil. Fiammetta fingered the hair, loving its soft brightness. She heard her
mother answering as if her voice came from a long way off.

"Naught to harm you, for I would not let it. I have still
enough power for that. Only I have had to promise, if he will let
you be reared as a Christian, to become the—the companion of
Dragut."

The child was bewildered. "Listen carefully," said her
mother, "we may not be alone again."

And she told Fiammetta of the precious inheritance of the
Faith for which they had all left Scotland; that Faith for which
so many had died since Our Lord himself had been raised on a
cross. "Rather than have that taken from you by alien teachings,
I myself would die a thousand deaths."

The child began to cry. "You are not to die—like father—"

"Hush, my sweetheart. What's past is done. God knows it is
the worst sin of all to take life, though it be one's own. How else
should I have gone on living? It would have been easier to stab
myself with a knife, and follow your father, whom I loved and
whose wife I was and, God will it, shall be hereafter. But I
knew that if I died in such a way we two would never meet
before God's Throne." She passed a delicate, tired hand across
her hair, tucking it back beneath the veil. "So I must live on, in
the way it has been written for me. Dragut is—not unkind."

She listened, with a child's mind only half understanding;
later, the meaning would become clear. She promised to say her
prayers, to say her rosary. She wept at her mother's going;
might not she come too? "Why may I not, if the Lord Dragut is
kind?" she begged. He had not minded her presence that first
time below deck on the Scots ship, or later. But the new cold
stranger that was her mother shook its head.

"Always you were self-willed, with your tutor and your
father and myself. Turn your will now to your faith and to God,
to Our Lord; that alone may sustain you, my poor child, for I no
longer can."

Even then she had not known real fear; not till the day they

came into a port where there were white square houses shining
in the sun and small boats coming out to greet the bustle of
arrival below decks. Presently Manoela screamed; old fat brown
Manoela who was no longer fit to fetch money in the market.
Later there were plaintive cries like those of a hurt animal, and
still later a splash in the water. She had never seen Manoela
again: would she, like father, gain Paradise?

Three

The little supper at Julius's house was a quiet success; nothing was overstated, but by the end of the evening it was evident that the Old Man's approval would be given to whatever might lead to a closer acquaintance between Juliana and his new protégé, Anton Muntz. At first Juliana had restrained her laughter at sight of the solemn young man, who clicked his heels on being presented; and the doctor's daughter, Miss Betsy Elliott, who had fewer manners, showed less restraint. The party had been kept very small, almost *en famille*, then Agnes, realising that the ladies would be outnumbered by the gentlemen, had invited Dr. Elliott and his wife and daughter—it was safe enough, as poor Meg Elliott had a sadly spotty complexion—to be present along with the Old Man, his wife Isabella, and young Muntz.

Timothy and Muntz arrived together from the yards, in the Bainbridge carriage. Both had taken time to change their cravats and to spruce themselves. Isabella Bainbridge, who in her youth had been a great beauty, wore purple satin trimmed with ball-fringe braid. There was a muted, if slight, air of gaiety in deference to Anton's mourning; after supper, which had been pleasantly lightened by the Old Man's anecdotes, Juliana, in a striped gown, was requested to play, and very prettily obliged with a rendering of one of Mr. Mendelssohn's *Songs Without Words*, which were becoming fashionable. Afterwards Anton sang, in an agreeable bass, while Juliana again accompanied him on the pianoforte. Agnes, watching, surprised a look of deep approval on the face of the Old Man. She was informed enough to guess why this party had been insisted upon; every day Julius, despite his reticence, came home with some tale of the progress the young German was making at the office in the yards. The men liked him and worked well under his orders, which were crisp and knowledgeable. In time, no doubt, he would be made a partner. This Julius had naturally not stated,

but Agnes had surmised it. Surveying the company, she was
surprised within herself to see such evidence of the Old Man's
plotting come true; his wife, his own cousin, had been a sister of
her own father, David, who in his turn had married a sister of
Timothy's. "We are all so closely related," thought Agnes,
"perhaps it has not been good for the child's health." And she
watched Juliana's immature figure, a little anxiously; if what
the Old Man had in mind was marriage with this German,
would her own child ably bear children? She herself had had a
difficult time at Juliana's birth, though less so than at Fiona's.
Fiona was not present tonight. It would have been most
inadvisable; in fact, one must put off for as long as possible her
meeting with the young German.

Farewells were made, at the reasonable hour of ten o'clock;
and Julius, exerting himself to be agreeable, waved the
coachman aside and himself handed his mother into the
carriage. The elder Bainbridges drove off, while Anton Muntz,
declining an escort, chose to return on foot to his lodging.

Fiona had seen the carriages arrive. She showed no more
curiosity than was usual; it was an accepted fact that she was
not to appear downstairs when company was present. She did
not know who had come this evening, nor did it matter to her.
For once she was not sketching or painting, and spent much of
the time brushing out her long hair, coaxing the spirals to fall at
last in long curls about her neck and shoulders, seen in the oval
mirror. Timpy watched her with reserved approval. How was
one to intimate to a young woman who could not hear a word
that to admire her reflection would give her too high an opinion
of herself? She packed the girl off to bed before the company
left, and herself sat alone in the forsaken room while, from
below, came strains of the music Fiona would never hear.
Timpy hummed the melodies to herself as she got on with the
spencer she was knitting; when young, she had been used to
play as well as Miss Juliana, but no young men had come to
sing with her. There had not been enough money, and at sixteen
she had gone out as a governess, an occupation which had
swiftly destroyed such looks as she had ever had. It was a good,
undemanding post here with the Bainbridges, and she had no
wish to be elsewhere now; all her relatives were dead. Perhaps,

when Miss Juliana married, she, Timpy, might not be considered too old, too out of date, to—But that was to anticipate, and life had taught her not to do so.

Four

Anton Muntz proposed to Juliana Bainbridge three months after making her acquaintance, which was considered a proper interval in which he might prove himself able to support her suitably. The Old Man had given his benison; Julius, when approached, had already been spoken to by his father and told that there need be no objection to the bridegroom because he was foreign; after all, Anton was half a Scot, and had shown himself to be industrious and also—Timothy did not mention this to Julius, who so sadly lacked it—possessed of the flame of creative genius without which Bainbridge's would never have become what it was; without which, no doubt, ships to America and Ireland would still be labouring under sail. Anton's alloy had received its tests, and had been found satisfactory; it would start production in the New Year, and perhaps, to celebrate the marriage—it was already taken for granted that the marriage would ensue—some form of directorship, of partnership, might be offered to so active and efficient a young inventor. Timothy's dream was about to realise itself, perhaps not as he had originally planned it; then, David's genius and his own were to have been channelled into a close family unit, intermarried through the generations. But new blood in the form of Anton Muntz was, by now, not unwelcome.

The proposal took place at Belland, Timothy's mansion at which those beyond the magic circle poked fun. It was situated in the Firth of Clyde, and boasted a frieze of statuary round the walls, a tower with a great clock, and a winter garden under glass. Beyond, roses were tended in season along the neat parterres. Here Isabella Bainbridge spent her days, in the pleasurable pursuits of being a country-based lady of leisure and means; she enjoyed driving her little phaeton about the lanes with their freedom from traffic, and Timothy generally left the larger carriage in the stables and made his way daily up to the city by water. In the evenings, he would return, dine, and play billiards, with guests, or else take his wife on his arm round the picture-gallery. This contained an ever-increasing number of masterpieces, for Timothy, blacksmith's son as he had been, had improved his knowledge with his means and was now, as the auctioneers knew, a force to be reckoned with in the sale of a Cuyp, a Lawrence, or even a Rubens.

The placid Dutch landscapes, browsing cows, and fleshy or aristocratic women were the chosen background for Muntz's proposal, when he had drawn Juliana, with the full approval of her family, aside with him after dinner by invitation at Belland. He had asked her, in his polite English, to show him the paintings again as he himself was not very knowledgeable. "I had no opportunity to see great art in Germany," he admitted. Juliana listened shyly. She had been told by her father that Anton had asked for permission to pay her his addresses, and it would not have occurred to her to disobey Julius. As for Agnes, she had said nothing; it would be at a later stage that she would instruct Juliana about a wife's proper duties. At present, as was correct in her maiden state, Juliana knew nothing except that to have a baby it was necessary to be married. She liked babies; she wanted to be like other young women of her own age; she had no objection to Anton Muntz, and it would be agreeable to please Papa and Grandfather.

So when Anton paused in front of a sunlit Claude Lorraine and said, pressing her hand which lay on his arm, "Miss Juliana, I have something to ask," she knew what he wanted, and was sympathetic with him about the difficulty of expressing himself. She helped him all she could, smiling gently. The great canvases looked down on them; beyond the windows, twilight turned to evening over this river which had made Timothy Bainbridge's fortune.

Anton was gratified by her reply and by her help; he kissed her hand, feeling triumph rise in him. Now he was to be taken into the Bainbridge clan, as one of them; and Juliana was a pleasing creature. When they returned to the nearby drawing-room, her cheeks were flushed prettily; Anton modestly announced the betrothal. Juliana saw with pleasure that when her future husband smiled, his teeth showed white. He smiles too seldom, she was thinking. I hope I can make him happy.

Already, amid the sounds of congratulation and the embraces

of Papa, Mama and the grandparents, she was thinking about the wedding itself, and of someone who was not here among the rest tonight. Whatever they might all say—and, after all, it was to be *her* wedding—she would insist that Fiona be bridesmaid. Poor Fiona never went anywhere at all. Anton had not even set eyes on her.

Fiona lay in bed and had a dream. It was not one of the dreams of blood, at which she sometimes cried out harshly in her sleep, to be wakened by Timpy shaking her shoulder, mouthing unheard words with lips indrawn from lack of the false teeth she wore by day. From fear and danger one almost woke to laughter then, except that that too was reprimanded; so many things she did were wrong. But in the place of dreams it was different. There she was a child again, a child with bright hair blown by a sultry wind, huddled against the bulkhead of the corsair ship which at last, after much voyaging, was to put her and her mother on land. Yesterday mother had come to her again and had said, "You can use your ten fingers for the prayers if you have no rosary. Do not forget it". She had been urgent and frightened, looking always back over her shoulder as though someone overheard. Fiammetta was more curious than afraid.

"What happened to Manoela, mother?"

"You must not ask." That was not the right answer for her, who always desired to know about everything. Manoela was gone, at any rate; and she herself no longer had a rosary. She said the prayers faithfully, less because she loved them than because she loved her mother. And mother was seldom with her now. Soon she was put in charge of a tall smooth-faced creature with fat thighs, whom later she learned was a eunuch. That was after they had disembarked at a line of coast which had risen out of the sunrise. The eunuch had carried her, Fiammetta, from the small boat to the shore while one of Dragut's men carried her mother.

Then in no time at all they were at Mehedia, with its creamy sandstone walls which were to encompass their lives for longer than anyone dreamed. There was a garden with cypresses, and other girls, some her own age, and many women. Most of them spoke French and Fiammetta was also glad of the Arabic she had learned from her tutor. Everything was strange, different from the ship, different even from the memories she still had of the gaunt castle at home; here there was languor, sunshine, ease, many perfumes of strange flowers, new matters. The Mistress of Girls, old and fat, was like a governess, but her punishments were terrible; Fiammetta learned of them in the first year. At first she was stubborn, because of her father's death and her mother's fate, and would learn nothing; then she began to see that it was in vain to fight, that she would never, by herself, win free of here. Soon another captive was brought off the ships; she was a little dark-eyed creature named Melissa, with a skin like a peach. Presently she was no longer called Melissa but Gulbehar, which meant Flower of Spring. Fiammetta herself was Safieye, the Bright One. She and the little dark-eyed girl soon learned to exchange words with one another in Maltese, Melissa's native tongue; the little creature was too lazy to learn Scots or French. While the rest slept they learned to whisper to one another in the dark; Fiammetta felt protective towards the younger girl and often helped her to avoid punishments.

That was after her mother had gone away.

How different it had been while she still lived! Fiammetta was allowed to be often with her, evidently on orders left by the Lord Dragut. They would sit alone, apart from the other women and girls, and talk low-voiced. Remembering it afterwards, Fiammetta was aware her mother had been desperately trying to teach her all she knew of the Christian Faith while she might still do so. The rest ignored them; there was jealousy of the Golden One, as Fiammetta's mother was called, because she had been chosen for the honour of bearing Dragut's child. Others in such a condition were dosed till they miscarried, but Dragut had desired the child of his Golden One. He himself had sailed again after landing the prizes from the Scots ship, and would not return till winter.

While mother lived ... if only she had known how short a time they would have together, she would have been kinder and not have grown restive at yet another rosary, another prayer to the saints or talk of the Trinity. As it was, sometimes she used to chafe to go and play and dance with the rest. Mother spoke to no one except to her, and did not move from her place by the wall. The new child within her made her heavy. One day, at last, Fiammetta was taken away and made to stay with the others for a day, a whole day and a night; and perversely, now that it could not be, she wanted to be with her mother. In the silence of the night a sound of moaning came, and in the new daylight Fiammetta wrenched free of the Mistress of Girls with her fat body in gauzy trousers and sequin-spangled veil, and went down to her mother; and cried aloud. For mother lay on a pallet made of straw, and by her was a tiny baby, with black hair; it lay still. Mother's face was waxen and she opened her eyes as if she had guessed Fiammetta was near, and smiled a little and said, "Water; bring me water, child, quickly". Fiammetta had run and fetched the water, from the great square tank where it was kept, and returned bearing it in her hands for she had no vessel. She thought it was to quench the sick woman's thirst, but mother had whispered, "Pour it on the child's head. Say 'I baptise thee in the name of the Father, and the Son, and the Holy Ghost,'" and Fiammetta obeyed her. Then her mother made the sign of the cross over the baby, and fell back with a little sigh, while her face suddenly looked like wax that had begun to melt and change. She did not speak again, and presently the women came wailing and cursing that a child of Allah should have been baptised as an infidel. But the baby died also. Fiammetta did not know when it had died, for she was weeping, more bitterly than in all her life she had wept, for the death of her mother.

After that Fiammetta was quite alone. There was Melissa who was friendly, but she was not the same as having mother; and there was a Circassian with pale eyes named Hafiza, whom both of them hated. There was no one now to tell her that the Faith said one must not hate, and to do so was better than nothing, better than remembering. Melissa tried to forget her parents also; she had been taken on the sea-shore where she had gone to gather shells, and the pirate ship had brought her here. "And my parents are old; they will weep for me." There was no one now to weep for her, Fiammetta; no one at all.

She consoled herself partly; there were things to be learned from the women and the Mistress of Girls; ways of painting one's eyes with kohl, or playing the curved guitar; or dancing intricately among the weaving patterns of limbs brown, white, black. From all the places where the Sultan waged war or exchanged barter these girls were brought by Dragut and others, as captives. Boys were less fortunate; they were castrated to become eunuchs, unless one especially pleased his masters by his warlike appearance, for then he would make a fine soldier in the Sultan's armies. From the Indus plains, from the Morea, Croatia, Hungary, elsewhere, they came; and life at Mehedia grew absorbing. There was the important art of making unguents from herbs, pounding the stuffs in pestle and mortar; one's lord, in due time, would be a warrior, and might come home wounded. Everything was, in the end, designed for pleasing a man; even the lessons on how to approach the lord's bed, kneeling first, touching the coverlets with one's forehead where his feet would lie; then writhing, without disturbing the covers, upwards between them, naked for the lord's pleasure, slave to his will. All the girls learned such things, for all would be given to a bridegroom. Perhaps he would be the Lord Dragut himself, though he grew old, and the tale went that he lived only for his wars now, no longer for women.

Juliana had opened the door and came quietly into Fiona's room causing her to open her eyes. She came and sat down on the bed's edge and spread out her hands, quietly smiling. On one finger was a bright diamond, glowing in the lamplight. Chuli was talking, talking so rapidly that Fiona could not, as she sometimes did, understand a word or two. There was a rose-colour in Chuli's cheeks; she was happy. Fiona lay idle, then put out her hand and fingered the ring. Once she had had a brighter stone than this, a great fire opal, slid on her finger on a far shore. ...

"And you must be my bridesmaid, and the wedding is in three weeks, so they will be coming soon to fit you for your gown, and oh! you will look so beautiful!" Juliana said. "I wanted Anton to see you before now, but now he must not do so until you are in the pretty dress. I do hope it does not rain on the day, it will spoil everything. It is to be a quiet wedding, because of the mourning; only the minister in the drawing-room, a few friends, and a small reception afterwards. I myself like it better that way."

She bent and kissed Fiona, and went out. The other girl closed her eyes, but the dream would not come again. She had lost it, that world in which there were sounds, speech, music; now she was like an animal, trapped in a cage, deaf and mute.

After her mother died at Mehedia, there had followed the years of the hardening of Fiammetta's will, until she grew into a woman. Looking back, it seemed that it had been an easy enough matter to have opposed herself, constantly and steadily, to all that was alien to her early upbringing, her remembered faith that had been her mother's. Yet many of the things they taught her at Mehedia would be useful to her. She learned the lore of the Arab doctors who sometimes, though never in person, taught the women by means of their eunuchs; in this way she learned that a wounded man feels less pain, and is in less danger, if the knife that cuts away his mangled flesh is hot; and that goat's serum scraped beneath the skin of the foot will deliver one from the peril of certain diseases. She learned to paint her nails as well as her eyelids, to preserve her smooth creamy skin with oils and essences; to comb and dress her bright hair which was like no other in all the harem. Yet all the time she was aware of an undiminished shrinking from the touch of the eunuchs, those unnatural creatures whose manhood had been taken away from them so that their chins remained beardless and their thighs grew fat. She did not show this shrinking; it was unwise to do so, for the eunuchs attended on the woman and bathed them, and would have reported her to the Mistress of Girls for any mutiny. Nor after the first year, when she was punished often, was anyone in the women's quarter aware of her continued hatred of all that the life meant. Her father and mother had loved one another as equals; here women were chattels of the flesh only, dependent on the whim of a master; their lives were often less highly valued than a man's camel. In this awareness, Safieye of the Bright Hair attained puberty; now, when the Lord Dragut should decide on a husband for her, she was ripe for marriage.

She remembered the times Dragut had sent for her. On each occasion her body was washed in rosewater, her hair carefully combed and essenced, and a gilt cap put on her head. She knew that the Mistress assumed Dragut might want to make love to her; but he did not. Once she came before him as he reclined on a low divan with a dish of fruit by him; his great drooping moustaches were still black as jet, the ring still flamed on his finger. It was difficult to believe what she knew to be true, that this man was past seventy years of age and had spent the summer harrying the islands in the Mediterranean.

He signalled to her to kneel by him and bade her help eat the fruit; she had a child's hunger still and gladly obeyed. She knew she ought to hate this man who had killed her father and violated her mother; but she could not. He was silent, and it was not her place to speak. Her fingers strayed towards a lute which lay there, left by one of the slaves in case Dragut required diversion. He noticed the direction of her hands, and nodded briefly.

"They say you are proficient in making music, Safieye. Play me the melody your mother knew; it was written by a king in love."

She pretended not to understand; sudden and sharp, the memory of her mother singing *Tayis Bank* came to her, within the confines of the little cabin on the Scots ship, sunlight filtering in on her green gown. It was difficult to restrain tears. She shook her head and began to play a tinkling, superficial Turkish tune; but the old man gestured her to silence and deeply, surprisingly hummed the melody as she remembered it. After that she could no longer pretend ignorance. The liquid notes of the lute sounded, in the African garden, a love-song written eighty years before on the banks of Tay. Before they had finished she too was singing. "You did that well," said Dragut. "It might have been your mother's voice. Many women have given me pleasure, but only once have I loved; and she is dead, and you are of her flesh." He reached out and stroked her hair as though she had been a small dog, then told her to go. She last saw him still lying as she had left him, his face beneath the turban shaded by his hand.

By the time he sent for her again, Melissa the Maltese girl had grown comely. When they had first brought her off the corsair ship she had been frightened and crying, but she was so no longer. Before long she and Fiammetta had a secret bond because of her faith. It was a comfort to the younger child to count the mysteries of the rosary on her fingers, after the lamps were out; comfort, too, to have Fiammetta for her friend, Fiammetta who knew so much more than she did about this alien place with its permissions and its punishments. "Say nothing, and learn all they can teach you," the older girl whispered. "One day we will be set free."

"Oh, but how, how, Fiammetta? I am so far from my family here, and they couldn't pay as much ransom-money as I would fetch in the slave market, Hafiza says." Melissa, called Gulbehar, let her dark eyes fill with tears. Fiammetta hushed her into silence. "Why believe that little Circassian cat, who will say anything to make you miserable because you are prettier than she? You know well enough we won't be sold in the open market now; we are destined for husbands in high places, chosen for us by the Lord Dragut. Why else would he trouble with our education? And, remember my name here is Safieye; all of them have forgotten having Christian names except you and me."

The two girls' friendship grew, and they continued to talk together in Maltese, which Fiammetta began quickly to understand; it was less difficult than Greek. But they must speak Arabic openly; native tongues, like the memory of homes and families, were frowned upon in the women's quarter; it was unlikely that any future master would require them to know more than Turkish, the Arabic, and possibly a little Greek for use with slaves. They were little better than slaves themselves. But despite everything, as summer passed into summer, the certainty that she would one day be free stayed with Fiammetta, and coloured her every action and thought.

Dragut sent for her again to his private garden in the spring of 1563. By this time she was, in the opinion of the Mistress of Girls, overripe. Her skin was clear and fine as rose-petals, not freckled as so often befell those with such hair like fire; she could play the lute, guitar and zither, could dance agreeably and was conversant with the etiquette which governed the pleasuring of one's lord in bed. Had not Roxellane, the foreign wife of the Great Sultan, been shown his will by his casting of a handkerchief upon her shoulder? Yet Safieye had never been called upon to give pleasure even to Dragut. The Mistress's eyes—her name was Hadasseh, and in her youth she had been a succulent Jewish girl, but that was long past—daily cast her eyes on Safieye's magnificent, global breasts with anxiety lest they should begin to drop or wither with prolonged virginity. So when a second summons came from Dragut after very long she served Safieye with a draught of bitter herbs known to have aphrodisiac properties, to induce compliance if the Lord Dragut wished at last to avail himself of her now that she was grown.

But Dragut sat beneath the cypresses in his garden and stared not at Safieye, but at the pointed reflections they made in his square tank of water. When the gardener had laid out the ground he had wanted to instal fountains such as the Lord of the Two Worlds, Suleiman the Magnificient, had playing in his garden at Constantinople. But Dragut had replied with a sailor's common sense.

"Conserve the water in a tank; it's scanty enough," he said. "Plant me a row of cypresses and another of orange trees, and I will be content to sit in their shade out of the sun." He did not add that this was because his birthplace in Anatolia, which he had not revisited since he was a boy, had had cypresses growing on the slope of a hill. Looking at them now, and at their image in the water, he could recall all of his life since then. There was his early adoption by a Turkish army-captain, his later progress as a Mameluke, a bombardier; the way he had later made enough money, by wrestling in the streets of Alexandria, to buy a galliot and put to sea; the glittering, challenging sea had always claimed him. From then on had come fortune, without reverses in his pirate-forays except twice; the first time, taken prisoner by the Christians, he had been made to serve a full year in the galleys till old Barbarossa, the Mediterranean corsair and his friend, could ransom him. Then later, raiding the Maltese islands with his own brother whom he loved, the inhabitants had killed the latter and burned his body on a high pyre on a hill, despite Dragut's pleas that they return it to him for burial.

"But *I* returned and raided the lesser island till there were no crops growing, and harried the greater till there was scarcely a young man free. And there I had a premonition that the wing of death should brush me at last, that it is written that I too shall die in those islands."

Love and death! They were written; one could alter nothing. He became aware that the young woman Safieye, the child of his Golden One, was standing again before him. He saw, as always, that she was beautiful and desirable, but he did not desire her for himself. He smiled, and gestured with a thin brown hand that she might approach, and kneel by him.

"Do you still play the king's melody?" he asked. His eyes, still clear despite his great age, noted her breasts, limbs and body and that she was graceful as a young tree. This pleased him, knowing the plan he had in mind.

She had nodded. "Yes, Lord. Shall I play it for you now?" It no longer hurt to play her mother's melody; she had died long ago.

"Not now," he said, "and no longer for me. You shall play it to a king as is fitting."

"A king?" Her green eyes had widened their pupils so that they seemed dark. She hid her feelings well, he thought; other young women would have squealed and laughed in triumph.

"I have found you the greatest lord in the world, Safieye," he said "the Lord of the Happy Constellation himself, Suleiman the Magnificent, the Lawgiver, seated on his throne in Istanbul. His favourite wife is dead and he has known grief through his sons; two were traitors and the third is a sot. He has a desire to breed new sons from a young, fair and wise woman. I have told him that you, Safieye, are like a young tree in spring; that you have breasts like ripe fruit and can play also and sing, to divert him in his leisure hours. He has not many."

He smiled, unheeding of her silence. "You will sail," he said, "with some of the others when the tide is ready to float the Kustir Aga's ship from Venice. It also bears precious stuffs, dried fruit and oil. Hafiza the Circassian shall go with you also, the Maltese girl who is your friend; she has a Greek bridegroom waiting who has shown prowess in the Hungarian wars. And the little fat one Yaya from the islands, she shall go—you see I know them all." He moved a little, and trailed a finger in the water, making ripples. "It was thought at first that if we were to provide you as a wife for Selim the Sot, he might give over his wine-drinking, which is forbidden in a son of Islam. But it has been thought better to have him killed as soon as it is certain you will bear a child. He would make an unfit ruler and is not a source of pride to the Osmanlis, as your son may be. You have a queenly future, Safieye; may you be found worthy of it, and of your mother."

She had trembled; perhaps it was the action of the bitter drug, making her senses disobey her mind. Would they give her such

a draught on her marriage-night with the old man who
governed both East and West? "The Holy Scriptures taught
that woman was taken from man's side as an equal, but I must
writhe upwards from his feet," she thought. And afterwards,
when she was pregnant by the old man, Selim the Sot—he must
be young—would be killed. They did that with bowstrings
looped about the neck from behind. Suleiman the Magnificent
had killed other sons in this way. She had heard of it from
Hafiza, who got it from the eunuchs.

"You do well to tremble; but think of it and you will be
proud," said Dragut. He had turned away from her and was
watching the cypresses. The hue of his moustaches was touched
with silver now, at last; behind them his face was bland and
walnut-hard, as though age could not affect it. It was the same
face she had seen first on the deck of the Scots ship, when his
sword was wet with her father's blood.

She rose, knowing he wanted her to go. "I am sensible of the
honour accorded to me, Great Lord." What would happen if she
said she refused it? A whipping on her soles, the enema-
chamber?

"See then that you are worthy. A wise woman rules a ruler."
He inclined his head in farewell.

She made an obeisance, and went. The shadows of the
cypresses were lengthening in the garden; it was almost the hour
of muezzin. Tonight she would say her rosary on her fingers
again; how long now till Istanbul?

And so the merchantman set sail. At first the young women
were excited, even flattered, at their cushioned quarters and the
attention of the eunuch, Wazir, who had been put in charge of
them. The silver sea ploughed past; they could watch, and guess
where they might be, and scan the sky for fears of storm. But all
was smooth and orderly until one day when, as often happens at
sea, uneasiness came aboard. The cargo, said to be worth eighty
million ducats, heaved and groaned in its protective bales of
linen cloth. The stacked wooden crates with their figs and dates,
pressed olives and Genoa velvet and silk, the mighty containers
full of oil and wine, concealed the living freight sent by Dragut,
Viceroy of Algiers, ex-pirate, ex-freebooter, in gifts to his
Sultan, Suleiman the Magnificent, greatest soldier in Islam,

conqueror in many battles, now growing old on his jewel-fretted throne in the city of minarets by the Golden Horn. The seven most beautiful women the Barbary Coast could send sat huddled together, all except one a prey to sea-sickness; they could no longer bear to watch the sea beyond the high square windows swirl opal, then silver swiftly with the coming of night. There was no word from Wazir; only one bright star shone calmly, fully down on the metallic, restless sky and sea. There seemed sudden danger in the very air of the night, scented risks and strangeness in the silence of the ship as she voyaged on, towards the islands with her escort following to the number of twenty galleys. When at last a hail came it was like a given signal. Fiammetta sprang to her feet, letting the guitar she had been fingering fall from her painted hands. The hail came again; and then there were the sounds of trampling, hurrying feet above decks, a crying of high voices, a clash of swords at the last. Safieye of the Bright Hair listened, her kohl-darkened eyes narrowed with knowledge and unafraid. This was as it had been on her father's ship. She knew what to do.

She said in Arabic "It is a Christian challenge. Presently they will fight." Her hand, too long and thin for the Turkish ideal of beauty, thrust back her hair. The other women began to chatter and mourn softly amoung themselves, like doves, their white limbs stirring on the cushions where they had lain for three days, complaining of the discomfort. Hafiza the Circassian watched Safieye resentfully, her own lips pouting and pale without their paint; she was the worst of the victims of sea-sickness.

"Who speaks of Christians? And what will become of us if they win? At heart you're an infidel still, Safieye, and I believe you wish the ship ill and all who sail in her." But with that a bout of vomiting overtook her and she turned on one elbow, voiding clear liquid from her stomach. Afterwards she fell silent. The other shrugged, bearing her no ill-will nowadays; if they reached Istanbul, Hafiza would not be of importance. Yaya and little Melissa sidled up, slipping small hands into the bare crook of Fiammetta's arm. "Hafiza is jealous because you have the first place," they murmured, and the words were so soft that the Circassian did not hear them from her bed. Above them by now the trampling and shouting had increased, and it became evident that the ship was surrounded. Beyond the windows a grey web of land, spun thin and seeming to hang between sea and sky, was visible beyond the islands of Zante and Cephallonia. At the window the women could see the nearing bulk of a strange ship; smaller and slighter than their own, but bearing a crew whose targes shone in the dulled light as though flares illumined them.

"Holy Mother of God, they are come to rescue us," murmured the little Maltese, and her hand tightened on the other's arm. "Oh, Fiammetta—"

"Do not speak of it yet, till they come aboard." The woman with bright hair waited, every muscle in her body expectant and taut; the disastrous sounds from above on deck, the rasping of metal and booming of shot, did not cause her to cry out, like the others: she had heard them before. The Maltese girl sighed a little with fear, and clung more closely.

"I'm not brave like you; the sound of the firing frightens me." Tears shone on her face and Yaya's, shown up by the lighted flares. The guns were booming constantly now, both from above and from the attacking ships. "There must be more than one," thought Fiammetta. Behind her the women had begun to sob and wail.

"Allah and his Prophet preserve us! What will become of us now?" But Fiammetta did not answer. She was thinking aloud, smiling a little while the guns sounded.

"I thought the prison had closed upon me for ever. Let the Christian come; I will welcome him."

Still smiling, she turned to face the hanging leather curtain which made their doorway; and was still thus when a powder-stained knight, one of the crew of three ships under command of La Romegas, Knight of Malta and leader of this foray, burst through the curtain and loudly, mockingly proclaimed to the questing men the presence on board of seven ladies, destined for the Grand Turk.

They came below hatches quickly, leaving the ripping open of cases and bales and sealed jars of wine. These could be unloaded at Birgù afterwards, for the island, by strict order of the Grand Master La Valette, was laying in all available stores against a coming siege. At mention of La Valette's name a remembrance of their vow of chastity assailed the Knights; they did no more

than seize the unresisting women, bind them by the wrists if it
was needed, and lightly and easily, as though they had been
bundles, lift them on deck and pass them down the waiting
ladders, by hands used to rougher freight. The night's cold
struck the women's lightly-covered flesh, and many of them
were shivering and crying by the time they were herded into the
small-boats, then to the galleys. Once therein, they found that
their quarters were by no means as luxurious as they had been
on the merchantman, that property of Kustir Aga, chief eunuch
of the Sultan's harem. Thrust down now on wooden planks,
their soft flesh grew chafed, making them weep and regret the
vanished cushions on which they had lain complaining since
Algiers. Nor would there be sherbet served to cool their thirst in
the new day's heat, which soon rose again as the little ships,
towing their limping prize, sweated back to Birgù harbour.

In his own cabin the Chevalier Romegas laughed, both by the
instinct of the corsair which was in him and by reason of the
dilemma he foresaw for La Valette when the Sultan's ladies
should be unleashed on him in his fortress. "But what was I to
do with them?" Romegas foresaw himself explaining, innocent-
eyed, to the Grand Master. Once or twice he himself went down
to take a look at the captive women, marvelling at the plump,
lazy quality of Eastern beauty and staring, for his vow of
celibacy did not forbid him to stare, at the creamy breasts of the
Circassian, half-veiled in transparent stuffs which were limp
already with the sweat of the encounter so that one might look
on them as if the woman were naked. All seemed passive, as if
resigned to become the property of whoever should take them;
that, the Chevalier supposed, was the accepted fate of Moslem
women, who were not nurtured to think of themselves as in any
way immortal except, no doubt, for those houris who
embellished the carpets of the faithful in Mahomet's Paradise.
"Well, as no such reward awaits an honest Christian knight it
would be as well to see to the conserving of the fruit and wine,"
grumbled the Chevalier. And he did not avail himself of the
nearness of the women or allow any of his crew to do so, to the
disgruntlement of the common sailors, who looked on them as
spoils of war.

When they were taken off the galleys into the small-boat

preparatory to being landed at Birgù, it was late. They had seen
nothing of Malta on arrival, for the grand sweep of the harbour
was blotted out by darkness; only here and there, in the velvet
night, a light shone, thickening the places where the rock,
yellow by day, lay against the sky. The water was like oil,
smooth, tideless and warm; it splashed about the boat's sides and
dripped from the oars with a plashing sound, scarcely disturbing
the quality of the glassy surface as they rowed near shore. The
harbour was deep, and as the boatmen alighted to pull the ropes
into the jetty, water reached their waists. Suddenly there was a
faint splash from the stern of the boat; someone had dived
overboard. A memory of pale stuff streaming, like a cloud, came
and then was gone. There was cursing, and much flaying about
with searching oars; few of the men could swim, but evidently
the woman who had gone could do so. Getting the rest on shore,
and counting heads by the light of a lantern, they found that it
was the red-haired girl, whose name someone said was Safieye,
who had escaped. Her friend, the little Maltese Melissa, cried
and sobbed constantly in the native tongue; at first they would
not listen to her, but later when someone did, it was with
interest enough. If this was Birgù, her father was the merchant
Paul the Greek, she said, and would pay much money to have
her delivered to him safely and still virgin. But they told her
everyone must be sent to await the pleasure of the Grand
Master, who would be by no means pleased at having women
again on his island after shipping all of the island wives and
daughters off to Sicilian biscuit factories; afterwards, everyone
would be disposed of according to his decisions.

Fiammetta swam with rapid strokes away from the boat, feeling
herself at home in the water already, having kicked off her
silken slippers already sodden with the sea-water in the
scuppers. Her clothes hampered her; when she had dived and
won from sight, she struggled free of the short embroidered
jacket, the sash, the flopping gauze trousers which impeded her.
Now she was free as air; they would not catch her. She felt the
water caress her naked flesh like dark silk, after there was no
longer the first necessity of putting distance between herself and
those in the boat. Now other sensations crowded in, and also a
kind of sixth sense, which told her that few except herself could

swim. She kicked out freely at last, and trod water; looking back, the harbour seemed a mass of dancing flares, reflecting the disturbed surface in yellow kite-shapes flung and tailing downwards towards darkness. Fiammetta laughed, stretched her limbs and swam on.

Presently her limbs thrust against rock. She gasped a little; the sudden contact had grazed her skin and the salt water nipped painfully. Rubbing the wound, she rested by the rock awhile, sensing its flatness and the way it had, in one place, been scooped out into a large circle as if to hold some object taut when wound about it. She noted this, idly and without immediate interest. She did not know what would become of her, but even now it was as though all the impurities of the years past were being shed from her, cleansed away by the caress of the water with its light current. She had the sensation of complete freedom, of having been born again. She let go her grasp of the rock, filled her lungs with air and swam on. Ahead was a deep cave. It seemed that she had always known there would be shelter for her, somewhere to remain while events shaped themselves. The starlight, and the half-effaced flares from the water, guided her on her way. She knew the boatmen had stopped looking for her. "They think that on an island they will find me readily enough, or else my dead body carried in to shore," she thought. She heard herself laugh, and her teeth gleamed against the wet veil of her darkened hair. Then she spared a thought for Melissa, little Gulbehar, her friend, and muttered a prayer to the Virgin that the child might reach her family again unhurt. Having prayed she felt certain that the prayer would be answered; it was as though a silver thread linked her to heaven and heaven to Melissa. She felt power in herself, in her mind, her limbs. Now she was nearing shore.

She waded out naked at last. The cave's shelter yawned above her, thrusting mysteriously towards inner darkness beyond the rim. Fiammetta pulled her wet hair forward to cover her breasts and body, and for the first time a shivering uncertainty took her. Why was she so certain of being protected? Should she not have stayed in the boat? Perhaps the men of the island here would not respect her; she remembered hearing at Mehedia that all the peasant families had been shipped off the island a year ago, because the Grand Master feared war from the East. There would only be nursing nuns left on the island, ready for siege. Perhaps she could reach them and help there; or ...

"May God and His Mother aid me to avenge my father and my mother," she said aloud, and for the first time since childhood felt warm honest tears running down her cheeks. There was nothing but rock here to lie on; she lay down, and in a short time slept, no longer hearing the whispering sea against the cave-walls. With the day, it would be shown her what to do.

The Old Man gave Anton and Juliana a handsome wedding-gift; a trip to the United States of America in his newest steamship *Isabella III*. Juliana laughed when she was told.

"I am a sad sailor; I shall be seasick, and Anton will spend his time in the engine-room."

She had settled contentedly into the state of a young woman about to be married. The house was in some confusion with the coming and going of the dressmaker, Miss Pringle, and in due course this lady knelt before the bride with her mouth full of pins to fit the wedding-dress, which was of India muslin with hand-goffered pleating at sleeves and hem. "After all one never wears one's wedding-dress again," Juliana had said when Agnes expressed doubts as to keeping the pleats sharp. She was to wear the very veil which Agnes had forsaken in the long-ago time when she ran away with Edward Tilney. It had in fact never been worn, as the second marriage to Julius had not, of course, been white. As for Fiona, she submitted with impatience to the fittings of her lilac-coloured gown; Timpy and Juliana had to hold her hands lest she thrust away the poor dressmaker.

"She will never understand what it is all about," said Timpy with finality. "It was a great mistake to have chosen her as your bridesmaid; you know plenty of other young ladies."

"Papa and Mama have given their permission," said Juliana flatly. In fact, the permission had had to be battled for with each parent separately; in the end, her own quiet will had prevailed. She was confident that she could teach Fiona what to do. "It is only a question of her following me across the drawing-room, and taking the bouquet from me while everything proceeds." She and Fiona would practise with flowers from the vases, she thought with determined triumph; fighting for Fiona had left her no time for the qualms every bride should feel. The wedding

day was not only to be *her* day, but her sister's. It was time poor
Fiona went about a little, now Timpy had schooled her not to
make those dreadful sounds so often. "She is so lovely that if
only she would keep quiet, she would be no different from a
thousand other girls, who never speak when their elders are
present." For poor Fiona to proceed in the way of those others,
and marry, would not be possible "but she may come and stay
with Anton and me, at least for a little; he has agreed to let her
have the attic room." For they had already found their house, a
smaller one than that lived in by Agnes and Julius, and only a
few streets away; one might call on Mama often. The house,
like the bride, was being fitted out; curtains, carpets, beds,
chairs, sofas were already there. Linen and china and silver
would be provided among the wedding-presents. Juliana, who
had never known what it was to be without enough money,
made plans with a happy confidence which somewhat shocked
her affianced bridegroom. Anton had been taught thrift all his
boyhood. But he was filled with pride at having made his way
and attained his position as a Bainbridge betrothed, and made
no attempt to stem Juliana's enthusiasm. In fact, it gave him
pleasure to watch her; excitement made her animated, and gave
colour to her face, making her less of a plain little mouse than
she had at first seemed. He looked forward to his marriage.

One day the Old Man had sent for him; it was just before the
public announcement of the betrothal. Timothy was at his desk,
as he had been that first day. As before, he rose and extended a
hand to the young German.

"I am pleased with you, Anton," he said simply. "You have
done well in the position I gave you, and will do better yet. The
design of the new hull is an improvement. You like your work,
do you not? I need hardly ask."

Anton bowed and smiled. Indeed he felt at home here among
these men with the rough guttural accents that were so like his
own tongue; the acrid smells of sweat, ink and worked iron, the
creating of great chains for lading, the belching of fire in the
furnaces, the sounds of working, and hammering, made him feel
at home. "I have never regretted leaving Germany," he
answered quietly. "I am honoured that you say to me what you
have."

Timothy was staring at the great daguerreotype of David
Bainbridge which hung above the mantel. "Once long ago I had

such a one as you here," he said. "It was when we were both
young men, and my cousin and I started with a name for
strength and precision, a yardful of scrap, and no contracts. I
could not have done without David then. He had the vision; I
toiled over the practical work, and together we made a team.
Since he died I have continued as he would have wished. I think
that if he were here now, he would be glad that you are to
become one of the family, as you are one of the firm." Together
they stared at the brilliant, sensitive face of the man who had
died because he brought death; presently Timothy turned away.
"It is a long time ago," he said, and began to shift papers on his
desk. He bade Anton be seated and commenced speaking about
a draft for a new engine they were presently at: the two men sat
immersed in talk, and were interrupted by Cochrane, the second
clerk, whose duty it was to bring up tea to the Old Man at
eleven o'clock daily. Today, he had had the foresight to place
two cups on the tray. It was a tacit intimation that Anton was
now of importance.

The wedding-day was cool, with only a hint of rain pending;
perhaps they would set off before it fell. Juliana was dressed in
her gown and veil, with the bouquet from Anton in her hands.
She went to show herself to her mother and then up to Fiona;
the latter was in her bridesmaid's dress, standing while Timpy
fitted the matching lilac bonnet over her thick bright hair.
Juliana laughed, and kissed her. "How well we both look!" she
said. "Come to the mirror, and see yourself."

She took Fiona's arm, and together they went to the pier-
glass, where their two young faces, and frilly gear, made a
pretty reflection. Fiona smiled, which she seldom did, showing
her teeth which were dingy. A sound came in her throat, as if
she would have spoken of her pleasure, but Juliana, laughing,
put a finger to her lips. "No sounds," she murmured, and shook
her head. Timpy watched them. She herself had trimmed her
dark gown with braid, and had on her best bonnet. She was
near tears; she was fond of Juliana, and hoped Fiona would
behave herself; it had been an exhausting business getting her
ready. Juliana came over, and kissed her cheek.

'Don't cry, Timpy; it will all be the same as it has always
been, except that you and Fiona will come to stay with us."

Timpy smiled with closed lips; she had caught a glimpse, once
or twice, of Juliana's young German bridegroom when he came
to the house, and was not certain that she liked him; but nobody
would have been good enough for Juliana. "I am sure I hope
you will be happy," she said tremulously.

"Happy? Of course, Timpy; and when my children are old
enough you shall be their governess." Timpy crimsoned; an
improper thing to have said! In fact, Juliana still knew nothing
except that babies came when one was married; she had turned
back to the mirror to arrange her veil, and was unaware of the
governess's discomfiture.

They came into the drawing-room. Anton was already there, his
bowed head facing the minister, who stood ready, the Bible by
him. There was no music—this was still considered ungodly at
such times except by the most progressive—and Juliana,
followed by her sister, made her way in silence on Julius' arm.
Julius looked well; this kind of situation let him employ his
dignity. The Old Man and his wife, certain workers from the
shipyard, and the few friends who had been asked, stood
watching. Agnes, in a handsome feathered bonnet, sat beside the
doctor and his wife. The groomsman was Mayo, one of the
firm's draughtsmen whom Anton had asked to support him on
this occasion.

Anton turned to look at his bride. There was Juliana, in her
veil and goffered gown, his Bainbridge bride that he had worked
for; and behind her was another, whose bright hair showed
beneath a ridiculous bonnet, for it should have been blowing
free with the sea behind it, while she herself, she, Fiammetta—

"An-thony."

The harsh sound pierced the silence; no one could pretend not
to have heard. Fiona Tilney stood staring at the man with grey
eyes; the flowers dropped from her hands to the carpet and lay
there spilled. So long ago, yet she could still remember; this was
the one for whom she had sacrificed everything, life itself in the
end; whom she had loved as it was no longer possible to love
anyone, seen again, known again, here.

He did not move. He knew her; how could it be otherwise
between them? What was he to do, caught in this trap? He had
the sense of being out of time and place; neither himself nor that

other, far from the actuality of the stuffy room where one could
not any longer hear the sighing of the sea. ...

He saw someone move outside his range of vision; it was
Juliana, who had halted in her progress for an instant and now
offered him her hand, smiling; odd that Fiona had known
Anton's name, perhaps she knew more than anyone was aware!
One must behave as though nothing had happened.

The hand was real. He held it as though it anchored him to
life. The minister began the wedding ceremony, plain and
without liturgy; this was Scotland.

"We are gathered here together to witness the marriage of
Anton Karl Muntz to Juliana Agnes Bainbridge ..."

There was a soft crumpling sound, and Fiona slid to the
floor. Instantly the groomsman, and Dr. Elliot from his seat,
came to lift her and carry her out. A pity to spoil the ceremony!
The poor creature must be got outside as soon as possible, into
the air. Juliana turned round, distress on her face. Julius said a
few words in a low voice, and she turned back; Fiona was in
good hands, as Papa said, and there was nothing one could do.
Afterwards, she would insist on seeing her before leaving, to kiss
her and make sure she was well tended. She heard herself say
the words which made her the wife of Anton Muntz. Afterwards, her mother embraced her. Agnes had remained calm. It
might have been foreseen, only Juliana was so stubborn, that
poor Fiona was unsuited to be a bridesmaid; but otherwise
everything had gone off well. She did not even notice that the
bridegroom's face was white. Had she done so, she would have
put it down to the emotion of the ceremony. Germans were
known to be sentimental.

And so Anton Muntz was driven off, after what seemed almost
perfunctory cake and madeira, with the Bainbridge bride
towards whom all his ambition had been directed until ... until
that other had come and stood there before him as had not
happened for many centuries. Yet it seemed only an hour since
he had seen, had touched and spoken to her, and more, much
more; the urge to catch her to him as she fell had been
overwhelming enough to cause him to step back from his place

at Juliana's side, with a cry rising in him which his dazed mind did not at once accept.

"Fiammetta! Fiammetta!"

Five

The great merchantman's living cargo stood huddled on the Maltese landing-place awaiting the decision as to its fate; the thinly-clad women shivered in the transient chill of early morning. Looking about them they saw, straggling down to the water's edge, the town of Birgù with, towering above, the giant yellow pyramid of Fort St. Angelo. A handful of market-sellers and peasants travelling early with their vegetables or goat's cheeses had collected, having heard news by word of mouth of the Turkish ship and its capture. They eyed the women idly, without lasciviousness. Greater interest was aroused in them by the sight of the ship's bulk, towed as she had been like a great helpless beast just inside the harbour and anchored, for many days of storm to come, below the wall of St. Angelo itself. A firing of salvoes caused the women to murmur with fright; the sailors, who still held them captive as though ready to drive them like sheep in one direction or another, consoled them.

"It is the salute to Our Blessed Lord," they said, and pointed to where, above the Fort, a painted Calvary hung in its stone shrine. "Every ship which carries guns salutes Him, on arrival and on departure." The man who had spoken crossed himself, staring up at the painted figure with its crown of thorns and the two weeping figures at its feet. A silence fell among the women, sensing some strangeness they did not understand. The air and water settled after the eddying of dust aroused by the salvo. Only little Melissa, the Maltese girl, remained staring up at the figure of Christ, her smooth profile rapt and content. She had lost her first anxiety and urgency on arrival; sooner or later, her parents would be told and would come for her.

Two young men had stood for a while nearby; both were of medium height and sturdily built, and wore the stripe-woven shirt and loose linen drawers of peasants. They guarded a cart drawn by a white mule, her thick eyelashes lowered against the

sun as she waited patiently. In the cart were vegetables, not yet
wilting in the day's heat, and a great pumpkin cut open in one
place to show its ripeness. The taller of the two young men took
the mule's reins from the other; jerking his head towards the
waiting women, the second made off in the direction of the
town.

"Sell what you can, Luqa, and take the money to my uncle if
I don't come back quickly," he said. "It is the little Melissa, I'm
certain; I shall go to old Paul and tell him, though how to do it
without his wife knowing is another matter; if I am wrong, it
may kill her."

"Tell old Paul anyhow; he is a man of sense," said Luqa
Briffa. He stroked the mule's neck while watching the other go
off down the street. It might be, it might not be, Melissa the old
Greek's daughter; Luqa kept out of direct trouble and did not go
to ask her, lest the Order's sailormen lodge a complaint that a
Maltese had been too familiar with their captured booty. Let old
Paul look to his own belongings. "But I pray for his sake and
his wife's that it is so," Luqa thought. "Five years they have
mourned her as though she were dead, ever since the day she
went to gather sea-shells on the north shore and was no more
seen, nor her maid neither."

He stared at the girl who might be Melissa, but had his
attention diverted by a sight which befell every Friday at this
hour; the Grand Master, leaving St. Angelo in procession on his
way to the hospital. The procession rode on mule-back, and the
clatter of shod hooves sounded clearly in the half-empty streets.
Grand Master La Valette rode ahead, and the Knights Grand
Crosses and almoners behind him, all clad in their hospitallers'
garb of black square cap and long dark gown. Once at the
hospital, all would share, no matter what their rank, in
dispensing food and comforts to the sick, serving them off silver
dishes. Luqa watched the erect figure of the Grand Master in
silence, holding his own mule steadily while the procession went
by. Like other islanders he had no great love for the Knights,
but when they went to the hospital they were doing good and
minding their own affairs. "I also will mind mine," thought the
young man, and returned to smoothing the little mule's coat and
keeping an eye on his vegetables. Would Toni keep him here
long?

But Toni Bajada, who ran swiftly, reached the old Greek

merchant's house in a matter of minutes. On the way he had discarded the idea of evading the merchant's wife; she would find out, in any case, and there was little time to waste. "Paul Grech!" he called. "Paul Grech!" using the dialect-name for all Rhodiot Greeks who had followed the Order to Malta.

The old man was already downstairs with his ledgers; he came to the door when Toni called, eyes blinking against the morning sunlight. "Not so loud, young man, you will wake my wife; she is in poor health and sleeps late, having spent half the night praying. What do you want that you are calling me so early?" But as Toni told him, and his face showed incredulous joy, the old woman's figure—she was too old to have been sent to Sicily—crept into the room; she was still fastening her *faldetta*. A gabble of questions followed; how had he known it was Melissa, where was she now, how soon might they have speech with her? "Talk less, good wife, and come," said the old merchant, and taking his wife's arm set off with her at a pace that left Toni Bajada behind. He lingered deliberately, not wanting to intrude on their reunion. If it were indeed so, it was the work of God and of His saints; that only child, born late, had been taken from them with a cruelty that seemed purposeless, leaving their lives dark and empty. Perhaps now the old woman would take hold on life again, and old Paul see his grandchildren about him before he died, if the Grand Master let Melissa stay here. "Let it be so," said Toni to his own saint, that other Paul who had once been shipwrecked on this island. Toni Bajada had often felt himself to have an affinity with the adventurous Apostle, who many times had taken the young man under his especial care.

There was no doubt left, as soon as the old couple approached the harbour; Melissa, turning from contemplation of the Calvary, cried out "*Missieri u ommi*, my father and mother!" and flung herself into their arms. The sailors, attempting to restore order, tried to separate the old pair from their daughter, though half-heartedly; tears of joy were running down old Grech's cheeks. "Tell your Grand Master I will pay him all of what I have and gladly, if only she may be restored to me!" he swore, and everyone laughed a little; the old Greek was known to have amassed much money since he followed the Knights here

from Rhodes in the old days. The stir and laughter died, then
rose again as the old woman, scandalised, swore her daughter
should not walk through the streets half naked, and where was a
decent mantle to cast round her? One was found; and lastly
there came on the scene a Spanish commander on his way back
to the Fort with word for the Grand Master when he should
return, and Grech pled with him to be allowed to take the girl
away. "We will attend to know the wishes of His Highness as
soon as may be."

The Spaniard, whose name was La Cerda, nodded coldly; he
knew Grech by sight and by repute, and his dark, heavy-lidded
glance flickered momentarily, with an awakening of interest,
over the plump forms of the young women. "They are to be
taken into the Fort," he said, "till I have word from the Grand
Master regarding their disposal. I will take it upon myself to
permit you to remove your daughter."

The Grechs went off joyfully. Dejected, the remaining few
women were herded up the steep ascent that led to the great
entrance-arch and stone defence curtains. Melissa's parents,
bearing her home thankfully, screened her with the borrowed
cloak from stares met in the awakening streets on their way; a
young girl was a rare sight now on the island. A chatter as of
magpies came from the small crowd left behind, as Toni Bajada
returned, joined Luqa, slapped the mule, and made off to the
town with their wares. Soon the place was as it had been, except
for the great ship lying at anchor below St. Angelo.

Fiona's faint, or coma, lasted longer than usual; lasted, in fact,
till after the bridal couple had left and the last guest had gone
from the house. Afterwards, Agnes, who seldom visited her
daughter, went upstairs, still clad in her wedding bonnet. She
stood looking down at the bed where Fiona lay, unlaced and
with her shoes removed. Timpy sat by her, rising to her feet
when Agnes entered. She said nothing, for there was nothing to
say. It had been a quirk of Miss Juliana's to have the poor thing
as bridesmaid; now, it was over.

Agnes stared down. As a rule, she forbade herself to think of
Fiona's father or of the brief, wild, foolish passion there had
been between them, that had resulted in this creature whose
affliction came from the brain. Oh, they'd had physicians to the

child in earlier years, even Julius, close-fisted as he was, paying
the fees, but it was all useless. With a deafness that came from
the ear alone they might have done something, but this was
unreachable, incurable. If Fiona had looked like her father,
what added pain to be with her now! But there was nothing of
Edward in his daughter; *he* had had a shock of straight brown
hair, a brown beard and laughing eyes. This changeling, this
threat to Agnes' own security, was neither hers nor Edward's;
Fiona came from some strange place beyond time. A queer
thought, but sanity vanished when one was brought face to face
with this first-born of one's body. The allusion made Agnes
flush; she evaded the rush of feeling by speaking to Timpy.

"Should the doctor be fetched, do you think? She should be
sitting up by now, and awake." The dark-red, gold-tipped
lashes lay on Fiona's cheeks without stirring, except for the
heavy breathing; her lips were parted. A pity she had never been
trained to brush her teeth properly; but it had been impossible,
like so many things. Timpy did very well.

Timpy was answering the question, in her careful way.
"Doctors have done little enough for her before; leave her to
recover in her own time, that's best."

Agnes did not question the decision. She inclined her head
and turned away, going majestically towards the door. The
governess looked after her. Poor soul, she was thinking, for all
her fine feathers, she has her own troubles married to a man
like that; half a crown a week pin-money, and that was to
include cakes for tea. Better to be poor with one's own shilling.

Fiona stirred, and it seemed as though she were murmuring
words; that was not possible. Timpy bent her ear lower and
satisfied herself it was only gibberish. The poor lamb! It was a
pity for her.

Julius was angry, and made his wife feel it; the scene at today's
wedding, *his* daughter's wedding, had been her fault. Fiona
should not have been permitted to appear. Fiona should never
have been born; the long-ago sin had been brought back to
weigh down Agnes' spirit. He saw to it that this was done.

"I have said little, over the years. But in future, she must not
leave her room, except in company with the governess. I will not
have this house made a laughing-stock."

Agnes looked at him, suddenly seeing him as if scales had dropped from her eyes; or was it that she saw him as she had always known him, truly, to be? If only he would not say "leetle". ...

"It was a pity it happened," she said gently. "But Juliana I think is happy, and Anton—"

"The father is satisfied," said Julius curtly. Happiness was a term that eluded him; when had *he* ever been happy? Not permitted to do as he would with his life, forced to marry—he put it in this way to himself now—forced to marry a woman who had gone out, like a bitch in season, to mismate, and the fruit of the mating lodged with him, Julius, for life. It was as well Juliana's affection for her half-sister showed some practical result, such as taking Fiona off their hands and letting her live, with the governess, in the new house the couple were to occupy on their return; there was plenty of room there.

Six

She awoke to bright sunlight, etching the mouth of the cave and sea beyond. In the shallows a man's figure showed darkly; he was wading towards the entrance. He was stocky, and the sun gleamed on thick brown hair. He wore the open shirt and coarse-woven trews of the Maltese peasant. He had not seen her.

Swiftly, like an animal, she let the shadows claim her, shaking out her salt-heavy tresses and crouching behind them and the shelter of the rock. She was ready for attack, and her hand, seeking a small stone, curved round it while her teeth gleamed wolfishly; with the stone, she'd do him injury if she must. But his gasp of indrawn breath, when he saw her, was sudden and genuine; a shyness came over his face, and he averted his gaze.

"I am hungry," she told him, thanking God Melissa had taught her the dialect. "Will you get me food? I have no money."

He nodded; his reactions, she saw, were intelligent and swift, not those of a fool. "I have a boat here in which I have caught some fish," he said. "In the back of the cave there is driftwood; will you light a fire?"

He reached in his shirt and drew a tinder from it. As he did so, a crystal locket borne on a black cord swung out, catching the sunlight for an instant before his brown hand thrust it back. He flushed a little, and fingered the place as though it held a crucifix.

Fiammetta laughed. The locket had held a curl of hair, silver-gilt in colour and fine as a child's. "I have no clothes," she said. She seemed to take it for granted that he would aid her. He nodded, slowly; unlatched his shirt, and tossed it over to where she was. She wrapped it about her body thankfully, feeling it warm from his contact and from the sun. "What is your name?"

she asked him. The shirt covered her to below the thighs; gracefully, as though savouring the pleasure of warmth and the ability to show herself freely, she came out to the mouth of the cave. Beyond it, the sun shone on a glittering sea; there was no sign from here of the captured ship.

He told her that he was Toni Bajada. "I am a swimmer," he said, and for the first time he smiled, showing teeth white and uneven in his brown, light-eyed face. He had a powerful, muscular body; a down of dark hair covered the chest and arms, but his lithe quick quality was more than animal; she had the sensation that he knew things in advance, by use of some sixth sense. She laughed again, feeling an affinity for Toni. "I too," she said. "I swam round from the harbour last night, past the fort. See! I grazed my leg." She showed the place to him.

"There is moss which I and my friend Luqa Briffa bring from a rock on Gozo when we have a boat. It is good for wounds," he said. He touched the leg gently. In all their dealings she had the feeling that he thought of her not as a woman, but his equal. This pleased her. "It is nothing," she said. "The salt water cleansed it well enough yesterday. It will heal quickly."

Toni Bajada nodded, admiration in his light eyes. "You swam from the harbour?" he said. "There are not many swimmers on the island except the Maltese. I have heard, though, that Greek women swim."

"I am not Greek," she said. She flung back her hair and met his glance squarely. "I would aid the Grand Master if I can," she told him. "Soon now enemy ships will come. I heard much talk where I have been. I have that which I must say to His Highness alone. Will you help me to reach him?"

"I?" he said. "I have no traffic with the Knights. It was not my wish that they came here, in my father's time, maybe my grandfather's."

"Yet you love God, for St. Paul brought the faith early to this island." She was still using lessons learned from Melissa. "Would you have it fall victim to the Turk? It would be better to make common cause with the Knights, though their pride may have offended you." She thought of the cold celibate commander of the ship which had taken them. "They fight for Christ," she said, "as you would surely do."

"Who are you that you know all these things?" he said, and

for the first time fear showed in his face. Despite her talk of the Christian faith she had the look, standing there, of one born from the sea, Aphrodite the lovely and terrible; her full breasts strained aginst the latched shirt, and her long slim legs ended in small feet whose nails shone like sea-shells. If she laid an enchantment on him he, Toni, might wait here for a lifetime that seemed like an hour; and win back at last to Mdina to find it in ruins, and Bianca dead or an old woman. He shivered in the bright sunlight; such things had befallen others. But Fiammetta smiled and laid her warm, human hand on his arm.

"Give me your knife, Toni Bajada," she said. "I want to cut off my hair."

He could not question her or plead, and he gave her the knife, his prized possession; watching, with regret, as the heavy masses were lopped off and slid, limp with the salt in them, to the cave floor. "We must burn that," said Fiammetta, and together they piled driftwood and weed at the back of the cave and, when Toni's tinder had caused it to crawl into greenish flame, burned the hair in the fire. It caught suddenly; Toni wrinkled his nose at the pungent smell.

"Let us eat now," he said. "I will bring the fish." He brought his catch and they cooked it, flat on the hot rock, and ate their fill; Fiammetta having gutted it with the knife in her hands, resembling a boy with her rough-cropped hair. Toni glanced at her now and again with a shy and increasing admiration; this quality, which was not love, he had never before accorded to any woman. Although she had told him none of her story he knew that they trusted one another. Suddenly, when their meal was over, she leaned forward and made the sign of the cross on his breast.

"It is good to have the freedom to make that sign again," she said. "In the country where I was born—far away from here—a stranger is welcome in one's house and is asked no questions, neither where he has come from nor where he may be going. That has happened to me here, and it is a kindness I will repay with my life if I must."

Then she began to give him swift instructions. "Lose no more time than you need," she said, as though knowing that he, like all Maltese, must sometimes idle. "Soon, within days, news will reach the Sultan of the loss of the great merchant-ship bearing his bride." She smiled. "His anger will be terrible, for he has been made to look a fool. I think that as soon as he may, he will send a great fleet against Grand Master La Valette and his knights. And so I must see the Grand Master, tell him all I know, and make him accept my help even though I am a woman. But of that we will speak to nobody until I am in his presence. Find me a man's dress, Toni, with a dagger at the belt that I can carry in my teeth when I swim."

And she laughed, and he also with sheer exhilaration of the plan; he felt more carefree than he had done this whole year, doubting as he had done the progress of his suit with Bianca, for although she was willing her father was not, and none of the nobles of the capital high on its rock had obeyed the Grand Master in any matter. Now he began to trouble himself about Bianca's safety even in Mdina if the Turks came, as they often did in smaller raids. "I will die in her defence if I may," he thought. Then his practical peasant's mind came to his aid; would it not be better, when the Turkish fleet came, to fight here on the beaches, near to his own medium, the water?

"God will arrange all," he said to himself. He made his way out to where the boat waited, leaving Fiammetta in the cave. He knew where he might borrow clothes for her which were not those of a peasant. The swift light oars struck the water as he rowed steadily back to Birgù.

The man to whom Toni Bajada would go for clothes was a young Scot who had come out in the previous year and whose name was Anthony Graham. Graham was in a peculiar position in that he desired to enter the Order but could not, or not yet; his parents, having obeyed only the Scots law of handfasting and their own hearts, were not here considered fully enough married in the eyes of the Church to allow that their son had been born in undoubted wedlock. No candidate with doubt on his escutcheon might become a member of the Order, not even if he were the by-blow of an emperor. So young Anthony Graham, with the impatience of his blood, awaited word from the Pope as to the possibility, or otherwise, of his reception; and in the meantime made himself useful about the Grand Master's secretary Sir Oliver Starkey, in whose house he stayed. Starkey was a kindly man who treated the young Scot as a son; Anthony felt an attachment to him which would only worsen any adverse

news from Rome. But the times were, without doubt, too
pressing for the question of one young man, of minor nobility, to
be considered soon by the Curia; days and months had already
passed while Anthony waited and recited his Offices daily in
preparation for the time when—as must surely happen, otherwise why had he been born to no purpose?—he should be
admitted as a member of the greatest Order of Knights in
Christendom. He tried in other ways to make himself worthy;
he had never looked on a woman in lust, although his dark,
pale-skinned good looks, clear grey eyes and curling hair made
many women look so on him. Toni Bajada accordingly grinned
at the thought of gaining such a one to aid Fiammetta's purpose;
it would remain to be seen whether Anthony Graham would
laugh when it was all found out.

Anthony Graham had first made the acquaintance of Toni
Bajada and his kin under distressing circumstances; it had been
when the renegade Scots knight, John James Sandilands, had
been turned over to the secular arm for justice and had been
hanged, drawn and quartered in Birgù market square. This
happened rarely and when it did, the fall of a great and haughty
Knight was manifested in a yell of hatred fit to chill the blood in
one's veins. Pressed back against a house-wall by the milling,
shouting crowd, clad in his anonymous plain mantle, young
Graham had felt sick. He had that very year, with high hopes,
journeyed out from Scotland by way of France, aspiring to join
the Order; by the time of his arrival the flaw had been
discovered, and he was already humiliated by the delay in
establishing the legality of his parents' marriage. Sir Oliver
Starkey being kind, Graham did his best to repay the kindness;
carrying out, while holding no certain office, the tasks of
secretary, errand-runner, sometimes even servant, taking himself down to the market for fish and cheeses and rough loaves
when the Spaniard who did such things was busied elsewhere.
For the Tongue of England, once so great, had few enough now
to fill out her numbers from a Protestant land, and young
Graham was welcome to Sir Oliver in all ways. For this reason,
and not of intent to see the hanging, he was in the market-place
that day.

Sandilands would make no confession nor did he now repent

publicly of his crime, which had been sacrilege. During his term in prison he was one of the few who had never, at any time, carved a submissive cross into the soft yellow rock of the deep cell, showing that they died in the faith of Christ. All Sandilands had left was a precise and beautifully carved rhyming epigram in Latin, bitterly concerned with the treachery of friends and the triumph of evil. It would survive as his memorial. Now, as he approached in the cart, fruit, stones and even eggs were flung; an expelled Knight was an object of less worth than a maggot, lower than if he had never risen high. Anthony watched while the condemned man was conveyed to the gallows, to die blackly without comfort for his soul; and as the cart was pulled away from beneath Sandilands' feet and the crowd gave its wolfish roar, pulled out his beads and prayed, with all the strength he might, for that fellow Scot he had never known. The mercy of God might well reach Sandilands now, in the instants between life and death; and if one prayed—

The executioner's knife slit the belly of the swinging body and raked out the bowels with a hook. There followed the bloody and gruesome form of death perfected by Edward I of England against that bravest Scot of all time, William Wallace. But Sandilands was now beyond memory of his great compatriot, and doubtfully in his company. When all had been done, and the quartered body exposed and flung into the street, the crowd thinned quickly now the day's sight was over. From corners and alleyways thin forms crept; the dogs of Birgù, ready to tear at the waiting meat. Within moments of the departure of the crowd they were there, pulling the flesh off the bones.

Anthony Graham leant unsteadily against the wall, white-faced and retching. The heartlessness of the people shocked him as much as the manner of Sandilands' death. What had happened to turn the gentle Maltese into a crowd reminiscent of the howls in a Roman arena? How near to savagery were all men Christ died to save? "He acted in a moment's insane fury, and has paid for it a thousandfold," he thought, remembering Sandilands' stripping of the church of Birgù, for which he had died. He could not bring himself to leave the support of the wall yet, though the smell of carrion in his nostrils sickened him.

A touch on his arm made him start; it was a Maltese lad of about his own age. The light eyes in the brown face were friendly. "I know that you come from the houses of the Order,"

Toni Bajada had said in halting French, keeping his voice low in case of eavesdroppers. "Will it please you to come and rest in my uncle's house a little while?" He spoke humbly, as though the other were to do him a favour thereby.

Graham let himself be led into the old peasant's house. It was the first time he had been inside a Maltese dwelling. Seated by the open door of the small, whitewashed room, a cup of rough red wine between his hands, he felt shame assail him; both that he should have given way to queasiness at Sandilands' death which after all had been just, and that he should have let himself been taken pity on by a native. The mask of aloofness, which was already Anthony Graham's defence against the world, slid over his face and posture; he laid the cup courteously down, with a word of thanks, and rose.

"The sun is hot," said the old man who was Toni's uncle. "Rest here awhile." He spoke in the dialect, which Graham could not yet follow; but his meaning was clear enough. The young Scot answered by way of Toni.

"Tell him that I value his kindness, but I should not be a stranger to the smell of blood. It is one of the tasks of the Order to fight God's battles." In any case, he reminded himself, though he did not boast of it, he had already seen service in the wars of France. He felt his assumed importance descend on him; the old man and the young regarded him shrewdly, both smiling.

"No one fights the worse for having a tender heart," said Toni. He lifted the door-curtain for the young Scot to pass out. After that they met frequently, about their business in the streets of Birgù, and spoke together on occasion despite Anthony's haughtiness. Their acquaintance could even have been called friendship by the time that Toni Bajada, seeking for a man's dress for Fiammetta down at the cave, knocked on the door of Sir Oliver Starkey's lodging and asked for speech with Anthony Graham.

"But why should you want these things?" said Anthony. He had wedged back the lid of his chest of possessions and had brought out, after some searching, a black velvet doublet, rubbed in places; a clean shirt with a laundered ruff, and a pair of reasonable trunk-hose. "These are mended," he said, "and the shirt I can ill spare. Will you return it to me? The rest do not matter."

"The person for whom the clothes are intended will do so, no doubt, in time." Toni was smiling as if some inner gaiety illumined him. "Can you not trust me? We have known one another for a year."

"Time is no matter," grunted Anthony. Then he touched Toni's shoulder to show he jested, and thrust the clothes towards him. "Take them," he said. "A dagger I cannot spare." Toni found one later, in a booth in the market-place. He lingered meantime, his arms full of young Graham's garments.

"One thing more," he said. "Can you ensure that the person wearing these clothes may be admitted to the presence of the Grand Master? The matter is one of urgency."

Anthony frowned, feeling himself involved in the mysterious matter more than he liked; it was of value to comport himself seriously and correctly during this waiting time. Any behaviour described as other than prudent might delay, even prevent, his admission into the Order. He compromised, and said he would inform Sir Oliver.

Toni nodded, satisfied. Sir Oliver Starkey was highest of all in the counsels of the Grand Master, and if Fiammetta's cause was of value he would see that she was brought to La Valette. "I will return in an hour, then," he answered, "bringing—your shirt."

He laughed inwardly, thinking how greatly Graham's unwillingness would have been increased had he known, and seen, who was to wear the shirt. The young Scot was so circumspect it was a temptation to tease him.

When Fiammetta received the clothes, she noticed a mark on the shirt; it was red, made of red thread, sewn carefully into the linen. When it was on her it covered a part of her breast. She looked down in curiosity; there was a device sewn there, almost worn out with many washings; it looked like two birds, one above the other. There was a motto which read *"Ne oubliez."* Do not forget ... but what?

She felt a strange trembling, as though the touch of the shirt bewitched her. It was like the trembling she had felt that time in the garden at Mehedia after the Mistress of Girls had dosed her with herbs, thinking Dragut might want to make love.

She sat soon enough on the edge of Anthony Graham's bed, wearing his clothes. It was all like a dream, had been so since she saw the face, that of a dark angel with grey eyes, glimmer in the half-dark of the cool hall. At sight of him, she had forgotten Toni Bajada and had not thanked him for his help. Absently, she admitted now that it was likely enough they would meet again in so small an island. That did not matter. ...

"What is the device on your shirt?" she had dared to say. She had to know; but why? He had not given her time to think of it, but had answered calmly "It is an eagle attacking a stork, the badge of my family since a Scot named Grim, long ago, overcame the Romans on their own wall and left a place named Grimsdyke." His rare smile had showed, then he had fallen silent. With the silence, the thing that had befallen her gathered force, threatening to overwhelm her. It was a thing that one could not help, or prevent, or ... Ah, to know more of him! She placed her hands on her black-clad knees, staring at a darn in the hose, to still their trembling.

Anthony had left her seated and had gone to his prie-dieu. Like every other aspirant to the Order he chose to recite a set number of Offices each day; after offering his guest wine he had excused himself for this reason, saying Sir Oliver Starkey was at present out of the house but would return in time for his food. "You may wait here till he comes," he had informed Fiammetta. He spoke in halting Maltese, as though the newcomer were a servant, as though one of Bajada's acquaintances could not but be so; this, although it meant her disguise was effective, made Fiammetta angry. She had not dared to tell Anthony Graham yet that she was a fellow-Scot, still less a female; waiting for him to finish his prayers, she tried to tell herself that this was the nearest to privacy with him that she would ever contrive. How shocked he would be when he found out what she was! She wondered what explanation Toni had given him for having required the clothes; she should have asked the Maltese before he left, and now it was too late.

She stared at the back of Anthony's head, noting its narrow symmetrical contours and the way in which the ears were set, small and fine, close to the bone. His hair grew down waving to a peak at the back of his neck and beneath its cropped sleekness, the flesh was fair as a child's; she would have liked to set her lips to it. He had a straight slim back, narrow hands and long straight legs; his grey eyes when they had rested briefly upon her had been cool, but when he smiled at Toni she had seen that he had sound teeth. He was too grave for so young a man, she thought, knowing even as little of men as she did; she would like to make him laugh, to see the teeth flash in his face like Toni's. But she had had no such feeling for the Maltese as she had for this man. She knew well enough what it was, for all her training at Mehedia had prepared her for it. "That last time they made me go to Dragut in the garden, they gave me a drug that was bitter, and made me tremble," she thought again. That same trembling was still with her, and what she wanted was to lie on the bed and let Anthony Graham make love to her. She faced the need squarely, knowing that it was impossible of fulfilment.

Presently Graham interrupted his prayers and turned his head to find her regarding him. Her eyes were bright with tears and it occurred to him that perhaps he had been inhospitable. "Are you hungry?" he asked, still in Maltese. It was possible that Sir Oliver would be delayed, and it would not do to keep a guest, of however small importance, famished. But the red-haired boy for whom his clothes were too large suddenly shook his head and answered him in Scots.

"No, I am not hungry. How long will it be till Sir Oliver is here? I must see the Grand Master; it is of importance."

Graham rose from his prie-dieu, filled with astonishment that the lad should be a Scot and also amused at his air of importance. "Sir Oliver will not be longer than a day and a night, and if need be you may share my bed till he comes," he said. He would have asked more, but the boy had turned his face away, the colour flooding up over it. Was he in tears, so tall a lad? If the message for the Grand Master was indeed urgent, perhaps he should take the visitor up to the Fort. In Sir Oliver's absence it was difficult to know what to do for the best, and he did not want to appear either unduly forward or timorously backward.

He went to the door, calling for the Spanish servant. "Where is your master?" he said. A volley of explanations and shruggings, gesticulations with the hands, and head-shakings followed. Anthony gathered that it was possible Sir Oliver might be with the Grand Master in his garden-grotto at the top of the Fort, where many matters were discussed almost daily. It was better, no doubt, to make the effort of going to search.

He jerked his head, a little impatiently, at the boy. "Follow me and we will go to try and find Sir Oliver," he said. He would make no promises about taking the other to the Grand Master, in case he could not carry them out and be made to look foolish. Not to be made ridiculous had assumed large proportions in Anthony's mind this last year; he was, as a result, a little pompous.

Fiammetta followed obediently, thinking how tall he was. She herself would hardly reach his shoulder.

Jean Parisot de la Valette, Grand Master of the Order of St. John, sat as had been supposed in his garden-grotto with his friend and secretary, Sir Oliver Starkey, by him. Both men's heads were bent over a map drawn in sepia ink on vellum, showing in some detail the contours of Malta and Gozo, the smaller island. Behind them, the shade cast by the little grotto combated the intense heat of the noonday sun. It had been carved, like the prisoners' carvings, out of that same soft yellow rock which was the foundation of the giant cone of Fort St. Angelo itself; in the shade behind the two knights' greying heads, Corinthian pillars reared delicately. Beyond was a garden, where in his rare leisure La Valette could walk; twisting creeper and mulberry, pumpkin-plant and tall red lilies, grew there. Below, the great fort spiralled down, curtain upon widening curtain, to the harbour. It was not possible to see the sea from here; the inner garden was walled off, as though to give the Grand Master respite from his incessant searching of horizons. He raised his head now, hazel eyes narrowed as though they saw beyond house-wall and gate-arch. His finger still pointed at a star-shaped fort in the plan. Sir Oliver studied the place, brooding above his narrow beard.

"It is true that, as you mention, St. Elmo could be the crux of any siege," he said, still staring at the place below La Valette's finger. "But who is to say that the Turk, if he comes, will not attack from the south-east or even by way of Mdina?" He spoke consideringly, as one who had known La Valette long enough to question his decisions; and as an old friend will, the Grand Master humoured him. He smiled, the act giving life and light to his long, shrewd, bearded face.

"Good Oliver, you are filled only with the doubts of any intelligent man. If the Turk comes, you say? I tell you he *will* come; as he came before, at Rhodes. You are not yet long enough in our Order to remember that."

His eyes changed and grew bitter and he himself remembered, in the way dreams still came to trouble his sleep, the fall of Rhodes, island home of the Order for more than two centuries; the valiant defence over half a year, and then, at last, the capitulation through treachery by a Greek swimmer; the parleying with the infidel, and then—on that last day of all with the snow falling whitely down—the massed ranks of the Turks, waiting in ordered silence while the old Grand Master, Villiers de l'Isle Adam, made his way out with his following to the waiting ships which would take him and his Order into perpetual exile. La Valette, who had been a young Knight then, remembered his own helpless anger as the snowflakes had settled on the collar of the old man's cloak, melting and soaking his thin white hair and neck; it was pity enough, so the young Sultan Suleiman the Magnificent had said, to see so gallant an old warrior expelled, at his age, from his home. Young Suleiman, resplendent with youth and a white brocaded mantle, had called on the old man at the conclusion of truce; had left nothing undone to add to his comfort except that he took the heart out of him; he took away Rhodes. Rhodes with that stronghold that should have been impregnable, ancient Rhodes of the fertile fields and orchards! How hard it had been to exchange her for this grudged and barren rock, to which eight full years later they came as strangers, forever wearing black cloaks as mourning for the loss of Rhodes!

"Yet we were glad enough of the Emperor's gift of this place, after so many years of wandering unwanted through every court in Europe. Once here, besides, the old man knew he could die in peace. When my time comes, I pray that I may be buried nearby him; he was a gallant soldier in war and, at all times, a wise leader."

He had not spoken aloud, and Sir Oliver Starkey knew his friend too well to ask what his thoughts were. He himself left

the study of Fort St. Elmo to study the Grand Master. He loved
La Valette, although the man was not lovable to everyone, his
cold, all-seeing intellect having in its single vision one aim, and
one only; the preservation, against the infidel, of the Order in
Malta.

"What makes you so certain that the Turk will attack?"
Starkey said gently. In his heart he knew the question itself was
folly; for years past the Order's galleys had harried the Grand
Turk at sea, taking merchandise and prisoners by the thousand.
It did not need the Grand Master's ironic shrug in reply.
"There is also the late affair of the Kustir Aga's merchantman,"
La Valette murmured, jerking his head in the direction in which
the great ship was now secured; down below the north wall of
the Fort, just within the calm harbour.

"The ladies?" said Sir Oliver. Again La Valette shrugged;
women did not enter his reckoning, and it fitted his estimation
of them that all, except nursing nuns, had now been shipped off
the island. "On the next boat to Sicily, to Don Garcia," he said.
"If the Viceroy has no use for them, they can find work in the
biscuit-factory." The Order maintained the factory in Sicily to
provide diet for galley-slaves.

Sir Oliver laughed outright. "You are not gallant," he said.
"One of them was intended as the Sultan's bride, so they say. A
biscuit-factory?"

"The Sultan's bride escaped from the small-boat, and swam
away with the current," said La Valette. "As for the others, it is
true they cannot all go. The Greek child was restored to her
parents on the wharf—a piece of good fortune for us, Oliver,
knowing the Maltese!—and since then they say one of the
Circassian girls, who is not a good sailor, has fallen into fits like
one possessed of the devil. They say she may not live. I have
sent her down to the good Sisters of St. John, with one of her
own nation to succour her. That leaves few." His tone grew
impatient suddenly. "Enough of this, Oliver! There are more
urgent matters, those of defence, to attend to. I think that to
instal barrels of salt water *here*, and *here*, in St. Elmo would be
a precaution, in the event of incendiary flames heating the
armour of those who can then jump into them behind the wall.
That is all ready; and the stores, and the line of reinforcement.
How we are to get the fresh men across by night, and ferry back
the wounded—"

"Are you then so certain that the Turk will attack St. Elmo at all? What if he attacks Birgù direct? He is no fool to waste time and ammunition on a small, hastily-built fort which does no more than guard one entrance to the harbour."

"Haste has been our curse, it is true," said the Grand Master. And the soft crumbling stone here, he was thinking, lifted too readily from the thin earth ... There is no more soil on Malta than will grow a plant with shallow roots. And yet we have done as well as we could, in the time. "There may be time still," he said aloud. "Sultan Suleiman will not have word of his great ship's capture, and the loss of his bride, for some days yet. Thereafter he must fit out his navy, decide on his commanders, call his troops in from Hungary and the Morea. You will have time, Oliver, for the task I would assign to you, if you will undertake it. It will be difficult, long, and possibly thankless."

"God's orders and yours are my life. You know that well enough. What is it that you would have me do?"

"Go to the courts of England, France and Spain; to the heretic, the murderess, the madman. Demand help, money and men and ships, for us here in Malta. Put it to them, to these people, that Christendom is at stake as much as it ever was in the days of the loss of the Holy Places in Jerusalem, for this is the last bastion of the Faith. Plead with them in your good Latin, Oliver; there is no one else in whom I could so place my trust. If you fail, then no man could succeed."

Sir Oliver Starkey bowed his head. "Monseigneur, I will do your bidding; that is without question. But recall that, hardly two years past, Elizabeth of England hanged and quartered three of our number because they would not perjure themselves against the Catholic Faith. Think also that the possessions of our Langue, the great Tongue of England, have been squandered and sequestered there among a grasping set of court-clerks and butchers' sons, so that I now have Spaniards to serve me instead of Englishmen and must pad out our hollow places in the Langue with whom I may."

"You have young Graham, whose cause is pending in Council. Take him with you when you go. It will be better than to have him kicking his heels here, brooding on whether his father and mother were or were not in wedlock when they conceived him." La Valette forced himself to jest a little, knowing that Sir Oliver saw, as he himself saw still, the face of young Adrian Fortescue the Order's Knight and martyr, looking up heavenwards from the waiting gallows as though the skies opened to show him the throne of God. "May their brave souls rest in peace," Starkey muttered. "To set foot in England will be a harder thing than once it was, yet I'll go ... ay, and kiss her hand that signed the warrant for that death, and many another."

"She may well sign an order for a round sum in gold, do her conscience prick her accordingly," said La Valette. "It must be attempted, Oliver! Nothing is too hard for assay in this coming war between day and night ... why, here is young Graham now, and another with him."

Both men left their thoughts and their staring at the map as the guard, who had been at the outer gate, saluted and asked if Graham and his companion were to be permitted to enter the garden. "Yes, let them come," said La Valette. He had forgotten the late talk about England and did not watch as the two figures, one tall, the other slight, advanced: his gaze had returned to the map again and he was once more engaged in the study of Fort St. Elmo. Anthony Graham advanced, dropping on one knee in the Grand Master's presence; behind him the red-haired, black-clad, slight figure did likewise. Graham had forgotten the boy, as he always forgot all other matters when in presence of Jean Parisot de la Valette. The nearness of so great a man, leader of the ancient and exclusive Order he had come overseas in the hope of joining, dazzled him; yet a down-to-earth quality in the Grand Master's manner dispelled illusion, forcing Graham to see himself as he was. Remembering that his legitimacy was still suspect, he cursed his parents, undutifully, for their Scots handfasting. If they had only waited till it could take place in church, no matter how hotly they loved one another! That unseemly passion—as his aunt, who had brought Anthony up with grim rectitude, had told him—had been their downfall; his father had been killed in a duel before he, Anthony, was born, waged with an erstwhile rival suitor for his flighty, pretty mother. And *she* had not survived Anthony's birth. A sensation pricked at the backs of his eyes which he knew with horror to be tears: he dared not look up in case the Grand Master saw him and knew him for a weakling. But as though he knew and understood the young man's feelings La Valette talked on, smoothly and with as much wit as if they were at home in his native Provence. He had a gay tongue when he was not burdened with worry.

"Monsieur de Graham, I regret this delay in your reception as much as anyone; for I have had reports of your fair prowess at arms. Also, I knew your father when he came over with the young King James the Fifth to the Court of France, to seek a royal bride. That was in the days when the Order, unhappily, had no home; now Malta is ours, and I am glad that you are here to defend her should the need arise. You resemble, I may say, your father greatly."

"He is dead, Monseigneur."

"I know it, and regret it."

Anthony spoke hotly. "Monseigneur, if the Pope's Holiness were only to send word regarding the validity of my parents' marriage! Both lived and died in the Catholic Faith despite all change in Scotland; in that land, the handfast way of marriage takes place often, and the heirs of such marriages are recognised. If I—"

La Valette held up a hand. "I know all that, and so does His Holiness. But he is ... pressed with other matters at the moment." He spoke drily, and young Graham was suddenly ashamed of himself. "Monseigneur, accept my sword in your service whether or not I may fight as one of your Order! The Turk may soon assail these shores; they talk of it even in the streets."

"If there was ever any doubt on that matter, the captured merchantman of Kustir Aga has resolved it," murmured La Valette. He signalled to Anthony to rise. "In less time than it will take to fit out a full fleet Sultan Suleiman will be upon us for vengeance—as once at Rhodes. This time, though, we will accept no terms."

His eyes strayed to where, on the near wall, hung the banner the Knights had brought with them from the Stronghold of the Hellhounds, thirty years before. The clenched fist which was the device of Villiers de l'Isle Adam showed clearly. "If you did, as I, remember the fruitless journeyings for aid after Rhodes, the bitter bread of charity from unwilling powers! This proud Order was great when the first Crusaders rode to the Holy Land, and now—" He spread out his hands, and said no more; but all present knew what was left unsaid. At last, grudgingly given and with the devil's brew of Tripoli as makeweight, this little, barren rock of Malta, so different from fertile Rhodes of the great forts that Villiers de l'Isle Adam, journeying here at last to die, had wept when he saw the island rising hard and naked from the sea. "But we have made it ours, have planted and builded and strengthened here; and I for one will leave my bones bare on the shores before I will abandon it to the infidel, no matter with how great an army."

He remembered the Scots boy standing in front of him and with a gesture of his fine-boned, practical hand brought himself back to the present. "Yes, I accept your sword gladly, Monsieur de Graham! I would do so—" he smiled—"were you a villain, a cut-throat or a galley-slave who had escaped his chains, so hard pressed are we for men and arms. But knowing you for a brave fighter I am glad you will stay with us: or rather that you will return to us, for I am going to send you away."

"Away, Monseigneur?" Anthony's face was white. "But I had hoped to remain here, and serve as a lay-brother or help with the fortifications." He heard a quickly indrawn breath from the red-haired lad behind him; what the devil had it to do with *him* ? He flung out a desperate hand towards the grotto's window, where from below there came the incessant sounds of digging, digging, piling of stones. La Valette's orders had been to work night and day at perfecting the defences with such poor material as they had; only the barren soft rock, inferior mortar, inadequate tools. Already, the two great forts of St. Elmo and St. Michael rose to the east of the island, and communications ran from north to south between them at St. Angelo, the main fort above Birgù.

"You shall return," the Grand Master said quietly to Graham. "But now I want you to accompany Sir Oliver here on an important mission to England, and elsewhere. You will be of more value to him—even as a Scot—" and La Valette's lips twitched—"than someone not of those islands. Also he tells me that you make a diligent secretary. That is as much a part of war now as to fight. Will you do this for us?"

Anthony flushed. "Monseigneur, I am at your command in all things, as much so as if I had been sworn into the Order. But, I beg of you"—he stammered in his emotion—"let me return here in time to draw my sword in your service, and if need be, to lay down my life."

"There will be many lives laid down," said La Valette.

As Graham drew forward his compatriot their glances met for the last time; the young Scot had the sudden impression that the Grand Master was carved in marble. There had been a coldness about his last statement as if he reckoned men only as cannon-fodder; yet Graham knew that was not so. Nobody was gentler or more approachable than this Provençal knight who, by dint of long service and many brave deeds, had at last won to the leadership of one of the most ancient Orders in Christendom. Graham had himself seen La Valette, in the knights' hospital, tend the sick and wounded and dispense alms to the island's poor. The shrewd, dry face could show compassion over a stinking, suppurating limb, a deadly wound or fever: but now La Valette spoke of lives to be lost as though he had assessed and reckoned them. "No doubt he has," Graham thought.

"Stay awhile," said the Grand Master. "I know that Sir Oliver means you to accompany him back to the lodging." He smiled. "Does it astonish you that I know all I do so precisely? I tell you, the success of a campaign depends on the ability of its commander to remember small things."

Fiammetta, in her boy's clothes, knelt before the Grand Master. Her head tilted upwards on its white neck; looking at his face, she found herself surveying him as she would any man. He will not show mercy always, she thought; he is not a fool, and he will discard even chivalry unless it serves his purpose for the time.

"Who are you?" La Valette asked her. His eyes had narrowed; almost, it was as though he had penetrated her attire. She kept her gaze fixed on his and answered boldly, knowing that he would have no time for those who were fearful or hesitant.

"A swimmer, Monseigneur." She used his title as she had heard Graham do. "I have already swum the harbour, and found a flat rock carved to hold a chain. I can swim long distances without tiring. It is my wish to serve Monseigneur in this way, in the coming war; perhaps when the galleys come, I can swim out to them and release prisoners. The galleys that will row out from Istanbul hold many Christians aboard."

La Valette grimaced a little; he himself had served a sentence in the galleys. "That is well known," he said, and frowned.

"From whence do you come? When did you arrive in Malta? I know nothing of one of your description, although—" and his glance slid sideways to where Graham waited, ill at ease—"do I not recognise the clothes?"

"Monseigneur, I know nothing further of the matter!" began Graham hotly, but the Grand Master silenced him. The boy with red hair flushed and dropped his gaze. "I asked Toni Bajada the swimmer to get them for me," Fiammetta said. "It is not his fault, Monseigneur. He has done no harm, nor has Monsieur de Graham."

They spoke French. "That is questionable," said La Valette. "Did you come naked from the sea, my friend?"

"Monseigneur has guessed it. But I could not have come as I was, or how would I have been received here?"

The red-haired boy then unlatched his doublet, simply and without affectation, like a woman about to nurse her child. When the opened halves were pulled back it was to expose clear, high breasts beneath the pleated linen shirt. No one spoke for a moment; behind the revealed girl, Graham drew a quick angry breath. Presently La Valette nodded, and Fiammetta laced up the doublet carefully, then knelt on, a prisoner waiting for sentence.

"You have courage, Safieye the Bright One," said La Valette, "or perhaps impudence."

"Monseigneur, that is only what they called me at Mehedia. My name is—Fiammetta."

He made no comment. "Why did you give yourself the trouble of escaping from the boat, and having to beg clothes before you could come here? The rest of the women are well housed and will come to no harm. Presently they will be sent to the Sicilian mainland, where by rights—" his glance flickered over her—"you should join them. Wantons, as you may not know, are whipped in Malta; what other reason have you to stay?"

"Monseigneur is angry, because I have made him receive me by a trick. But to say that I am wanton is false. I have no parents, Monseigneur. The Turks killed my father and my mother, and our servant, and the sailors on our ship who were kind to me. I myself was taken and kept to sell to their Sultan, which fate I have escaped. If Monseigneur could only forget that I am a woman and remember that I can swim, which his own men cannot, which the Turks cannot! No swimmers will be sent here by Sultan Suleiman because it is not honourable, in war, for a man to have the means of retreating in such a fashion. Knowing this, am I not worth more than one fighting man to you? And I would die willingly in the cause."

The Grand Master was still frowning; both he and the English secretary stared down at the map on their table to avoid staring at the woman. Women were to La Valette a matter to be left out of reckoning: the celibate vows of the Order were so strict that no knight need even have been married and hope for admission. Other, looser ties were frowned on; La Valette himself lived the life of a monk, as did those close to him. "Your presence here—" he began, remembering the treacherous women swimmers of Rhodes.

"Monseigneur, I can salve wounds also, and nurse the sick. I remember many things the Turks taught me. There may come a time when you need willing hands in the hospital. And I know the Turkish tongue, Monseigneur; many a time I may hear something useful and bring you news of it. Do not send me away with the other useless ones to the mainland!"

"Then you may stay, if you will forget that you are a woman and expect no one else to remember it, in this war."

"I have already forgotten, it, Monseigneur." But even as she spoke she was sharply aware of young Graham, and his anger, behind her. La Valette was still talking, as one who had accepted the situation˙ and resolved to treat her as one more recruit to his army. "Do not expect quarter, or any mercy, from the Turks if they take you again. Do not expect us to regard you as a hostage worth ransom. I myself have served in their galleys; but your fate would be far other."

"I know it."

"Can you live on short rations? Food is already scarce among us, and hunger makes cowards even of the brave."

Her face was radiant. "Monseigneur, I can catch and eat fish and perhaps bring some in to relieve you. There are sorts that if one eats, the bowels turn to water; but I would not be mistaken twice, and one survives." She watched the effect of her words on the Grand Master and Sir Oliver; she had dared to be flippant, to lift the solemn mood of everyone. In the end, both men laughed; threw up their hands, shrugged, and nodded.

"It is agreed, then," said the Grand Master. "And the place

where we may find you? Have you provided for that also?" His eyes regarded her with a cold admiration; she was practical, he thought, unless it was all boasting; if so, she would not live. He moved impatiently, anxious for the interview to come to an end; there was much else to do.

"I can live in the cave where I now am, and Toni Bajada knows where to find me," said Fiammetta. "Since you sent most of the women and children away last year there is no one else to watch when I come and go."

"So be it, then, and God go with you," said La Valette. He nodded dismissal, and before they were out of the gate had returned to his map, and its problems and probabilities. With next day's tide he must be ready to send Sir Oliver Starkey, and Anthony Graham, on their journey to beg swift help from the rulers of Europe.

Seven

Suleiman the Magnificent reclined on his cushions in the summer-pavilion he had long ago built himself by the Sweet Waters of Asia. In all seasons of the year he could find coolness and diversion here, except today; today it was hot, with a lax heat that even the Nubian slaves, fanning peacocks' feathers on long staves behind his head, could not dispel. Now and again the Sultan's grey eyes, with their whites made yellow by illness, turned restlessly as if to seek the source of a breeze, a draught. Back in the city, he was thinking, it might be less hot, with some sudden sea-wind blowing up from the sweep of bay at the Golden Horn, among the aspiring minarets of Istanbul queened over by Hagia Sophia dome. "Nothing, not even this place, pleases me forever," he thought, and moved his head restlessly so that the jewel in his turban, a matchless ruby, gleamed. His body, the body of an old sick man now, was clad in rich stuffs; the cushions on which he lay were made of silk dyed in bright colours, woven ell upon priceless ell from the mulberry-worms of far-away T'sin, and brought hither by caravan. The spices among which they had been wrapped exuded a faint, delicious scent as Suleiman moved: but nearer was the smell of age and death found in his own body. Sometimes he would wake in the night with a sense of outrage that he, once young and splendid, the master of any horse they could bring, the master of his own janissaries, he who loved power and magnificence so that his will governed Islam like a vice, should grow old and die like other men. What was it the Khan of Poets had written about him?—

> *Across the face of earth thou hast hurled the right,*
> *From east to west thy armoured champions have borne*
>   *it,*
> *As sweeps a sword.*

But it was of no purpose to regret his vanished youth; he was old, and time brought wisdom, they said. Surrounding him now were curious and precious objects of all kinds, brought by water from the city for his diversion; the silken-coated Araby hounds who would obey no master but one, and grotesque dwarfs brought from the deep, steamy jungles far south of Africa's deserts. With them had come giraffes and elephants, carved stools and heavy painted beads and masks fashioned from clay. Suleiman had always liked to surround himself with such things, any new acquisition being a matter of brief and keen delight; then one grew tired, in these days, more quickly. He sighed, moving his long horseman's hands idly on the carved ivory divan-rests; there was a weariness in his flesh which was not due to the heat; it had first come when Roxellane, his Russian wife, had died. Roxellane had been troublesome, treacherous also, like her children; he should have had her put to death with their two sons Mustapha and Bajazet. He frowned now, to hide the sadness that showed in his eyes. Why should it be so hard to replace Roxellane? She had had no notable beauty, only the sharp attraction of the vixen for him. That had been refreshing; other women were too readily yielding, flattered him too much, having been taught that he was the representative of Allah on earth so that they forgot he was a man. Would this new woman, this Safieye of the Bright Hair his old friend Dragut was sending him, fulfil the rumoured promise of her early years? At that time he had sent to the Barbary Coast to find a wife for his son Selim, only later deciding, as Selim proved unworthy, to take Safieye for himself. Dragut had long ago described her as having the wisdom of one twice her age and a wit like a knife's edge, as well as—for wise women were often ugly—beauty, a skin like new milk, full alabaster breasts, hair bright as the sun. "However long one may spend in her company it is impossible to weary of her, for her eyes change in colour like the changes in an opal, and her spirit is that of her father who was a sea-fighter and died with great courage. She would be a fitting bride for the Lion of Islam himself, and for his son she will be as a jewel on the finger of his right hand." So the wily old corsair had written; but after the execution of Bajazet his brother Selim had drowned himself ever more deeply in drink. Then Roxellane had died; and he, the Sultan, had decreed that he himself should breed sons on

Safieye to replace the perfidious sons of Roxellane. He had
forgotten his ageing body in pursuit of his will; if Allah judged
it good, he would live to see Safieye's son a man.

He had awaited her arrival now eagerly for many weeks,
knowing—the captains of his little ships had told him—that she
had set sail in the great ship of Kustir Aga, bearing cargo east
from Venice. But although the shapes of many craft, great and
small, came sailing past the Horn they were none of them the
merchantman; Suleiman knew her well enough, her great orb
and crescent which were his own symbols flashing gold from
afar in the light of the sun.

The waiting had become intolerable; he struck his hands
together for a slave, who came and knelt. "Fetch the lady
Mihrmah my daughter to me. Send the covered barge to her
house-steps in the city and wait there till she enters it." After
the slave had gone he almost recalled him, regretting the
impulse that had made him send for Mihrmah after so long. She
would be a dismal sight these days with her widow's clothes and
her air of mourning for her husband Rustum and her two
brothers. What woman had a right to question his actions?
They were creatures that did not even enter Paradise; had
Mihrmah said a word of treason he would have had her
strangled long ago with Bajazet. But she had said nothing. He
would make her speak with him now, when she came.

She was brought to him from the barge two days later, eyes
unfriendly behind their kohl. She had a long list of complaints
in her whining voice; her old nurse Gajn Siva had been captured
by the Christians years ago and no one had as yet done anything
about it; and the ship of Kustir Aga, which carried merchandise
for her as well as a young bride for her ageing father, was late.

"If the Christians have taken her also, there will be great
wailing in the Serai," she said spitefully. "Everyone's money is
carried in that ship, in bales of Venice velvet and Castile
leather. Why, my father, do you not send galleys out to escort
her home? It is well known that the seas swarm with enemy
vessels, which do their will everywhere with no one to prevent
them."

"Hold your tongue! Answer only when I question you. Have
I fathered a wildcat?" And at the remembered roar of anger in
his voice she dropped her eyes, and pretended submission; but
he was not deceived by her. Roxellane her mother had possessed

just such a trick, sayirᴖ some outrageous thing and then dropping the painted lids over her strange light eyes in pretended innocence. She had had, he remembered, a harsh voice, like a peacock's, despite her gentle lute-pláying. Perhaps Safieye of the Bright Hair, who also made music, would understand the value of soft speech and silence. The Sultan sighed. To have conquered half the known world and still to lack the final knowledge of the secrets in the minds of women troubled him.

They had left the Place of Sweet Waters and had returned to Istanbul by the time news came of the great ship.

Before then there had been restless rumours in the Serai, the women's quarters concealed from view behind the latticed corridors dividing them from the main court. About the latter, as though disturbed by the prevalent unrest, courtiers stood in clusters ceaselessly, not taking their ease on cushions as was customary in the heat of the day. A savagery stalked abroad, causing seasoned warriors like the Sultan's son-in-law, Mustapha Pasha, to whet their swords. A young Greek sanjak from the Hungarian wars, Philip Lascaris, seeing the way of life in the outer court for the first time since being released from military school, noted the whisperers in corners. He himself would have welcomed activity, for he preferred a clean and open campaign to this smooth conjecture; but he had been brought here in reward for his prowess on the plains beyond Vienna, and had been promised a bride from the Aga's ship to enjoy for nine days before returning. She was Maltese, he had discovered, and had been educated by Dragut in Tunis. He reflected on it, showing no personal curiosity, for such would have been unbecoming in a soldier; the status marriage gave him would increase his field-value and for this reason alone, the prospect pleased him. In his lifelong training he had not learnt to assess himself as other than a part in a great machine. To play that part efficiently satisfied him, at present. Was it not taken as a sign of weakness in the history of the great Vizier Sokollis that, at one time having shown good progress at school, he had refused the embroidered prize offered him, demanding instead to be allowed to visit his parents who had waited for years, having come from afar off, outside the great gate of the school?

Philip's upbringing induced him to feel genuine scorn for this weakness. To serve the Sultan, the Shadow of Allah, one shed away all lesser ties and affections. He himself was fortunate in that he could recall nothing of his origins, though he knew from his own fair complexion and grey eyes that he came from the West.

A buzz of chatter sounded at the door of the courtroom. Philip turned, and the Sultan on his jewelled throne stiffened also at the sight which greeted him from the doorway. Into the great court, silk draperies billowing round his fat thighs, waddled Kustir Aga the eunuch, hands tearing at his tunic. Philip raised an eyebrow; the creature's face was pallid with shock, and, having prostrated himself in the customary three obeisances before the Lord of the Happy Constellation, the Sultan, he had difficulty in making himself understood for agitation and the wobbling of his chins.

"Lord of the World, Defender of Islam, Name of Allah upon Earth, Mighty Caesar, I have been robbed!" And behind him, as if to echo these sentiments to the full, there arose a great wailing from behind the lattices of the Serai; it was as Mihrmah had foretold. For the many unseen ladies had invested deeply in the illegal French wines, the figured Genoa stuffs and Spanish leather the merchantman carried, and the wind that bore news of the loss to Kustir Aga had borne it also to them, in their seclusion.

The court blenched, fearing as always the anger of the Sultan. Suleiman had risen from the carved throne, the rouge he always wore nowadays in public concealing the yellow pallor of his face. "Has an army perished, Kustir Aga?" he demanded. In that instant, looking down on the fat grovelling eunuch, he conveyed the close-lipped contempt of the whole man for one who is forever less than a man. Then he struck the throne-rests, at last taking in the import of the eunuch's mouthings.

"The merchantman with my bride? Taken by the Knights of Christendom?"

Then Suleiman the Magnificent, finest soldier of his age, victor of Rhodes and Tabriz and Algiers, shouted his orders, as though he were made young again by the very anger in his heart. "Piali! You will be my admiral. Mustapha! You will command the land-forces. Dragut, whom they call the Drawn Sword of Islam, shall be sent for to avenge his daughter, my bride. You, Lascaris, Hassem, Salik, who are worth many swords, shall sail with us, for I myself shall go to capture Malta, that thankless rock, as I took Rhodes a generation ago. Had I not then shown mercy to the infidel there would have been peace on the seas these thirty years. There shall be no mercy now."

Then he summoned his Divan, his advisers; and once assembled, Mustapha voiced the general feeling, making a speech of which he was so proud he had copies of it made by scribes to distribute to his acquaintance. It called on the Sultan to make war against the Knights of Malta both by land and sea; echoing everything Suleiman had already said except that, in the end, being no longer a young man, he himself was prevailed upon not to set sail in person.

Only the echo of his fierce anger sounded still, as though the very sun's light stemmed from the throne of Islam and would be darkened at the ruler's command. Blinded except for the necessity for vengeance—death in battle being the finest a warrior can command, for he will go straight to Paradise—a great cry went up, eclipsing the gentle continued murmuring behind the lattices.

"Death to the infidel! So perish the Knights of Malta and all their Order!"

There would be nothing left, they swore, by next year, but a razed and empty rock above the sea.

Eight

Anton and Juliana returned from their two months' honeymoon to take up residence in the new terrace house, which Agnes had staffed with four servants. China, linen, silver waited for the offices of the bride, who was carried over the threshold amid friendly laughter from the servants and assembled family. Juliana, in a pork-pie hat and sealskin pelisse with matching muff, had gained poise and serenity during her absence in the United States. "The hospitality we received was extraordinary, Mama! I have never met such kind people. Anton made many business friends, and I—" Shyly, she let her description of life in New York tail off until she should be alone with her mother, so that Anton, despite his taciturn talk, should have leisure to dwell on the associates he had made and the interest he had aroused by certain sketches made, before the marriage, and sent off with the couple by Timothy. Julius drew down his long upper lip; trust the father not to provide a two months' stay in America to no purpose! He grudgingly admitted that many business contacts had been made, and the promise of a new contract which pleased the Old Man. Juliana, presiding prettily over a first dinner-party consisting of the relatives only, disclaimed any knowledge of what was beyond her sphere. She had simply been called upon, and had returned the calls of the American wives, whose dress was of a wider variety than any known over here; she talked in an undertone to Agnes about it, and perhaps would dare to place an artificial rose in her hair during a winter party, as they did in New York.

Of other things, including her husband, she said little; it would not have been proper to say too much, even to Mama. Anton seemed to have made his way in the company of the cigar-smoking American shipping magnates, while their wives voted him courteous if not talkative at the little dinners to which they had been invited. He in fact said little at any time, and

Juliana tried not to let her mind dwell on the bewildering hours in their bed, when matters took place which to her were unpleasant, though Mama had of course warned her of the necessity for submission before the marriage, but not—not in detail; one could not imagine matters of the kind taking place between one's parents, and yet it must have happened. Her small body had been unable to support Anton's ardours, and when she thought of it, which she tried to do as seldom as possible, she felt a sense of failure. Perhaps all wives were so.

"How is dear Fiona?" She had looked, in vain, for her half-sister at the threshold ceremony; surely Timpy could have brought her to see the new house, and their entry? But Agnes placed a finger to her lips when Papa was not looking, and Juliana realised that the unhappy accident at the wedding was not forgotten. She waved the party farewell from her own newly claimed threshold, and took Anton's waiting arm to turn back into the house. She addressed him timidly.

"I thought Mama looked well, did you not, dearest? She is to come tomorrow for tea. What a pity it is that you will not be here! But I expect that at the office, they will have a great deal for you to do; they must have missed you sorely."

Anton smiled with closed lips. He had come to terms with himself and with his marriage; the physical side held no mystery for him; when he was seventeen his father had supervised his initiation with a healthy German whore. Juliana gave him no such satisfaction; she showed no response such as he would have wished. He took his rights upon her, associating them as he must do with the rights he possessed, now, with Timothy's compliance, over Bainbridge and Company; on the marriage, he had been made a partner. The matter of Fiona he had deliberately put to the back of his mind, not attempting to explain to himself the uncomfortable occurrences at his wedding. Juliana was flesh and blood, even if the blood ran thinly; he was fond of her, she would be the mother of his children; he had all a man need wish for, a comfortable competence, pride in his work, and a pleasant home to which to return at the day's end.

On their first night in the new house, he turned to his wife and took her with a passion that frightened her, though she did not cry out. Afterwards she lay awake, distractedly trying to recall passages from the Bible which would justify this extraordinary physical act which made a marriage. It was impossible to think of confiding in anyone, least of all in Anton himself, concerning her timidity. Perhaps she would learn to be a better wife in time; and meantime, there were so many delights to be attended to, during the day; her delicate china, the repoussé work on a little spoon to match a silver dish which held whipped cream, the servants to order in her own way, everything as it should be. ... And Mama was to come to tea tomorrow. They would have plum cake, of course, preceded by bread and butter done in little thin whorls, exactly as it had always been done at home. And she would wear her striped dress; stripes were fashionable even across the Atlantic. What a long way they had come together!

She turned her head to look at Anton at last, but he slept, well satisfied. What a dear he was! She did not regret her marriage, any other man would have been the same in such ways ... and otherwise he delighted her.

Presently she slept also.

Agnes came to tea next day in the feathered bonnet she had worn at the wedding. She looked very handsome, in fact what she was; the chief embellishment of Julius Bainbridge's existence, and she brought a message from Julius. She managed to get it out between bread-and-butter and cake, while Juliana poured more tea; the little hand never faltered.

"Papa would like it if you would take Timpy and poor Fiona soon."

Juliana nodded, so briskly that the fragile lace cap, which as a married woman she might now wear, trembled upon her smooth head. "Why, Mama, you know we shall be delighted! When may they come?" It would be pleasant to have the days filled, and Fiona much nearer than she was while at Papa and Mama's, when one must always dress and go round to see her. Poor Fiona! Perhaps she could make her life a little pleasanter, a little kinder. Papa—

"You have not had time to ask Anton yet," put in Agnes doubtfully. If Anton refused, as he had it within his rights to do, she herself would, she knew, be blamed. Dear Juliana was so goodnatured, a little impulsive, perhaps. ... Surely everything was going well with the marriage? The dear child seemed a trifle pale and listless; perhaps. ... But if it came to *that*, Fiona and Miss Timpson could always return to the house. Even Julius would not raise objections, for such a reason, if it were true.

Anton came in to drink a glass of sherry-wine with his wife before dinner, and was informed by her of the day's event, and to what she had agreed.

"I said we would be glad, dearest. You do not mind it, do you? Poor Fiona is no trouble, and there will be Timpy to look after her, and they need not have dinner with us if you do not like it, although when you are away all day at the yards, it will perhaps be in order for me to have them down here with me?" She spoke gently, not anticipating any rebuff from Anton himself. But he was angry, a fact she had never contemplated. He set down his glass with force.

"Is this my house, or is it not? Am I a mere interloper?"

"Oh, dearest Anton—I had not thought—when Mama came, and put it to me, I did not know you would mind, I said they could come, it was perhaps wrong of me—"

"It was wrong indeed. My opinion matters nothing, I suppose, in my own house."

Her lips trembled. "Then they may not come? Of course it is for you to say, dearest, it is only that Papa ... "

"Your father undertook her responsibility when he married your mother. That is her home and she should stay in it." Anton could not explain the blind panic that rose in him; to have the creature here, under his roof! And yet, with any sense of the ridiculous, it must be evident that this argument, if it were one, could not go on; he could not disoblige Julius, or Agnes, without offence to Timothy. He was caught in his own trap; those Bainbridges!

He went over to where Juliana sat, and kissed the clear straight parting of hair in the centre of her head. "Forgive me, dearest. Of course you shall have them here, if it will please you. But in future, consult me first about all matters put to you by anyone; it is our home, is it not? And I do not like to share your company in the little time I am able to see you."

That pleased her, and their dinner together was amicable. He must accustom himself to the fact of Fiona under his own roof. The governess did not matter.

Nine

The room which Fiona was to occupy pleased Juliana, who thought it less dreary, more full of light, than the room in which she had spent her days at the old house. It had been painted, like all the rooms for the new-wedded couple's homecoming, with two coats of fresh cream-coloured paint; and although the slope of the ceiling made the space smaller than Juliana would have liked, she had chosen, without knowing who was to be the occupant, a wallpaper which she thought would please Fiona; it was made up of a pattern like recurring bows of differently coloured ribbons. The window which gave on to the back green—an oblong space of rough grass, where the wash-house was—would be cool in summer, and unusually for a room so high in the house, there was a small grate. The new-fangled bathroom was next door, with Timpy's room adjoining.

They came that same week, with Timpy's meagre belongings contained in a banded trunk. Fiona's drawings, her crayons and paints, and her easel, were carried round by two of Julius's servants, and conveyed upstairs. When everything was in its place, Juliana brought a vase of fresh flowers, purchased from a vendor in the city, to place upon the table where Fiona would work. She watched her sister's face eagerly for any sign of pleasure; but Fiona only smiled good-naturedly, with closed lips. It was difficult to know, at any time, what she was thinking; that was accounted for by the way everything she did was watched and corrected; poor Fiona! "At least it shall not take place here," Juliana told herself firmly. This was to be Fiona's home; she must be made to feel welcome in it.

Matters were somewhat delayed in this intention by Timpy's feeling unwell. She had no headache, she said, only an aching sensation *lower down*. Pressed to indicate this indelicate place, she was prevailed upon at last to point to her abdomen. Juliana had her put to bed and a stone hot water bottle brought to place upon the sore part. Perhaps it was indigestion, from which Timpy often suffered; but as time passed her cheeks became a flushed and patchy red, and she seemed heated. Juliana sent for the doctor, who felt the offending part, was evidently not disturbed, and prescribed light food if the patient would take it. But Timpy would take nothing, and after the doctor had gone away the flush subsided, and she cried out sharply once and then said the pain had gone, but she felt drowsy and would sleep. When Juliana tiptoed into her room after dinner—Fiona's had been sent up to her on a tray in her room, mindful of Anton's feelings—the sick woman's breathing was light and uneven, almost as if she hardly breathed at all. Troubled, Juliana sped downstairs to consult Anton; should she have the doctor come round again? He had found little amiss last time, it was true, but—"I think myself she is very ill," said Juliana hesitantly. Anton readily agreed to have the doctor again, and when that personage returned he shook his head, looking gravely down at Timpy who by now was murmuring aloud, like a person in fever.

"What is the matter with her?" asked Juliana fearfully. "Might it not be an infection which would attack the whole house!" But the doctor calmed her fears on that score; as to the other, he could do nothing. "I considered, when I last saw her, whether it might be so or not; in either case, there is nothing to be done."

"Nothing? But surely Timpy—" she caught her lip, and looked her appeal at the doctor, whose glasses glinted in a baffling way above his beard. So much knowledge, and all that could be done for Timpy was—nothing.

"If it is desired to remove her to hospital—"

Juliana was shocked. "To hospital? Oh, no, I will gladly nurse her at home! Poor Timpy is like one of the family; I cannot remember a time without her." This was true.

"It is kind in you, so newly returned," said the doctor, and he issued instructions which Juliana knew, in her mounting fright, to be useless; freedom from disturbance, beef broth if Timpy should wish to take it, fresh lemonade beside the bed in a jug. None of them would help Timpy, tossing now and again and then, at other times, lying still as if—as if—Supposing she died in the night? "How thankful I am that Anton is here," Juliana told herself with the age-old trust women place in their men. "He will know what to do."

Anton knew. Timpy died at half-past four in the morning. He at once had the doctor informed and when the certificate of death had been given, directed all arrangements for the funeral. "You must not wear yourself out," he said gently to a red-eyed wife. It had occurred to him only lately that perhaps his good little Juliana might be already in a delicate situation; with that possibility in mind, she must not be allowed to overstrain herself. He arranged for one of the servants to attend Fiona, lay and light her fire and bring up her meals and hot water; he himself never saw her, for he had gone daily to the yards before she ever showed herself downstairs.

Timpy's funeral was simple, and a positive prohibition expressed by Julius against Fiona's attendance at the ceremony prevented them, again, from meeting. The coffin was lowered below the ground in drizzling rain, with only Julius and Anton and the undertakers present; the women had remained in church. Reflecting on the necessity for a headstone later, and wondering what Juliana would suggest to put on it—the dead woman had no relatives—Anton had small leisure to let his mind dwell on who, now devoted Timpy was gone, might be found to look after Fiona. It was out of the question that his wife should do it, though he knew she would be eager to offer. They must look about, perhaps advertise, for someone suitable. With this in mind, he stepped into the black-hung carriage and drove away. The rain continued to fall on Timpy's fresh-turned earth.

Fiona was unhelpful with the women who came, one after the other, in reply to Anton's advertisement. There had been a variety of applicants, some apparently suitable, with experience of like cases; from among these Anton chose an Irishwoman who was convinced that the girl would be led by affection. "The poor thing knows nothing of God, sir," the woman said, her slightly protuberant blue eyes fixed on Fiona as on a brand to be plucked from the burning. It was, to Anton, a revelation, especially as he took his own religion largely as a matter of course and convenience: How, in fact, would one convey the

notion of God to a creature who could not hear? Fiona had, he
knew from Julie's speaking of it, often been taken to church
with the family in younger days, with Timpy at her elbow. But
she could have understood nothing and benefited not at all. For
the first time the girl's full loneliness was brought home to him;
he tried thereafter not to think of it.

The Irishwoman survived for a week, though at first Juliana,
when he came home in the evening, admitted that they had had
a distracting day. "She seems to understand that poor Timpy
will not return, but doesn't brood over it, though it makes her
restless. I found a little portrait of Timpy when she was a young
girl—she was pretty, isn't it strange to think?—in her trunk
among her things, and I went up and put it on Fiona's mantel.
She stared at it, and I think knew who it was."

But on Sunday, when Anton was in the house, and the smell
of roast beef and potatoes rose from the basement kitchen after
church and before their midday meal, Fiona began to scream
hoarsely. The sound echoed through the house. Juliana put a
hand to her throat, then gathered up her skirts ready to run
upstairs. Anton prevented her.

"Leave this to me," he said sternly. "What if the neighbours
can hear? This must not be tolerated."

He made his way swiftly upstairs, but by the time he had
reached the third floor there were other screams added to
Fiona's, and he entered the room to find her trying to gouge out
the Irish companion's eyes. She was screaming still, her lips
drawn back to show the discoloured teeth; in his anger and
horror, Anton felt no personal awareness of her. He went to the
struggling women, brought down Fiona's wrists, and briskly
slapped her face. There was no sound now except for the
defeated Irishwoman's sobbing; Fiona had fallen quiet, her lips
parted, and she stood still, staring at Anton, tears spilling over
from her eyes and running down her cheeks.

He contented himself with ministering to the companion,
taking her back to her room and ordering that the servant
should take up sherry on a tray, and food after it if she felt too
disturbed to eat with Fiona. But afterwards he heard her for
himself.

"I've said nothing, sir, because all my life I have believed in
the power of love and the love of God, even to such poor
creatures who cannot know as we know ... who cannot. ..."

Her plump bosom heaved with outrage, and she burst out "There have been things, scenes—I can't describe it to you, sir, a gentleman, but in my opinion she should be locked up, with a warder, though it's a hard thing to say." The redeemed eyes glared up at him; he suddenly felt thankful that he himself was not a deaf-mute under their sole power. "You think, then," he said carefully, "that she is crazed as well as deaf?" The word bedlam was old-fasioned; he revolted from it and from the picture it presented.

"I only know that I can no longer deal with her, sir, if you'll forgive me. Gentle enough she is with your lady wife, who seems to be the only one as can do it. I'll ask you for my fare back home, and no wages." He gave her her wages, and saw her off. He was assailed by a terrible conviction; apart from Juliana—who must on no account, despite what the woman had said, be left alone with Fiona for an instant—there was only one person, lacking Timpy, who could deal with Fiona. Her parents? They had shelved responsibility for her; if the incident had happened under Julius' roof Fiona would have had a whipping, perhaps worse things: the problem was not solved. She was unafraid, he suspected, of any form of physical punishment, and there were few who could reach her mind. Juliana, perhaps, by constant gentleness and unaffected love, could do so; and the other ... the other was himself.

Three servants slept together in the tiny bedroom with its barred window, which led into the basement where they worked most of the day. The coachman and his wife had quarters above the stables; a fourth servant, the tablemaid, came in from her home each day. She was a tall silent woman, with a pasty face. Anton sent for her. She came, as always, with eyes lowered.

He asked her directly "Are you prepared to sleep in the room which used to be Miss Timpson's, and to aid Miss Fiona if she should be troubled during the night?" That was all, he persuaded himself, that would be necessary, and Juliana must take another servant with her for visits during the day. He had no fear that she would disobey him. The story of the gouged eyes he had kept from her. He would keep other hurtful truths from her, if need be. He added to the servant "It will increase your wage." He named a sum.

The woman—her name was Lily Soames—agreed, still without raising her eyes. He had an uncomfortable feeling of complicity with her. Beggars could not be choosers; he would not risk another physical assault, perhaps injury, and damages.

That day, Lily brought her few possessions and put them where Timpy's trunk had been, and slept at night in Timpy's bed. Thereafter there was no disturbance; as he had guessed, Fiona was happiest left alone, lacking the persons she most wished to see; Timpy, Juliana, and ... himself.

Juliana came to him one day. Her face was pale and she suffered from sickness in the mornings; he was convinced now that she was carrying his child. He had said nothing to her; it was her mother's place to instruct her, but meantime he had abstained from intercourse with her in their nights together. Like most women, he thought, she was relieved, though she would not show it. He felt affection towards her, more strongly than for anyone since his father's death. When the child came, he would treasure it.

She seemed shyly eager that he should go upstairs to Fiona's room. "I want you to see what she has been drawing," she said, and smiled. "No, I will not tell you."

He mounted the stairs; Fiona was out, with the servant, for her daily walk. The light in the room dazzled him after the darkness of the stairs, and he had to go forward to the easel before he realised what it held.

He looked at it. It was a portrait of the head of a young man, in crayon. The hair was shorter than his own and round the neck was a narrow ruff. His own grey eyes looked out at him; his own mouth was there, unsmiling, secretly haughty. She had caught the expression well.

He felt unease grip him, staring at his own likeness when he had been ... in another place and time. He went to the easel, stripped off the paper from its block, and crumpled it between his hands. A fire burned in the small grate and he put the drawing in, standing till it had writhed and twisted into unrecognisable ashes. When he came downstairs again Juliana was waiting, still smiling.

"I thought it looked like you," she said. "Fiona notices everything; I think that if she were able to hear and speak, she would be very clever; cleverer than I." Her smile grew rueful and he knew there was nothing coy or self-seeking in the statement as it might have come from another woman. He was pleased with her; she represented stability, security, as opposed to a foot on quagmire.

He consulted Julius, against his own inclination; but he would have blamed himself had he not done so. The man was adamant: it might have been expected. Fiona must not return to her stepfather's house.

"I have sheltered her and paid for her education, such as it could be, and her upkeep since she was an infant," Julius said, standing with his long fingers resting on his watch-chain, precise and still. Behind him—they talked in the office, being alone—rose the same sky of shifting cranes Anton had observed that first day he spoke with the Old Man. Now, he knew the Old Man's son was having his revenge for insults, real or imaginary. He had been passed over; had been forbidden his own chosen career and then forced to make way for a man much younger, more apt, more dedicated; for that Anton would never be forgiven. Then, too, there was revenge against the dead Edward Tilney, who had abducted and sullied Julius's Bainbridge bride. Before he even said the words, Anton knew he would say them; in this case they did not speak of a bedlam, but, with deadly and accurate naming, a mental asylum for Fiona. "If she may not stay with you, she goes there."

He could not abandon her to such a fate. She must stay on with him and with Juliana.

Ten

It was a year before Fiammetta was able to return Anthony Graham his shirt: and that was the year during which the Sultan's fleet made ready. Despite the anger which would have made the old man set sail forthwith, even he could not contend with the winter storms. No one expected the Turkish fleet till late spring or early summer.

During the time Anthony and Sir Oliver were fruitlessly riding the roads of England, France, Spain and Austria and Poland, Fiammetta inhabited her cave. She made it homelike; many islanders had lived all their lives in the caves before being shipped to Sicily. She found ways to earn a living on this island where nobody was idle now; often she would catch fish, marketing it at once in a flat basket which Yaya, the girl from the ship who had been allowed to stay, made out of weaving stems of the cactus-like plant which grew everywhere. With the money they bought clothes, bread, eggs, a comb, a knife.

Yaya had been lent to Fiammetta from the beginning. The day after Anthony had gone off she had been dejected, dragging her feet through the market to the convent hospital, where Hafiza the Circassian still lay sick. She had seen her there, and had witnessed the twitching of her limbs and the foam running from her mouth. It was difficult to remember the spiteful, dainty little cat who had carried tales and garnered gossip at Mehedia. Everyone knew by now that she would not live. "When word came that the Grand Master would send all of us, myself also, on the boat to Sicily Hafiza screamed that she could not take to the sea again," said Yaya. "When they would not listen to her she fell down in a fit, and lay as she is now, and they brought her to the convent and let me stay with her." Yaya told the story without emotion, wiping the saliva from Hafiza's loose mouth. Twice daily the nuns would bring food, which the sick girl could not keep down; but Yaya ate it gladly. She was like Melissa in a way, whom no one had seen since her parents took her home; but Yaya was little more than a child, like a small fat partridge, with creamy flesh and bright enquiring eyes. She was good and helpful in all practical ways, for the Mistress had trained her well; but she chafed on the island and was glad when permission came for her to go with Fiammetta. As for Hafiza, she was slow in dying; the nuns would come silently to help nurse her, say a prayer for her, then go as they had come. Once the Prioress herself came, wearing on her shoulder the cord of the Order of St. John and on her habit the great cross. She was a cheerful, placid lady who told Fiammetta that she was welcome to come and live in the convent if she chose. But Fiammetta knew that one day instructions from the Grand Master would reach her in the cave, and so she slept there. Sometimes, if the weather was bad or if Yaya had an ague—Fiammetta herself never ailed—they would go to the convent for warmth; they would launder and borrow the flat-iron there, and in return would help with the lay tasks or carry dressings in the hospital. Fiammetta found that much of the lore she had acquired at Mehedia was already known to the nuns, who had it from the Arab doctors hired by the Order in times of peace. They knew here, for instance, about the use of the hot knife; and they boiled their silver platters to clean them. For some reason, accordingly, there were no outbreaks of infection in wounds and most of the patients lived. Fiammetta kept all such information in her mind; it helped to ease the ache for the absence of Anthony Graham. Why should she think of him so much, when they had only met in deceit and parted in anger? Whatever the reason might be, she thought of him, prayed for him that he might return safe. With the flat-iron she pleated his shirt afresh; there had not been the opportunity to give it back to him before he sailed with Sir Oliver. She kept it by her as she slept; when she woke, and stretched out her hand, the cool linen lay there. Would he, by the time he returned, have forgiven her for deceiving him? She had learnt enough now to know that he wished to enter the Order. That meant that the love of a woman would profit nothing; yet she continued her prayers. Perhaps when he returned he would have forgotten his anger, at least.

Hafiza died on the twelfth day. It was not permissible to bury
her in consecrated ground and the two of them, Yaya and
herself, watched while the linen-bound body was lowered into a
hole dug in the stony earth, a little way out of Birgu. Now and
again Fiammetta would pass by the place on her way to the
market to sell fish; already wild mustard was flowering on the
turned earth, so that nobody would know a grave was there.
Yaya would not pass by the spot even in daylight, however; she
was timid, and seldom left the cave except to go up to the
convent. Her upbringing had made her shy of being seen, and
when she went out she veiled herself. But usually she was
content to sweep out the cave-floor, when Fiammetta was away,
and keep the straw of their beds turned and fresh. She was a
clever cook and made many dishes out of caught mullet and
lampuki, using the herbs that grew by the shore and a crockery
pot they had bought in the market.

The Grand Master called all his knights to assembly by
mid-May. There were those from far places who could not come
in time; all over Europe they were hurrying southwards over the
mountain passes and by sea. Lacking the latecomers, the muster
still showed strength; through the streets rode the Viceroy of
Sicily's reinforcements, sent by order of Philip of Spain. Their
leader was Juan de La Cerda, his full lips compressed. He had
been bidden to ride out to Fort St. Elmo and complete the
ravelin there, afterwards manning it with his men. All over the
island the defences rose, bent backs of Maltese workmen
digging, raising walls and reinforcing weak points. St. Elmo, in
the mind of La Cerda, was weak. "Its accustomed garrison is
only six knights," he thought. He stared ahead at the brash new
shape of the yellow fort, rising from its headland; and averted
his gaze, fixing this instead on a plump young woman who
walked through the streets with her head and body veiled, but
not with a *faldetta*, so that one could see her shape free of that
coffin-like appendage. La Cerda's native hot-bloodedness rose in
him, at this time when uncertainty nagged at his mind. Later,
when his men were disposed about their posts, he found out the
direction of the young woman and when she might be alone. It
was unusual for her to come into the town, he was told. Indeed
the Grand Master had left few such diversions, ordering

everyone who still without good reason remained to take themselves up into the ancient capital, Mdina on its hill, and shelter there behind its walls. An oversight, perhaps, that this girl had not been sent? It was unlike the Grand Master to be anything but thorough.

La Valette had indeed excelled himself, in these waiting months. He had demolished such of the harbour-town houses as might be targets for attack; he had apportioned wells, doling out an exact ration for those who remained. Later he was to poison such wells as the enemy might use; but meantime, it was uncertain which way the campaign would direct itself. Prepared for either direction, La Valette stood ready, and never idle. A spy who had escaped from the African coast had brought him news of the size of the Turkish fleet and when it might be expected to sail for Malta. Meanwhile the Grand Master conscripted labour, built walls, strengthened the forts, stored corn in great underground bins. These tasks were not yet all done.

Sir Oliver Starkey returned. The news from Europe was bad. The rulers of Christian countries all had their excuses. Elizabeth of England, raising her strange jewel-like eyes to his face with an appearance of candour, had told him lies; the truth was that she dared send no aid to a Christendom which, she well knew, would have had her ousted long since in favour of her cousin the Queen of Scots. Sir Oliver had forced himself to look on Adrian Fortescue's murderess without flinching; at her refusal he bowed, and took himself off. It had been even more difficult for Anthony Graham to bend the knee to Elizabeth; as a Scot, he resented the differences with his own Queen. Then there had been the long arid ride to Spain, where in the shadowed arches of the Escorial dwarfs scurried, friars told their beads and the King's mad heir picked the wings from living flies for his diversion. Philip II himself had sent a handful of men and ships by way of the Viceroy of Sicily, but only provided all expense was borne by the coffers of the Order. France was third, and more unfortunate still; the Medici Queen told a coarse joke to Sir Oliver, squeezed the muscles on young Graham's arm and ridiculed Jean Parisot de la Valette, who she said should be at home defending his native Provence where

there was more to do than on a foreign rock which mattered to
no one. The Holy Roman Emperor had his excuses; the King of
Hungary fondled his mistress's breasts in public while they
talked. There was no help for Malta, for Christendom, from
any Christian ruler despite the fact that if Malta fell, Europe
itself would be in danger. In the end the two men came home.

Fiammetta heard of their coming, but did not seek Graham
out. She remembered La Valette's warning about wantons, and
she did not want to be whipped and sent off the island. But her
heart yearned to be with Anthony again; perhaps one day, by
accident, it would happen. She waited, and went on with her
life as she had chosen it; given the choice again, she would act
no differently.

The Grand Master had heard his secretary out regarding the
useless journeyings, and at the end merely said "We must trust
in God." As if to show this trust, he assembled the knights in
procession to the convent church of St. Lawrence in Birgù;
walking on foot, for all the cavalry had been sent up into the
hills to permit of a sweeping downward attack when the need
came. The black cloaks in mourning for lost Rhodes stood thick
in the church, like crows' wings assembled; on every knight's
shoulder a cross gleamed, hundred upon hundred. La Valette
knew well enough that he would not speak to all this
brotherhood again. He stepped forward in the nave, and spoke;
his voice rang out like a young man's.

"It is the great battle of the Cross and the Koran which is
now to be fought. ..."

They listened; they pledged themselves. Then Mass was said
and they filed up to the altar, each knight in his turn receiving
the Host. In the minds of those present there was not yet fear—
that might never come—only uncertainty, the sense of the
waiting unknown. But by the Grand Master's words every man
had been fired to a clearer image of himself, all grosser things
purged away; each one present felt, at this moment, "that
contempt for death which alone can render us invincible."

Anthony Graham had stood to watch the knights go by;
bitterness was in his heart that still, after all these months of
journeying abroad, no word had come from the Curia that he

might join the Order. He turned away, for the church was full; and thrusting his passage among the diminished crowd in the streets found himself confronted by Fiammetta, this time as a woman; in a shift and a loose full skirt of coloured stuff woven on the island. She wore a flower between her breasts and her hair, which had grown almost to its full length again, hung loose and shining on her shoulders. She smiled at him, timidly.

"Monsieur de Graham, I have your shirt laundered for you. I heard that you had returned." She would not ask him more of it; his face was not that of a successful ambassador.

"My—" At first, he had not known her; resentment rose in him for her desirable beauty, which had not been apparent when she was a crop-haired creature wearing his clothes, a year ago. Fear that she might arouse desire in him made Anthony cautious and stiff. He answered her with courtesy, but coldly.

"I do not need the shirt," he said. "After today all of us will be in armour. Bestow it on whom you will." He turned away; but a sight of her fallen face assured him that he had been churlish, and he cast back over his shoulder, less curtly, "Leave it at the lodging, then, next time you pass by."

He made his way swiftly back there, bitterness still in his mind; soon, he forgot her.

Eleven

Toni Bajada had straightened his aching back, and had looked down the row of conscripted workers to where, rising slowly in the unceasing sunshine, fortifications of rough yellow stone ran. The stone had the crumbling softness of hastily quarried stuff; there had not been time to bring down enough of the good Zouqur stone of which the fortesss of St. Angelo was built. For the first time, a creeping doubt assailed Toni. How soon would a volley of shot destroy these quickly-erected walls? "The forts they have finished at St. Elmo and St. Michael are no better," he thought. "One can carve one's name in the rock itself with a knife, as though it were cheese."

Grumbling sounded constantly down the lines of bent backs; the Maltese had had to leave their fields before gathering the harvest last autumn and now, when that had all been brought in by old women, there was the spring sowing, still not started. "*They* think we are slaves to do their bidding, without lives of our own or land to tend," muttered a man near Toni, a middle-aged farmer from the inland country. "I myself came down to Birgù to get a price for goats' cheeses; now, and I should be back home long ago, this Grand Master of theirs lays hold on me, taking away my mule, and bids me lift his stones into a wall against the harbour. Who will milk the goats with my old woman lying sick in her bed? Life is hard enough without making it harder. Why should we be sent into Mdina either? The nobles there will not help us."

"Here, old man, heave your stones!" cried Luqa, Toni's friend, from two places off; he came and slapped the farmer lightly across the shoulders. "There'll be no need to milk your goats, Marcantonio, once the Turk gets them and you; sixty goats and pigs they killed on Gozo last sea-raid, slit their throats and left them on the road bleeding, then set fire to the houses. It is not only the Grand Master on whom they make war." "*Aie,* it is the Grand Master's quarrel." But the surly man bent more willingly to his stone-heaving, only spitting aside in sullen fashion when, a few moments later, La Valette himself, inspecting his boundaries, passed by on foot, followed by Sir Oliver Starkey and two of the knights. One of these, the Spaniard Juan de La Cerda, looked down at the stone-workers sneeringly, and spoke to his companion behind his hand. They were finer than their leader; the Grand Master's armour was dusty, and it was evident that he had not spared himself in his instructions for positioning the stones; even now he bent, showing one man how to place his boulder more adequately. But La Cerda and his companion were freshly shaved and attired as though for a tourney. Old Marcantonio made a gesture as they passed, thrusting out his first and last fingers.

"And the devil go with them," he said, bending to his stones. "I do not build their walls because I like it; I build them because I must. But he, the Grand Master, is a good man who will turn his hand to anything and not be soiled. My he-goat is of more use than the rest."

"They will be brave in war," said Luqa Briffa. "It can happen then that folly is forgotten, and only the best in a man remains. That happened in the Holy Land, long ago in the Crusades. In those days the knights guided and befriended parties of pilgrims through great danger to the Holy Places, and nursed them when they fell sick. That is how the Order was founded."

"Have you a grey beard that you speak at such length? They still do nurse the sick. My old woman's brother Vicenzo had an issue in his leg, and they lanced it for him so that the issue came out. And until he was better they fed him twice daily off silver. The Grand Master himself used to come round in his turn on Fridays, and cleanse the wound and feed Vicenzo and others. That is why I say he is a good man who—"

"If he is a good man, you should be happy to serve him, Marcantonio, instead of grumbling about your old woman and your goats."

"On with your work there!" yelled the overseer, a Donat whose half-cross glimmered faintly in the sunlight, yellowed with dust. And the Maltese bent to their lifting again, each man with his thoughts.

Paul the Greek was waiting for the Grand Master when he
returned from inspecting the walls. They exchanged courtesies
habitual to both over the past thirty years, ever since Paul as a
young man had chosen to follow the knights from Rhodes. Now
he was bent and balding with the years spent over ledgers in his
shop; but the finding of his daughter had caused new happiness
to shine in his eyes, and he showed a contrast to the harassed La
Valette, still covered with dust from his day's tramping over
barricades and down ditches. "I will not detain Monseigneur,
for he is busied with great matters," Paul said. But he hesitated,
and it was left to La Valette to aid him with the next part of his
speech.

"You had a thing you wished to say to me, Paul?" He went
over to where he habitually sat, and cast off his great cloak;
pouring from a flagon of wine for himself and the Rhodiot, he
handed it to him informally, and they pledged old friendship.
"This is watered," said La Valette distastefully. "It may be long
enough before we can drink good wine again together." He
smiled; the other's dark eyes regarded him steadily.

"Perhaps in God's Kingdom there will be wine," Paul said.
"The infidel pledge one another to meet again at the Red Apple,
the Eternal City. But even there they must only drink water."
He set the wine-cup down, wiping his beard on the back of his
hand. "Monseigneur, I came to ask you if your goodness you
will permit me and my wife and daughter to remain in our
house in Birgù instead of making for the hill-city or even for
Gozo, as you have ordered. We—"

La Valette frowned. "It is for your own sakes, Paul! By the
end of this coming siege there may be no Birgù. As it is I have
demolished certain houses, at crucial points in the firing-line
that will come. There should be no one left here, by the time the
Turk is sighted, but fighting men and defenders."

"Monseigneur, I may be old, but my hands are strong. I can
build walls as well as the young men. My own house I built
myself, when I first came here from Rhodes in the time of the
old Grand Master, and took a wife. I saw Senglea rise; to me it
is a new town still, as you, who followed de Sengle, are a young
leader." Both men laughed, and Paul threw up his hands.
"Why send me to die of idleness in Mdina? The Order has
meant my work, my life, to me here in Birgù. Give me leave to
stay, and serve you while I have goods and life remaining."

"And your wife, and your daughter so lately returned? Would you see them in danger?"

"My wife and daughter will stay where I am," said Paul. "If we die, it will be together."

"So be it," answered La Valette. He laid a hand briefly on the old merchant's shoulder before Paul went out into the light of evening.

Fiammetta had returned to the cave at dusk to find a dishevelled and weeping Yaya; that day a tall man had come in, thrust her against the rock and ravished her. At the end he had left a coin. Fiammetta stared down at the coin, her own mind empty with shock and seeing only, as small things to be remembered afterwards, the Grand Master's leopard, falcon and cross stamped on the silver. "Was he a peasant?" she asked, knowing in her heart that he was not; the peasants respected their women. No, Yaya said, he was too tall; clean-shaven with a darkly stubbled chin and, beneath his hood of dark stuff, hooded eyes and a full red mouth. He had spoken in some rapid tongue she did not understand. "I did not know what he wanted, and he thrust me back and put a hand over my mouth. I bit his hand and the blood came." She turned away and began to knot together the broken laces of her bodice. Her eyes and mouth were swollen.

"You must leave here," said Fiammetta. "He may come back."

"What will you do, then, alone?"

The dear child, to feel for me, she thought; and if I had not come to the island she would be safe in Sicily. Her fists closed abruptly and she made as if to cast the silver coin from her into the sea; then she checked her gesture. If the man were ever found, she could show it. She bit her lip over the certainty she had that the ravisher was a Knight.

She turned to Yaya. "I will keep a knife by me, have no fear," she said. In her mind was the need to relate the tale to Toni Bajada. He, more than anyone, would know how to help Yaya now that she could not stay in the cave and would not, for shame, return to the convent. For many reasons, Fiammetta did not want the news to reach the Grand Master. He would, perhaps, forbid the women to live longer by themselves; and the

times were too urgent for dissension and punishment. The
scattered bones of Sandilands were still recalled in Birgù, and
lately La Valette had had a renegade hanged by the heels. She
shivered.

"You too are afraid, though you will not say it," said Yaya,
and two bright tears spilled out of her dark eyes and ran down
her smooth wet cheeks.

Toni was vehement: not only must Yaya leave the cave, he said,
but Fiammetta also.

"I must stay," she said again and again. Toni lifted his broad
shoulders and spread out his hands, his eyes to heaven.

"I know what I will do with you both," he said. "I will bring
mules in an hour. For the time at least, you shall come with
Yaya." She nodded at that; for the present, she could not leave
Yaya to travel alone.

Toni brought the mules as darkness fell and the lights from
the town's remaining houses spilled reflected in the water. The
two girls mounted in silence and let him lead them as he would;
his direction never faltered. They made their way past the town
and inland, towards where the crumbling soil and rock climbed
ever upwards, slowly into darkness. Once Fiammetta murmured
her surprise at his certainty on the rough ground, and he
laughed. "I know this way blindfold," he said.

At last, in the cool dawn, they saw a walled town rising, its
clustered towers and house-roofs above them pointing skywards
in the new, golden light. "What is its name, this place?" asked
Fiammetta. She felt the night's weariness and cold, the sadness
over Yaya, depart; the beauty of great age was about this city,
different from the raw new forts and coastal towns. Toni's
upturned profile was rapt, the dark hair stirring in the breeze of
morning.

"This is Mdina," he said. "Sometimes your people call it
Notabile, or Città Vecchia, the Old City. Nothing ever changes
here. It was our capital when the Normans came." He did not
add that still, in Mdina, each winter was said a mass for the
repose of the soul of King Roger of Sicily, dead four centuries.

Fiammetta did not ask further questions and Yaya remained
silent as Toni led them across the drawbridge, hailing the inner
guard who answered readily. Everyone knew Toni Bajada.

Within the thick walls, beyond a moat, the tall houses were packed together alongside narrow streets. Up one of these they rode; at last, Toni knocked on a studded door in a wall.

"This is the house of Inguanez," he said, as though it were the house of God. Presently the door was opened to reveal a long stone-flagged passage leading to a courtyard in the midst of which was a tree, spilling white blossom on the stones. They led the mules inside and saw them tethered by a Maltese servant. Toni exchanged a few brief words with the servant, who saluted and disappeared within one of the doorways of the inner court. Presently he returned, beckoning; they followed him.

A winding stairway led to an upper room, in which a brazier burned although it was summer. A young girl with silver-fair hair bound in a fillet lay on a couch; she did not rise, but smiled very sweetly, holding out both hands to the newcomers. Toni Bajada possessed himself of one of the hands and knelt and kissed it. He did not leave go of the girl's hand as she spoke and she seemed content to let it lie in his brown palm.

"I am Bianca," she told them. "You must be weary all three, for you have ridden all night. Will you have breakfast while we talk?"

She beckoned a serving-woman, who had waited at the further side of the room. "Fetch wine, olives and bread," said Bianca Inguanez. She nodded to the young women to be seated and, when the food came, they ate together. As they did so, Fiammetta watched without appearing to do so. The love of Toni for the daughter of the house touched and puzzled her; he stood now waiting, like a dog, never taking his eyes from the delicate figure on the couch. Fiammetta remembered the secret crystal he wore, with its strand of silver-gilt hair. How could he, with his robust common sense, persist in so hopeless a love? For it was so by every standard Fiammetta knew; the Maltese aristocrats of this ancient walled city did not .wed their daughters to peasant fishermen.

They spoke of Yaya as soon as the serving-woman had cleared away the remains of their breakfast. Toni had already told Bianca the story, speaking low in rapid Maltese; a fleeting expression of horror and pity showed on Bianca's exquisite face. Presently she turned to the two girls and said in careful French, so that Fiammetta might the better understand, "Will you stay with me? Will you both stay?"

Fiammetta told her courteously why she could not stay, and thanked her. Yaya, who had sat throughout with her dark eyes withdrawn and opaque, as though she were a bale of merchandise to be disposed of, had to have the invitation repeated in dialect; by the end she rose, came over and knelt before Bianca.

"I will stay with you, lady, and be your servant always," she said. She lifted a portion of the hem of Bianca's embroidered robe and held it to her forehead. Fiammetta knew that, in the language of the Serai, this meant submission to a new owner; how many things they had in common, the Christian and the Turk!

But she was already torn by a pity of her own. The lifting of the garment's hem had revealed the small twisted foot of a cripple, encased in a silver sandal. It was no longer needful to wonder why Bianca had stayed on the couch.

Riding back again down to the coast the two kept silent for a while, Toni with his memory and Fiammetta, with her habit of seeing small things to be remembered, staring at ripening pumpkins on a farmhouse roof, their colours orange, striped green and gold in the sun. Below, terraced fields sloped with their thin harvest down into the blue distance which held Birgù. Gaunt goat-like sheep wandered in the way, their udders heavy with milk although it was hardly past morning. This was a different world from that of the knights with their forays and privileges and occasional sordid crimes; different also from high-born Mdina with its enclosed aristocrats remote from the war. She ventured to ask Toni what would happen in Mdina in the event of a Turkish siege.

"Nothing," he said, and his tone held bitterness. "The *notabili* will not change. They have never done so in more than a thousand years. They resent the Knights, as we peasants did at first. But for us at the coast it means that we have money to spend from the trade they bring and that we are employed sometimes as servants. Nobody is as poor in Malta as they were before the Order came. But *they*—" and he jerked his head back towards the Old City while still guiding his mule forwards on the rough road—they will go on as they did long before the coming of Roger the Norman. The Order's cavalry will be housed in Mdina because it is commanded, that is all."

"And you?" she said, knowing that he would understand. He flushed a little under his brown skin.

"Bianca's father, the Count Inguanez, does not favour me because I am of the people. But he thinks so highly of his daughter, knowing she is as wise as she is beautiful, that he does not prevent her from receiving me in his house. And after this war, who knows? Perhaps if I am of great use to the Grand Master he may make me of some little importance so that the Count may not be ashamed of marrying me to his daughter."

He said no more, and Fiammetta noted that he had made no mention of Bianca's crippled foot. Possibly the Count Inguanez might be glad enough to have his invalid daughter tended by so devoted a lover. She looked at Toni's strong muscles as they showed beneath his skin, remembering how he was like a tiger swimming in the water; and thought of his honesty and bravery and what a fine lover he would make. Yet she herself could not love him, for she loved Anthony Graham who was in thrall to an Order of celibate knighthood. A bitter smile twisted her lips, and the strange many-coloured eyes, staring ahead, grew bright. Love, despite all she had been taught about it, was as arbitrary a master as the Grand Turk of Constantinople, the Grand Master of the Order of St. John; there seemed no way of commanding the heart.

Three days later they sighted the Turkish fleet, by dawn's light spreading fanwise, making for the south.

Twelve

Anton and Juliana slept in a bedroom on the first floor of their new house; below were the reception rooms, below again the basement, reached by a long flight of stairs. A further flight led up to the top floor, where Fiona and Lily Soames slept and where the bathroom, a tiny windowless room apologising for itself, was situated. Generally Anton shaved with hot water brought up in a brass can from the kitchen boiler by one of the servants; it was lighter and more convenient to use the jug and wash-basin in the bedroom, relieve himself in the commode provided, then go down to breakfast. He would not have admitted to himself that he disliked climbing Fiona's stairs. All he need know of her was the occasional sight of the servants taking up or bringing down her food-tray; her eating habits were not pleasant, as she could not hear the sounds she made. It was better for everyone if she continued in the ways to which she had been trained in Julius's house, although kind-hearted Juliana would willingly have had her company more frequently. Of an afternoon, after the house-cleaning had been supervised and she had changed into a fresh gown, she would take her sewing up to Fiona's room and sit by her there till it was time for Anton to come home from the yards for tea. Their days settled into a pattern, and Juliana knew at last that she was going to have a baby. She had been shy of telling Anton, hoping that perhaps her mother, who had given her the assurance that she was pregnant, would break the news to the family. But Agnes, as always, kept out of any discussion; she might have been a pattern of discreet behaviour, as though atoning all her life for that single indiscretion long ago.

Anton had shown no surprise when Juliana had told him, merely taking her gently in his arms and kissing her forehead. She was relieved and happy that he knew: at nights, nowadays, he did not make love to her, and this pleased her also, though she kept silent regarding it even to her mother. She became gradually aware of the changes in her body; it was a subject so delightful and mysterious, so unfit to be mentioned and yet bringing so much joy to her, that she hugged her knowledge like the very child itself. Fiona, of course, did not know of it: there was no way of telling her. "Be careful when you are in her company," said Anton, and he still insisted that she take one of the maids with her for their sewing-sessions; he had never forgotten the terrible outbreak during the brief stay of the Irish companion.

A problem arose as the New Year approached; all the servants were to have two days' holiday, and there would be no one in the house but themselves. The cook had provided everything ready for their own New Year feast, exerting herself so that, one would have thought, the holiday itself would have found her too tired to enjoy it; like the other servants except Lily Soames, she was devoted to her young mistress. Mrs. Muntz was so considerate and gentle, and remembered—this was in the cook's own words—that servants were folk. Yet she had dignity and would not have tolerated rudeness or laziness about the house. Mr. Muntz had a jewel of a wife, was the opinion of the pair in the stuffy little basement bedroom, when they talked together after the lamp was out. Both women prepared to turn themselves into retainers of long and faithful standing. As for Lily Soames, no one had ever known or cared what she thought; she had never been popular, said little about herself, and to have taken her away to sleep nearby that poor half-crazed creature upstairs suited the kitchen very well. The coachman and his wife would stay in their quarters over Hogmanay, when the rest went home; but it was understood that, as in other establishments, the carriage would not be required by Mr. Muntz, who was taking his own holiday from the closed yards. If he and his wife went visiting, or if the family—as was going to happen this year—came to visit here, everyone would walk.

In fact, Juliana felt tired; lassitude overcame her at the thought of the large meal which must be served to their guests, Agnes and Julius and, because it was their first year, the Old Man and his frail wife Isabella, who were paying them the signal honour of a visit. The weather was not cold, as one would have expected it to be in January; it was almost humid, with no wind; heavy and still, with perhaps a threat of thunder in the air. Juliana made her walks with Fiona very short, spending some time afterwards with her feet up on the sofa in the sitting-room, as Anton instructed. He took great care of her; what a pleasure to have him at home for two extra days! But she also had a secret she shared with Fiona, who was to be permitted—in fact, Juliana had insisted on it—to come down for New Year's dinner. Miss Pringle had excelled herself in the making of a very pretty gown for Fiona to wear. "Now that she is to stay with us, she shall no longer be put into everything that is ugly," thought her sister loyally.

Anton was intrigued with the Scots New Year. "Hogmanay, they call it?" She had nodded, smiling. "It is a strange word," he said, "like a religious festival, perhaps from pagan times. In Germany we keep Christmas instead. Here they do not heed it." He himself would help Juliana bring up and serve the meal heated on the kitchen-range the maid had left ready set, with only a match to put to it. Later, when Agnes came, she helped also; correct in bombazine over which she tied an apron. Dinner given to Timothy and Isabella must always be a success, and Julius had instructed her to give all the assistance she might. He himself stayed upstairs, warming himself by the bright coal fire and drinking madeira with Timothy. Delicate Mrs. Isabella sat with them, her fine features set off by silver hair which had once been gold. Her beautiful hands bore many rings, which gleamed as she moved. Timothy was as proud of her as if she had been a bride. Theirs was a lifelong love-match.

"And how is Fiona?" Timothy's wife asked her son. Julius made a little bow before replying and again compresing his lips. "Juliana insists that she come down today," he said. "I must apologise in advance for her eating-habits; she cannot hear the sounds she makes. I have long tried to have her trained suitably, but with little success, I fear."

"Why, there will be so much cheerful talk that we will hear nothing," said Isabella hastily. She glanced at Timothy and their eyes met. Both were ashamed of their son's treatment of the forlorn girl who had until lately been in his charge, and were glad that she should at least be allowed to show herself today. "She is a pretty creature," said Timothy, "and, I believe, talented in drawing and painting." He did not add that that must have come from her father. Years of entertaining distinguished company at Belland had added to Timothy's innate tact. His wife smiled serenely.

"You must have her down to the house, dear, and show her the gallery."

"She will not appreciate it," put in Julius drily. "Her own efforts are almost illegible, if one may use the word. She amuses herself with crayons and paper, like a child."

Meantime, Anton came in, and the party waited until Agnes and Juliana should join them in the madeira-drinking. Outside the sky was yellow-grey. "A disappointing afternoon," ventured Julius. "They are coming now."

The door opened and Fiona entered, on Juliana's arm and followed by Agnes, who had been persuaded to wait behind until the full effect of Fiona's new dress should have been shown to the gentlemen and Isabella. There was a moment's hush, as though all present had drawn a breath; Juliana herself smiled radiantly; her darling was a success! Fiona looked supremely beautiful; that she was more so than Juliana mattered nothing, today or at any time. She wore the dress superbly, her full bosom and tiny waist set off by the narrowing strands of black velvet braid which embellished the gown itself; this was of dove-colour. It set off her bright hair, which Juliana had brushed and combed carefully and had arranged in the fashionable style, with a knot pinned low on the nape of the neck and hair brushed over the ears. Fiona wore a pair of her sister's earrings, tiny pearls each with a drop-pearl swinging. Old Timothy, who admired all beauty, came forward and took both Fiona's hands, bent from his thin height and kissed her.

"You are very lovely, my dear," he said.

"Lovely!" echoed Isabella Bainbridge. She rose from her place and came to where they stood, kissing Fiona warmly on the cheek. Tears stung her eyelids; such a beautiful girl, and with that dreadful impediment! But one must not be sad today. She drew Fiona down beside her on the sofa, and held her hand while she talked. The child must not, even for an instant, be made to feel unwelcome or an intruder.

"Dinner is ready," said Juliana. Agnes put in a word.

"Dear Juliana has worked very hard; *too hard.*" The final words conveyed the special news. Everyone rose to aid Juliana in the seating and serving in the dining-room. No one noticed Anton in the general activity. He made himself think of his tasks in assisting the guests, pouring wine, carving and serving the great turkey which Juliana had basted so lovingly in the oven, passing round vegetables, plum-pudding, oranges, raisins. He did not look at Fiona again.

The guests stayed, without any untoward happening, to bring in the New Year with cake and wine. As Anton and Juliana waved them farewell from their doorstep the late night was still, almost as warm as summer. Juliana turned away to go indoors when her parents were out of sight. "What a dear old man Grandpapa is," she said. "He was so kind to Fiona, which Papa is not."

"You are weary," said Anton; her small face was pinched now that the flush brought to it by the wine had disappeared. "You must go straight to bed; leave everything until the morning." He closed the heavy door; outside, the sky was lit by no stars. A dark, heavy Hogmanay!

Shortly he went to their room, where Juliana had already undressed and lay in bed. He got in beside her; she was almost asleep, and her face, innocent as a child's, inclined on the pillow towards him before he turned down the lamp. Next Hogmanay their child would be with them; and he must not, again, permit her to work as hard as she had done today, bending over the heated stove and carrying plates and silver. A ridiculous custom to get rid of the servants on the very night they were needed! Tomorrow, also, the women would be away.

He himself must have slept, because what wakened him was a crack of thunder. It was followed by lightning whose strength showed through the closed curtains, flashing into the room; what a night! The rain had started and was pouring down in torrents, and his thoughts, seeing Juliana still asleep, went unwillingly to Fiona; was she afraid, under the roof and alone? She would not hear the thunder, it was true, but she would see the flashes and the rain. It was not pleasant for any woman; he remembered even his mother, who feared nothing else, had been nervous of it. He slipped out of bed without waking his wife— how soundly she slept!—and, thrusting his feet into his slippers, made his way quickly out of the room and upstairs. The lightning flashed again, revealing its forks, lighting up the whole staircase as he ascended. It gave the familiar everyday objects a ghostly significance of their own; the China vase with dried grasses, the lacquer cabinet which had been Julius and Agnes' wedding gift and had been placed at the turn of the stairs where it might show to advantage. He hurried on, concerned now lest Juliana should be awakened by the thunder while he was absent. He would reassure himself as to Fiona and then hasten back downstairs.

He came to her door, turned the handle and opened it. The rain drummed on the roof, making a louder noise up here. She was standing by the window with the curtains drawn back, staring out at the night; the lightning lit up her white-clad figure and loose hair. The plashing of the rain wet the sill; she had opened the casement; the mad creature, she had opened the casement to let the water in!

He went to her, and took her by her soaked shoulders to try to get her back to bed and out of the rain. Then it happened. He could not have said why, or how; such things were beyond him in that moment as everything else, sanity, convenience, decency, faithfulness had gone. He knew that he seized her and held her fast to him, that their two bodies merged into one. He lost count of time and identity. The rain drummed down, and they were lovers. They were lovers as surely, in this hour, he knew they must have desired to love before.

Later, in the silence that followed the storm, he crept downstairs, leaving her lying on their bed, eyes wide open. He made himself go back to Juliana's room and prayed she might not have wakened to wonder where he was. She had not; the gentle face on the pillow lay still, her even breathing scarcely raising the sheet. Guilty and wretched, he made himself slide in again beside her, hearing her murmur in her sleep a little; the movement had half wakened her. "Anton."

"Yes, my darling, I am here." What was he? A lecher who had betrayed her, submitted to the lure of that other of whom again, by now, he dared not think? How could he have behaved so at this time? How? He forced himself to think of the morrow. The servants would not have returned; he would make early coffee and take himself out of the house, pretending that he had private work on which to catch up at the office. His zeal for the yards was well enough known not to be questioned in such a way. He would drink the coffee in his study, again pleading

work. He could not yet face Juliana's candid gaze across a
breakfast table, let alone the sight of Fiona.

Juliana miscarried of her child on the third of January. Among
other matters discussed in whispers by the distressed family was
Anton's behaviour; he had knelt by his wife's bedside and wept
without comfort, like a child himself. In a way this was
satisfactory, as showing that the young man did truly care for
dear Juliana; at the time of the marriage some had thought that
he made it out of ambition rather than affection, and had
hitherto seen him as cold, formal and self-seeking in his
connection with the Bainbridges. But this genuine grief proved
quite another state of affairs. Finally Agnes came to him by the
bed, wherein Juliana lay under sedation white-faced, eyes still
red with weeping. The doctor was still here, Agnes whispered,
and would like a private word with Anton in the study.

The professional spectacles gleamed over the beard, as they
had done at the time of Timpy's death. Anton felt desolation
beset him; was he to be told that Juliana too would die? And if
it happened, he would have all of the rest of his life to live
without forgiving himself for ... for ... But at least nothing he
had done had brought on the miscarriage; that had been caused,
he was certain, by unaccustomed work two days previously
when all the Bainbridges had come and gorged themselves. He
regarded them, from a place far back in his mind, with a
universal hatred. But at least Juliana did not know what he
himself had done.

The doctor was deferential, one hand held in his waistcoat
where a watch-chain gleamed; the gesture reminded one of
Julius. The complacency, also, which Julius would surely have
had in no uncertain fashion had he been allowed to follow his
chosen bent was there; the doctor spoke of intimate things as if
they were graphs on a chart.

"Your wife is in a delicate state of health, and will be for
some time."

"I know it." Had the fool brought him in here to tell him
that? Juliana bleeding, fainting, crying out with the cramp that
assailed her and then, when they had got her to bed, the pains,
the smell of blood. ...

"What you do not know, for I did not myself know it until

now, is that she has a heart condition, which needs absolute rest. It may improve, but until then—"

The inevitable advice followed; no intercourse. Juliana and he must live as brother and sister, there must be no hope or talk of more children until—when?

The doctor was pompous; he was not personally involved. "A few months if all goes well, possibly even a year. She must have every consideration if this lamentable occurrence is not to repeat itself. Some women bear children easily and with the minimum of inconvenience until the birth; your wife is not and never will be one of them. I repeat, she is not robust, and must be treated meantime as an invalid, with every possible care, especially to ensure that she does not remain in low spirits. That in itself is a hindrance to return to health."

And so he must handle Juliana like a porcelain doll, and for himself, must be continent. The irony of it came to him as he showed the doctor out of the house, and struck him afresh as he turned away from the closing door and saw, above on the staircase, leaning hard against the banisters, Fiona. Her green eyes were fixed on him and her full breasts thrust themselves provocatively above the wood. He stopped in his tracks, unable to do other than stare at her in return. What, now that Juliana was ill, was to be done? Would Julius take her after all perhaps? An institution ... no, he could not!

He became aware of a second presence; the woman Soames, standing at his elbow. He asked her sharply what she wanted.

"Only to say how sorry I am about madam, sir." She must be English, Anton thought; the Scots did not use "sir" and "madam" readily but preferred one's name. "All of us in the kitchen are sorry, sir. If there is anything we can do ..."

Why was it that the message itself, kindly enough, sounded false? He was suddenly assailed by a certainty that the woman knew what had passed between himself and Fiona. Impossible, on the face of it, but ...

He turned away. He would go back to Juliana, too sick at heart to battle with forces he could only partly understand. He also had looked forward to their child, had wondered whether it would resemble him or Juliana, whether or not it would be a boy, the Bainbridge heir. Now, God knew when there would be an heir, or if there would be one at all.

Thirteen

Philip Lascaris, the young man who had stood in the Sultan's throne-room when the ill news came about the merchantman, was standing now at the rear of the Turkish Admiral's barge. Above him, streaming in the light wind that had come up since the fleet left Navarino, was the Sultan's horsehair emblem, fastened in a great ball of gold above the silver Crescent and Panel. Its presence signified that below decks—idle at the moment, surfeited with last night's unaccustomed feasting— were the Janissaries, the Sultan's bodyguard. Philip had seen, only this morning, their grey steeple-shaped caps cluster and jostle for a sight of the gift of jewels that the Admiral, and Mustapha Pasha the Commander-in-Chief, had made them to mark the commencement of this campaign. The young man frowned; in his opinion the gift should not have been made. The Janissaries, tough as horse-leather and dedicated to hard celibate living with a bale of cloth for part payment yearly, were like excited children when given a rich reward. Out of hand, lapsing from their own severe standards, they could be dangerous; old men remembered the bloodthirsty uprising in the Sultan's youth, which he had quelled.

Philip pricked an ear for sounds of quarrelling or any unusual silence, but all seemed in order; the beaten slave-gongs, struck once a minute, carried their echo down wind to where, behind Mustapha's great figwood ship with its gilded prow, there came the galleys, each full with its quota of fighting men. Seen from here, the Spahis' red pantaloons gleamed against the blue of the summer sea. The oars dipped rhythmically. Towed merchantmen, as great as the one they had lost at Nauplia some days before, followed each with its cargo. Young Lascaris let his frown deepen, for that episode disturbed his mind which was trained to logic and economy. The lost merchantman, having on board seven hundred Spahis and much ammunition, should not have gone down. What had happened? It was unthinkable that the captain should not have desired to sail with the fleet.

Philip's face, lean and hawklike beneath its white turban, hardened a little and his grey eyes grew remote. When, as had just happened, a doubt raised itself in his mind, he found it valuable to remember his boyhood training in the Enderun, the Sultan's school of tribute children. There no softness or indecision had been allowed to interfere with one's daily, yearly routine, inevitable as the cold water which gushed at dawn from copper taps into marble basins in order that one might wash. The boys were taught to obey orders unthinkingly; to be ready to die, as to live, for the Sultan. Philip himself had been closer to Suleiman there than ever since, even in the throne-room; once by night, when he should have been asleep on his pallet bed in the dormitory, he had seen the Lord of the Two Worlds pass by, a sconce of lighted candles held high for him by a slave. He wore a plain mantle of grey felt and to the boy, watching behind his lashes as the tall figure neared the bed, his face was wistful; with sensitive features, a poet's rather than a conqueror's. Yet this was the victor of Hungary and Rhodes, the Person of Allah upon Earth; one should hardly dare look on him. Philip had closed his eyes in respect and then, hearing an exchange of voices at the foot of his bed, had listened; he could do no other. Yet he was more than ever careful to show the expression of a sound sleeper; the man whom the Sultan addressed was the Master of Boys, who would administer a whipping tomorrow if there was need. Philip felt his heart beat fast as the group failed to move on; why had the Sultan paused by *his* bed?

"This is young Lascaris, whose ancestors once ruled the Empire of the West." The musical voice held no query; Suleiman knew every child in the Enderun. "How does he progress?"

"Average, less studious than some," replied the Master. "He excels at sword-play and is obedient to command. There was a time when he asked too many questions, but he was younger then."

"All boys ask questions," said the Sultan. "See that he is given the chance to use his sword, if not his head." And they passed on, while the red light behind Philip's eyelids faded, leaving his heart still thudding in the dark. The Empire of the West! His ancestors had ruled it, had ruled Istanbul until the

Sultan's own ancestor had driven them out! He should be ashamed of that, not proud; and yet from that night he had felt different from his fellows.

There was another difference; he had always known how to swim. He could not remember when the first cool caress of water under his body had come, except that he had been very small, not yet in the Enderun, not in the power of the Turks at all; there had been hands gently bearing him up, and then presently he had been able to do without the hands, and had felt his muscles obey him like a fish, swimming. But one must not speak of it here. Only cowards could swim; it was a coward's way of escape. He had never spoken of it.

This was easy, for no one had ever discussed his origins with him in the Enderun. He could not remember having been brought there. At the back of his mind was a remote memory of snow-capped mountains, a gilded dome, the sea; women's soft arms nursing him and babbling to one another in the Greek tongue, which he still recalled vaguely. That he should be a Greek was nothing extraordinary; Piali the Admiral had come from Belgrade, and Sokollis, the great Vizier, from the mountains of Croatia. Origins did not matter in the Enderun, but prowess did. It was necessary to excel in whatever aspect of education one had chosen. Some chose horsemanship, others swordplay, still others clerkliness or the understanding of the minds of men. All of the boys gave themselves totally to the choice, and never discussed memories, home or kindred. Philip had felt himself no different before that night of the Sultan's visit, but now ...

Well, now he was a swordsman in the employ of the Sultan. He stretched out his hand, and looked at it; and was suddenly aware of the supple strength of his whole body, from the soles of his feet to the shaven crown of his head beneath the turban of Islam. A war against the enemies of Allah was just and right. He could whip himself to ready anger again by remembering his lost bride who had been chosen from among those on the Kustir Aga's ship. He knew nothing of her but her name; Gulbehar, Flower of Spring. By now she should have been bearing his child. He would never now see her, and she was in any case unfit to mate with him after being deflowered by infidels. He would avenge her. His hand clenched, slowly, against his linen tunic; he did not hear a soft-footed slave approach. It was the personal slave of Admiral Piali, bearing a request that Philip come and drink sherbet with the Admiral under his silk awning, before the noon sun grew hot.

The monotonous clanging of the gongs seemed fainter and readily forgotten as he reclined by Piali, both of them enjoying the draught from the fan waved behind them by an African slave. "The sherbet is refreshing," said Philip politely.

Piali grunted: his sense of comfort was marred by indigestion after too heavy a share in the previous night's feast. "Well, it was cooled in your Greek snows brought down in jars from the mountains of Epirus: they won't melt, I daresay, before this war is over."

"You think the island will surrender quickly?"

"Bound to: a barren rock! Rhodes took six months, and their fortifications were the marvel of two centuries and built in lasting stone. The Stronghold of the Hellhounds! It was well named." Piali sipped his sherbet more comfortably; almost, he had persuaded himself that he had been at Rhodes, in the Sultan's youth, alongside him. "Besides," he added, returning to the present, "we have picked troops in every division; the orders were that all unwilling men should buy themselves out. Two-thirds went back home, as you know, after Navarino! It left us rich." He laughed, tossing back his head with its flabby cheeks. "Also, it was by the Sultan's orders that all swimmers had to go. There is to be no escape from the enemy; all must fight to the death, ours or theirs."

Philip lowered his eyelashes to hide any betrayal of the fact that he also should have gone. He was certain no one knew of his ability to swim; years now since he had done so, no more than a childhood memory! He was relieved, nevertheless, when a diversion came; a slave again, with a written message from the Commander's ship. Piali took and read it, murmuring excuses; then his face, still reddened with last night's intake of food, darkened to the shade of apoplexy. It was difficult to picture him as the abandoned peasant baby Sultan Suleiman had rescued from a ploughshare outside Belgrade.

Presently Piali stuttered, not looking at his guest, "There is word from the Sultan that we are to await the arrival of Dragut Rais before action is decided. How long will that be? And ... by the Prophet. ... ? But he spoke no more, only beat his clenched fist against the gilded wood of the awning's support, making the silk folds tremble. He crushed the missive in his hand; later, by way of gossip, Lascaris heard that what it had contained was a further order from the Sultan that Admiral Piali was to be subordinate in all things to Comander-in-Chief Mustapha Pasha. This arrangement had not been known when Piali left Istanbul.

But Lascaris kept silence, as he knew well how to do. No words would comfort so angry a man; in any case, he did not like Piali enough to want to comfort him. He was aware of some relief at the mention of Dragut; that doughty old sea-robber would be of great value in the campaign.

So he assured himself, and so, in time, did the rest of the fleet; and to the eternal sounding of the gongs the rowers made their way into a Christian sea, and on the sixth day sighted Malta.

Fourteen

In the first Turkish land-clash two Christian captives were taken, a French Knight and a young Portuguese novice. They had been riding out on a sortie to dispel the Turks encamped on the Marsa, having berthed their ships to the south. Mustapha Pasha was short of temper; he had already had occasion to taste the spirit of the Knights' reply to invasion. It was true that men were cheap, but he had lost too many, in cavalry clashes and in other ways. His instinct told him to attack Mdina on its hill, from which parties of harrying riders constantly swept down. But there was the evil necessity of conferring with Piali, and Piali had already persuaded him that Fort St. Elmo must be reduced, thereafter turning the great guns towards Birgù and Senglea. Piali, after all, although Mustapha's subordinate, was in charge of the ships without which they would be stranded on this island of poisoned wells and scanty food, bare rock and barren fields from which the harvest had vanished. Curses on the astute Grand Master who had it all gathered in, the animals destroyed or taken into the towns, the inhabitants removed elsewhere from their razed dwellings! There was nothing for the troops to lay hold on; for every hard-won stony mile there were already Turkish dead, lying on the primitive roadways which had been here before the history of man. Yes, Mustapha was in a vile temper when they brought him the Knight and the novice; and neither would speak for any persuasion. What about the sitings of the Christian guns, the strength of the posts about Birgù, Senglea, Fort St. Angelo? Nothing, only silence, and the young men fixing their eyes on the glory of the May sun setting behind the sea, then crossing themselves as it grew dark.

After he had turned them over to the torturers Mustapha Pasha paced the ground, listening for screaming. It came; no man could fail to scream under the bastinado. But when the soles of their feet were beaten to jelly the two men had still given no sign as to where it was best to attack. "Let them have the night in which to think," smiled Mustapha. Often, as he knew, in the cool dark, the throbbing of fearful wounds, the period for reflection, unmanned even a Knight. Yet he had greater hope that the novice would speak first. He was disappointed; but next day, after further beating with rods, there came jerked information that the weakest place in the Order's plan of defence was at the Post of Castile, below St. Angelo.

"If you are lying, you will pay the penalty," said the Commander-in-Chief. He would give orders to attack at that point. Lying on the stones which even in mid-May were already giving out intense heat, Adrien de la Rivière smiled through his pain. He had sent Turks to death by the hundred; it did not matter now what became of him.

La Valette himself stood on the Bastion of Provence, watching the advance on the Post of Castile.

Behind him were Knights of his own nation. In time of war the rivalry between each post, each country, was intense; it became a matter of honour for each to outdo the other in bravery, wounds, death and glory. Part of the famed zeal of the Knights in battle was for this reason; the other was that, in making their vows, they swore to wage war on the infidel unceasingly wherever they might find him. They had found him now, and he them; advancing across the slopes of the near, low hills was Mustapha's army, in clear and jewelled array.

"Terrible as an army with banners." The old phrase came to La Valette as he stood there, his mind strangely empty; this was not his first battle, and he was devoid of fear. Although he knew he presented a target, standing there, he would not withdraw; the men saw him, he knew also, and were heartened by him, old as he was.

The standards of Mustapha Pasha's army waved like coloured kerchiefs; from here, the curious tall caps of the Janissaries, the scarlet of the Spahis, their heron's plumes, all mingled and converged like a great waving moving tapestry of death, so that one no longer thought of it as made of men. "Monseigneur, they say certain of the troops are drugged with hemp, so that they know nothing except to fight to the death," said the Grand Master's young page shyly. He was proud of standing here with La Valette; he would not have changed places with any Knight in the army.

"They need no hemp, though it is true enough of the madmen, the Iyalars," he told the boy, without turning his head. "But every infidel lives to die in battle against a Christian, as you know."

"But we also live to die in battle with the same intent, Monseigneur." The boyish voice distracted La Valette's thoughts; he motioned him to be silent.

Muffled by distance, they heard the Turkish gongs; they had made such music across the Hungarian plains and the deserts of Africa, to victory. "Hold the fire till they are within range," said La Valette. He was aware of the stirring unrest behind him, of men eager to ride into the fight.

An unbidden clashing came; a party of young Knights had burst through the gates, in defiance of orders. "Let them go," said the Grand Master, and reluctantly ordered out three divisions. Let the young hotheads draw their first blood! They would find soon enough that to wait was the harder part, the better, in this war. Why had he not attacked during the landings, they had asked him? He remembered the eager upturned faces as they knelt, those young men of Provence and Auvergne who had come, ready to throw away their lives in an hour's hand-to-hand fighting. They lacked the knowledge that to have done as they wished would have been to throw away numbers of which he was still woefully short. No, he must conserve all strength in St. Angelo which was made to resist the heaviest siege. ... They were not surrounded. "Mustapha would have encircled his reinforcements round to the west and south, whereas now, by the mercy of God and the bravery of two prisoners, he is in strength against Birgù," he thought. He had more to rely on than his own shrewd assessment of that matter; two deserters from the Turkish lines had already come across to tell him what he wished to know concerning their numbers and the decisions of the council of war.

"Piali is a fool," they had told him roundly. "He is full of his own importance and the fine rig of his ships. He will not risk them in anything but a spectacular engagement, thinking it will bring him glory. He was even afraid of gales in the bay as we crossed over, but old Mustapha told him it was too late in the year. Piali is no sailor, only a bladder full of air. But Mustapha is leather-hard, and has won many campaigns: nor will he have mercy."

"As to that, we ask for none and we will give none," said the Grand Master. And he had sent them to be fitted out with weapons and armour by his own men of Provence; they would fight well enough against their late masters.

After the gates had been shut behind the advancing divisions, the thunder of the guns crashed out. The Turkish banners rose and fell near enough to read the embroidered passages from the Koran on their silk folds. One was brought in before the end, together with a gold bracelet that had belonged to an officer. Below the walls arquebus-fire still ran, and muskets poured out shot. The Janissaries' reply was their long hand-artillery. Beside La Valette a soldier dropped dead, killed by an enemy musket; and the Grand Master heard the sudden sobbing of his little page, whose neck had been grazed and bled sorely. He withdrew, knowing he himself might have fallen. It was time to recall the impulsive ones who had gone out; the Turkish attack far outnumbered them and were beginning to press them hard. He ordered retreat. Clearly, as the trumpets shrilled out above the beating gongs, the Christian force withdrew within the gate under cover of gunfire from their own side. There were many wounded, but laughing and glad of the encounter: they held their wounds for bandaging without complaint. "Forgive us, Monseigneur! We left many more dead than they did." He could not upbraid or punish them.

Soon, the Knight who had captured the gold bracelet came to show him the motto it bore. *I do not come to Malta for wealth or honour, but to save my soul,* it read. "And we?" murmured the Grand Master.

Then he turned to where, in the clear light of evening, the uncounted Turkish dead lay on the field. The Christians killed had numbered twenty. They were brought back with honour, for burial in the grave of the first dead.

The Post of Castile had been well defended. They watched the payment, the fate of Adrien de la Rivière and his companion the novice Bartolomeo Faraone. They were raised up in full sight of the Christian army they had saved, and there crucified.

Mustapha was without mercy, as had been said. The war had begun.

Fifteen

Fiammetta had little time for solitude in the cave after placing Yaya safely in the care of Bianca Inguanez at Mdina. At first she had expected the return of Yaya's ravisher, and had a welcome ready for him with the knife at her belt. But he did not come. Toni Bajada did, dividing his time between the cavalry attacks on the Marsa camp below Mdina, carrying word from the Grand Master to the Governor of the town and back. No one else knew the trackless way up into the hilly midst of the island so well, or could evade the Turkish guards who by now were constantly posted there. "They sleep sometimes," was all Toni would say. But, one day, he came with another message; the word she had been waiting to hear.

"We are to swim out to the galleys?" she said before he could tell her. Toni laughed. "You are quick. Yes, we swim tonight. There is no moon."

So together on that night, and on other dark nights, she and he would plunge into the harbour-water still not cold after the heat of the day; and swim out beyond the great chain the Grand Master had had dragged across to impede the entry of enemy ships and conserve prizes. Sometimes, resting on the pontoon of rafts attached to the chain, they would take stock of the half-lit towns and forts in the bay; the great light above St. Angelo shone out boldly, as if to boast of its impregnable strength. "Will the Turk ever attempt St. Angelo?" she breathed to Toni, near her in the dark: sound carried.

"He may attempt it; he will never take it, until everyone inside is dead, and that will not happen without some few losses to the infidel. St. Angelo's guns point in all directions and at all heights, and they have curtains and ditches so cunningly contrived that it would take more than human onslaught to capture them. It is the only fort the Grand Master has had time to build resembling what they had at Rhodes; the rest are different. St. Elmo has not even any passages dug beneath to allow for reinforcements or secret messengers; any message will have to be rowed across the bay, or brought by swimmers."

"Then we may go there?" She gazed across at Fort St. Elmo, seen in the darkness only by the lights at its walls. They had called it after the saint who was the guide of sailors; in its lonely siting and with its pale gaunt bulk, it resembled a lighthouse. Toni nodded, grunting an affirmative so that she could hear him.

"The Turks are massing for attack and they have sited their guns high above the Fort, where it will be difficult to move without exposing oneself to fire. The two ridges of rock beyond are ill-placed, as the Grand Master knew, for siege, but there was no time to level them. Time and money he has always lacked. Now we must go, if you are rested."

They poised for the dive, and together they reached the water beyond the rafts. Fiammetta knew, for he had instructed her carefully, where the galley was to lie tonight that they would make for, and what she was to do. She already knew her part well enough; at her belt, by the knife she always carried, lay a file which Toni had given her, saying it was from the Grand Master's armourer. "On no account leave it with them, though they will beg you to, the poor wretches," he said. "There are not enough files to do all the work we have waiting for us."

The galley-slaves were chained in rows of fifteen a side, living and sleeping on their benches. The smell of their ordure rose in the night as the swimmers approached the long vessels where they lay at anchor. Living and often dying, chained thus, like animals, were many the Christian Knights had known, some of the very Order itself, captured in the incessant sea-war that raged in the Mediterranean. Unless there was hope of ransom a man would die at his oar in the end, worn out after years of living purgatory under the overseer's whip; the great oars of many pounds' weight were rowed by the men's strength alone, equal numbers to each oar. They were the living heart of the galleys, the means by which ships moved in peace and war; sail was seldom resorted to. A slave could row, break water, back swiftly, make the long ship advance and retreat to command. Only the other day a Christian Knight had pursued Admiral

Piali's ships by such a feint, causing a quick backwater so that
his small ship turned on the eddy, making for the Turk, who
had fled back to harbour. The Knight's slaves had been Turks,
forced to pursue their own kindred. It was the way of war.

Fiammetta and Toni Bajada reached the ship's side; drew
breath a little, then whispered softly "Who would be free?"

It was the signal. A stirring and rustling as of dying leaves,
no more, came from the men, their eyes gleaming in the faint
light of a deck-lantern. It hung at the poop, to light the overseer
as he came, now and again, with his own lantern to see that all
was well below. Now he was elsewhere; a chained man bent
and aided them aboard as best he might. Fiammetta felt the thin
arms grasp and steady her, the sickening smell of ordure among
which she must kneel, unseen and silent, to free as many as she
might. She worked with the file unceasingly, resisting attempts
by the poor devils to snatch it for their own use later; during the
hours of darkness, their only hope, it was not possible to wrench
loose more than two or three men. These dived over the edge as
soon as they were free of the chains, making a slight splashing
which might alert the overseer. It was at last not possible to risk
staying longer; the dawn was about to break, and Fiammetta
knew that she must leave quickly for the sake of those there had
not been time to save. Sounds of cursing from those still held
prisoner came from the galley as she left, already lights shone
out, and she knew that the men they had left behind must soon
give information to save their own skins from the flaying lash.
But now she struck out through the water, free and with her file
safely held between her teeth. Before they were halfway to shore
a volley was fired from the ship, startling the water and the
pearly light of first dawn. Five of the men they had saved won
to shore; the sixth was dead when he floated in at last, his head
shot away by the firing.

"It was better to die quickly than to remain," said the rest.
There was no time to find out who they were or how they had
come to be in chains; they were taken to the Fort instantly and
given food and clothing. Later they would build walls, or fight.

Fiammetta once had to go out to the ships alone, for Toni had to
take a letter to Sicily for the Grand Master. He set out for the
north shore where he was to meet a fisherman who would carry

it through the watching Turkish sea-patrols by night. Fiammetta, left behind, wound the linen strip about her head that she used to cover her hair, oiled herself for greater ease in the water, and swam out. This time, though, she freed only two men before the alarm was given. Leaping overboard, she heard the hail of gunfire about her; the light of a lantern was suddenly shone in her face, and she felt hands grip her. Struggling, she slid from the overseer's grasp and he seized her by the head, where the linen gave him purchase. She stabbed upwards with her short knife and at the same time pulled away the linen, so that her hair fell fiery and loose in the lantern-light as she made her escape. She heard the astonished curse from above her, and the shout of "*Aie*, it is a woman!" as she struck out for shore.

Thereafter they knew of her, the tale of her red hair spreading among them and growing to be a legend, so that it was said to be long enough to cover her from head to heels and burned a man's fingers if he touched it. They called her a witch, a succuba, the Grand Master's mistress, other names. They said only a silver ball of shot could kill her, for she was impossible to capture or to wound. These tales came back to La Valette by the mouths of the men Fiammetta and Toni rescued; shortly he sent for her, and told her she must no longer swim out to the ships. "There are plenty of Maltese swimmers who can carry on the task," he said. "You I can use in other ways." He told her what they were; shortly, a night ferry would be needed to and from St. Elmo, to take reinforcements and bring back wounded men.

"I will go gladly," she said. "But I will cut my hair again; the Turk almost had me by it, one night." She knew regret at the thought of cutting it, because of Anthony, but the Grand Master shook his head.

"Do not do so," he said. "There is a superstition among the infidel regarding you; they say you are made of fire. Do not betray to them that you are mortal; the rest of us are mortal enough." And he smiled for the first time. Then he placed a hand to his eyes; he was racked with torment over the defenders of St. Elmo, having resolved that they must die to a man to delay the onslaught on Birgù.

Sixteen

Philip Lascaris stood on the reinforced site of Mount Sciberras, having inspected the gun-emplacements there. His feet sank softly into the new earth that had been carted up; on the further side of Fort St. Elmo, barriers of ever-scarce brushwood, sacks, and more earth had been raised to allow the snipers there to pick at targets. It was the hour of noon. That day, Fort St. Elmo had come under fire at last from their carefully planned gunsites, and should fall in a matter of hours.

Philip repeated this hope to himself, hearing again the confident tones of Mustapha Pasha, who had made the statement earlier in the day. Since the attack had been begun against his wishes old Mustapha had accepted the inevitable, becoming more of a driving-force in Piali's plan than Piali himself. He had stumped over the ground where they were to drag up the cannon, himself directing some of the emptyings of earth brought from the camp-site two miles distant. "There, and there; stamp it down. A few feet one way or the other may make all the difference to the time wasted in this part of the reduction; then we can close in on Birgù."

Piali had returned sullenly to his ships, whose appearance he was concerned to preserve rather than spending the day watching fortifications raised on the island. Word had come that Dragut Rais was setting forth from Tripoli, and should be with them within the next few days. Nothing would escape the eye of the old corsair, and Piali made it a matter of pride to have his gilded woodwork gleaming, his silk awnings displayed without a crease, his decks scrubbed to milky whiteness. He was exercised over the salvo he would fire on Dragut's approach; it was to be extravagant, in the manner of the Christians when any great commander arrived at the scene of war. The Sultan had commanded that Dragut be received with all honour; well, it should be done.

Philip had watched the Admiral go without regret; a heaviness was upon him, no doubt because of the heat. The smoking rounds fired hour after hour at St. Elmo had crumbled the uncertain walls, again and again where the shot had crashed against them; then, from inside, came rebuilding, as if machines and not men worked behind the screening stones. All day they had sighted and fired; all day the unseen repair-gangs had mended, patiently and immediately, those places which had been shot away, till they were whole again; though smaller. "Given enough time we shall shrink this fort till it is the size of an apple," grunted the Turkish gunners on Sciberras, making wagers with one another as to the time it would take.

No, it was not the unseen defenders of St. Elmo, though all day he had wondered what manner of men they were, and there was the earlier business of the attack on the Post of Castile into which Adrien de la Rivière had tricked them ... were the Christian Knights, all of them, valiant as the two men who had died?

"If that is so it will be a long siege," Philip told himself. He stared down at the besieged fort in the noon heat, watching as the guns shattered it, no longer hearing their incessant thunder. Before his mind's eye was the body of de la Rivière, nailed to his cross, flies crawling about the pierced wrists, the pulped feet. Where had he himself seen such a figure, head drooping to the shoulder, arms extended, a crown of thorns on the brow? Too early for ready memory, he must have been shown Christ's Crucifixion as a child. That prophet whom the Koran honoured had indeed been crucified, though the fact was not noted in the sacred writings of Mohammed. Some awareness of the other faiths of the world for which men died came to Philip, uncertainly; but there was no one to whom he could speak of such things. Unless ... Selim.

They had been cursing and spitting on the figure on the cross as it hung here; he himself had drawn back in the shadows, having respected the dead Knight's bravery. He hoped de la Rivière were indeed dead; the torture of ·hanging thus, expiring every breath in pain, and the thirst and wounds, would make futile any wish to live, and he would never walk again. Philip had waited, meaning to thrust a knife into the body's side to end the torment, forgetting where he had heard that that was done out of mercy in such cases. A pierced side. ... As he waited he

heard another voice, near at hand, murmuring with the vanished crowd of onlookers, but differently.

"... *et lux perpetua luceat eis.*"

Philip had looked round; it was old Selim, the released
galley-slave who sometimes brought him his sherbet at the camp
on the Marsa. Selim was so old and bent it was hard to hear
him at the best of times; how did he know Latin?

"Selim!" His command had rung out sharply; the old man
stopped in his shuffling tracks. Philip went up to him, and as he
cringed in fear laid a reassuring hand on his shoulder. The eyes
looked up at him warily, as if in memory of the overseer's whip.
Sudden self-reproach took Philip, and he spoke to the old man
gently.

"Don't be afraid," he said. "I will not punish you."

Why had he said that? What was it he implied he understood, perhaps agreed with, in the mind of Selim? *Let light
perpetual shine on them* ... The Christian paradise was
situated differently from that of houris and carpets to which a
faithful son of Islam could look forward, especially if he died in
battle. The reward of the dedicated, for which one fought, for
which one had always lived, until—

"Go now," he said to Selim. He went up to the crosses to
ensure that both men were dead, and found that there was no
need to thrust the knife into their sides.

He had spoken to old Selim at times thereafter; about what? To
say the sun shone, that the defence of the Fort was stronger than
they had at first supposed, that it would take many days now to
reduce it? To ask for water? Selim knew where to find some
that had not been fouled, and from his secret source one could
drink cleanly, not succumbing to the dysentery that soon
troubled the Turkish camp from La Valette's carefully
adulterated wells. No, for the most part Philip would ask Selim
about himself, as one never did, should not do, with a slave;
what he had been before he was taken and sent to the galleys,
something of the life he had led there, cruel enough to turn him
from a strong man to a moving skeleton in seven years, so that
he had been released for duty ashore. "That happens to some,"
Selim told him. "The rest die, or ransom is paid. But the Serene
One knows all this already."

He knew; or did he know anything? Now and again some
matter of which he had never heard, had never troubled himself
about hitherto, came from Selim. Before the campaign was ten
days old he and the slave were allies. Against what? Philip
Lascaris would lie awake in his tent by night, trying to fathom
the matter.

Fiammetta plied her oars steadily in the dark water, making a
ripple for other boats to follow. The weight of the numbers of
armed men made the craft heavy. It was smoother and easier to
ferry them across the bay in this fashion than to try to send
them by land. No one spoke; sounds carried; they were as they
had been when they had first come on board silently, without
speech. Their dark cloaks covered their armour lest it shine in
the light of the moon. They took little heed of their rower,
cloaked and hooded as she was. It had not occurred to anyone
that she was a woman.

The Fort drew near. All day again the Turkish cannon had
thundered, raising clouds of smoke and dust that made it
difficult to see the walls in daylight. Now, even by night, their
mended places showed; Fort St. Elmo was already like a ruin in
appearance. "Pray God their rock-cisterns are not cracked with
the blast, or there will be no water," said a voice, whispering.
No one answered. Fiammetta directed the boat towards the
arched door in the wall facing Birgù. Here, nightly, the
reinforcements were landed under cover of darkness and silence;
here also the wounded who could no longer fight would be
withdrawn. She knocked softly on the rock, remembering the
signal; two quick taps, then a pause, then tap again.

The door in the wall opened. A tall man in armour stood
there, and she knew that this was the Chevalier de La Cerda,
who was to be ferried across to the Grand Master to report on
progress of the siege. She took less heed of him than if he had
come alone, for there were many wounded; some aiding one
another, some carried down to the water. No man at death's
point was to be sent across; he must die, and leave room in the
boat for a less seriously injured man. So had decreed the Grand
Master.

"He is hard," Fiammetta thought, without resentment. She
remembered the two crucified men whose death they had all

witnessed from Birgù. The Grand Master had made no effort to ransom them. No doubt he was wise. Grasping her oar, she thrust the new-loaded craft back into the water. The door in the wall had closed. It had not been feasible to have speech with anyone inside. Were they in good heart? If she might only ask the Chevalier de La Cerda, seated in the stern of the boat. ...

They lurched a little; it was a wave, breaking from the disturbed pontoons in the tideless sea. Fiammetta steadied herself and caught sight again of La Cerda, clutching out at the boat's side to steady himself. One of the wounded men gave a little moan of pain; and the world spun about her.

I must, she told herself, row on, as if nothing had happened; as if I had seen nothing, these last moments, except the guide-light at the harbour.

And she rowed, knowing that it might, after all, be possible that La Cerda had damaged his hand early in the siege, so that he had had it bandaged some days ago. Otherwise, Yaya had bitten it savagely.

She waited until the last of the wounded men had been safely bestowed. La Cerda waited also, sedulous in his care of them before going, as he must now do, to the Grand Master. Light had begun to break before they were all disposed; already, from across the water, the renewed firing on St. Elmo sounded, seeming as though it would blast away the tatterdemalion walls. Those she had rowed out in the night would be at their posts already, manning the guns, rebuilding shattered positions, picking out snipers in the early morning light without showing themselves above the further ramparts.

Fiammetta stepped forward, having looked at La Cerda closely, and flung back her hood. The coin he had given Yaya was in her purse which hung at her belt. Coolly, in face of his staring, she opened it, and held out the coin in her palm.

"I hope that your hand is healing, Knight de La Cerda," she told him. "We, my friend and I, have no need of your money."

Then she turned and left him, remembering his flushed face and parted, full red lips. She had given him no time for the denial he would have made, and the coin lay between them in the dust. Behind her, she knew, he found his dignity again, as he had done on the boat; and walking with his accustomed hauteur went up to St. Angelo's outer guard to demand entry to the presence of the Grand Master, who expected him at daybreak. He had been shaken, a little, by the young woman's accusation; what was a woman doing at the rowlocks? It agitated him, disturbed his mind which he had tried to keep steady; the devil was in the message he had to deliver.

He found La Valette surrounded by his Council, even so early. This, in addition to the shock he had just sustained on the boat, made his manner uncertain. He felt that La Valette was waiting for words which would not come. The eyes of every man in Council were upon him, and yet, unwillingly, he could only remember the girl in the cave, mouth gaping in fear till he had laid his hand over it to silence her. If word of that escapade ever came to the Grand Master's ears no valour in war would avail him. His confidence was undermined; when he spoke, he could not repeat the words carefully rehearsed by old Le Mas, the officer in command of guns at St. Elmo. "Tell them we will fight to the death and gladly," the big old man had said. The remembrance of the cheerful, weather-beaten face beneath the siege-helmet faded from La Cerda's mind in the light of current necessity. "St. Elmo is doomed," he heard himself mouthing to the Council. "The walls are crumbling to powder against the continued onslaught of artillery which, it is well known, have reduced stronger fortresses. Everyone inside is exhausted from lack of sleep, from working constantly to rebuild the walls."

"How long can the fortress hold out?" demanded La Valette. He had not moved or altered expression at La Cerda's speech. He played with his great seal now, tracing the engraved lines of the leopard with his fingers.

"Perhaps eight days," replied La Cerda. "Eight days at the most." Could they, in fact, withstand the onslaught for so long? It was impossible to walk upright along the outer defences any longer, and the toll of daily wounded was as great, in proportion, as that of a besieged town. Even La Mas, the indestructible, had wounds on him. I, though, thought La Cerda, have only the wound on my hand.

"St. Elmo is like a sick man worn out and at the end of his strength," he said suddenly and angrily. "Even a doctor can only give him hope."

There was a stirring among the Council; then the Grand Master rose.

"I myself will be your doctor," said La Valette. "If we cannot cure you of fear—" his glance, slow and contemptuous, raked the Spaniard, so that La Cerda felt the hot blood rise in his face, "we will at least ensure the safety of this vital link against the enemy."

Babel broke out; under no circumstances must the Grand Master risk his life! La Cerda found himself thrust aside, rejected and ignored, in the press of anxious councillors. He saw Sir Oliver Starkey, with all of the Grand Crosses, besiege La Valette; the medley of hands, gestures, tongues testified to his own discredit. His fierce Castilian pride rose for moments, then subsided miserably. Why had he spoken thus, instead of asking for reinforcements as he had been instructed at the Fort? These were forthcoming in any case; by the end of a quarter-hour, fifty Knights had volunteered to relieve the force at St. Elmo.

La Cerda stepped forward as the names of those who would return to the Fort were called.

"I will go back," he said. They shrugged, and admitted him to their ranks.

On the twenty-ninth of May the defenders of St. Elmo made a sortie. Leading it were the gallant Le Mas, followed by many who had been rowed over in the last passage; and the Chevalier Medrano, who captured the Turkish trench. Back up the slopes of Mount Sciberras the infidel was pressed; from his vantage-point the Grand Master watched, knowing by this sign that the defenders had not lost heart.

But now the Janissaries came, with their keening battle-cries and waving swords bright in the day's sunshine. By sunset they had recaptured what was lost, and taken more; the flag of the Crescent flung itself out on the summer breeze from a point where gunners, knowledgeably placed, could pick off the defenders inside the Fort at leisure, like ninepins. And more came to hearten the men of Islam; news that Dragut's ship had set sail from Tripoli with fifteen troop-galleys. Now they would have a worthy leader.

Anthony Graham had been one of those rowed out with the fifty volunteers. He had not been in Fiammetta's consignment; but he caught sight of her slender figure plying the oars of the boat ahead. During the crossing some traverse fire caught the boats, and four or five were killed; this had begun to happen nightly. A feeling that he recognised as anger came to Graham at the knowledge of a girl's presence in such encounters. Surely the Grand Master had enough Maltese to row his craft and swim for him! The bravado of that speech she had made long ago, in his clothes, came back to him now. Never since then had he thought of her as a man; and he had, he knew, thought of her often.

But he forgot Fiammetta on admission to the dark arch of the gate in St. Elmo's wall. The night swallowed him up, and she herself returned with the new wounded to Birgù.

Dragut the corsair had set out with his muster at dawn on the first of June. By the following day he saw, yellow with heat in the sea-distance, Malta and Gozo rise.

The old man stood on the bridge of his three-decked galley, a light awning, furnished with cushions, behind him to give him some shade if he cared to recline. But he was impervious to intense heat or cold and all through the time of noon, while his generals dozed, he paced the bridge. Watching him, it was not possible to think of him as being nearly eighty years of age. His body was still upright as a tree, and the knotted brows and long moustaches had no dye to lend them colour. Dragut's skin, beneath the whiteness of the turban, was bronzed, clear of wrinkles except for a fine network about the eyes. These were narrowed, hard as agates, and gazed constantly out to sea. "He has the plan of campaign in mind," the sailors whispered, watching him.

In fact Dragut had ceased to think of the campaign, whose progress he had already mapped out in the expectation—in which he was to be disappointed—that Mustapha Pasha and Piali had awaited his arrival as they had been ordered. The sight of the shining stretch of sea, of Gozo rearing her thin ribs in the distance, made him remember, firstly, his brother who had been killed in the raid there twenty years back; and, secondly, the only woman he had ever loved in his life. The premonition that he himself would die here, which often came, did not trouble him today.

He thought of the woman, his Golden One of the Ship, finding to his grief that a clear memory of her features eluded him. It was as though she had withdrawn herself from him as soon as she might. Until the day in the Venetian strait when he had fought and overcome the little Scots merchantman, Dragut had never seen a woman with golden hair. They said it brought ill-luck. He recalled her standing frozen-eyed, clutching her child, below in the little cabin after he had despatched her red-headed lord, who had fought well; it had been an honour to send such a man to his account and to take possession, thereafter, of his woman.

Why did he reproach himself still? He had treated her well, had even listened to her conditions of surrender as though she had been a man. On that day when he had carried her and the child aboard his own ship, she had promised that if the child were to be brought up a Christian, she would give herself to him. As far as he knew they had not forced Safieye in any way to become of Islam, after her mother was dead; dead, bearing him a dying child. Before that he had sailed with her to raid Sicily, the Sardinian islands, anywhere where his men might have loot and cease to grudge the time he spent in her bed. But soon he had to leave her at Mehedia because of trouble in Tripoli; all that winter he had been busied with it, only once taking leisure to ride up into the hills; and there was the woman among the rest, crouched by a fire, her body curved with the weight of pregnancy as he had decreed. The little red-haired girl had still been by her, and ran to him; Safieye had never been afraid of him. Where was she now? He had known blind anger when he learned that the ship which carried her to Istanbul had been taken by the Knights. Well, she would be a Christian still, if they had spared and had not ravished her. Would he see her again, on the island here or in Sicily, if she had been sent with the rest? He did not know.

"They are firing now," said one of his commanders named Sinan, who had come up to the bridge. "Was it not stated by the Sultan that there was to be no firing before the Lord Dragut's coming?"

The old man smote the ship's bar. "Mustapha is a fool," he said. "Why do they attack so near shore? Surely the firing should have come from the hills behind, from the Marsa itself, once Mdina was surrounded. That way their Fort St. Angelo could have fired in the air, for all we would offer in the way of a target. Lower the boats! I'll go myself to find out what the screen of smoke means, for with two fools in command the sight of a wise man may hearten the men, at least."

He had already set aside the memory of the dead woman and her daughter. He sniffed at the scent of burning powder in his nostrils, like an old dog ready for the fight.

The Turks captured St. Elmo ravelin the day after Dragut's arrival.

The old man had taken up his quarters among the troops. "He is one of us," they said among themselves. Mustapha Pasha and Piali, avoiding one another's glances, had withdrawn by dusk to their silken tents on the Marsa. Whispers ran round the camp as to Dragut's anger with them both. "He told Mustapha Pasha he was an imbecile to have attacked shorewards, and that the salvoes he fired to welcome the arrival were so much wasted shot," they said, grinning. "But since it is too late to surround Mdina, did the old man say we were to withdraw? No! He is down here among us, and is building an earthwork to hold additional guns which will fire crosswise at St. Elmo, surrounding it on all sides when our batteries thunder out. St. Elmo must fall now, the Lord Dragut says. See how he jests down there among the men! He went over every yard of the ground himself, this evening; and he is eighty years old and has just landed from Tripoli. Surely a year in the galleys in youth must harden a man in great age!" And they recalled the legends of Dragut which followed him about the Mediterranean; how he had raided Naples under the separate noses of Charles V's generals and viceroy; how he had carried off the whole population of Reggio in Messina, and Gozo itself, into slavery. "And the fool he made of the great Christian admiral Andrea Doria, dragging ships overland to evade him at Djerba, and on the way capturing his reinforcements when the admiral thought he had him trapped! Ah, Dragut is as great a corsair as ever

Barbarossa was in his day; it is worth more than all the troops he brought to have him here among us."

The watchers on the other side were assured, by the redoubled fire against the walls of St. Elmo, of Dragut's presence among the enemy. For the first time, firing did not cease with the coming of dusk.

The Fort seemed incandescent now. From it a livid light shone on the watching figures in Birgù, and there seemed no hope for any living soul in the holocaust. "They will all burn," thought Fiammetta. She crouched down by the wall, seeing her boat rock uselessly; none could cross to or from the other side tonight against the fury of the guns. The water was like disturbed blazing oil, reflecting the lit star-shape of the Fort as though in fragments. At any moment its form must surely crumble in the white heat; and yet it held.

Dawn came, in silence; the guns had fired on until well after dark. In the new light, a Turkish reconnaissance-party explored a breach in the Fort's outer wall. Inside they only saw sleeping exhausted sentries; no one fired back.

Dragut was awake. When the advance-party returned with their news he gave the order to take the ravelin. Within moments the Janissary guard was out, with scaling-laddes, moving like one grey swift shadow in the quiet of morning. They swarmed up the outer wall. A yell broke the dawn; and up and over, like a great wave, the robed figures ascended, smothering the breached wall like flies so that its very shape was lost. Then, from within, the Christians opened fire.

A Knight named Lanfreducci was in charge of the portcullis guns of the inner Fort. He had slept, and instantly with the yell of the Janissary charge awoke; in the way in which one half slept, half lived, but swiftly acted these days, knowing that the exhausted body functioned only for that purpose. He fired, repeatedly and accurately, at the swarming Janissaries, seeing them fall. He held the gate until the last survivor was within the Fort and then let down the portcullis, swiftly with a smooth-running oiled clangour of spiked metal. The great teeth pinned the first few of the enemy runners to the ground and there they lay, pulped redly below the fast-closed bars of the grating.

Inside the Fort, wildfire and hoops had been made ready from the beginning. Nobody remembered, or cared now, that the hoops were said to be the invention of the Grand Master himself. They were set alight and thrown flaming over the wall at the scaling horde; their robes afire, the Janissairies fell backward in a sheet of flame, screaming as they roasted alive. Wildfire was thrown, released from the sudden, despairing strength of arms long spent with famine, wounds, weariness, but for this moment throwing with force and precision. Trumps and gunpowder, bursting with some delay in the folds of the chosen targets' robes, left a patchwork of torn scorched linen, twisted metal and guts where there had once been a man. At the end of the day there were countless festooned remnants of humanity, limbs and intestines, packed into breaches in the wall.

"Lions of Islam!" A Janissary had been born, trained, lived to die, in this manner and at this moment. Behind, a monotony of dervish-voices recited the belief, constantly instilled, that a man who fell in battle against the infidel went straight to paradise. Some struck a blow against the half-seen defenders who—protected miraculously by walls which under fire had seemed no stronger than butter, and had held together, constantly re-formed, by the hands of the dead and dying—poured pitch down into their eyes, burning and blinding them. Others fell without a blow struck, their hands lopped off at the wrists as they clutched the crumbling edge of the upper wall. Others again never reached the wall itself, but fell to join the ditch of piled dead who were beginning to stink in the sun's heat, so that by noon the smell of putrefaction rose high about the Fort. Piali, who had come to protest to Dragut about the number of guns commandeered from his ships for the new cross-battery, turned his head fastidiously away towards the sea.

"Yes, they stink," said the old man savagely. "Two thousand Turkish dead to breach one ravelin! But it will have been worth the cost, for now we can train our guns inwards and cover the infidel wherever he moves." His fierce eyes scanned the smoking ramparts above him, and he cast the next words over his shoulder without looking back at the Bulgarian, whom he despised. "No need to grudge your guns, Piali! If this fort does not fall we will become a laughing-stock to the world. How many do you estimate are in there still? Not a tenth, not a twentieth of our two thousand, and yet they have held us at bay

now for four days. It would be better to send us your ordnance
and tow away your ships. For there can be no withdrawal till
this siege has been raised, and no man among us will be
welcome yet in Istanbul."

Piali scowled. He was too greatly aware of his own fancied
importance to admit his mistake in skimping Dragut's order of
cannon, as he had moreover failed to realise the need for
preventing reinforcements to St. Elmo under cover of night.
Now, however, it was different; he would let nothing through by
water, not even the small Maltese sailing-boats which fought
with surprising resistance when one reflected on the grudge
these people should have against the occupying Knights of St.
John. Peasants had no reasoning, Piali reflected; and in this he
omitted to recall that he himself was of peasant blood.

But it was of no comfort to recall anything at the present
time. How incensed the Sultan would be when he heard of the
losses at St. Elmo! Someone's head would roll; and Dragut's
estimate of four days, if they had known, was only the
beginning.

In the small chapel of St. Elmo behind the portcullis-gate, the
stone-carved Trinity looked down on a dead Knight. He had
dragged himself mortally wounded, at the close of that day, to
the altar alone; and when the rest came to give thanks they
found him, and his face was peaceful. "He would not let us
succour him, when we ran out to him at the last," they said.
"Knowing that he must die, he called on us to save ourselves, for
we were still fit to fight. Now he is with God."

They knelt before the altar with stiff and wounded limbs, still
in the heavy siege-armour in which one ate and slept nowadays.
The faces beneath the raised vizors were puffy with ill-health,
scarred with fierce wounds, burned with wildfire. Yet they
lived; and kneeling here before the little red flame of the
sanctuary-lamp renewed their vows to die in the cause of Him
Whose Presence fortified them in this place.

Yet now there were some among them whose courage
flickered like the draught on the lamp, making the flame sway.
Why, they asked themselves, did not the Grand Master send full
aid, or else instruct them to withdraw from St. Elmo? They had
fought as no men had fought before, had faced overwhelming

odds for longer than should have been possible by human reckoning. Were they to be abandoned here in this daily holocaust that must soon light itself for the last time?

And the murmur swelled among some of them, even in the chapel itself. "Tell the Grand Master that he must evacuate St. Elmo!"

Seventeen

Toni Bajada had journeyed to and from St. Elmo many times by night; he had as a rule no need of a boat. He knew the half-mile of water as a campaigner knows his map; each current and breakwater, each hidden rock; the places where one might pause and rest briefly, unseen by the increasingly watchful night patrols. Since the arrival of Dragut Rais, these had intensified and it was no longer profitable to row reinforcements across. Luqa Briffa had reported, also, from the north that the old corsair had prevailed on Admiral Piali to deploy a constant patrol of boats between the Sicilian strait and the Gozo channel. "They turn face at dawn, and spread out again towards the south," Luqa had said. Toni grinned in the darkness. The island fishermen knew ways to Sicily despite the new vigilance of Piali's men. Not a single message from La Valette had fallen into enemy hands.

His face hardened now as he pulled on the oars; he was to bring across a messenger from St. Elmo. More than anyone else to be found daily about Birgù Toni knew of the conditions at the Fort; the near-panic of the common soldiers, who by now could scarcely be induced to man a breach. The Chevalier Medrano, whom he was to bring over tonight, had cheered the men somewhat by giving them their pay and some playing-cards. "But it interrupts the game if a man has his head blown off." Toni anchored his boat below the rock now, and climbed up towards the door in the wall.

Medrano was ready. During the return journey they spoke little; Toni was aware of the harsh sadness of the old soldier's face, and would have ventured to cheer him if he might. But he was still shy of his difference from the Knights of the Order, who would on occasion address him as though he were a servant, and so he said nothing. The voyage was uneventful, no shot breaking the water.

Medrano shortly faced the Grand Master in Council, standing where the wretched La Cerda had stood some days previously. La Cerda was now in gaol; he had returned to St. Elmo, but had given way increasingly to his fear, edged himself out by night again with a pretended wound, and had been detected on admission to Birgù hospital. "Confine him," said the Grand Master tersely when he heard of it. The contagion of fear might spread; better for La Cerda to keep it to himself in his solitary cell, studying, if he wished, the verse carved last year by John James Sandilands *in carcere.*

Nobody thought of La Cerda now. Faces were tense about the council-table; for some reason no one watched Medrano, who had come from the Fort, but all eyes were fixed on the face of the Grand Master. He it was who would decide the fate of the men across the bay, as he decided that of everyone on the island. The weight of decision resting on his shoulders was like that of Atlas who held the world; but he was not bowed with it.

Medrano made his speech, prepared after much bitter thought and consultation with those whom he had left; not only the irresponsible, the panicking men, but the men of granite; old Le Mas, the Bailiff, Broglie, others who had defended St. Elmo from the beginning. "Tell him that it is untenable!" was the general cry. "Tell him we should evacuate the Fort, mine it, blow it up in their faces, and return to help defend Birgù. Without reinforcements we cannot hold out, and many are killed now coming across or else will certainly die while they are here. Why perish like rats in a trap? Tell the Grand Master we will withdraw, and fight."

He told them. He addressed the whole Council, but like theirs his gaze was fixed on the one man whose word could turn the scale; that old man, erect, spare, silver-bearded. The light behind his head dazzled Medrano's tired eyes; the features were unseen; the Grand Master was immobile as a statue. Was he made of stone? About him the Council had begun to murmur in agreement about the need for withdrawal from St. Elmo. Why did La Valette make no move?

He spoke then, coldly. Like all his sayings each word had the weight of a word from God. The silence in the hall beat like wings.

"We swore obedience when we joined the Order," he said. "We swore also on the vows of chivalry—" he stopped, his voice thickened a trifle, then went on—"that our lives would be sacrificed for the Faith whenever, and wherever, the call might come. Our brothers in St. Elmo must now accept that sacrifice."

Toni Bajada was accosted by a figure in a cloak and hood as he waited by the harbour for the Chevalier's return. It was Fiammetta, her face drawn and pale in the dawn's light. She plucked at his sleeve.

"Tell me," she said, "of Anthony Graham." Toni told her, without comment as to the state she revealed in herself, all he knew; last time he had seen Graham had been when the latter sat down, drunk with wine after lack of sleep guarding the breaches, to play cards with one Spaniard and two Frenchmen from Auvergne.

"He has taken some wildfire-burns, like everyone; but his eyes are safe," he told her, remembering the bandaged hands of the men laying out their old-fashioned bells, leaves and acorns, for the cards Medrano had managed to find for them were not new and were well thumbed. Fiammetta gave a queer little sound between a sob and a laugh, and thanked him. "I pray for him daily, hourly," she said. "Surely there is value in prayer. I pray when I am in the cave, in the boat, in the hospital. Perhaps when he comes across to have his wounds dressed, I—"

"No more can come."

Her eyes widened in horror. "Then—"

He turned away, speaking roughly to hide his pity for her. "You cannot stay longer in your cave." he said, "Mustapha has sited a battery opposite it. Nor will there be further work for you in the boats. Best go to the hospital, and wait there for word. There will be enough to do."

"Yes," she said. She turned away, moving stiffly. Then she called back to him where he stood by the boat.

"Sometimes I am at Melissa's house, at Paul the Greek's, in Birgù."

"I will remember." He saw the doors of the council-chamber open and the dark cloaks spill out, like released great birds out of a cage. He bowed his head at the approach of the Chevalier Medrano; would he return to St. Elmo? "Not only I, but fifteen others," said the old soldier. "It is right that you should know of this; the Viceroy of Sicily will send no aid till the twentieth of

June, and then only if St. Elmo still holds. Therefore it is our duty to hold it."

He added that there would be fifty men sent down from Mdina as soon as they could come. Would Toni go up to the capital, on his return, to hasten them?

"We assume that you will win your way back across the bay safely," Medrano smiled. Toni took little heed of this reference to his known immunity from attack. He thought with sudden, undeniable longing of the comfort of Bianca's presence, the cool sight of her, a slip of new moon before his eyes, even only for instants. "It is as though she gave me strength to continue, frail as she is," he thought. "Perhaps she too prays." But again he said nothing as he rowed the Chevalier, and his volunteers, again across the water while it was still dark, followed by rafts with the remaining men.

That day there was a further attack on St. Elmo, like fire playing about a melting candle. The light was bright enough for gunners at St. Angelo to pick out and shoot the snipers between them and the flames.

At midnight a messenger disturbed the Grand Master. It was an Italian Knight, bearing a message from the defenders of St. Elmo. They begged to be allowed to sally forth and die. "Do not send further reinforcements," they said, "they are no more than dead men."

The letter ended "We kiss your hands."

"They must not make the sally," said La Valette.

Vitelleschi, the Italian who had come, looked at the man before him with the stupefaction of tiredness. It occurred to him that the Grand Master himself could not have slept for many nights. At whatever hour one came, he was always ready, that old man, seated at his table with a quill in his hand, writing, or studying the map of campaign. The eyes turned on Vitelleschi at this moment showed the fevered brightness of one who has lived at an unnatural pace for many days; like a delicately balanced machine, La Valette was in constant action, in no danger of stopping before it was time; then, he would stop dead. Vitelleschi felt his own hesitation, his very weariness, recede by reason of his nearness to the Grand Master. It was like the woman who plucked the hem of Christ's garment and was healed; how much more virtue could yet come out of this old man? The Italian's resentment, which he had shared with some of the men in the Fort over their long duress, left him. Henceforth he would be at La Valette's orders. If the garrison were to remain and roast alive in St. Elmo, and he one of them, they would remain.

"Wait!" said the Grand Master.

He rose from where he had been sitting and with his quick terse way of giving orders, soon had three Knights standing robed before him. They were all from different Langues.

"You will row out, and bring word back to me of the condition of St. Elmo," he told them. Then he turned to the Italian again, the shadow of a smile on his lips.

"A soldier's duty is to obey," he said. "But the laws of honour cannot necessarily be satisfied by throwing away one's life when it seems convenient."

And he ordered them, again, to stay at their posts in St. Elmo.

The commission made its report; by the majority of opinion of one member, the Fort could be held for a few more days. It was known that everyone in it must die.

The Grand Master had neither slept nor rested. When the commission returned he was sharp and brittle with extreme tiredness; but he listened to what they had to say. Then he called for Sir Oliver Starkey. The English secretary was always at hand, like a faithful shadow; it was not known when he himself ate or slept. He was calm, while by now the Grand Master was like a naked sword; Sir Oliver wrote evenly, while the voice above him gritted with anger as it dictated the words which were to be sent to shame the restless ones in the Fort back to their obedience.

"A volunteer force has been raised," Sir Oliver wrote to dictation. "Your petition to leave St. Elmo for the safety of Birgù is now granted." There was more; flaying the disobedient Knights to an extent that might have branded them as cowards despite the suffering of many days. To a man, they would resent it; to a man, they would now refuse to leave. "Men whom I can trust implicitly!" Who were these if not themselves, after all that they had undergone?

That night, after returning from Mdina, Toni Bajada swam out and back from St. Elmo with a letter. It bore the signature of all the Knights, assured the Grand Master of their obedience to his commands, and contained a request not to relieve them. They would stay, and die for the Faith.

Eighteen

On the thirteenth of June a Spanish trumpeter leapt the walls of St. Elmo and deserted to the enemy. "They are at their last gasp in there," he told them. There had been two major bombardments in the last two days. Eagerly, he described the shortage of whole men and the weak nature of the Fort; if only further reinforcements could be prevented, the handful inside would soon surrender a hopeless task. "Raise the ravelin a little more! That way you may fire on them at your leisure."

"If you are lying, we will kill you in a different way from that we use for heroes," said Mustapha. "Cowards and brave men do not die among us side by side."

The Spaniard was led away in fear. Dragut took Philip Lascaris by the arm and led him down to share his own meal among the gunners on the site. "I would not break bread with Mustapha and Piali, for our minds are not as one," he said. "But you, my son, have the eyes of a thoughtful man and I know of you as a warrior."

They sat in a sheltered place, looking out over Dragut's newly reclaimed battery which had been already breached by, and won back from, the Christians. "A worthy enemy," said Dragut. He broke a portion of ship's biscuit and passed it, with a platter of the sour red cheese the Barbary galleys had brought, to Philip. The stench of dead bodies did not impede Dragut's hunger. He ate neatly and sparingly, as old men do. Philip watched him covertly, marvelling at the action of so aged a commander. Dragut had been born in a century which was now myth, before maps had been clearly marked or the world acknowledged to be round. Now, as had already been written of him, he was a living chart of the Mediterranean. "To listen to all his memories would be an experience without equal," Philip thought. The old corsair wiped his hand across his mouth, and called for sweetmeats. "Piali sent these across," he said. "He swears they are made from honey brought out of the Carpathian mountains. To me all honey tastes alike; but they're pleasant enough. What think you of the campaign, young man?"

Philip flushed. "Serene One, may I say what is in my mind?"

"I have commanded it of you."

"It might have been thought that, being so small an island, it would have surrendered more quickly."

"Ay, and so would it have done, had the fools surrounded it as I bade them. I may speak to a man of your rank as I would not to the men. In Grand Master La Valette we have a wily adversary. That is a man of iron, and what he decides is done, no matter how many die. I have watched it and marvelled, even since I came. Before that, surprise would not have been too late. Now—" Dragut spread out his hands, shrugged, and called for water in bowls. He rinsed his fingers fastidiously and Philip did the same.

"You know of La Valette?" asked the young man. Needless to ask; Dragut knew of everything.

"I have exchanged courtesies with him," said the old man drily. "On the first occasion, I took him captive to serve in the galleys; on the second, he did the same to me. 'Fortune of war, Monsieur Dragut!' he said as they led me off. I looked him in the eye and said 'And change of fortune, Monsieur de La Valette.'' He bore me no rancour, and I bear him none. Barbarossa ransomed me from the Christians after a few months; I took no harm but a sore backside, which healed."

He struck his breast with a curiously preoccupied gesture. "Barbarossa combed the Mediterranean before my time; I served with him as his lieutenant in the end, as you will know. He taught me seamanship; there is no ruse of his I haven't practised and perfected, during all these years at sea." He turned his head and grinned at Philip, the wrinkles deepening round his eyes. "By the Prophet's Beard! There are tales I could tell you; but never in all the lands I've laid bare have I had the certainty which comes to me, again and again, on this accursed rock."

"What is that sureness, Serenity?" Philip's eyes were watching the guns against the sky; so much shifting, digging and replacing, all of which the old man had himself supervised day after day. But the guns of Fort St. Angelo could still blast here

across the bay, even fire vertically up in the air so that
cannon-shot ricocheted on the further side of St. Elmo. Soon—

"That as it is written that I must die here, I do not think that
I shall see the end of this siege."

"Serenity!" But the old man had not the air of one who was
ill or in pain. He shook his head, fending off Philip's anxious
rejoinders. "No, no, no; I am in health. But in the way that such
knowledge can come to one, I know that I shall soon die. And
when that happens, or rather before it, I want certain wishes of
mine carried out; neither Piali nor Mustapha will do this when
I can no longer command them."

His eyes lingered wistfully on Philip, who bowed his head.
He was flattered and touched that the old man should have
singled him out; several of Dragut's blood-relatives had come
with him from Tripoli. "I will do all I may," he promised, and
Dragut began to speak rapidly in a low voice, as if already he
felt his time to be running out.

Philip listened, and by the end felt that he had been
transported into a child's country, a land of faery and of genie.
Perhaps after all the old man was growing childish. To
remember at this time the daughter of the woman he had loved,
to the extent that if he were dying, she was to be brought to him
with his ring as a sign! And this in war!

"Will you swear it?" said Dragut. "The ring was given me
by Barbarossa."

"I swear by the Prophet." He would do his utmost. He would
cause Safieye of the Bright Hair, once she was found, to be
given a safe-conduct from the Christian side to Dragut's tent, if
he were dying. He would send the talisman Dragut instructed
him to send and ... afterwards, see that the woman departed
again safely.

He left Dragut seated alone in sight of his rebuilt battery,
eyes fixed on the positioning of the guns. If it were indeed his
fate to die here, he had accepted it calmly. Soon dark fell and
Mustapha, in face of the scorn the old corsair had poured on
him for having let reinforcements through to St. Elmo by night,
blazed forth his guns across the harbour-water, and the
renegade Spanish trumpeter, taking advantage of cover, made
off.

Nineteen

"Six thousand and ten," muttered Pepe di Ruvo, soldier at the Fort. "Six thousand and twenty. Six thousand and thirty."

Anthony Graham glanced sideways at his companion, not saying anything. Pepe had been beyond hearing speech for several days. He had made up his mind that he would count every single round of shot fired against St. Elmo, and at the end of the day he marked it down in his diary. Six thousand; seven thousand; six thousand and fifty.

Graham himself had grown used to the noise of near firing; it was the same as being deaf. He and the rest would move about cautiously, noting one another's movements, which served instead of words. It was impossible, had been impossible for many days, to make oneself understood by ordinary talk.

Yesterday the Grand Master had been able to smuggle over wine and bread. As a result everyone felt less hungry than of late, for the bakehouse in the Fort had long been shot to pieces and the baker was dead. An unappetising mess of watered flour, badly cooked over a fire, was not a substitute. Anthony knew that never again would he take lightly the existence of bakers, wine-merchants, farm labourers with vegetable carts, women with milk-pails. Never again? He would not see them. All that had been taken for granted all one's life was gone now; gone for ever.

It was accepted now by everyone here that they must die. The prospect even held a certain lightness about it; as old Le Mas said, lumbering round with his good-natured bulk encased in siege-armour so that he resembled a giant turtle, "Is our Paradise so much less satisfying than the infidel's? He has known rewards; those in store for us must be delightful beyond words, for no priest has ever described them."

Le Mas had come to stand beside Anthony an hour ago; watching the course of the guns, seeing the figures of old

Mustapha and older Dragut over there on the battery, picked
out—ironically—like the coloured figures of saints in a church
altarpiece. They stood there hour after hour, Dragut watching
the activities of his gunners closely. When a point had been
breached or a surge of men sent across in the way of the fire the
old man would alter its course, swiftly as though in command of
one of his own galleys. Like galley-slaves the gunners obeyed
him, idolising the aged commander who cared nothing for his
importance and stayed among them night and day. Also, they
knew—and the Fort by now knew also—that Dragut had
caused to be turned away two ships sent, at last, by the Viceroy
of Sicily, loaded with troops for the relief of the siege. "But not
enough, knowing him," Anthony thought grimly, remembering
the vacillating countenance of Don Garcia de Toledo when he
and Sir Oliver had bearded him just before the last stage of their
fruitless European journey. "With him there will never be
enough, and it will never be in time. They say he promised aid
by the twentieth if we still held; we will believe in that when it
comes. All he could say to the Grand Master was that the
Order's galleys must be returned to Sicily! What a parsimonious
fool! Who was to man them?" But there was no one to hear, let
alone answer, his question; beside him Pepe still continued with
his counting. It had again reached the seven thousand mark.

Then silence fell. "What has happened?" said Pepe, like a
child. His voice rang out in sudden, squeaky resonance against
the beating quiet; all the guns had stilled. Down by the ravelin a
messenger, known by his banner, was walking out from the
Turkish lines. He came to a place where all might see and hear
him, then let his voice ring out to the walls above.

"Defenders of St. Elmo!"

He might be a Greek, or an Italian, from his speech;
pompous and slow, doing his utmost with a foreign tongue and
his watching masters behind him. How many of all the nations
of the earth had the Turk captured and raised as infidels? This
man's skin was light. A jeer came from the Fort; always, the
womanish attire of the Turkish soldiery raised ribald comment
among the Christians. "Defenders! The Lord Mustapha in his
great mercy swears that any who wish to leave St. Elmo this
night shall have a safe conduct. By the tombs of his ancestors, by
the beard of the Prophet, he swears it; may he be brought to
eternal shame if it is not fulfilled."

More jeering; the Grand Master's letter had steeled the resolve of every burned, exhausted, wounded man. "We stay here!" they yelled. And then "Look what you're standing on, dearie! Don't dirty your gown!"

For the ground was yeasty with decomposing Turkish bodies, black in the heat. "How many thousand has the enemy lost here?" murmured Pepe. "I wish I knew."

The hail of shot from the walls of the Fort disconcerted the messenger even more than the discovery of what he stood on. Grabbing at his robes, he leaped in the air as the shot danced round his ankles, running ignominiously back to his lines, while a shout of laughter sounded from St. Elmo. "Tell old Mustapha Pasha he can—" "Tell old Dragut—" The messages were obscene, half drowned in shot. Shortly the bombardment began again and this time, as if in revenge for the treatment of his messenger and his oath, Mustapha ensured that the firing did not cease at any time of the night, so that the tired men who had just fallen asleep for moments must raise themselves again to reply.

"Does the Grand Master hear it all?" Anthony wondered. In the clarity that exhaustion brings he knew that was probably so; that La Valette, watching from his own place, heard every round of firing as precisely as Pepe di Ruvo had done. Pepe would not count many more; next day he was killed where he knelt, priming his cannon.

During the night Le Mas came to Anthony again; there had been a message as well as the bread and wine. "And fresh incendiaries," said the old man cheerfully. During all that time of unquiet when the few younger Knights had been pressing for withdrawal, Anthony had never seen the old Colonel other than calm. He seemed tireless, imperturbable, lion-brave as everyone knew from his reputation and his late attack on the spur that time the enemy had attempted bridge-building. Now he turned Anthony to face him, looking thoughtfully at the young Scot's wildfire-burns. "You have manned the walls well, Anthony Graham."

"Less well than some." Emotion always made Graham taciturn, and the praise brought him near to tears. The Colonel clapped him briefly on the shoulder, bade him be seated, and himself sat down ponderously by him; any movement in the heavy armour he wore was slow and unwieldy, and he lived in it night and day.

"They tell me you went with Sir Oliver last year," he said without preamble. "There has been word from His Highness regarding a further visit to Don Garcia at Messina."

"Don Garcia? That blown bladder of air? Excuse me, sir; I have seen him. He will delay until it is safe to come." Anthony blushed at his own forthright words, noting at the same time the punctilious fashion in which Le Mas referred to the Grand Master by his princely title. *To him La Valette is both prince and lord*, he thought; *and to me?* But the time of siege had blunted his own ambition; one lived or died, it no longer mattered whether as a Knight or no.

"Will you go to Messina as our spokesman?" said Le Mas quietly. "As you say, you have met Don Garcia; you know the ways of courts; and you have seen, none better, how matters stand here at St. Elmo."

"I?" At first the prospect of freedom, of escape, surged over Anthony like a great cool wave; then his flush deepened.

"Sir, I cannot leave others here, who have fought as well as I. You know well what a few days, perhaps hours, will bring to all of us."

"There is life in us yet. The Grand Master requests that you go." To Le Mas, such an order was to be obeyed unquestioningly. Graham bowed his head.

He could not leave that night or the next. During the unceasing bombardment the Turkish losses had been so huge that they had called a council of war, stung to it at last by the death of the Aga of the Janissaries in the late attack. At the council Dragut held sway; he used it to right several wrongs in the method of reducing the Fort and the use, or misuse, of the Turkish fleet. Shortly the high voice of a mullah raised the troops to ecstasy again with promises of paradise; firstly there were hurled into the ditches crazed figures which were hardly men, drunk with hemp. Their round targes and gilded helmets flashed in the sun; they had been born only to die, in this manner and at this hour. Chanting they came on, and were hewn down in their hundreds; then there came the Janissary assault. The grey wave subsided;

and in the exaltation raised by past days in the men of St. Elmo it seemed that nothing could conquer them except the hand of God. By night they had again left the ditches full of dead, and the great circle of the fleet drawn up in the bay began to withdraw, like wolves licking wounds after an attempted kill, ready to renew attack.

Next day they came on again. It was clear by now that so long as any fresh men or sustenance could reach St. Elmo it would hold out, crazy and riddled as it was. "So many thousand picked troops dead, and the Aga himself, all for a fortress which should have fallen in—what was it?—four days?" Dragut gibed as he moved away from Mustapha, who in the last days had admittedly tried to emulate his courage and had come down among the men. But Dragut continued his own overseer, giving his own orders to the men who were raising, on his instructions, the highest palisade of brushwood and earth yet attempted for protection against the snipers from the Fort, the long-range gunners of St. Angelo.

He moved down as the cannon roared out; and when the reply came could be clearly seen among the gunners. A crashing of sound, a curtain of thick shot, followed as the old man turned to say something to Philip Lascaris, who was behind him. They were within the range of fire; it did not show courage, Dragut had always said, to appear to hide oneself from the Christian roundsmen.

So Dragut fell. A cannon-ball had struck at the ground beneath his feet in the last salvo; hurling upwards into the faces of those who stood there were sharp stones as well as earth. A stone struck Dragut on the right side of the head, felling him. Blood gushed from his nose and ears, suffusing the robe he wore over his armour and also staining that of Philip, who had caught him in his arms as he fell.

"Cover him with a cloak," said Mustapha. "His death will dishearten the men."

But Dragut was not yet dead. That evening, with the going down of the sun, they carried him back to the tent on the Marsa which he had only visited so far by day, on occasion, for conferences. They laid him there and bound up the wound in his head, for he was still unconscious and they feared he would die without speaking again. But presently his eyes opened and he appeared to search about him. Philip, who was still in the tent, came over and said clearly, "I will remember, Serene One." He bent, and drew the ring from Dragut's finger. Then he turned and went out. The old man's eyes closed again and he appeared to sleep peacefully.

Twenty

The crowd moved, swayed, parted and prayed aloud, the women clattering beads in their fingers, while their great black hoods screened one from viewing the procession in the street. "Who would have thought that the Grand Master would keep Corpus Christi in the midst of war?" But on the whole the crowd seemed pleased that this should have been done. Wars came and passed, but the Body of God must still be honoured; and, after all, what was the end of us in any case except death?

Beyond the deceptive calm of the defended harbour, St. Elmo still flaunted its banners of the Cross, hanging limply now in the windless air. Irregularly, sounds of the bombardment came across to Birgù. "They will not cease till they have pounded the Fort to ashes, but how could they have known it would take as long?" Fiammetta asked herself. She could survey her thoughts from a separate place to which long weariness of body and mind accustomed her; daily, she awaited news that Anthony Graham was dead. Even now, at this moment, the last round of firing might have killed him below a breach in the wall; but no, she would have known. She prayed still; but other women were praying for their beloved ones, and so many had died in spite of it, were still dying.

"Here is the Grand Master now," said Toni Bajada. He had come up behind her, moving silently as he always did; one minute he would be there, the next gone, slipping under water or through the enemy lines. If he bears a charmed life, why may not others? thought Fiammetta. Then she crossed her fingers over one another; it was attempting Providence to ask for that, for Anthony.

La Valette carried one of the standards of the canopy above the Host, the other three being supported by Knights Grand Crosses of the Order. All four wore armour under the ceremonial cloaks; only the Bishop, who carried the monstrance in

the centre, was clad as always on great occasions. The brilliant
colours of his chasuble and mitre gleamed in the sun which
struck rays from the golden monstrance. All of this will be
desecrated and burned if the Turk comes here, thought Fiammetta; the Hand of St. John itself thrown on the streets, the
gems prised out of its reliquary. Yet would that matter when all
who cared for such things would in any case be dead? This
might be the last time the Host was carried through the streets
of Birgù.

"Why do you shiver?" said Toni. "Have you an ague?" He
noticed everything; his tone to her was that of an elder brother.
Fiammetta shrugged. "Have you seen Bianca of late?" she asked
him, after they had genuflected to the Host as it made its way to
St. Lawrence in Birgù.

"Say nothing, but I go again tonight—perhaps. There are
ways I know. Yaya is to have a child; did you hear of that? At
first, Bianca says, she was resentful; but now she is happy. The
child will grow up in the house of Inguanez, and it will not
matter there who was his father."

"Poor Yaya," said Fiammetta, "but she will not be so
lonely." Half of life seemed to have been lived since the day they
had all ridden up there to the narrow walled streets, the roofs
and towers. God's hand had stirred among the living cargo of
the Sultan's merchantman, scattering its members to east and
west. Hafiza was dead, Melissa secluded from the world by
parents who would never let her out of their sight again. She
herself, who had no home, no family, what would her fate be?
"It does not matter," she told herself. It was impossible to think
of a time when there would be no war.

Later, the Grand Master took a white napkin and placed it on
his shoulder, knelt and began to serve dishes of food to the
waiting poor. Watching the inscrutable, bearded face, Fiammetta wondered what his thoughts were. Did he live for the
present and his duty only, seeing nothing beyond that old man
with his running sores, the old twisted woman in the *faldetta*,
the thin orphan craving for a meal? His gestures as he served
the bread and meat were gentle and graceful; he might have
been the very Christ he served and not a commander at war.
"What a man he is!" murmured Toni beside her. "Whatever he

undertakes, it is with his whole heart." He stared across at the Grand Master, admiration in his light eyes. The stresses of the past weeks had removed all trace of lingering resentment for the Knights among the Maltese. This was a war of truth against evil; everyone had a part to play. Toni left Fiammetta still watching the ceremony, slipping away from her without saying goodbye.

Later, on the night of that same day, she could not sleep for the thunder of the guns. At some hour she put on a cloak and went out, down to the harbour, staring across at the fire-drenched Fort. She had been there perhaps a quarter-hour when a hand was laid on her arm and her name spoken. She stiffened, but made no sound. The man wore full armour and she could not see his face.

"The Grand Master would have speech with you. I sought you at the house. I am to take you to him without delay."

A sudden flare across the water lit up his face under the helmet; it was the Commander Gurial, a Spaniard in charge of a key post in St. Angelo. Earlier she recalled him as a dark, laughing devil, ready for any mad ploy. Now his laughter had long gone and his madness held direction. He was known to be in the Grand Master's most secret councils and even to be the source of many of his plans. He escorted her silently through the empty streets.

The hour was late, but La Valette was at his writing-table. As she entered, he handed a despatch to Sir Oliver Starkey, who sanded it and sealed it with the great leopard seal. Both men were gaunt with lack of sleep and their eyes feverish with purpose. La Valette nodded to her briefly.

"I have an assignment for you which may be the last," he said; as always, he treated her like a man. "What I have to say to you must be repeated to no one. If you are asked concerning it by the enemy, use your wits and remember that you are a woman."

The coldness of the speech froze her, for a moment causing her to underrate what he said; when would she meet the enemy? Her eyes held the question, but she said nothing. Sir Oliver made a sudden movement of the hand as though he would intervene, but the Grand Master silenced him with a gesture and spoke on, as though he ordered a line of battle.

"You will comb your hair out tonight and wear no hood.

Then you will get in a boat with a lantern heading it, and row
out alone to St. Elmo. There—"

"Monseigneur, I am not afraid; but for the past two nights it
has been impossible to reach the further side. The Turk has
gunners trained day and night, which he did not do earlier."

"Do you teach me my business?" demanded La Valette
angrily. Again Sir Oliver Starkey intervened. His manner in
adversity was gentler than the Grand Master's, who resembled,
in these days, a fierce old mastiff; he came over to Fiammetta
and led her into the warmth of the lamp. La Valette watched
and, at sight of the shining light on her hair, his anger seemed
forgotten and he nodded eagerly. "Yes," he said, "like that; you
must row out like that, with the lantern-light on your hair so
that they may see who you are."

"Safieye of the Bright Hair," said Sir Oliver; he was smiling
a little sadly. Fiammetta stared up at him in amazement. "That
was my name in the house of Dragut, at Mehedia," she
stammered. "How did you know of it?"

"If in no other way, from Dragut, who has murmured it in
his delirium these few days past. He cannot die till he has seen
you again; they have sent a message that you are to be allowed
to pass through the lines, with one other."

"And return?"

They did not answer. Fiammetta stood still for moments.
Why did they want this? she was wondering. It was nothing to
them whether or not Dragut died with his wish granted. There
must be some other reason, something she had not been told.
She countered for a while, assembling her wits.

"How do you know that it is not a ruse?" she asked them.
"They know that I have swum and rowed for you, and that in
this way they can lay hold of me for—for themselves. Dragut
may well be dead by now, an old man with his skull shattered.
They told me how that happened by the ravelin. They will want
to conceal his death from their men till St. Elmo falls."

The Grand Master made no reply; his eyes glinted coldly. He
gestured to Starkey and the Englishman brought over an object
in his hands which glistened in the light of the lamp. It was the
fire opal, set in the ring she remembered which bore signs from
the Koran. Even now she drew her breath as she looked at it,
remembering how she had first seen it on Dragut's hand while
his sword was wet with her father's blood; then later in the

place by the pool. The Jewel of Barbarossa, the dead corsair who had been the scourge of the Mediterranean when Dragut himself was young! And at his death he had caused it to be sent to Dragut. She closed her eyes; behind the lids came the sight of the Mehedia garden, the cypress and orange trees.

"You know this?" asked La Valette. Fiammetta nodded, and he smiled grimly.

"You can see that, after all, our own spies are not inefficient. Anyone wearing this symbol may pass safe through the Turkish lines by order even of Mustapha. It is perhaps as holy an object to them as the Black Stone of Mecca. When you reach St. Elmo, anchor the boat by the door in the wall as you have been used; a man will come out to you, and you will take this ring from your finger and put it on his, to ensure his safety. Then you will give him this scrip, which he will conceal about him." He took the sealed despatch from Sir Oliver. "That is all; except that, as you alone will meet this man, you must know something of what his mission is to be. Pray that he may accomplish it."

"I will do so, Monseigneur. I ask your pardon for having doubted."

"That is nothing," he said, and for the first time his face and voice softened towards her. "It is my unhappy need to spare no one in this matter, but neither would I spare myself. Your companion will make his way through the Turkish lines to Sicily, where—as only he is qualified to do—he can make vividly clear the conditions in Fort St. Elmo to the Viceroy there, Don Garcia de Toledo. If his tale does not move Don Garcia to send help quickly, then nothing will. You yourself will be taken to the tent of Dragut, for it is by means of this bargain that the safe-conduct for my messenger was promised. You understand clearly what you must do?"

"I understand, Monseigneur."

She stood erect, and poised; to Sir Oliver she seemed like a still flame. "Who is to say that courage is only a matter for us men?" he thought. In the manner of the courtier he was, he bent over her hand and kissed it; but La Valette laid both of his on the girl's shoulders in blessing.

"May God go with you, Fiammetta," he said. Tears sprang to her eyes. Quickly, lest either man see them, she turned and made her way out alone into the dark.

The boat was ready. Dipping the oars in the strangely silent water of the harbour she heard their creaking, a little. Slowly the inferno that was St. Elmo drew nearer, a redly-glowing mass reflected in the water; the fires made by today's battle had not yet subsided. As she rowed beneath the walls heat met her, as from a giant's expiring hearth. Everywhere about her was silent, as though no one watched; yet she knew a thousand eyes beheld her as she rowed across the bay. The lantern's light which hung from her boat illumined her hair; it also shone, for her brief wearing of it, on the great fire opal of Dragut and Barbarossa. "Yesterday they shot at the oars of Luqa's craft, killing two rowers," she thought. There must indeed be orders from Mustapha not to fire.

St. Elmo's rocks loomed, with the silent swaying of the water like a requiem for the dead who lay above her, Turkish and Christian piled together in a medley of death. The last glow of the fires, the light of her own lantern, shone on a limb here, a severed trunk there, its blood-vessels cut and gaping. She avoided her gaze and anchored the boat, as she had been told, below the gate as on other nights. No wounded would come out tonight. The gate of the dead stood in its arched shadow; when it opened she thought a dead man waited there, wrapped in the whiteness of his bandages. But he moved, and the door in the wall closed after him. He stepped into the boat, and she knew him for who he was.

"Anthony!"

For instants the world, the water whirled about her, then was still. She saw his eyes fixed upon her; but he did not speak. She drew the ring from her own finger and tried to set it on his, with a little sob at the contact of his body against her hands. But it was useless; he could not wear it, his hands were tied up in linen and he moved stiffly, as if on puppet-strings. "Wildfire-burns," he said briefly. "They will heal. Compared to most in there, I'm a whole man. They took the cavalier today."

The sound of his voice made her tremble. She saw him turn and brood at the receding Fort as they pulled out. He had stowed the ring in his doublet. She made herself row on steadily, round beyond the bay.

"Did they draw lots to let you go?" she asked. It still seemed like a miracle that he should be here; he, of all men whom she had expected never to see again! He drew a sharp breath and she knew that she had unwittingly flicked at a raw place in his mind; to leave the rest in St. Elmo, all of them wounded or unfit, had seared him more deeply than the fire.

"No," he said expressionlessly, "it was by the Grand Master's order, brought across by Medrano when he returned. I had formerly, as you know, been to Don Garcia with Sir Oliver; and it was thought that when he saw my state now, and heard from my own lips what had befallen the rest, he might forget his caution."

The ruined hands spread themselves briefly in a shrug. "He must send aid soon, or not at all," said Anthony. He scarcely seemed aware of her presence in the boat, nor did he question her as to the reasons for her voyage alone into the Turkish lines. Bitterly, she told herself that she meant nothing to him; and yet how could any woman do otherwise in face of the memories he endured? Perhaps no man who had lived through St. Elmo's siege would ever again be quite as other men. But who else was to survive? Who else? He heard her caught breath.

"How will I know that you have won through to safety?" She could not forbear the question; whatever she herself might be called upon to endure in the infidel camp, she could bear it only if she knew he were either safe or dead. Uncertainty would be worse than madness. She saw the bandaged head turn.

"You ask me that?"

"I ask it. You must know that I love you." She made the statement calmly, keeping up the rhythm of the oars. They only had a very little way to go now. Graham continued to look at her; his mouth might have been smiling. But when he spoke it was only to answer her question.

"I will light a fire-signal when I have reached Mellieha Bay. Toni Bajada should have a boat there. He is making his way round the island from the west, by way of Mdina; he will bring word from the governor there for His Highness. Once we are ready to sail I will light the fire—Fiammetta."

He spoke gently, as though for the first time he saw her as she was. "What have I to do with love?" he said. "Even were we not at war, my hope is to become a Knight."

"No hearth-fire is for me. Do not trouble yourself; only, do not forget me. Your device says *Ne Oubliez*."

"How could I do so?" he asked, and as they drew near he put his wounded hand again in his doublet and drew out the ring.

"By rights you should wear this, not I. You are braver than any man, Fiammetta."

She smiled, and gave him back the ring; his words were honey, to be garnered in her mind during whatever might come. She was comforted by the thought that he was to meet Toni Bajada. The heartening thought of the Maltese whose agile body and quick mind death or accident could not touch came to her. She knew Toni was already a legend on both sides for the manner in which he could accomplish impossible tasks, like disarming a Turk without wounding him and thereafter taking him prisoner to work on the walls.

"They are waiting for us now," said Anthony. "If this is farewell—"

She took his bandaged hands, and kissed them. In the darkness, on the shore, figures loomed as they drew in. Anthony had pulled the hood of his cloak over his head to hide the bandages; wrapping its folds about his hands, he allowed himself to be drawn full into shore before stepping from the boat. The Jewel of Barbarossa gleamed; a raised torch borne by a Spahi shone on it.

No word was spoken. They regarded one another for what might be the last time, standing there amid the waiting enemy with the water lapping about their feet; she still and silent, the brightness of her hair hanging about her like a veil. Graham watched as they led her away with ceremony, surrounding her with torchlights to keep her feet from stumbling on the rocks. A little way off a mule waited, to take her to Dragut's tent on the Marsa.

Graham stood there while she was led off, and watched her mount the mule. He was filled with a curious humility at the declaration of her love. He was less than a man, no doubt, to allow her to go; but there was his duty. They had left him alone in the darkness, and under cover of it he made off, swiftly and with strength of purpose enough to let him forget his burned limbs and weary body. The torchlight had not faded before the rock was again empty; he had passed through the lines as though he were a ghost that no one had either felt or seen.

At dawn the bombardment started again. Soon there was no memory of truce on either side; the full fury of the Turkish onslaught was again directed on St. Elmo, and again the defenders held off, as though by a miracle, the massed attacks of troops and firing of mighty cannon; they fired from the batteries and the ships which had closed in at last in crescent-formation near the shore, like sharks massing.

It grew light as Fiammetta was led at last through the camp by the Marsa. She saw that there were many sick; the Grand Master's early foresight in poisoning the wells had brought dysentery among the Turks, and hundreds were unfit to fight. But there was no shortage of food such as must be endured in the Christian camp; the flap of Mustapha's silk tent, opened to let in the morning air as she passed, revealed piled grapes and figs on a salver, waiting for the commander to refresh himself on waking. A retch of hunger troubled Fiammetta; it was many days since she had eaten enough, any more than the other inhabitants of Birgù.

But when they brought her to Dragut's tent there was food for her; fruit, sherbet and the pressed flat flour-cakes soldiers bake on fires. She made herself eat a little, while the slaves undressed her. They brought warm scented water and immersed her in it, combing through her hair with flower-essences; bathed and refreshed, she felt her body wrapped about at last with gauzy stuffs, her feet thrust into white leather slippers. It was like a dream of sudden luxury between horror to come and the remembrance of horror borne. She did not look at the slaves who groomed her; they might have been eunuchs or men.

Once there was a voice in her ear. "Lady, take heart. I am a Christian, and I will help you. Do not turn your head this way. For a year they held me in the galleys, and then when I grew too weak they brought me ashore as a body-slave, for I am old. I it was, under orders, who took the Jewel from the finger of Dragut and had it conveyed to the Christian general. If I can serve you further, I will; when the old man dies you will be in danger. Remember my name here; it is Selim." She slid her eyes round and saw a gaunt old man, with stumps of yellow teeth. She would know him again. "I must go now, they are beginning to watch," he murmured, and made off, bearing away the water in which she had bathed.

They came then to lead her to Dragut. She found time to wonder at the slackness in the camp, that the old slave should have had leisure to speak to her unobserved. She wondered also how many Christian prisoners were in the camp; it was known that Mustapha took none by custom. These men must have been with the Turkish army for years, perhaps from boyhood. How many of them remembered the Faith in secret, like Selim? It might not be impossible to find friends to aid her here.

Dragut lay on the silken bed he had refused in health; they had carried him up here by litter from his chosen place among the gun-batteries. His face had lost its lines and hollows and was smooth; below the mustachioed lips the jaw sagged, and his breath came snoringly. Near his hand, so that he could both touch and see them if he wakened, were the two gifts Sultan Suleiman had sent him when he made him Viceroy of Tripoli and Algiers; the jewel-studded Koran, the gold scimitar. Neither had comforted Dragut these last days; it was seen by his servants, and the Arab physician who came to bandage his head-wound, that he was restless and wanted something, or somebody, who was not here. As Fiammetta entered they murmured "Safieye, Safieye" as if to tell the dying man his wish was granted; often the ears failed last of all, when one could no longer see. But Dragut's eyes opened; they were suffused with blood, yet as Fiammetta stood before him with the early sun shining behind her through the opened flap of his tent, he smiled, and raised one hand a little. A great sigh rose among the watchers; he could see, he had smiled, he might live!

Safieye of the Bright Hair took her place by his bed. During the days which followed she hardly left him or even turned her glance away, except to watch for a fire-signal' from the north. After two days, it came.

The sounds of firing from St. Elmo had ceased for many hours. The silence carried in it some sinister, unforeseen thing. During the time of quiet the leaders of the Turkish army came, one after another, soft-footed, to pay their last homage to Dragut, the Drawn Sword of Islam. He lay for the most part as he had done when he fell wounded by the breach; now that the swift rush of blood from ears and nose had slowed and darkened, the pace of his life slowed also. It had not been thought he would live for one more night. Yet he had lived through three and four; dozing for the most part, as old men will sometimes do to

conserve the weak flicker of life that is in them. Only in Dragut
the life had flowed so strongly, panther-swift, that to see him
now was like looking down on a stranger. They stood there,
with unashamed tears in their eyes, Mustapha, Piali, the rest in
their turn; not heeding the woman's still figure by the tent-wall.
After they had come and gone Fiammetta still sat on there,
watching the rise and fall of the old man's breath, hardly
enough to stir the coverlet. There would come a time when it
would no longer move with Dragut's breathing, and by that sign
they would know he was dead. There might be no other change.

Once or twice he had spoken. After a time she was not certain
that he still knew of her, though he seemed to derive comfort
from her presence. At first he had shown her he liked to see the
tent-lamp shine on the brightness of her hair; she had stayed
where he could watch it, before his sight began to fail. But once
he had roused himself to speech and had said clearly "Golden
One, does the child stir yet in your womb?" and had flung out a
hand as if searching. She had placed her hand in his and let it
lie there till he fell into a fitful sleep. He spoke no more, but the
hand comforted him. Another time he had beaten lightly on the
coverlet, as if he were hearing a melody played in his mind; she
sang to him for a little while, having no lute. Otherwise, there
was nothing she could do for him that was not done by the
constant ministering of his slaves. They served Dragut gently
and gladly, not letting her touch him otherwise.

Last of all in the procession of commanders a young man
came. His eyes were grey and though he wore a turban, he took
heed of her, not, as the rest had done, looking on her, if they saw
her at all, as part of the tent's furnishings, without ears or mind.
He said his name was Philip Lascaris and that he commanded
five hundred in Mustapha's troop-galleys. "What will become
of you when he dies?" he asked in a low voice. They stood
together looking down at the gaunt drained face of the dying
man. A weariness as of her own death came to Fiammetta; she
had not yet thought of what would happen to herself.

Lascaris spoke quickly, quietly. "Let no one suspect that I
have spoken to you of this," he told her. "Mustapha will value
your life at less than a pin once the old man is dead. He will kill
you, and not quickly, for all you have done to thwart him in the
past during this siege. What you must do, as soon as the old
man dies, is to leave the tent and make your way down to the

water before anyone knows that you are gone. Once there, you
have a chance to get back to the Christian lines."

"Dressed in this fashion?" She looked down at herself, clad
in the white, revealing garments of the Serai. I'd not get ten yards
from here before they fell on me, she thought; she had noted the
lascivious glances of the Spahis on her way in, but they had
dared do nothing while Dragut lived. A shiver took her; would
it not be better to die under Mustapha's orders than let herself
be raped to death? Yet perhaps that itself would be his order;
she had heard of such things. A shudder took her, watching the
ebbing life of the frail old corsair; he had so much strength even
in his name that that alone protected her, but when he was
gone. ...

"Trust me," said Lascaris, and it occurred to her to wonder
why he should do this for her, a Christian and his enemy. Why
should she trust him rather than Mustapha Pasha? But the
sight of the grey eyes, with some pain in their depths that she
could not understand, reminded her of Anthony; this reassured
her against all reason. Whatever the man's motive might be in
helping her, he was suffering in his mind.

An hour later the old slave Selim who had been a Christian
appeared, with a concealed flat package for her. When she was
unobserved she opened it; and found a turban ready folded, the
scarlet pantalooms of a Spahi, and a curved knife. The sight of
the last gave her confidence; whatever Lascaris' reason might be,
he had given her the means to protect herself, and he had sent
Selim. She slipped the pantaloons on beneath her clothing when
she could and thrust the knife in her girdle, covering it with
draperies; when the moment came there would be nothing to do
but wrap the turban round her head quickly, and go out.

There came a day when the guns fired on for four hours,
shattering the quiet of the morning. In the tent where Dragut
still drew breath, it was as though a storm thundered beyond the
Marsa. Twice in that morning Fiammetta went to the tent-flap
to look for news, seeing beyond the back of the Spahi guard who
stood there the hordes of untended sick on the camp-ground
with the smell of their infected ordure rising from the refuse-
ditches. There seemed nothing new; except that, the second
time, in the still air of noonday, came the sound of a bell. It rang

out at solemn intervals, with a clear deep note. It was the great bell of St. Elmo.

"Then it is their last hour," she thought. She stood there, hands clasped together below her breast, praying silently for the defenders' souls. So few must be left now; during the past few days, she had heard Piali say in the tent, they had thrown up ladders to every part of the Fort so that there was not a yard of it where battle was not raging. And all night, as usual, at intervals, they had kept up the firing so that the exhausted men inside would have no sleep. So few, and those few wounded; when the enemy gained the Fort he would find them unable to stand, fighting where they had been placed in chairs to support the weight of their armour.

The bell tolled on; tears were running down her cheeks. Anthony Graham was safe; but soon the Standard of the Cross would be torn down, the Crescent flutter out above St. Elmo. This was the eve of the Feast of St. John, patron saint of the Order. Could cruelty satisfy itself further than that the Fort should fall on this very day? "Mustapha would plan it so," she thought.

But it was good news to the enemy; a murmur of joy was spreading through the camp. Soon runners came to the tent to bear the news to Dragut. Fiammetta drew back into the shadows, nearby the bed, her face hidden.

"The Christian fort has fallen," they told him. "Mustapha has taken no prisoners. Allah be praised for such a victory and that we are able to bear it to the ears of the Drawn Sword of Islam."

But Dragut lay still, and at first they feared that he had not heard them. Then he raised his eyes and made a small gesture of pleasure with his hands. A bubble of blood burst between his lips, and soon he lay dead. Afterwards they said that he had lingered on to hear the news of the fall of St. Elmo.

Within instants a great wail sounded for him within the camp; it sounded out beyond the tent and the disease-stricken plain of the Marsa, and beyond to where Mustapha Pasha and his officers were disposing of the bodies of St. Elmo's defenders. Corsairs, busy with their attempted saving of Knights for ransom despite Mustapha's decree, looked up and said to one another "Dragut is dead." Then, as it was the will of Allah, they returned to their affairs; and that night lit a blaze of bonfires across the hills in mockery of the Feast of St. John.

Across the harbour mutilated bodies drifted; silently, swimming unseen nearby, were nine survivors who had managed to escape from the Fort and would live to tell what had befallen there these last days. Among them was Toni Bajada, who had returned by night from his journey to Mdina and the north, having seen Graham set off in a boat made of skins bound with cord which had been dragged overland by Toni and another. His own protective fortune stayed with the Maltese lad now, almost as if Bianca's crystal talisman contained it: guarding him from the Turkish arquebusiers as he made his way off through the water.

Within moments of Dragut's death Fiammetta had withdrawn from the tent. In the consternation of wailing that had arisen no one noted her; as she went, she stripped off her outer woman's garb, winding the turban about her head and grasping the curved knife Selim had conveyed to her, and which had stayed hidden in her girdle. Once beyond the tent's shadow she hurried, head down, trusting not to be accosted. The Spahi pantaloons were loose-fitting and let her take great strides like a man. By the time Mustapha Pasha sent for her, she would be beyond reach of his orders. The wailing for the dead Dragut sounded in her ears more faintly. She gained the crest of the low hill at last, keeping away from the bonfires, and made on out of sight.

Twenty-one

"I can hear the carriage now; Papa is always punctual. Are you certain, dearest, that you will not accompany us?"

Anton excused himself; he had work to do in connection with a new paddle-ferry to Ireland in which his alloy was to be used, and although it was Sunday he could not get it out of his mind. Also, he disliked Julius and the prospect of being shut up with him for an afternoon's driving did not accord with his inclinations. He bent and kissed his wife, warm in her sealskins.

"Do not overtire yourself, my dear. Enjoy your afternoon; give my love to Mama." She laughed, and put a hand up to his face.

"How could I tire myself sitting in a carriage? I am glad it is a fine day. I wish Papa had agreed to take Fiona; but he does not like to—to see her, as you know. Look in on her if you have the leisure; Lily Soames has gone to visit her mother, and Fiona may be lonely."

He bowed, smiled, assisted her to the door on his arm; saw her bestowed in Julius' carriage, waved the party off; and went back inside the house with a sensation of panic. He had not known—there was after all no reason why Juliana should have told him—that she had given Soames permission to visit her mother. It was difficult to picture Soames as having a mother at all. But he would shut himself in his study, and immerse himself in plans. Since the night of the storm he had not allowed himself to see Fiona unless it were unavoidable; she spent the mornings with her sister in the downstairs parlour, then went back to Soames' custody for the rest of the day. After tea, when he had come home, Juliana rested; she had begun to improve in health, and there had been a pretty colour in her cheeks today. The episode in the storm might have been a bad dream, involving someone else. He had closed his mind to the memory of it.

He turned, and beheld Fiona herself regarding him from the staircase. Her hair was loose, and hung on her shoulders; she wore her grey gown. She did not move or alter under his scrutiny; she simply waited. He felt a weakness assail him, and at the same time tried to act roughly. He gestured to her to go back to her room; what was she doing here? But she did not move. It was as though she had heard, had waited for the carriage to leave. Her green eyes were fixed on him. He felt a flicker in his loins, and knew that he was again in danger. She must go away! She must!

He climbed the stairs to where she was, and tried to turn her by the shoulders. The warmth of her body beneath his touch unmanned him. He kept hold of her, and they mounted the stairs together. When they came to her room, the key—he had ordered that one should be made—was on the inner side of the door. He took it, and turned the lock. Fiona began to unfasten her bodice, and lay down on the bed. He stood indecisively for some moments, then went to her. It might all have been planned, he heard his mind saying; he could not resist her, or save himself.

Twenty-two

Philip Lascaris had entered the captured Fort of St. Elmo immediately behind Mustapha Pasha and the High Command. The smell of fresh blood already mingled with the sweetish, cloying odour of decay from the piled bodies about ravelin and ditches. Fires still smouldered from the four hours' resistance that morning, before the signal for surrender had been given by Medrano at last. Everywhere the dead lay, hacked in pieces. The Turkish troops were already stripping the headless trunks and limbs, bearing away the heavy siege-helmets and great two-handed swords. "The Christian commander, an old man named Le Mas, was seated in his chair when we came in, for he could no longer stand; he died wielding this, but we soon made an end of it all." An eager Spahi spoke, hoping to win approval from his superior for the news. It was no longer possible to single out the remains of old Le Mas, torn to pieces in the final onslaught in which he had sat, sword at the ready, to face the enemy for the last time. Philip stared down at the sword, held out to him between the tough brown hands of a man who had suffered nothing in the siege. "It is heavy," he heard himself saying. "The old man must have been strong."

"He could no longer stand for his wounds, Serenity. None of them could stand. Who would have thought that such a resistance could come from a handful of seated men?"

Mustapha Pasha wrinkled his nose at conditions in the Fort. The Christian Knights had lived here, by day and night, in their own ordure, like galley-slaves; never having enough leisure to take off their armour to sleep, eat, relieve themselves elsewhere than in this place of battle. Sudden anger flared up in Mustapha, making his face patchily red. "By the Prophet! If so small a son has cost us so many men, what must we pay for the capture of the father?" And he looked across the water at Fort St. Angelo, unscarred as yet and bristling with gun-batteries

which had continued to fire high in the air during the late siege
so that the cannon-balls fell down like rain beyond St. Elmo
itself, wounding and playing havoc among the troops drawn up
on the further shore. A wolfish grin spread over Mustapha's
face, showing the light eyes above hard as pebbles.

"Come now!" he said. "There is still a thing to be done. We
will go into the chapel. That is where the last handful ran out,
waving their swords; we will send a clear enough message by
them to their Grand Master."

St. Elmo chapel had been stripped. All of the sacred matters, the
vestments, the tapestries which lined the walls, had been set
alight by the last defenders and reduced to ashes. Such of the
Host as had not been consumed they had buried beneath the
flagstones of the floor. No one now took leisure to search
beneath. Where the sanctuary-lamp had glowed steadily all
through the days of siege, there remained a metal ring, now
empty. Mustapha jerked his head in a brief command; a
Christian Knight, whether living or dead it was hard to tell, was
dragged forward and tied up by his heels to the empty ring. A
yell as of hounds in a pack came, as a cross was carved out of
the man's naked breast with a knife-blade and his heart exposed
redly in the flayed cavity. "Cut off his head," said Mustapha.
"It was the fate of their patron saint whom they honour. How
many more are left alive? Four? A sizeable raft; tie them all
together by the wrists, and float them across on the current to
the harbour, with their crosses upon them." He was smiling;
cruelty pleased him, making him feel the more powerful now
that Dragut was dead. He watched in silence as the rest of the
sentence was carried out. The four living Knights made no
cry for mercy; one turned his head a little as the cross was
carved into his living flesh. The eyes met those of Philip
Lascaris, who stood watching. He closed his own, assailed by a
pang of nausea for the first time in a life of many battles.

When he opened his eyes again he fixed them on the stone
pediment over the altar. This was the place where these brave
men had worshipped, which had given them such strength as to
resist to the death through hunger, privation, lack of sleep,
burns and extreme pain. Nothing was left for a Christian here
now but an escutcheon with the cross—always that, he

thought—and roses carved in the pale stone; above, a bearded figure looked down, having seen all from the beginning. What was the figure? Philip was ignorant of sculpture; the Prophet in his writings had forbidden the portrayal of man by man, so that in Philip's experience there were only scrolls of hidden meaning, arabesques and distorted shapes lacking reality. He told himself that his ancestors, the Emperors of the West, would have worshipped at such an altar as this; they would have known that watching figure, with its curious three-cornered headdress or canopy. His ancestors would have died as these men did, bravely and without a groan, for this cause.

He followed Mustapha out into the sunlight and saw how they treated the bodies of the Knights; headless, lashed together with arms outspread, thrown down to float across the water, the carved crosses bright with congealed blood. "This was all?" said Mustapha. Philip made himself answer, feeling the sound unreal; the world about him had acquired a sharp intensity that had not belonged to it when he wakened that day. He was no longer fully aware of the Turkish commander. "All," he replied from habit, "except some few who escaped by diving into the water; they were Maltese, the men say. I did not see it."

"How many?"

"Less than a dozen. It happened when the assault was made on the inner Fort. They will be in Birgù by now." He looked over at the town; between, the tied white corpses floated uncertainly, their wounds washed clean by the sea. There might, he knew, have been others still alive, smuggled away by the corsairs for ransom: he said nothing of that, astonishing himself; why had his sense of duty failed him?

The smell of death, the sight of it, settled as the dust ceased to stir about St. Elmo. Presently, the standard of the Crescent rose where the Cross had been. A cheer sounded from the Turkish ranks. Philip found his own lips parted silently.

Among the many dead found in the Fort were several Jews. Their presence baffled the high command; had these not been reviled by the Christians? "No doubt they were forced to come here and bear arms," said Mustapha. But Philip knew that the Jews had been in that part of the Fort which could have been manned only by volunteers. On a moonless night they could have revealed a breach in their wall to the enemy, shown him where to climb. Yet they had died, defending St. Elmo with the followers of Christ. What was this curious faith?

Twenty-three

In Messina in Sicily the bordellos spilled down to the sea, and by night there was noisy carousal. Anthony Graham heard it, marvelling at the differences in this babel of sound to the memory of St. Elmo. There nothing had been heard but the incessant cannon; here there was a confused murmuring in a dozen foreign tongues, often a burst of drunken song or women's high voices screaming. He found it disturbing and, still, he could not sleep. In the back of his mind was the knowledge that no firing had been heard in the distance since yesterday, the eighteenth of June. What did the silence hide, over the narrow water?

Near at hand lay ships, lying idle because the Viceroy, Don Garcia, would not give the word to man them. Filling the bordellos and taverns were men who, many of them, had come from afar to help relieve Malta, but who were not allowed to sail.

"To wait is politic." The recent memory of Don Garcia's cautious face, its hair and beard carefully combed and essenced with orange-flower water, came to Anthony again. Today he could have gritted his teeth at the Viceroy, spilled forth in so many words what his aid might have meant had he sent it sooner. But to wait was politic. He could imagine the reply impatience would receive. "You are young, Señor Graham, and youth is hot-blooded. But in my position I must uphold the trust placed in me by His Majesty the King of Spain." And turning then to the portrait, hung on the wall, of Don Philip himself, in rose and silver hunting-dress, his dog by him and his short legs encased in high soft boots of blond Castilian leather.

Nothing would be done, despite all his own patient argument, his diplomatic silences, learnt from Starkey. Useless to point out to Don Garcia, as he had tried to do, that one must risk a little to gain a great reward; that one might even be halting an infidel tide from sweeping across Spain itself, undoing all the life's work of Philip II's ancestors, Ferdinand and Isabella the Catholic Kings who had driven the Moors back to Africa last century. This was too great an issue for Don Garcia; he dared risk nothing. "Have I not sent my own son to the Grand Master as hostage?" he enquired plaintively. "You have seen him, my Federigo? He is well?"

Graham had lost patience. "Your Excellency, I have seen little but gunfire, wildfire, wounds and war. I have no knowlege of anyone in Birgù. If Your Excellency would land even a few hundred men by cover of night, to march down the west coast and across to Birgù itself, they would avoid the sea-patrols which follow a regular nightly pattern between Gozo and the Sicilian strait." Echoes, repeated words; where had he heard them? He was too tired for them to have come from himself. Now—

"We will see," was all Don Garcia would answer, and he rose to signify that the interview was at an end. Anthony had left, his disgust hardly tempered by the melancholy in the Viceroy's eyes regarding his beloved Federigo. Even now, would-be volunteers still howled below the viceregal windows, calling night and day to be given ships.

Graham moved restlessly, feeling in himself a thing he dared hardly acknowledge; a new and terrible desire to go out, down to the bordellos, and lie with a woman. The urges of his body troubled him and had done since release from the long duress of St. Elmo. Under such unnatural conditions men became strangers to themselves, he thought; such a thing had never happened to him before. What would his grim Scottish aunt say, who had reared him in the faith, the hope, that one day he would redeem his parents' lapse by dedicating himself to the service of a celibate Order? Now, remembering his childhood, he almost understood; always, in every least thing, directed to that end, his natural wishes and tendencies discounted! He had been kept at his books, like other Scots boys; if he showed a desire to idle, he was beaten; it was the devil tempting him, he was told, and any luxury, even warming himself at a fire, was frowned on. He had ended by fearing softness and beauty of any kind, seeing in it the face of his unknown mother who, he had been told, died for her sin of lust. Now he, her son, had that same lust rising in him, despite all the warnings; should he succumb? It would be welcome enough to go to one of those women now, forget the blowsy painted face and lay one's head between a pair of soft breasts, forgetting duty till morning came.

But with the morning, it would be too late; he would have betrayed himself.

He had walked as far as the harbour when a hand on his arm made him halt. It was a tall Knight named De Robles, whom he had met that day while waiting for the Viceroy. De Robles had the calm, cheerful aspect of a man who is undeterred by any human obstacle; he reminded Anthony of old Le Mas, left behind in St. Elmo to God knew what fate. They sat down by the water's edge and the Chevalier told him, swiftly and under oath of secrecy, that they would sail with the tide. "Never think that you failed with Don Garcia! Your Scots tongue, I don't doubt, has seared him where our courtly phrases failed. Moreover, you were able to describe conditions in St. Elmo at first hand; that has shocked him."

Some few hundred picked men, De Robles said, were to be sent out to Malta with two ships. They were to skirt round to the north-east to avoid Piali's patrol-fleet; but if St. Elmo had fallen meantime, they were to make back to Messina. "What, by the saints?" swore Graham furiously, and struck his clenched fist against his palm, forgetting his hands' hurt. "Sooner I'd leap overboard and attempt to make for shore, though I'm no swimmer."

Like a flicker of flame, the memory of the girl Fiammetta came to him. With her by him, he could reach land; it was a strange thought to have to rely for such things on a woman. He had never seen one naked; vaguely, he saw her strong white limbs, and a mystery that was her body, swimming by him, upholding him. If she—

"You would not be alone," said De Robles grimly. "You'll join us, then, at dawn? Silence must be kept regarding it; we may only board seven hundred, and none of these others—" he jerked a head contemptuously from where light spilled out from the bordellos—"will be in a state for the march."

After the Knight had left, Anthony sat by the water till

sunrise. He was thinking again of Fiammetta, as though the thought gave him comfort; and thanking God that he had not gone that night to a whore. Perhaps the hand of God was in this matter for him; though to dwell on it confused him. Don Garcia himself had assured him that there had still been no word from His Holiness the Pope about his own legitimacy of entry to the Order. At one time the news would have broken Anthony's heart; now, it brought no feeling, but he was tired; this inactivity would rest him for the morrow.

By dawn he had gone down to join the rest where the shadowy bulk of great ships thrust against the sky. "They say there will be mist," De Robles told him. "That is good for us if the captain knows his soundings."

Anthony watched the dark shapes of men filing on board in the wraith-like morning. He himself was assailed by a feeling of hope, and felt no more bitterness.

Twenty-four

Dusk had found Fiammetta stumbling, running, over the stony terraced ground which rose always, showing her, before the sun set through the mist, that she was going inland. Direction of purpose had left her and she was concerned with nothing except to put as much distance between herself and the Turkish camp as she could. Later it occurred to her that she would have been better to take to the water. In daylight, the scarlet trousers of a Spahi would single her out against the pallid rock, a clear target for the Maltese snipers who lurked here behind every ridge, every ruined farmhouse. They would have no mercy on the enemy, for he had none on them. Only days since, before she left, there had been a tale brought into Birgù of a pretty Maltese girl a sanjak-bey had carried off, and when a party of her kinsmen rode out to rescue her he had cut off her head with a single sweep of his curved sword, bearing it away, swinging by its long black hair, like a trophy of war at his saddle-bow.

Fiammetta hid herself, therefore, all next day, and only when it was night again crept forth, her limbs cramped and her stomach empty. Once she found brackish water, lying in a surface pool that might stem from a well; but she dared not drink from it, lest it was one of those which the Grand Master had poisoned when the Turks first set sail for the island. He had been right; she had seen the sickness on the Marsa.

She stumbled on, many times falling and bruising herself in the blind dark. Towards morning she sniffed the fresh odour of the sea-shore again, and thanked God; while she was near water she was safe. She scattered a group of the island's thin brown sheep as she thrust her way through them, vainly attempting to seize one for its milk; they were wild and would not stay for her. By now she was light-headed with fatigue and hunger, no longer capable even of concealing herself from lurking danger.

But on this deserted side of the island no one saw her that she knew of.

The seas where St. Paul had been shipwrecked long ago were white with rising mist. Out of it a small country chapel reared at a place above on the high cliff; she made her way there and, stretched out before the altar where a light burned, slept. She awoke refreshed, though still hungry; and found the pallid wreaths of mist drifting about the chapel-floor. When she ventured out, it was thick everywhere like a blanket.

She turned westwards, hoping to make her way with care to where, on a clear day, one could see the island of Gozo rear ahead past the channel. There also they had suffered so cruelly from Dragut's raids that the sight of a stranger, garbed as she still was, might cause them to shoot or fling stones without asking questions until afterwards. Perhaps, instead, she should attempt Mdina, where Bianca Inguanez would lend her clothes, and then go back to Birgù. But before that, somehow, she must eat, even if it were only clams from the rock. She groped her way down to the shore; and presently collided with men's figures, coming up suddenly from the water.

"By God's blood, a Turkish dog so far north already." The voice was robust and coarse, speaking French with the accent and swagger of the Gascon. Hands seized her, then thrusting about her in search of her dagger found her soft breasts, and cursed again with surprise while she cried out that she was a woman, a Christian.

"What does a woman and Christian on this road alone? Here, *mon chevalier*; look what we have here, clad in Turkish trousers!"

More men had come up, their beards bedewed with the wet from the sea-mist. Fiammetta's captor held her, struggling, her arms pinioned behind her back; in the fight her turban had worked loose and her hair fell about her shoulders.

"Stop that, and let her go!"

Fiammetta found herself looking up at a tall Knight, fully armoured and wearing the cloak of the Order. "Madame," he said courteously, "I am the Chevalier de Robles, in charge of this expedition. We are on our way to Birgù. Come with us, and direct us."

"How can she do so in the mist?" mocked the first man, who seemed in awe of no one. "She may lead us straight into the arms of the Turk. Find out her direction, *mon chevalier*, and her name if she has one. Why that dress?"

"All in good time," said De Robles gently, seeing Fiammetta's drawn face. "Madame, have you news of St. Elmo?"

"Yes, and all therein." Something in his manner warned her not to speak further. He nodded, grim and unsmiling.

"See that you say nothing of it. I lay that charge on you if you march with us."

"I am silent, *mon chevalier*." She was also tired, cold and hungry. Would they give her a piece of bread from their provisions?

She began to ask; but more figures were coming up from the shore, featureless in the enveloping mist. "You who take orders like a soldier, then, march," said De Robles. He beckoned a man to put a cloak round her shoulders to warm her, for she shivered in her thin garments with the release from fear. The man came closer; he was tall, almost as tall as the Chevalier. A cry escaped her, seeing him for the first time clearly; beholding her, he drew a long breath.

"Monsieur de Graham!" She was almost shy: it seemed a miracle.

"Fiammetta!"

She could not believe that he was real, that they could have met thus on a chance shore. She was aware of another thing; in some way that had changed him since the night they parted, he was no longer resentful of her womanhood. She accepted it with a sigh of thankfulness that left weariness and hunger behind. They might have been alone in that instant, together in a sea-mist at the end of the world. Without saying more, he wrapped half his cloak round her, keeping the cord still about his own shoulders. During the stumbled march south along stony ways they walked close, he supporting her tired body by an arm about her waist beneath her breast. From someone had come a portion of ration-biscuit, made in the Grand Master's Sicilian factory. Fiammetta munched as she marched. She was happy. The others jested at first, then forgot them, Graham and Fiammetta. Once on the march well begun, he told her, in a low voice, all that had happened since he had parted from her to join Toni with his hide boat and set out, alone, for Sicily.

He had done speaking. Through the sound of the marching columns they looked at one another, she seeing the burn-scars half healed, he watching, covertly, her face. He knew so little of love that he would not have thought of his glance as that of a lover. She, schooled at Mehedia, knew differently. Instinctively she writhed closer to him, and felt him withdraw. Her disappointment was so bitter that, to cover their silence, she blurted out a thing which lay on the surface of her mind.

"What of the Jewel?"

"I still have it." She heard the relief in his voice at being extricated from what, after all, had meant embarrassment for him. Tears stood in her eyes. She felt him plunge a hand in his doublet and take out the talisman, saying strangely "I should put it on your finger. It is for you, not me, to return it to the Grand Master."

She felt the ring slide on her hand, where it fitted loosely. She could not see, for her tears and the mist, its bright fire. A thing was made clear to her on this journey; when the time came for Anthony to don the cloak of the Order the Chevalier wore, she must not stand in his way.

If she had known, he was still thinking of her; and of the thing he had just done. In such a way his father had put a ring on his mother's hand before witnesses; they had said to one another "I take thee for my husband, for my wife." That was Scots law, but not, evidently, the Pope's. When this siege had run to an end he himself would once more have to await word, patiently and with no impediment.

"The Grand Master should have boats for us, if the messengers have done their part," someone said. Fiammetta heard them idly; if the Grand Master had promised a thing, he would do it. She herself had lived for a little while and had died. She was no longer aware of distance or time when they came at last to a village, and the mist merged into evening. In the dusk boats waited in silence on the water. She felt Graham, his hands impersonal, lift her into the boat and then seat himself apart from her, leaving her his cloak. She must have slept on the way across to Birgù harbour, and did not realise their danger in crossing or the miracle it was that they, who were to be known as the Little Relief, had won at last into shelter with no men lost.

"What ails Don Garcia de Toledo? Is he a Turk at heart?" enquired Sir Oliver Starkey. "To have sent those men, with orders to recall them if St. Elmo had fallen, but by God's mercy the mist came down and deceived the Sicilian commander of the boats! They kept silence regarding the fall of the Fort, though it seems they knew of it. We can use fresh men."

"Don Garcia serves a cautious master," said La Valette. "Philip of Spain has never moved swiftly. When all's over, if fortune favours us he will rejoice with us in our victory. Until then we can make shift for ourselves." He went on to murmur some remark about Don Garcia's son Federigo, who seemed, from his activities in the siege to date, to be a pleasant and courageous young man. "Is a divided mind a blessing?" asked the Grand Master. "I cannot tell. To me there is a goal to be won for God's honour, and all other matters are less pressing."

Sir Oliver had begun to smile, over by the window. "Sir, they are waving banners to mock at the Turks on the further bay, who let them through last night without so much as a shot fired! It warms the heart to see our men so joyous. I would Don Garcia himself might witness it, and his master."

Neither man had referred again to the other event which had not been so joyous; the arrival, with the languid current, of the headless bodies of the defenders of St. Elmo, flies crawling in the dried wounds carved in the form of a cross.

La Valette had indulged in an act of reprisal. Toni Bajada, swimming swiftly, had brought him news of the bodies before they floated in. La Valette was down by the shore, with crowded watchers, when they did so. He had not shown anger. What he felt was in its cold depths more terrible than any outburst would have been, or pity for the dead men alone, knowing the burden of responsibility he himself carried. There was wailing on the shore; friends tried, often vainly, to identify a scar here, a mole there. By the end some of the bodies were still nameless. La Valette went to his guardroom and there ordered a turnout of the Turkish prisoners. These were kept in the passage below St. Angelo by night, brought out in chains at daybreak to help build the walls against the coming siege of Birgù. They were paraded now, eyes blinking from recent darkness; they knew nothing of what had happened.

The Grand Master executed them, in full sight of the people of Birgù; one man for each dead man of St. Elmo. As the heads, shaven except for a single long lock of hair, fell severed, they were cast to the gunners. "Fire them back!" said the Grand Master. And the cannon sounded. As the grisly loads hurtled across from the cannon-mouths, in splashed blood, cracked bones, spilled brains at last to Mustapha's waiting horde, the people of Birgù and the garrison of St. Angelo called out the names of the dead of St. Elmo. "One for Le Mas! One for Medrano! One for de Broglie! One for. ..."

It was impossible for Mustapha, on this occasion, to reply in kind. He had taken no prisoners.

Two days later word was brought to the Grand Master that the woman who swam and rowed waited to see him. She was brought to him, still in her Spahi trousers. He saw that she looked pale and haggard. She held out an object in her hand; Dragut's ring lay there, with the Jewel of Barbarossa scintillating in the light. La Valette shook his head, briefly diverted from his anger over the deaths of St. Elmo.

"There will be no reward for you after this war, and perhaps death during it," he said, "and you have done well." He questioned her briefly about the state of affairs behind the Turkish lines. She told him of the sick men on the Marsa, and he nodded, satisfied. He did not ask her concerning her own escape; it was of no interest to him. "Keep the jewel," he said, "as your marriage-dowry, or your portion if you enter a convent. When you look at it, remember that I am not ungrateful."

She was shown out, the ring again on her finger. She had given him no thanks. When she was out of sight she gave herself up to bitter weeping. There would be no marriage for her, she knew; neither would she be a nun.

Twenty-five

Lily Soames opened a shabby purse and dropped in a coin which lay in her hand. She had turned it about with some satisfaction before bestowing it, letting the thin daylight play on the gold; it was a half-sovereign. In the purse were several; she had never had as much money before. She had no temptation to spend it; for one thing, folk might suspect something if she were suddenly to appear in a new bonnet or a fur pelisse. There was no fear of Mrs. Muntz, but that sour-faced Mr. Julius she had never liked, he had an eye as sharp as a needle.

She put away the purse, and sat down in her wooden chair to turn the matter over in her mind, much as she had turned the money in her fingers. All she needed do was not ask questions— there was no need, she knew everything that went on, when Mr. Muntz came upstairs and when he left, returning to the first-floor room where he slept alone now that Mrs. Muntz' doctors had advised that she have a bedroom on the ground floor, because of her heart. It usually happened when he was home from the office, and his wife was resting before dinner. That was the time of day now, and he'd been in there twenty minutes; soon he'd come out, lock the door with the key outside, and go downstairs again to what he called his office, where he was thought to have been all the time. "I have certain things to see to, dear," she'd heard him saying to Mrs. Muntz after tea. Certain things indeed! And that other, as mim as you please, had been downstairs sewing with Mrs. Muntz all of the morning. No morals, that one hadn't; there was no way of getting them into her head, when all was said. But she enjoyed what went on; oh, yes, more than once Lily had heard, towards the end, the high harsh stuttering cry of ecstasy. It was never too late to learn; she herself didn't know anything about such things, they weren't proper. But a half-sovereign was a half-sovereign; and all she had to do was be discreet, he'd said so.

They lay together on the bed. He had taken Fiona today
forcefully, using no gentleness; within his mind was a kind of
resentment. *This is what you wanted, isn't it?* And he had used
her to the full; after all, he might have gone into town and taken
some casual woman; a man couldn't live forever like a monk, as
he must now do with Juliana. He downed the memory of his
wife and fondled Fiona's breasts; they were large and creamy,
the breasts of a woman with a body made for this. If she hadn't
been sheltered for so long, first by her parents and later in his
own house, she'd have come to it long ago. He felt desire rise in
him again and went into her, once more; her thighs opened
willingly. Two months now they'd been at it, almost daily,
when he could get away; without Lily Soames it would have
been difficult to be sure no one would come upstairs, but now if
so, she'd warn him in time ...

He surrendered to the enjoyment of·the act, thrusting hard,
aware of his jerking buttocks driven by a force which was
beyond and yet within him. She lay passive now, her green eyes
wide open and fixed on his face, body no longer taut, arms and
legs clinging to him. Except for one cry she had been silent, not
even calling out his name which she knew and used at times.
How the devil should she know his name when all about and
within her was silence?

They lay in surcease at last, his mind already removing itself
from her. Tomorrow he couldn't come up; Agnes and Julius
and two business friends and their wives were coming to dinner;
Juliana liked these intimate parties. Fiona wouldn't be brought
downstairs; as well. She might do something which would give
the situation away; he tried, for both their sakes, not to be with
her when there were others in the room. Dear Juliana thought
he was rendered uncomfortable by the presence of her half-
sister, and made tactful arrangements so that they seldom met
downstairs. Dear Juliana. But this ... this was magic. He had
never known that one could journey as far in enchantment by
means of a woman's body, a woman's response. "If she hadn't
been deaf she would have made a courtesan," he thought. He
thumbed her flesh, sensing the pleasure it gave him. She grew
restless; however long he stayed within her, she clung to him
when he had to go; clung as if he meant all of life to her. What
would happen in the end? He sometimes asked himself,
prudently; but prudence had no place here. As well not to look

into the future; the present was wholly delectable. His work at the yards went well, moving with the ease of oil because he felt physically satisfied for the first time since his marriage. She had done that for him ... Fiona.

He nuzzled his head against her breasts, feeling their buoyant yielding. He felt her arms tighten round him again. She smelled pleasant, of Windsor soap. Lily Soames saw to that. Why think of Lily at the moment, remembering that she waited next door, a silent witness, knowing, knowing? It would be better to lie on a beach with Fiona, or else in a cave, hearing the sound of the sea. What had put that into his head? Soon he must go back downstairs, change and be ready for dinner.

Twenty-six

The gaunt shapes of trees remaining in the Grand Master's ruined garden on the Marsa could be seen from here by day, wilting from gunfire. No one now had leisure to remember the welcome shade of the garden; once there had been mulberries there, oranges and palms. "One cannot think of a time when any of us may walk in idleness again," thought Anthony Graham, posted as he was for the time being by the gunners of Sanoguera. It was not thought strange for him to be under a Spanish commander; defending the Post of England in this year of 1565 were Spaniards, Frenchmen, Italians, Maltese, Jews. The Reformation in England and Scotland prevented open aid to what men there now called the Pope's concerns: "but he does not concern himself with us either," thought Anthony, aware of the crucifix round his own neck. No doubt His Holiness could not commit himself any more than other rulers, even of Catholic countries, had felt themselves able to do.

Shading his eyes against the dust and heat, Graham stared across to the four new gun-emplacements of the Turks. Their crawling incessant labour was like that of an ant-heap, forever piling and building regardless of the crushed bodies under the weight of stones. There was a placement behind St. Michael's square fort across the strip of narrow water, others by French Creek, a fourth on Corradino heights. One noted, remembered, reported, adjusted one's own calculations for the length and height of shot. Some day wars would be waged only by this, a mathematician shifting gun-batteries. Now and again the singing whine of cannon-balls would sound overhead and the figures on the ant-heap carrying earth and brushwood to their destination would falter and disappear. Soon there would come a toppling of the remaining trees in the far garden and after that, the hillside would be flat as a grave.

Don Francisco de Sanoguera came himself at noon. "How is

it?" he asked. "The Grand Master says the fire-signal from Mdina continues. It should be possible to get some of the Maltese through the lines by night."

"There is a man down on the shore now below St. Elmo," replied Anthony. "He is signalling, I think."

Don Francisco shrugged. There was nothing further one need know with regard to what happened on the peninsula of St. Elmo. The ragged ruin of the destroyed Fort stood, bearing the Crescent in a light wind as though in embarrassment. Below, the single figure continued to stand and gesture. At first they thought it was a Turk taunting them; but why did he stand alone? "The rest are busied enough in mounting their brush-wood-platforms," grunted the Spanish Knight.

"I think that he has a message for us." Graham half turned at a touch on his arm; it was Fiammetta, sent with the noonday ration of bread soaked in wine. She handed him and the Knight their portions without comment. Anthony saw her make her way down the line of gunners, handing each man his bread. They took it with a jest; they knew and respected her. She made her way back again with the empty basket. Young Don Jaime, Sanoguera's nephew, bowed with Castilian courtesy and offered to carry it back to the base for her. She smiled, and shook her head.

"You have your task here, and I have mine," she said. "That man on the shore—". Then she drew a breath. "Why, it is Philip Lascaris whom I met when I was in Dragut's tent on the Marsa. He gave me clothes to help me escape." Her voice rose in excitement. "He is friendly to us, I am certain of it! Only he cannot come through their lines."

"Are you so certain of his friendship?" Graham asked her. He could not, even in the urgency of the moment regarding the solitary Turk, forget her physical presence and the disturbance it aroused in him. The sun had bleached her hair almost to straw-gold and had burned her skin to the colour of a walnut; except where, as she moved, her shift slipped aside from one shoulder and he saw the cleft between her breasts, white as snow. An urge of desire took him; he turned his head away.

"What do you want?" shouted young Jaime to the Turk, in French, cupping his mouth in his hands. The lone man took a pendant fold of his turban and held it up, like the white flag of parley.

"I want to join you," he called. "Will you send a boat?"

"Blood of God, this needs higher orders than mine," muttered Don Francisco, and he sent young Jaime forthwith to the Grand Master to ask his desire in the matter. Jaime came running back quickly: the boat was to be sent. "But we have no boat," said Fiammetta. "There are none ready outside the chain defence."

She had begun to unfasten her skirt, ready to jump into the water. Sudden anger rose in Graham; why must she always be the one to risk her life? "Stay where you are," he said harshly, "there are men on board the *Gabriel* who can swim." He took hold of her by the arm, but she struggled against him.

"Let me go, he saved me then; why should I not save him now? He cannot swim, or not so far alone."

"Then let him sink." His teeth gritted; he knew he was being unreasonable, but she—

Meantime the Spaniards had shouted to Lascaris on the other side that he must swim across, for they had no boat. "Can you swim? If not, we will help you," yelled Don Jaime.

Lascaris was already stripping off his clothes and armour. "Name of all that is holy, he is wrapping his shirt round his head," muttered a gunner, who was watching. "Does the infidel keep his nakedness in his scalp?"

They had made ready to mock Lascaris, but Graham ordered them to be ready to keep up a protecting arquebus-fire over the swimmer's head. Already the platform-builders had sensed something amiss and were swarming down from their anthill to the shore. "Mother of God, let him come across in safety!" sobbed Fiammetta.

She had strained over the parapet regardless of their guns, and was watching the swimming man. Graham strode over and pulled her roughly down. "Do you want to be killed?" he asked her.

"Does it matter to you?"

"Yes, by God!"

They lay pressed together in the shelter of the wall; overhead the light gunfire sang, guarding Philip Lascaris in his journey across the bay. Part of the way over he began to tire; at once, three men of the *St. Gabriel* dived overboard, and making their way out to him with strong strokes brought him to shore. "He was about to sink when we reached him," they boasted afterwards.

The gunner who had mocked Lascaris, by name Balbi di Correggio, was ordered down with Don Jaime and the pair of them lifted Philip up. He was spent and exhausted, with the water running down his naked body and soaking into the ground. "You mocked him, Balbi," said Jaime. "Now you can give him your trousers."

Afterwards Balbi himself was to recount the tale. They had taken the infidel to the captain's quarters and had there offered him food and drink. "But he would eat nothing, it being a fast day over there, and although he had had his fill of water on the way over, as God knows for we all saw it, nothing would he take but a drink of cold water all day. They make hardy warriors enough on it in Constantinople; muscles he has on him as hard as iron, harder than my own. What did we do then? Why, what do you think? We took him along to the Grand Master. Don Francisco's orders were that he was to be allowed speech with no one else, though Madonna Fiammetta by the wall was hot to get at him, mother-naked as he was." And Balbi rolled his eyes and twirled the upward sweep of his mustachios, of which he was proud and which wilted easily in the heat. "Nay, I meant nothing towards Madonna Fiammetta; she's a brave lady, as everyone knows. What am I to do without my breeches? By the saints, Don Francisco himself shall pull me off a new pair from the first dead Turk we find, for I've a fancy for scarlet. Meantime I must make shift, I daresay, with none, for all my modesty."

La Valette had received Philip Lascaris, still clad in the motley clothes he had borrowed. Some of the suffering Fiammetta had seen in the young man's eyes on the Marsa had abated; in its place was defiance. These Knights, dark, strangely cold and, until today, his enemies, might hang him; but he had salved his conscience. The lifting of guilt left him lighter at heart than at any time since the early days in the Enderun, when they had begun to teach him to stop thinking for himself and to obey without question. Now he, himself, Lascaris, had acted as his own spirit bade him; and would do so again, for only in this way was his soul's doubt appeased. He could not say all of this to La Valette, who stood regarding him with that cold glance which saw everything. "Why have you come?" the Grand Master said.

"I wish to be a Christian, as were my ancestors."

The words were stilted in his own ears; the answer he had wanted to make would not come. I have seen the bravery of those who died, Monseigneur; some matter was there among them that we of Islam do not possess. Whatever it was that made the Jews also, who killed your Christ, fight and die as bravely as anyone else at St. Elmo, that is what brought me here today after many a night sleepless in my tent on silk pillows.

But he could not say it all. He looked mutely at La Valette, who nodded.

"You are welcome indeed," he said, and a smile lit his gaunt face. Later he came to Philip alone and they talked far into the night. There was nothing the young man knew of Mustapha's and Piali's siege-plans for the island that he did not lay bare. "And now my sword is for Christ, as once for Islam." He would perform valiant deeds, given the chance; but La Valette answered drily as was his way.

"You have left your sword behind on the shore below St. Elmo. We could have used it here. But the armoury-master shall provide you with another tomorrow, and armour to fit your body. It is as well that you are of ordinary breadth and height; it should not be an impossible task."

And leaving Lascaris thus assured that he was no unusual mortal, he bade him sleep, and himself retired.

One who did not sleep that night was Fiammetta. Her arm was bruised from Graham's handling of her, and she was troubled by desire for him; also glad that the thought of Lascaris' arousing of her interest should have made him angry. She let her teeth sink into the back of her hand, letting the resultant pain blot out her longing. To remember, to pray for anything except the progress of the war would be a sin in the eyes of the Grand Master, perhaps of God, whom Graham must also serve. But he would have lain with her that noonday in the shadow of the wall, in full sight of the gunners, had he been let. The Grand Master, who reckoned all things else, had left out of accounting the hungry need of a man and a woman for one another.

She turned Dragut's ring on her finger. During the day she wore it with the stone hidden against her palm. One day Graham had said to her openly, while he was manning the breach "You have not returned the Jewel to the Grand Master yet," and she had blazed out at him "Ask him of it! Ask him! Do you take me for a thief?"

But he would take her in no other way, nor should she ask that he do so.

Twenty-seven

"Mellissa!"

The young girl heard her mother's voice again, grown sharp with calling. She had heard it for sometime, though with her fingers in her ears on account of the renewed firing, so she could pretend that she had not. She stayed where she was, aware that, sooner or later, her mother would come to find her. "It is like a pet dog," she thought, "that they are afraid to let out on the street."

"There you are, my child. Why did you not answer?"

The wife of Paul the Greek had a flat basket on her arm from the small garden, where despite the siege she still managed to grow a few vegetables. "These are thin and poor," she grumbled, forgetting that she had asked Melissa a question. She laid down the straggling roots on the table, fetched a knife and began to pare them. Melissa sat still, watching her mother's face flush with exertion under the *faldetta* she had not taken time to remove on entering the house. If I offer to help her with the vegetables, Melissa thought, she will tell me I don't do it properly. Or else she will say there is no need for me to trouble myself with household tasks. She doesn't want me to do anything except stay where she can see me; neither does my father.

The guns crashed again. "I expect it will be our turn now, here in Birgù," said the old woman. She finished cutting up the carrots, rinsed them in an earthenware vessel which stood by the window, then set them out with hard-boiled eggs and bread, ready to eat when Paul came in. "There's little enough now to put on the table; no fish or meat of any kind. That girl you knew used to bring round fish for sale; does she not catch any these days?"

"Fiammetta's busy at the hospital by day, and at night she is to be one of the swimmers when she is needed." Colour rose in

Melissa's cheeks at what she would have liked to ask next; but before she could speak, her mother had tossed her head so that the folds of the *faldetta* tumbled like sails in the wind. "Swimming in the company of rough men! That's no task for a virtuous girl. I never did think she was the right company for you, Melissa; it's as well your lives have taken separate ways since God was merciful and restored you to us." Passing from the table to the door, she stroked Melissa's dark hair lovingly, not heeding the girl's silence. "Every single day, when you were missing among those devils, I said a rosary night and morning and asked Our Lady to keep you safe. Thank God and His Mother you're restored to us now, and will never leave us again." She went out, to return with a second water-vessel. "One has to be careful of the water; only so much we're allowed to use. I wonder if rationing will stop in the winter, with the rains? Perhaps they will have fought it out by then, or else gone to some other part of the island, away from Birgù."

Mother, mother, you live your life in a world of your own, Melissa thought. By the time Birgù is left it will be in ruins, like St. Elmo. Fiammetta had said that, last time they'd managed to have a word together. "The Grand Master will not yield a yard of ground while it can be fought for," Fiammetta had told her. "Everyone thought he was hard and pitiless in his insistence that all of the garrison should stay and die to a man in St. Elmo. But he knew well enough that each day which could hold off the Turks from Birgù gave us more time here to build and prepare for the main attack. Why don't you and your mother come out and help with the walls, Melissa? Some of the stones are quite light. And there's the hospital. In a day or two, if this bombardment continues, there'll be more wounded than we can deal with at our present strength. Come and help to bandage up the injured; the nuns will show you what to do."

Melissa had promised to ask her parents if she might come to the hospital, but already a day had passed and she had still dared say nothing. It was like a soft, enveloping blanket, this love her parents had for her, their miraculously returned only child; they even used her and spoke to her as if she were still the little girl who had wandered on the shore in search of shells one day, and had not come home. In a way, it was like being in the Serai still, unable to think or act for oneself, carrying out the orders of the Mistress of Girls. Only, of course, her father and mother loved her; that made a difference. "I wish they didn't love me so much," Melissa thought petulantly. It was impossible to go beyond the door of the house without them.

Tomorrow, perhaps, she would summon courage to ask if she might go and bandage the wounded; it was too late today. They'll only tell me I don't know how to put on bandages, she thought. Whatever I do or want to do, they tell me I'm useless at it. It's because they are afraid that anything, anything at all, will happen to separate me from them again. If that came about, they wouldn't be able to bear it a second time; they're too old.

"There is the firing again," said Paul Grech, bending his head in the doorway and blocking the light outside. He himself had worked on the defence-wall since early morning; he held out his hands, smiling.

"Why, they're bleeding!" cried Melissa. Sickness rose in her; she felt that way, she knew, at the sight of blood. She turned away and went to fetch a bowl in which her father could cleanse his grazed hands; but her mother had already fetched it, set it down in front of old Paul and scolded him for getting himself into such a state.

"And frightening the child; can't you see how white she is, she never could bear nasty sights. Give them here and I'll put salt on them; it stings, but it cleanses the wound. Melissa, my darling, go into the other room; you oughtn't to see such things, and it's for us to protect you from them."

She cleansed and bound up Paul's hands, while the guns maintained their thunder across the bay. In the tunnel below St. Angelo where the prisoners had once been kept, Toni Bajada was addressing the swimmers on behalf of the Grand Master.

"The time is coming when we Maltese may help win, or lose, the campaign. It will not only be a war of guns and armour, but of knives and teeth. We must preserve at all costs the barricade which protects the great harbour chain; if that is broken, the enemy can bring his ships with ease close into Birgù. When I give you a signal, it will be a tapping of drums, like the one the Order used to sound when they went out to their galleys to make a sea-raid. Wherever you may be in the town, you can hear it. Do not fail to come."

They listened and nodded, the swart stocky men, the lone woman with loose flaming hair and eyes that burned in a thin sun-browned face. Afterwards Fiammetta retraced her steps to the hospital. There was nobody there but the nuns and a few wounded, some of them still from the early days of St. Elmo and others, already, from the new bombardment of the towns. Melissa had not come. After looking round for her in vain once or twice Fiammetta forgot her. The flowerlike face of the Gulbehar of Serai days meant less to her now than the face of Anthony Graham. Even he receded in importance in sight of these wounded, whose hurts were so great and so bravely borne. She stayed for many hours, changing and soaking the bloodstained bandages.

The air was thick with dust from the demolition of houses overlooking Kalkara Creek. The Grand Master had ordered that this should be done to give no interruption to the guns, and he had sealed up the streets between the houses with raised barricades of rubble. The homeless slept in the streets elsewhere, in the churches, in the houses of friends if these still stood. Many took their mules with them if these had not been destroyed as eaters of food soon to be needed for men. Fiammetta had heard the pitiful crying of an old woman whose mule had been killed; earlier, the dogs of the town had been slaughtered, among them the Grand Master's own hunting-hounds that he had loved. Nothing lovable served war; she was to find her own love altered and twisted, changing to lust for the moment, the hour that remained. It was the same with Anthony, she was to find. During the course of one such day he came to her, his eyes evasive.

"I have found a room for us; come." He raised her up from the place where she was piling brushwood, hauling stones. He himself had manned a battery all night in anticipation of a sortie which the Chevalier de Robles had not yet made, putting it forward to two nights later. "Come, Fiammetta."

She was filthy, stained with dust and sweat; her hair was twisted up in a knot on top of her head to be out of the way while she worked. She had not eaten since the ration of bread had been brought round many hours ago. She let him lead her off, like a bitch claimed by its owner; the room he had found must have cost him money, for places were short and they were alone. There was no furniture except a bed and a table on which stood a jug of water, an inkstand and quill. He made her drink the water, sharing it with her; it was brackish, but the moisture eased her dry mouth. He unlaced her bodice then, making her lie down; all the time they had not spoken. She lay there feeling weariness flood her, shutting out other feeling; she watched him as he stood over by the window, closing the lattices. It must be dark for us, she thought, even though the sun outside shines at midday. Tears stood in her eyes; her own lack of feeling bewildered her. This should have come earlier, or later; not now. She closed her eyes, waiting for him to come to her, seeing behind their lids a memory of him as he stood there by the sill, face grey and drawn.

"Anthony—" She knew without being told that the desire for her flesh must have become a torment to him, increasing other torments; that she must assuage it as a duty, in order to restore him to himself as he had been. "And if the Grand Master hears, he will have me whipped out of Birgù." It did not matter; the future held nothing but blankness, like the red dark behind her lids. Yet now beyond the certainty that for the present, nothing mattered but to maintain oneself in order to stay the defence, as though lacking it the world would spin downwards into darkness, a sound came; beyond the shuttered windows, beyond Graham's advancing shadow, making her swing herself down from the bed and run to the shutters and fling them wide, letting the new sound in. Tap-tap of drums; the order for the swimmers to assemble, as it had been when Knights went forth crimson-clad to their galleys, masters of the sea. Tap-tap in the streets, and from all corners of the town they would come from their tasks to the appointed place, to receive instructions. Tap-tap, tap-tap. She began to fasten on her clothes again, bending to tie her shoe-latch before she thought of Anthony Graham.

"That is the signal." But he tried to prevent her; came over, as he had done that day by the wall, and took her by the arms, making as if to force her back to their bed, but her flesh stiffened and he let her go. "The signal," said Fiammetta. "How can I lie with you here when the drums are sounding?"

"They don't need you, a woman. There are hundreds of swimmers, men who do it daily for a living. How do we know, in this siege, if there will be another time?" His face was sullen and angry; despite her urge to be gone, she wanted to take it between her hands and kiss the frown from between his dark thin brows, lie down with him. To be fresh again, perfumed, as she had been in the Serai, ready to obey him as her master! But it must not happen. "Let me go, Anthony. I must go now, and you also."

"Go, then, as you will." And he flung away to the window. She did not look up to see if he watched her as she fled along the street; sobs rose in her as she ran, and the denial of her body's roused desire tormented her. But she downed the torment, feeling the other solace, a knife at her belt; and shortly found the darkness of the tunnel below St. Angelo and glimpsed the shapes of the others, Toni Bajada among them, who were to swim out that night by order of the Grand Master, to certain places made known to them now.

By night, the defence-palisade on Senglea spur had grown up, built by galley-labour and the willing hands of the Maltese. It was made from brushwood and iron. By the ninth night it was completed; forty-eight hours later the Turks attacked it from the water, armed with axes.

Toni Bajada led out his swimmers, knives in their teeth. The battle that followed was hand-to-hand, like fighting in the dawn of time; land-man against sea-monster, and the water red with blood. The Turks were driven back to the ships.

Next day they came again, this time with cables. They had seen the hoops of iron the Grand Master had had built into the palisade; loops of cable were flung about these and strained back to the Turkish ships to pull away the defences. Again the Maltese swimmers flung themselves into the water. Sitting astride the palisade they cut the cables through at last. By night they repaired the damage; like slaves working ceaselessly, meeting danger with teeth and knives. "It would have been impossible to be more courageous," wrote Balbi the gunner, who kept a diary. He had lived through the hot sun-steeped July days, watching the Turkish batteries disappear from the northern emplacements; later, they found Mustapha had taken a leaf from old Dragut's book and had dragged his ships overland, bringing them to face the protected harbour. On the third day came a combined sea and land attack with hundreds of small boats putting out from the opposite shore; three containing dark-clad holy men who chanted incitements to battle, then the jewelled commanders with their scimitars and fine muskets from Fez. Presently the red tide of battle rose, casting itself against the chain-defences like a wave, then faltering. Spilling out into the water the attackers came under fire from the Christian musketeers. Shields above heads, they broke through a part of the defence below Senglea; a powder-magazine blew up with a great roar and shower of fire. The men of the Barbary Coast scaled the walls heedless of life or death, charging in full face of the thundering cannon, their banners waving. Don Francisco de Sanoguera was shot down by a musket in course of turning the wave of attackers by his single sword.

And along the Grand Master's bridge of boats from one peninsula to another came reinforcements running, and turned the tide.

Gurial the Spaniard had a hidden plan, a secret battery of guns behind a blank wall just above the harbour. Nobody but the Grand Master and the gunners knew of it; they had lived and slept by their guns since the attack began. From the water, nothing could be seen but yellow stone. The upper batteries thundered out overhead; time and again the gunners, desperate for action, begged their commander to let them break through and fire. "Not yet!" said Gurial. And again "Not yet. The time will come."

It came. Mustapha Pasha, back on his ship, had reserved a final assault in case the first attack should fail or falter. They were Janissaries, those who had been held back even from the attack on St. Elmo. They were like restive horses who have been kept in the stable too long; day after summer day, they had whetted their curved swords and waited. Today fulfilment would come.

They set out. Implacably, across the water in which Turkish bodies floated now like monstrous weed, they came; nine boats, with the intention of landing their grey-clad cargo just above the point where the great chain guarded the creek. The sun glinted on their scimitars. Silence was theirs, wrapping them about in an eternity of smoke and fire; they were death itself, come to deal death. A thousand men were on board the boats, each man trained through all his life for this moment; to conquer or die in a bright arc of deadly steel. The beleaguered harbour waited. In that quarter-hour, all that had already passed might have been in vain. The nine boats glided in under the yellow wall.

"*Now!*" yelled Gurial. From the lifeless stone a sudden blaze of smoke and flame emerged as the gunners thrust the soft wall through, firing and firing at close range, unwearied. And the grey drifting islands of men with bright bared swords collapsed and crimsoned over as the boats sank in moments, blasted through with gunfire. The soiled water creamed about the bodies of eight hundred crack troops who had never struck a blow. In a hail of shot the last boat of all turned tail and scudded back to where Mustapha waited, saving thereby some few.

So the day ended. There were no prisoners taken. For every writhing Turk who lay dying or wounded there was someone who remembered St. Elmo; despatching them with sword or knife-thrust was no more then St. Elmo's pay. Later, in the cool of evening, the Maltese who had done as much as anyone to win the day came down to the water, and stripped off the silk turbans with their studded gems, leaving the shaven heads, with their single lock, lolling nakedly at the sea's edge. Purses they took, and swords; for a long time such women as there were, who had poured pitch and stones on the attackers as they scaled the breaches, took their toll in fine stuffs which they wound about them, or later gave to Our Lady's statues in the churches at Senglea and Birgù. But one cannot eat silk; and day by day the stores of food in the towns were dwindling, while those vanquished who survived went back to camp and refreshed themselves with ample provisions.

Fiammetta had burned her arms with pitch to the elbows, searing the skin of her blistered hands with hurling stones. After it was all over she fell asleep where she lay in the street; later, she went into the church to pray in the cool silence of early morning. It was scattered with women, most of them old, who had helped in the defence: the silence throbbed like a wound, and the memory of dark, wolfish faces, the whites of their eyes staring out as one poured down boiling pitch to blot them out forever, lingered long. The water was full of dead still, stabbed and burned and maimed and drowned. Long ago it would have

been a desperate, a dreadful thing to kill a man by blinding him
with hot tar. Now, like other horrors, it was everyday.

Within Fiammetta's range of vision knelt Philip Lascaris, the
hair on his scalp beginning to grow, like stubble. He had cut off
the long lock in the centre and soon, if he lived to see it, he
would have a crop of brown hair. She watched him genuflect
and go out. He was taking his new faith seriously. She gave a
quick look round for Melissa, who sometimes came with her
mother to pray. But Lascaris' erstwhile bride was not here.
Fiammetta had brought down her hands, which still smarted,
from her face; but she was not thinking of them. Those two
should marry; stranger things had been known. The possibility
was less remote now than it had been in the first days when the
great armada of infidel ships had come sweeping about the
island.

Love ... marriage. It was not for her. Anthony Graham had
not come near her again, though she knew that the English post
had survived the day's fight. He was still angry; or perhaps he
had had leisure to remember his ambition to join the Order. She
must not prevent him from that.

The Turks dragged back their barges by night to the place
where they had lain anchored before the attack. Hearing them
go, hope surged in the hearts of the people of Birgù. By night,
the churches were full; many went to tell their beads and pray.
Light shone faintly from the candles at the foot of the statue of
Our Lady of Pity and from the lamp above the sanctuary. It
outlined the women's black-covered heads and, here and there,
the whiteness of bandages from wounded men.

Twenty-eight

"I shall invite only the ladies, and you men may dine at your club." Isabella Bainbridge looked up to smile at her tall husband, on whose arm she was promenading the picture-gallery at Bellands. "Poor Agnes is a different person when she is unaccompanied by Julius, and as for Fiona, say what they will, I think the paintings will interest her."

Timothy looked down at his wife, savouring the delight she never failed to give him. Her slender figure was dressed in pale grey watered satin, with a lace collar and cuffs. Above it, her white hair was like a crown, with an engaging curl at the back of the neck where it swept up into a chignon, showing an expanse of neck clear and vulnerable as a child's. Timothy had tried to keep her from the storms of life, and the only unspoken sorrow they ever shared was the unlikelihood of Julius' inheritance of David Bainbridge's fire and genius. He was almost like a changeling, that son of theirs; but now young Anton Muntz had come Timothy felt as if he had a second. He would, when the time came for him to retire, hand over the business to Anton without qualms; the lad had already proved his worth in yard, office, accounts-room, and lately at the table of directors. Bainbridge's would continue in the forward tradition it had always held, and Bainbridge ships would be the finest afloat.

"I shall stay at home and spoil your party," said Timothy. "I should like to show Fiona the Tintoretto; it cannot fail to interest her." He had recently, as so often, acquired the priceless masterpiece by means of his international repute as a collector; frequently paintings were offered to him before they reached the auction-room. He looked with some pride at his gallery, built to his own design here some years back; in it were four Albert Cuyps, a Rubens, a Van Eyck Crucifixion and a De Hoogh, as well as the Tintoretto. Along the walls colour blazed and

shadows echoed the colour, and at the end of the gallery a great
lancet window looked out on the broad river where it met the
sea. Timothy was proud of his house, of his wife, of his
reputation as shipbuilder, connoisseur and host. Royalty had
dined here, and Isabella had been the perfect hostess. It was
almost magical to think that when they had married she had
been, granted, David Bainbridge's young sister with a lady-like
education and pretty ways; but he had been only an ironmaster's
son, learning his trade with his hands. The partnership with
David had brought out the best in both of them; and when
David died Timothy had gone on alone, till now, except for
Isabella. He touched her soft hair; he loved her deeply, and
when her laughter came it pleased him.

"Never fear that you will intrude," she said. "I am glad to see
you take a holiday from your everlasting account-books and
company meetings. Anton will deputise for you very well."

So on the day appointed Agnes, Juliana and Fiona came
down alone by water, all three dressed for the summer's day in
light-coloured gowns and straw bonnets.

Timothy admitted to himself clearly that he had remained at
Belland today half from curiosity, half from kindness, in
wishing to show Fiona the paintings. Looking back, he remembered snippets of information he had concerning her; how she
had for years been kept under Julius's roof in the charge of a
companion, seldom or never permitted to show herself in
company. He recalled her at the wedding, tantalisingly beautiful
in her bridesmaid's gown, only to see her faint and have to be
removed from the ceremony. All her life Fiona had been
removed, not spoken of, passed over as a regrettable incident, for
Agnes' sake, or Julius's, not brought forward lest anyone should
remember the elopement and her unsatisfactory parentage, and
God's punishment—this was Julius' phrase—on so unhallowed
a union. Yet Timothy had heard also that Fiona was interested
in sketching and painting, though Julius had grudged her a
drawing-master.

He was waiting with his wife on his arm as the party arrived
off the pier, and escorted them to his carriage which waited to
drive them to Bellands. Seeing its tower, containing the great
clock, and the walls surrounded by statuary (he was unaware

that others poked fun at the grandiose structure) and its gardens full of the colour and scent of roses, he was assailed by pride; it was as though he were driving down with Isabella to look at the rebuilt house for the first time, all his plans completed. It had only been a small cottage when they found it years ago, and now—

"It is a pleasant day," vouchsafed Agnes, magnificent in Saxe blue with matching bonnet-ribbons. They agreed that it was indeed pleasant, and Juliana expressed delight at the prospect of a walk round the garden before luncheon. Fiona's green eyes brooded; she looked excessively beautiful, for Juliana took the trouble to buy her pretty clothes, which Agnes had never dared to do. The girl looked her best today in a sea-green dress, which set off the colour of her eyes; it had small white flowers embroidered on collar, sleeves and hem, and her straw bonnet was also white, with a bunch of straw at the side which echoed the colours of the dress. Juliana looked at her with affection. Dear Fiona was happier, she was certain, now that she had come to live with her and Anton. If only he would agree to have her brought downstairs to meals! But one must never try a husband too far; it was pleasant, at any rate, to have her half-sister with her today, by grandfather's special invitation.

The roses of Belland bloomed, opening to the sun. Once Fiona bent over a huge pink Zephyrin Drouhin to savour its scent. Her eyes and sense of smell were not defective; a pity, a great pity, about the rest! Timothy Bainbridge would have liked to have her painted so, her red hair, lovingly combed that morning by Juliana into a fashionable chignon, attracting all the sunlight in the garden, and the leaves of the roses setting off her green dress.

After lunch, they repaired to the picture-gallery, Fiona on Timothy's arm. The rest watched the pair with affection; the old-world courtesy with which the Old Man treated his guest, handing her into the gallery as though she were porcelain, troubling himself to escort her and to point out, though they could not be explained, the choicest masterpieces. Agnes and Juliana were impressed with the new acquisitions, though they had seen the gallery before; ignorant as they might be of great art, they knew Timothy for a shrewd business man who would never invest in doubtful merchandise. "I knew very little until Timothy taught me," said Isabella softly. "That is the Van Eyck; the Flemish paintings are all in some way intimate, to be looked at in the warmth of a little room, while the Italian are for great palaces and churches."

They came to the Tintoretto, which was admired; Fiona put out her slender hand to feel the paint carefully. She had lingered longest over the Flemish painting; it was as though every detail of the tortured Christ echoed some chord in her mind.

They moved on, with Timothy still escorting Fiona; his blue eyes were kindly; she might have been a royal guest. "There is one here which puzzles me," he told the rest. "I bought it as a curiosity; what it portrays I do not know; it may be symbolic."

The painting was small, with the figures roughly portrayed and lacking in proportion; men and women were grouped on a shore, beyond which, on the sea, floated elongated naked figures decorated, or so it seemed, with red crosses. They made a human raft. Isabella shivered. "I do not like it," she said, "but Timothy—"

Suddenly Fiona gave a harsh cry, removed her hand from Timothy's arm and flung it across her mouth. She stared at the painting with eyes filling with tears. Then her face whitened and she slumped to the floor; foam appeared at the corner of her mouth. She lay there in silence, convulsively twitching; the knot of her hair had come loose and the brightness splayed down over one shoulder, catching the sunlight as it had done in the garden.

"I am sorry," came Agnes's voice, in annoyance. Fiona had embarrassed them in public again. How fortunate that Julius was not present!

They had carried her to one of the bedrooms where Isabella and the housekeeper, Mrs. Norris, eased the lacing below her gown and laid her head on the pillow. "Perhaps we should take off the gown, it is too pretty to be crushed," suggested Isabella. "Poor creature, what could have been the reason for it? The painting, perhaps, was not pleasant—"

The soft, uncorseted body lay exposed, outlined by the clinging chemise.

"It wasn't the painting, Mrs. Bainbridge," came the woman's

voice presently, at once respectful and grim. "Though I don't like to take it upon myself, she—the young lady—"

Pursed lips, a shaken head confronted Isabella. Then she was invited to place her hand where the housekeeper had laid hers, and was left to draw her own conclusions. When she stood up again, her face was as white as Fiona's. "I do not think there is any doubt," she said, and to herself "How am I to break it to Agnes?" It would be harder, in some unspecified way, to do so than to break it to Juliana. When all was said, Agnes was the poor girl's mother, and must take responsibility.

"When," she said tentatively to the housekeeper, "when would you say ... ought we to fetch a doctor to her?"

"It would be as well to have an opinion, Mrs. Bainbridge. But I'd say coming along for five months myself, and I've had four of a family."

"Let nothing of this be spoken of to the other servants."

"No, Mrs. Bainbridge. That would not be proper."

The woman turned, and left the room to order the coachman to go and fetch the doctor. Isabella stared despairingly down at Fiona's face; the girl was beginning to stir. What man could have been so wicked—and when—

"Do not fret yourself, my dear," she said softly as the girl regained consciousness; then scolded herself for a fool. Of course Fiona could not hear.

The doctor came, and confirmed the verdict. Before he left Agnes was sent for. It had occurred to Isabella to wonder how Julius' wife would receive calamitous news nowadays; for so many years she had been so sheltered, almost crushed, by the weight of Bainbridge respectability as to appear to have lost all feeling. Isabella was thankful that Dr. Bryce was with her to help break the truth to Fiona's mother. His bearded face grave, he announced the opinion he had that Fiona was to have a child. Agnes heard him out, neither fainting nor crying hysterically; she was either a woman without emotions, the good doctor decided, or else she had iron control of them. He might have been discussing a stranger with this majestic woman, not an afflicted girl who had been—one must face it squarely—taken advantage of, without anyone's knowing until now.

Agnes' lips moved at last. Julius must not be told. He would be very angry."

Isabella spoke sharply. "But she cannot go back to dear Juliana!"

"Juliana must be informed. She would insist on knowing what has happened, what the doctor said. She—I can hardly credit that this has happened while Fiona was in her sister's house, unless—"

She broke off. The two women stared at one another, the same thought occurring to both. The situation might be worse, far worse, than they had at first thought, a horrible scandal involving everyone in the family, unless it could be kept from spreading. "She may stay here," said Isabella. "Timothy will give his permission, I am certain."

"That would be kind in you. I will ask Juliana to have her sister's things sent down meantime, till we have thought what to do. Of course it must not take place where there would be talk; where can she be sent when the matter becomes obvious? Perhaps a convent in Ireland; I know of one which takes these unfortunate cases, though it is generally servants who—"

She broke off, lips parted, and Isabella's head turned from where she had been staring at the closed bedroom door beyond which Fiona lay. The doctor had gone. Suddenly they were confronted with a new aspect of the problem. Juliana had come out into the passage, her hands holding up the skirts of her pretty summer dress.

"What did the doctor say, Mama? What brought on the convulsion? Poor Fiona, she has had none all the time she's been with us. It must be excitement; she looked forward so much to wearing her best dress, and knew she was being taken somewhere pleasant."

Her voice fell away into silence; and Isabella said gently, "Come back into the drawing-room, my dear; we can discuss it there."

After all, dear Juliana was a married woman; it was not out of place to tell her, and she might have some comment to make which would lighten the frightful suspicion which had reached Isabella, and which, she was certain, had not escaped Agnes either. Agnes was not a fool, only withdrawn and perhaps uncaring. Her chief fear seemed to be Julius' anger. Perhaps it would be possible that, as Agnes wished, he need never know;

the child could be kept in Ireland after it was born; one must hope that it would not inherit its mother's affliction.

They told Juliana, who was sitting on a sofa with her face against the light. Her immediate reaction was unexpected.

"It is my fault," she said, and her tone was light and even. "It must have happened—it could only have happened—on the Green, where I or Lily Soames sometimes take Fiona walking. I myself have frequently left her while I walked further on, if she had something she wanted to look at, the willows or the river, or—or the washing on the grass where the women put it. Such things are a treat to her, for she sees so little day after day. It was careless of me, I know; the fault is mine."

They accepted it; the Green abounded with unpleasant characters, tramps who slept there, undesirables of all kinds which made it unsafe to walk among the trees even by day, unless one were watchful. Relief entered the air; that was the answer, a man on the Green. ...

No one noticed Juliana's hands, clenched so tightly that they left nail-marks in her palms. She continued talking brightly, superficially, glossing over the thing that had been found out. Yes, it would be better for Fiona to stay at Bellands until other arrangements could be made; she would send her clothes down.

I could not bear to have her in the house again, she was thinking. I could not bear it.

She left without seeing Fiona; the doctor had given the girl a sedative, and Mrs. Norris said that she was asleep. When it was time to catch the boat the carriage waited for the two women, and Timothy saw them on their way. He had been told nothing except that Fiona was to stay with them for a little while; he had expressed his pleasure, but Isabella would tell him the truth when they were alone.

"It would be advisable perhaps to send Lily Soames down with the luggage, as she has been used to Fiona for some time."

Agnes' implacable calm seemed as if it had never been ruffled; they sat in the lee of the paddle-boat's cabin, outside which there was a wooden seat. The slight summer breeze stirred ribbons on bonnets and bodices; there were few aboard except for themselves. This little boat did several voyages daily

up and down the river, being busiest in the mornings and
evenings when regular travellers such as Timothy Bainbridge
went up to town or returned home by water.

"Yes, Mama. I shall speak to Soames tonight; she will be
ready to travel down in the morning, and I shall enclose a note
to Grandmama."

Juliana did not look at her mother, seated staring ahead
along the river. Now that they were nearing the city there began
to be evidence of the busy shipyards, the huts, office buildings
and cranes and the occasional giant hulk of an unfinished ship
in dry-dock. Juliana saw none of it; she was thinking, with a
mind made sick with shock, of Lily Soames, who slept in the
adjoining room to Fiona and could not fail to have known of the
matter ... she must surely, when one thought of it, be aware at
least that Fiona had not been inconvenienced by a certain
monthly occurrence, for she collected her linen and brought it
down to be washed. She must know ... many things. Juliana
rehearsed in her mind, to shut out its misery, exactly how she
would address Soames tonight, so that the down-dropped lids
did not leave her in awe of the woman, who had always been so
silent. An honest woman would have come to her long ago,
saying something was wrong. She would be glad to see Lily out
of the house, and some arrangement could be made so that she
need never return to it. Perhaps she could escort Fiona to this
place in Ireland Mama knew of. Mama said little, but she was
practical.

They drew in sight of Bainbridge's yard. The workers were
still busy in the summer evening and Juliana saw, like a scene
in a play, her husband's hatless figure, deep in talk with one of
the riveters. Anton took the tool in his grasp and bent to show
the man some matter or other; his square, long-fingered
engineer's hands would be steady on the tool. Juliana did not
point out her husband to her mother. Mama was unobservant,
and was watching the river.

The carriage brought them home, calling first at Juliana's door.
She was aware of the polite necessity of inviting Mama to step
inside for a little while, but hoped she would not accept. To her
relief, Agnes refused. "You look white, Juliana," she said

unexpectedly. "Remember to rest as much as you can; it has been a tiring day."

"I will speak to Lily Soames, and then I will rest." She let the coachman help her down and knew a sensation of relief; her door opened to the sound of the departing carriage-wheels.

Juliana took off her bonnet, then asked the servant to send for Soames. The woman came downstairs from her lair at the top of the house. She stood waiting in silence, hands folded, eyes downcast. Juliana was brief.

"You will pack Miss Fiona's clothes, Soames, and necessaries for yourself; she is to stay for a little while with my grandparents at Belland, and you will be needed there to help look after her. You will leave tomorrow morning."

The woman spoke. "I hope it isn't for long, madam. I have to be near my mother." Again there was the amazement one felt that Soames should have anyone at all. "If word comes here about your mother, it will be sent to you at once," Juliana heard herself saying. She was anxious to get the woman out of the house; if only Lily could have gone tonight! But there was everything to be packed, and then—

"Shall I pack all of Miss Fiona's dresses, madam?"

"No, only her summer things." The rest could be sent later to wherever Fiona was going; no need to let this creature know more yet. "You may go now, and pack," said Juliana gently.

Soames raised her eyes, which were the colour of onyx, and for a moment gazed straight at her mistress with an expression the other could not forget; a kind of opaque contempt. She said nothing more; as well say nothing as everything, and they must both keep up the pretence that all was as it should be, that nothing amiss had happened in the house.

Lily Soames turned and went out. Juliana. felt a great lightening in her body, as if of a load shed; but there was the other feeling, the one she had been fighting ever since learning the truth at Belland, of having been kicked in the pit of the stomach. She felt physically sick with it; but she must learn to live with it. Perhaps as time passed it would hurt less; but now—

She suddenly put her hands before her eyes and began a deep and terrible sobbing, without tears.

Later, she heard Anton's step in the hall. She sat as she was, waiting for him. It would be necessary to look, speak, talk to him again; but she could not pretend to him as she had done to Soames, it would be impossible to live a lie for the rest of their lives, without trust, without understanding. Perhaps some of it had been her fault; she considered the possibility clearly; so that the time between hearing and seeing him enter might have been not moments but an hour. There was the brother-and-sister life they had had to lead since her miscarriage, and the fact that her room was now separate from his; there had been the temptation of a beautiful young woman close to hand. Fiona *was* beautiful; everyone had overlooked it, remembering only her deafness and the fact that she could not speak. But none of that would prevent ... lust. The ugly word rose in Juliana's mind as Anton entered, and came over as he always did to kiss her. She averted her cheek; the gesture was unconscious. He halted, stood up, frowned, and turned to the sideboard where a decanter and glasses were, pouring madeira for himself and for her. "Did you have a pleasant day at Belland?" he said. It was as though they were two fencers, armed not with swords but with cardboard toys. One could go on like this for a long time, thought Juliana. She answered calmly.

"Did you and Lily Soames know that Fiona is going to have a child?"

He did not move, holding the wineglass without a tremor; he set it down again on the tray, and turned towards her. "I did not," he said. "I—" suddenly he abandoned pretence and came to her; she rose up from where she had been seated, her small height facing him. "You know, then?" she heard him ask. "Juliana—"

"I think that I must have known almost from the beginning, but I would not admit such a thing to myself. When the news came today it was no real surprise; only—horror."

"I swear I—" He passed his tongue over his lips; swiftly, he drank a glassful of wine, then poured another. He brought her her glass. She shook her head; he went and set the glass down again on the sideboard. She saw the items on it strangely clear; a potted plant, a daguerreotype of their marriage, a pair of china figures of the Queen and Prince Albert. The plant had begun to sprout pale flowers with small dry petals surrounding them. It was as though the scene burned itself into her vision as if she had not seen it a hundred times before. Never, after this, would it be the same; nothing would ever be the same again.

He had begun to talk rapidly. He had not, he was certain, got Fiona with child in any of the later visits to her, but perhaps, the night of the storm, the first time—"You remember the storm?" he asked. "That was when I—"

He made a helpless movement with his hands. "If I were to tell you the truth of it, would you listen?" he asked her. "Would you believe that I did not lie to you?"

"I will listen; it is my duty, I am your wife. If you tell me the truth it will avoid hurting me again later." She spoke drily and precisely, like a much older woman. That she should have had to find out in such a way, he thought; in such a way! Later, he would ask how it happened; he himself was still in a state of shock, uncertain of his words. Hurt her? He would not hurt Juliana for the world and all it contained; it had not been to hurt her that he had visited Fiona day after day, but perhaps to spare her ... no, that was banal ...

He flung himself into a chair. "Then if you will listen, I will tell you," he said. "It is as if I had loved—or desired—Fiona in another life. If anyone had told me earlier that such things could happen, I would have laughed them to scorn. Now, you may laugh at me if you so desire."

"I do not feel like laughing, Anton."

"No ... nor I. Who I was in the other existence I do not clearly remember, except that there was a seashore and caves, and we fired cannon. I can recall the thunder of the cannon; it never ceased, and we could not sleep."

"Where was ... Fiona?"

"She was there. I do not know now how a woman could have fought in that war, but she was there, and fighting. I can see her now with her hair wet with sea-water, for she swam and rowed a boat. Once I was in the boat with her and it was dark. I can remember I was wounded. Then again I remember closing shutters on an empty street. And there was a man hanged; the dogs tore his flesh."

She did not, as most women would have done, pretend disgust and beg him to speak less openly; she was silent, and he knew that she was listening. "There was some obstacle," he said, "some matter that prevented our love, something that made me not free to love any woman, but what it was I cannot remember.

I wore a crucifix; at night I used to pray holding it. And there was a bright jewel the colour of fire. All this sounds like unconnected nonsense; if a child told me such a tale I would not believe it, and yet you sit there and hear me out, Juliana."

"A crucifix." She remembered the Van Eyck earlier today and the strange, unidentifiable painting at sight of which Fiona had fallen down in her fit. "Does it mean anything to you," she said slowly, "if I told you of naked men tied by the wrists to make a raft floating on the sea, with crosses red on their bodies? And a watching crowd?"

"Yes!" he cried. "Yes!" and bowed his head in his hands and began to sob like a child.

Presently, she went to him.

Twenty-nine

Philip Lascaris had been kneeling alone, aware of his difference from almost everyone here in the church in that he, an able-bodied man, had as yet taken no wound. The bitterness of solitude came to him, as it had often done since he joined the side of the Christians. Yet had he never been solitary among the men of Islam? It was impossible to recall now; like another life.

He met the other men at the battery, or at the side of the Grand Master. La Valette still spoke with him daily, valuing Philip's advice on placing of guns and whatever tactics Mustapha and Piali might well adopt tomorrow. He had, the young man knew, been pleased with some of the matters told him, and had acted on them, a sign that he trusted a renegade. "That is what I am," Philip told himself. He did not regret his action in changing sides, but his loneliness stabbed at him like the wound he could not obtain. All the folk here were kin to another, mourning when a neighour fell in the streets which had submitted to bombardment these ten days past; some would be praying, now, for lovers or husbands, wounded or dead. "No one prays for me," Philip thought. "If I were to die tomorrow, there would be no one to care." He knew it was true; La Valette needed him for information, no more; in himself he was nothing to anyone, and he had lost the guiding spirit of the Enderun. If he were to die, it would be no more than one other Turk lying dead on the shore, devoid of jewels and not worth stripping.

He spread his fingers before his face to hide the hot, childish tears that rose to his eyes. Beyond him two old women rose, genuflected and went out: they were devout, he told himself. This Faith that he had to learn again from the Grand Master's chaplain was a separate and personal thing, lacking the oneness of all those who prostrated themselves when the voice called from the muezzins at sunset. There, everyone was less than

Allah; here, in some strange way, God had come down among men.

The space left by the going of the two old women revealed a girl who knelt alone. The purity of her profile came to him, raised in rapture beyond the golden candles. "She is alone with her God, in the way I would like to be," he thought. "She knows no other state."

A sudden rebellion against the formality of this religion which still came stiffly to him hardened his resolve, and when the young girl rose to go he followed her unobtrusively. All her movements were graceful, like a young doe's. Desire took him; he would like to lie with the young girl, quietly, in a cool bed. If he could do so perhaps this fever of the mind would leave him. They had catered for such things in Constantinople, knowing that when a man came back after the wars he needed women's flesh for a time, provided he were not a Janissary. But he, Lascaris, had never even had the wife they had promised him. His lost ·Gulbehar, Flower of Spring, was gone forever, no longer a part of him.

"Melissa!"

The breath of a name was whispered close in the dark arch of the door as he reached it close behind. For an instant he thought he had crystallised the sound out of his own longing. Then he saw one of the old women, black *faldetta* framing, like a coffin, the anxious wrinkles of her face. She grasped at the girl's arm, fastening on it with determined fingers. Her backward glance included Philip impersonally in a hatred of all things which might come between herself and the girl. He stayed in the shadow of the porch, watching them go out and the way they went.

"Why did you delay?" he heard Melissa's mother say. "I thought you had come out with us. Anna has gone on; it's getting late." He heard the girl's murmured reply, echoed in the distance which had widened so swiftly between himself and her: some matter of finishing a rosary. She is lying, he thought delightedly; she was saying no rosary; her mind was not on her prayers.

Melissa. Was it a name often heard in these islands? It was beautiful, he decided. He remembered her smooth young limbs and unafraid shy bearing, that of a virgin. He made his way back to where the guns were, his lonely anger forgotten; striding swiftly, as greatly filled with purpose now as ever in the Enderun. He must find Melissa, where she lived, why her mother held fast to her, whether or not he might—without prospects for himself as yet, he admitted—persuade them that he was eligible as a husband. To say he had been captain over five hundred in the army of the Grand Turk would mean worse than nothing; worse still that he had ever been an infidel. He must learn to love Melissa's Christ.

The realisation of his diminished value stayed with Philip, making him less arrogant than before. By day he toiled at the batteries, refusing even to answer when a second renegade, who had deserted to the Turkish lines, taunted him from the other side.

It was then that the Chevalier de Robles, who had brought in the Little Relief, again proved his worth. After the night-sortie against the entrenched enemy in Senglea ditches, he built a double defence day after day, so placed that no one, until the outer wall was breached, would know of the inner. When after a fierce attack and much loss of life the Turks breached the outer wall, it was to find themselves not in Senglea but a trap; butchered in their hundreds, they lay dying and dead between the walls and out into the sea. The Turk was tiring; the new battery he had raised on Salvator did nothing but blast away walls that were rapidly built up again, as at St. Elmo. The only news that cheered the Marsa camp was that of the death of the Grand Master's nephew, young François Parisot, at the Senglea breaches; taking the incident as they would have done for themselves, they assumed great mourning in the Christian towns, perhaps a slackening of vigilance to allow for the passing of the dead youth's soul.

But La Valette, who had loved his brother's son well enough, did not pause to mourn. He turned instead to the plan he had of sinking more boats across the harbour, this time to make a bridge to impede attack when it came; and to build inner defences, after the manner of De Robles, behind the Posts of Castile, Germany and England.

Mustapha began his great bombardment of the harbour towns in early August. Already too much time had gone by in the progress—or was it progress?—of this siege of a small isolated rock which should have fallen in five days. It was becoming difficult to word the despatches to Istanbul, and the body of Dragut had had to be conveyed back to Tripoli without any of the pomp of salvoes which had so angered the old man when he sailed in. Mustapha's rage quickened also at the conduct of the Maltese. Despite the fact that he had had it from assured sources that these islanders hated the Knights who had usurped their territory, he had been able to induce no mass desertions despite the promise of freedom the island would enjoy under the Grand Turk. The Maltese, in fact, had been a damnable factor in the sea-war, swimming out to maintain their ramparts and to demolish communications between the ships. Toni Bajada, who still continued to cut through galley-bottoms and release slaves in the oar-bays with his knife, was legendary in the Turkish lines, a kind of evil spirit who would not be suppressed. It had been safer to send Admiral Piali north towards Gozo again with his fleet of ships, hoping that he would intercept any help sent to the Grand Master from Sicily. But despite the vigilance of patrols, four boatloads had slipped through by night, and fishermen were still eluding Piali and taking letters through from La Valette to the mainland, where a great force was said to be ready to embark.

Therefore Mustapha concentrated all his fury on the bombing of the towns. There were culverins for the lower reaches and great cannon above, which would fire stones of marbles so huge that a grown man could not embrace them with his arms outspread. They should blow the town and its defenders to powder, leaving nothing but rubble for Mustapha to land his troops on at the last, ready to run the flag of the Crescent up on a staff high enough to be seen from the remote capital behind its ancient walls. Mustapha assumed that as Mdina had taken no part in the siege it must be filled with those sympathetic to the invader, or at any rate disposed not to disturb him. When the truce was concluded and not a single member of the detested Order left alive on Malta, life in the native villages could go on as it had always done, except that there need be no further sea-raids.

So, early in the morning of that August day, he gave the order to fire; seeing the fuses crawl in the heat of the early sun so that the air quivered in columns above the gunners' brown arms.

Then from Sciberras, Salvatore, Gallows' Point and Corradino the cannon crashed forth, breaking in waves of unceasing thunder in the low terraced hills towards Mdina. Smoke rose, and its clearing revealed a jagged hole in the harbour wall, stones and dust cascading down into the disturbed water. "That will smoke them out," smiled Mustapha. He gave word that firing was to be unceasing, that day and each day thereafter, until there was nothing left but flattened ruins below St. Angelo.

Five times the Turks attacked during the bombardment, and were continually repulsed as before. And still, in the clearing of the cannon-smoke, Mustapha saw the flaunting banner of the Cross.

Thirty

Bianca Inguanez was learning to walk. Every day she would contrive a little more, first in her apartment, then, as she progressed out into the courtyard, where she would try to reach the tree, devoid of blossom now and hardening into fruit. Sometimes she would have to stop for pain, and lean on Yaya's arm; laughter took her that she would not allow to show, for what must they look like to a watcher, the pair of them, Yaya pregnant and herself a cripple? But nobody watched; everybody was about their own affairs. Bianca had persevered, and now after what seemed a long time she could stand on the tip of her twisted foot. That hurt a little; but when everyone down there was being blown to pieces, every able-bodied man and woman carrying wounds, how could she complain? She only thanked God that Toni at least had a charmed life; she prayed for him constantly. Sometimes, despite the war and his part in it, he would spare leisure to come to her, mostly by night.

Bianca could not remember a time when she had not loved Toni. His strength and gentleness had been a shelter for her weakness as long as she could recall. When she had been a child, he would lift her in his arms and carry her to the mule-carriage her father had had built for her in the days of peace, and together they would drive about the rough rutted roads with Bianca's maid jolting behind, and on a clear day they could look down at the sea. Toni spoke of swimming and diving in the sea, as though he were a fish; the child would listen breathlessly to his stories, wondering that anyone could be as strong and as brave. Later, when he asked shyly for it, she had cut off a curl of her hair and had it put in the crystal locket he always wore; she liked to think that it held his luck. He performed feats now that made him a legend, and she was proud; he would be remembered as a hero, and he must not love a cripple. So, as each loved the other and nothing could alter it, she must learn to walk, like other women, and not be a burden on him. If she could not overcome her lameness she was unworthy of such a man's love. So it would be overcome; after the tree, the stairs; twisting stairs, a few more every day, till at last she was able to climb to the flat roof where hens scratched as they did on all the other roofs in Mdina. It had been a great triumph and joy to look at the town from the rooftop; at last, at last she could go anywhere! Soon she must balance herself in a saddle, when the war was over and horses were to be had again. Fiammetta she was certain could ride; Fiammetta could do anything, row a boat, swim out to rescue men, carry messages through the Turkish lines. "She is the bravest woman I have ever known," Toni had said one day. Bianca tried not to feel jealous; she herself must show him that she too could be brave, in her own way if not Fiammetta's. Yet who knew? Perhaps the war would come inland to Mdina; when that happened she must be ready. So far, only the distant noise of firing had come, and no one saw anything beyond the haze of late summer's heat. How easy it was to forget that there was a war when life went on in its old leisurely way up here, where nothing changed!

The greatest excitement was Yaya's coming baby. "The old women say she is too big for just one, and that it will be twins," thought Bianca. She glanced at Yaya's enormously thickened body, wrapped in a loose robe. Yaya was happier now that the babies were coming soon, even though no one knew who the father might be. The old women—always the old women, who knew everything!—said they must be called Spiteri, because it had almost certainly been a Knight Hospitaller. Bianca had heard them whispering of it, black-hooded heads together, watching Yaya as she walked by with a pitcher. Yaya had her own dignity; almost, Bianca envied her. If she, herself, grew strong enough to walk and ride easily, would she one day have a child of Toni's? The thought filled her with happiness and increased her determination to walk further each day.

"But what impudence, to come here and ask such a thing! I hope you sent him about his business. Lascaris, you say? Not a name we know."

"My dear, he is not of this island," said old Paul Grech. "I know of his family, though you do not. They were once

Emperors of the West." He smiled a little behind his beard, watching his wife's changes of expression.

"Emperors." In spite of her anger she was flattered; the descendant of emperors coming here to ask for little Melissa! But, of course, it was not to be considered. "We've only just got her back. How could anyone be so cruel as to expect us to part with her šo soon?"

She rose in the restless way she had, and went to adjust the lamp where it swam in oil; the flame illumined her wrinkled face and gnarled hands. Paul sighed a little. She was an obstinate woman, his wife; God knew the girl should marry one day, so that they might yet have the gladness of grandchildren about them. But, as she said, perhaps not yet ... "There, wife," he said gently. "I told the young man that it was not a time to talk of marriages in this war, and that he had best distinguish himself in some way so as to make the Grand Master recognise him, instead of being only a deserter from the Turkish artillery. So he—"

"A deserter?" his wife šcreamed. "A Turk? Heaven forbid that he should set eyes on our darling alone! Where did he see her, this infidel?"

"In church. He is taking instruction in the Christian Faith. Truly, wife, I did not compromise us. I said to him—"

"God knows what you said, Paul Grech; you are always too trustful of everybody, they even cheat you in business. Describe this young man to me, that I may take good care he does not come near Melissa. In church indeed! He should have been attending to his instruction!"

"Well, so he may have been," said old Paul wearily. Beyond the curtain where she lay in bed, Melissa clenched her hands together in helpless anger. They might have asked me, she thought. It's like them to think, now, that I must be asleep. They might have let me see him, asked if I thought he would make an agreeable husband, now that I'm back in charge of Christian parents and not shut up in the Serai where one never sees the man till the wedding-night. When I was put on board the Kustir Aga's ship with Fiammetta I was to marry a young soldier in Constantinople. His name? Was it ... ah, surely it could not be the same?

She lay hot and cold with ecstasy, determined now to see

Philip Lascaris for herself. They should not prevent her from seeing him, try as they might.

Next day she said to them, "I am going to the hospital."

Tears, recriminations; it was all useless. Metal had been forged in Melissa and she was no longer the gentle malleable girl they had known. She would go, nothing should prevent her; and short of locking her up there was nothing for it but that the wife of Paul should go too, and accompany her daughter there and back again morning and evening, leaving her man to fend for himself during the day.

But there were many wounded now in the hospital, far more than had been foreseen. In the press of work to be done, Melissa's mother became separated from her child, fenced apart by the bustling habits of ever-present nuns. She took comfort; in a hospital, nothing much could go amiss with Melissa. Being a practical woman, she let her mind fix itself on applying dressings to the wounds as she was directed; only by the day's end did she realise how weary she was. She looked round for her daughter. But the little minx had gone home long ago; sick, the nuns said, at the sight of blood, but she had said she would be back again tomorrow. "And you also? We are glad of aid."

Paul the Greek's wife promised, and hurried off anxiously through the gathering night, thanking God the bombardment had ceased for the time: it had gone on all day.

Up the hill, some days later, the Governor of Mdina sat in audience with a delegation of the most distinguished *notabili* before him. The light slanted through the high narrow windows on chased silver goblets filled with Catanian wine, which they drank in a leisurely, formal way, passing the morning. They had come early, before the inhabitants of low-lying Birgù would have breakfasted; preserving thus the manners of an ancient civilisation, when the day's affairs were conducted before the sun grew too hot. Watching them, the Governor felt incredulity assail him, as it had done at intervals since the Order had posted him to Mdina two years since. Two years, a moment in time to these names as old as the centuries; Manduca, Inguanez, Apap, Bucana. They took no heed of him or any orders he might issue. He had learned to tread carefully, knowing their power.

Count Inguanez raised his whitening head now; he was sixty years of age, blond like his Siculo-Norman ancestors, and with their arrogance. "We have to complain about the disturbances in the streets," he said, "in particular after sundown. Undesirables, messengers from the harbour towns, bring with them unrest which is felt by your garrison, and sometimes all night one may hear shouting and the tramp of feet. Only the other day a Spanish deserter, who had come here by way of the Turkish lines, was tied to a horse's tail and stoned to death. Such behaviour is not seemly in our city."

"Mdina has been a place of peace and silence for centuries, until the Order came," put in Count Manduca, fingering the stem of his drinking-cup. In the distance, when he had finished speaking, came the crash of bombardment against distant Birgù. The Governor hid his ironic smile behind his hand.

"Noble sirs, the Order is immediately concerned with maintaining the Christian Faith on this island against the infidel. If Malta falls, peace will not follow. It is understandable if, in course of such a campaign, ancient peace and quiet must give way to gunfire and the tramp of feet."

"Sir, do you mock us to our faces when the Order brought this war on itself by the piracies committed at sea?" The two old Counts had risen to their feet, hackles stiffening like two cocks before a fight. Their lives were taken up with such matters, protocol and precedence, slights real and imaginary involving their pedigrees, their privileges in Mdina. The Governor soothed them with professional ease, at the same time inwardly cursing the slowness with which his own days must pass despite his cavalry's sallies; he had orders from La Valette to guard the old stronghold on the hill with his life and those of all his garrison. If Mdina fell, the whole of Malta might be in the hands of the Turk within hours. "They should have made here, first, not for St. Elmo," he thought, as if remembering an event very long ago. He heard the two old noblemen's restored courtesy-talk as if through a veil.

"Excellent wine, Mesquita!" A peal of distant thunder came; the Turk, he had heard, was firing cannon-balls of three hundred pounds' weight against the Birgù townspeople, while he sat here. If the harbour towns fell, and the enemy came marching inland, surrounding the walled city closely on all sides, then—

"Your good health, noble sirs. I am glad the wine pleases you." And so it ought, he thought; there is little left in Birgù. He forced himself to speak with them of everyday things; the indulgence granted by His Holiness the Pope to all who should take part in this war against the infidel, forgiving them all their sins to date if they died; the health of the lady Bianca, old Inguanez' daughter, which had frequently given cause for concern. At mention of her name the old Count's fine-boned face lightened; he was well known to dote on her and to allow her as much freedom as if she were a married woman. "But she will neither make any marriage I could arrange for her, nor will she go to the Ursulines to take her vows," he said indulgently. "When I am dead, what will become of her and her fortune? It is true that she is wise, and will not squander it nor take a spendthrift to husband; but I should have liked to see her disposed as befits her rank. Yet with her health as it has been from her birth, how can I force her to do otherwise than her own will? She is all I have since her mother died." He spread out his delicate hands resignedly; nearby, the Count Manduca looked down his long nose at the floor, where patterned tiles receded in coloured perspective into the distance. "Women need ordering, not permission to go their own ways," said the Count sourly. "With a name as old as yours, my friend, it is a pity to allow such freedom as might cause it, perhaps, to mingle with other blood less worthy." He knew, as did the whole town, of the lady Bianca's and Toni Bajada's attachment to one another.

"Noble sir, such a saying insults me and mine!"

The play, the cock-fight, had begun again; the Governor gave a mental shrug. They would boil up and simmer down again as they always did half-a-dozen times in the course of such a parley; at first it had amused him, now it wearied him. He longed for action, some positive command to go out into the field of battle, and fight. To sit rotting here, while these overbred turkey-cocks flexed their wattles, was no soldier's task.

He was glad when an orderly came into the room, whispering to him that a matter of urgency waited. Murmuring an excuse to the delegation Mesquita came out; to see two figures dark against the sun outside, tense with the importance of their errand. One was Toni Bajada himself; the Governor knew him well. The other was a tall young man whose brown hair had been closely cropped, and whose grey eyes looked out at him with a kind of defiance. "This is Commander Philip Lascaris," said Toni.

He himself interpreted for the Greek, who could not yet make himself swiftly enough understood in the Christian armies. Toni spoke quickly and sparingly, with a wealth of gesture. The boldness of the plan they had come to outline struck the Governor with the sudden freshness of a breeze after the long stagnation of the last weeks; he gave an exclamation, but was prevented from speaking by Lascaris's warning finger. "Others are coming," said the Greek slowly.

Behind them, the delegation of the *notabili* had risen and left the audience-chamber; it approached the hour of noon. The bluest blood of the island passed by in formal file, murmuring courteous leavetakings; Toni, colouring suddenly, gave the quick submissive salute of the peasant as old Inguanez passed him, only regaining stature when he had gone. "He must carry the lady Bianca off, if he and she do not wish to remain single into old age," thought the Governor. The great door shut at last behind the delegation. He turned again to the messengers of the Grand Master.

"It is His Highness's order, this full attack on the Marsa? You have it from him in writing?"

Toni answered swiftly. "Sir, how can the Grand Master entrust such a written order in these days, when Birgù and Senglea are a mass of crumbling stone and flame? He is out every day manning the walls and planning reconstruction and attack; early today, before we left, he led a counter-attack in person in the streets of Birgù. If we had been seized on our way through the lines with letters, the surprise of such an attack, which is its value, would have been lost. Make the attack quickly, sir, while the Turk's troops are busied on Senglea spur and across the bay pressing their charge home; that way their provisions will be cut off, and they will be in a state we ourselves have endured since the beginning of this war, with no refreshment or place of rest. There are many sick already on he Marsa."

After they had gone the Governor set about the instructions for action thankfully. Even if, as he suspected, the Grand Master himself had not personally ordered the charge against the

Turkish camp it was something to be done at last. He armed his men; and silently, to alarm no nobleman of ancient blood taking his siesta in the afternoon heat, marched out down the narrow streets, past the houses which since King Roger's time had turned blank walls to the gaze of the curious, across the bridge and over the moat. The silence continued as they made their way down towards the camp on the Marsa; desultory fires there raised single spirals of smoke, but otherwise there was no sign of life.

"This way," said Toni Bajada, who knew the camp by night well; times without number he had sidled his way through the sleeping lines, so carefully that not a dog barked. Lascaris too knew the camp. He kept the thought of Melissa before him, despite her father's discouragement the other day; it would prevent any moment of weakness wherein he might fail to slaughter some sick man once known as a comrade. He could remember, too, St. Elmo.

A great yell sounded at last from the released troops of the Governor as they pounded down, setting fire to the silk tents where the important wounded lay; flailing about them with swords and stabbing with short daggers, burning and spilling the vats of oil and the containers of flour and dried fruit. There should be nothing left for the returning hordes, whether they came as victors or vanquished. The sickly smell of burning flesh soon came from the holocaust of the tents, and the smoke and flames were fanned by a summer breeze which carried men's screams. Soon the Marsa rivalled the harbour towns in running blood, fire and death. The black columns of smoke billowed thickly, and in its shelter the ravaging army withdrew to Mdina by nightfall, swords blooded and hearts high from the kill.

Only one man was suffered to survive; old Selim, the Christian slave, whom Philip himself had rescued and carried off on his saddle-bow.

Mustapha had word of it all in the course of his five-day attack on Senglea; they told him the Viceroy of Sicily must have come at last; with troops to the number of eight thousand. Hastily recalling his Janissaries who had been on the verge of capturing the breached town, he sounded a retreat: to the besieged Christians in their tottering defences it sounded like the trump of God. Why had the Turk turned tail? Whatever the reason, later that day they gave thanks; while Mustapha and the rest bewailed the loss of tents, comrades and all their stores, in the blackened camp-site carelessly left unguarded since the attack on Birgù.

Later that day, the Governor of Mdina sent for Toni Bajada, knowing he would find him at the house of Inguanez. They talked together far into the night; the young Maltese still seemed tireless and indestructible, like the half-divine figures of old, Hercules and Aeneas. It was as though his enemies were right in saying no ordinary weapon could wound him; after today's hand-to-hand fight he was still untouched. He laughed when it was spoken of, and thought, "I have a chain of prayer wound about me, anchored to my heart," and touched his crystal locket, where the tress of Bianca's hair was turned towards his body.

Melissa had not yet found Philip Lascaris, in the hospital or elsewhere. Each day she meant to ask Fiammetta where he might be found, but feared such a question would be unmaidenly. She was even shy with the patients, doing no more than following the sisters of St. John to hand them dry dressings from a basket. That way she need not look too closely at the terrible wounds, which still made her sick, in danger of fainting. Some who came in were mutilated beyond recognition; others lacked limbs, and one man, horribly, had had his side shot away and the intestines showed coiled inside, but he was dead by the time they could come to look at him and his body was removed, for there was little room. After that Melissa had gone over to the door, to breathe the air. On the way back she passed Fiammetta, who was straightening a fractured limb while a nun pulled at the other end to supply traction; the man was screaming. How could she ask about Lascaris at such a moment? Perhaps the man *was* Lascaris. Perhaps, in any case, she herself would never meet him now. A sense of hopelessness came to Melissa and she began to miss days at the hospital. But her mother continued to go regularly; and nowadays would say on leaving, "Child, prepare the vegetables and see that your father has a meal when he comes in from building the wall," and would then go out, flinging her *faldetta* about her in the swift way she always did.

But there had been women among the wounded too; and there came a night following steady bombardment, when Paul Grech's wife did not come home. When next day Melissa ventured into the hospital to ask, she was told what had happened. "They found her on her way home yesterday, struck down by flying stones. She didn't live more than a quarter-hour after coming in; there was no time to send for you. She wasn't conscious; by God's mercy, she never knew what had happened. There are enough here who do know, and can't die as easily, free of pain."

That was true; and yet she sat down and shed tears for her mother, less because she had loved her than because she ought to have loved her more. "At least she won't be worried any more over what is to become of me," the girl thought. Then she went home, in that hour when the guns were quiet, through the splintered rubbled streets to break the news to Paul.

Thirty-one

Anthony Graham had manned the gunnery-platform himself following the deaths of the engineers in that five days' bombardment; at such a time, there was no difference between officers and men. He rammed the shot home grimly, setting the fuses without regard to his own safety and staying by the post day and night. His bitterness regarding Fiammetta seemed to have changed his whole life, even to making it of little value now. Perhaps she would hear of his death amid danger and would remember that he, also, could obey.

He had thrust to the back of his mind a confused regard for her; her instant obedience to the orders of the Grand Master had shocked him, though he himself would not have behaved otherwise. He admired her courage, but was it for a woman to prefer courage to love? Were they not, should they not be, soft things, chattels, fashioned to stay at home by the fireside, not run out hastily to the sound of a drum, ready to plunge half-naked into the water in the midst of a horde of swimming armed Maltese?

Yet he could not forget her.

His grudge against the islanders, among whom she preferred to be, caused him to regret less the absence of Toni Bajada. That young man had been drafted by now to the command of a posse of Maltese cavalry, guarding against the threatened reprisals to Mdina. Toni's place had been taken by one man after another whom Anthony might know by name, or else might not; Spaniards, Portuguese, Frenchmen, Jews, released galley-slaves of every race under the sun. Some of them could tell, between firing, of how Toni himself had freed them with his knife: others again had word of a woman with bright hair who had appeared in the water by night, let them file through their chains, and afterwards guided them back to harbour.

Legend; she was less reality now than legend. In a month, a

year, the tales about her would have swelled beyond credibility; how was a man to assess her? Could he himself picture her in a wife's role in his great empty house in the north? Yet she came from his own land, was one of his own kind. The thought of Scotland, of the snell winds and the snow, was as remote as other half-remembered things in this strange existence. The only reality now was gunfire, its thunder, the crash of basilisks hurled day after day at the crumbling walls, holes blown, sliding masonry shored up by brown willing arms whose owners themselves, as often as not, slid dead into the waiting water minutes after they had done their task. One had long ago ceased to be shocked or revolted by the sight of death. The faces of the living and the dead mingled, and a friend seen by chance might be greeted for the last time. Yet he himself did not die.

Such experiences had helped Graham overcome his dislike of Philip Lascaris, who now and again came down to the post where he was. Together, they had charged behind the Grand Master in his personally led attack to reclaim the breached wall of Birgù. In the hot, savage charge with swords wielded hand-to-hand, each man on one's own side was a comrade: and Lascaris fought well. Afterwards they had gone back together to the Grand Master's house in the town and, in his company, had drunk a ration of watered wine. Graham had sat nearby the young Greek, the pair of them keeping silence for a while; beyond, they could hear the voice of Sir Oliver Starkey vainly trying to persuade La Valette to withdraw for his own safety within Fort St. Angelo.

"The townspeople have had witness of your courage this day; it would be foolhardy to risk your life further, for if you are killed or severely injured it will be worth the capture of the island itself to the Turkish commanders," said the English secretary gently. But La Valette shook his head, easing the place where his casque chafed him between neck and shoulder. His knee-cap had been shattered by a flying ball; another had struck his back-plate over the right lung, but old as he was he had taken no visible ill. He might have been fashioned of steel and leather. He raised the flagon of watered wine with a gesture as courtly as though it had been the finest Gascony, and his guests royal.

"The townsfolk of Birgù take courage from my presence, as I think," he replied lightly. "God preserves those who may still be of service to Him. Fort St. Angelo is too far removed from the present theatre of war."

"Ay, well may they leave that till the last, knowing its strength," murmured Sir Oliver. He watched over La Valette day and night, fearing the Grand Master's heedlessness of his safety to an extent that made Starkey forget his own. The house La Valette had insisted on taking for himself was in the heart of Birgù, and the bombardment as day followed day laid it increasingly open to danger. The Englishman's face darkened with anxiety; what would become of them all if this man were taken from them? But suddenly meeting the Grand Master's eyes he found them filled with a serenity absent for many weeks. "God is watching over us, Oliver, as I believe," he said quietly. "Who would have thought that the Turkish losses would have been as great, or that we ourselves could have held them off for as long? No human strength could have contrived alone; as you know well, we have been unable to trust in princes. Sometimes the certainty comes to me that we in the conduct of this siege are carrying out God's purpose in a spoiled world, stripping away the lies and greed that surround all worldly matters and returning, perhaps, to the truth as it was in the days when our ancestors went forth to battle for Christ's tomb."

Ay, and by the end lost it to the Saracen among much greed and lying also, thought Sir Oliver. But he did not speak aloud, only keeping an eye on the dressing of La Valette's knee-wound, which still bled at intervals.

Anthony had led Lascaris on, as he realised later, to talk of Fiammetta. He heard, by no means unwillingly, of the days she had spent watching by Dragut's death-bed and of the manner in which Philip had aided her escape. The old man Selim, now Lascaris' body-servant, could bear it out, the Greek assured him. "But she could have done nothing without her own courage," he said. "Why has so beautiful a woman fallen on such evil fortune? She should be married to a prince, with her children about her." And, encouraged by the Scotsman's silence, he went on to talk of Safieye the Bright One, legendary among the infidel as well as here; of how she had been kept as intended bride for the Sultan, and put on the merchantman together with

Lascaris' own bride Gulbehar. That he had forgotten the latter since seeing Melissa in church he did not say; he was still occupied with the thought of Fiammetta. "What will become of such a woman when the war is at an end?" he asked. But Graham, assailed by taciturnity at the swelling of legend about Fiammetta, seized on the other name Philip had mentioned. "Your promised wife, you say? And she was captured by the Knights? She may be in Sicily now." Relief flooded him; he had not yet forgotten Fiammetta's anxiety the day Lascaris swam across the bay to them, nor how she had leaned over the parapet regardless of danger, ready to dive in and save the young man. His jealousy—he could see now that that was what it had been—of Philip receded; perversely, he now became anxious to befriend him. "It is a sad pity about your bride," he said sincerely. "Perhaps she will be restored to you safely when this war is at an end."

"I have forgotten her. I fancy an island girl, but her parents will not permit me to marry her."

"There are few young girls on the island. One is the daughter of Paul the Greek. She came off the merchantman."

"The merchantman? How could that be, unless ..."

Anthony laughed. "You had best ask her. Maybe she was your promised bride; stranger things have occurred." He shifted his stiffened limbs. "Toni Bajada should be here; he knows the family, as he knows everyone. Let us go, when night has fallen, into Birgù; maybe we will run into old Paul at his fortifications."

But when darkness fell there was no sign of building, and they walked the shattered streets alone. In the place where the merchant's house had been was a crazily leaning pile of rubble and stone, for Mustapha's basilisks had hit the place squarely. Among it was the balding head of Paul Grech, dead with arms outflung in an attempt to ward off death. There was no sign of Melissa.

She had crouched against the protective wall of stone, stopping her ears. All day the bombardment had continued without ceasing, seeming for the first time to concentrate its fire on their end of the town, as though the enemy had resolved systematically to reduce everything on the two spurs of land to final and desolate ruin. Not a house or booth remained where any had stood; there was only dust, rising in a yellow wall to blot out the things Melissa had begun, again, to find familiar. There had been the Norman church with its wide-sprung arches, the market-place where mules had once stood laden with carts of pumpkins and cheeses, and a flower in each mule's mane. The very first day she had come off the ship there had been Toni Bajada with his white mule. The thought of mules made her cry. There were none now, no single living thing left in Birgù; only dust, deafening noise, and the crying of the wounded in their bombarded houses, level with the ground.

She must find shelter. But where was she to go, now that the very street her father's house had stood in was gone? Perhaps the hospital would let her in. Today she had gone there again, for Fiammetta had come to ask her to go back. Everyone who could help with the injured was doing so, while the rest repaired walls. Fiammetta did both things, and others as well. She looked so wild and grim these days, with linen strips wound about her head and arms where she had burned herself in the firing, and her clothes stained with blood and dust from her constant tending in the hospital. Once there, Melissa had seen that this did not matter; the wounded men thought of Fiammetta as an angel. She was there day and night now that the swimmers had ceased to go out during the bombardment; acting as the nuns did, in their dark habits with the Cross of St. John on the shoulder. Papa—ah, dear Papa!—had told her the nuns were the only women the Grand Master had willed to stay on the island, for what they did; healing, feeding the sick with scanty rations, binding up and cleansing wounds, setting broken bones, disposing of the dead in common ditches. Melissa had again retched at the smell of blood, then at the sight of Fiammetta and a nun; they were carrying out a dead soldier, making the sign of the cross over him and laying him in the ditch where other dead lay putrefying because there was no leisure to bury them. "Later they will have consecrated graves, for each man has his name on his body," Fiammetta explained briefly. "Wind these strips for me, Melissa; there'll soon be more coming in."

Guns had started to crash again now, though it was evening. The wall on which she had relied leant forwards, subsided, fell at last with a lurching and crumbling of soft stone. Melissa sobbed aloud; she had never been as much afraid: even Fiammetta was no longer her friend. They had sent her home from the hospital today, as she could no longer assist without vomiting. "We have enough sick here," they had told her, and it was true. Now she was useless, unwanted by anyone; what would become of her? Even the church gone, where she used to go and pray; Papa and her mother both dead; nothing to be seen but dust, or heard but the cannon. Perhaps they would hit and kill her; but she was afraid to die. She laid her head on her arms, feeling the helpless tears run down her cheeks.

Then she heard a man's voice calling her name.

He had found her, his Gulbehar, in dead streets where the rubble of houses made a landscape without life. He had gone at first towards a shape there, a dead body here, thinking it might have identity. Always the cannon crashed beyond, piling up desolation till it fell with its own weight, burying living and dead together. Once or twice they found survivors, huddled in the cavern-like holes which were all that remained of buildings; two old women were seated by the corpse of a third, raising a wailing sound that was hardly heard above the constant noise of firing. In another place a dead mule lay, picked at by gulls. They rose screaming every time the cannon roared, then settled down again to continue the feast. The faces of the dead stared up at the sky, rejected one after the other as the two men passed. These were not soldiers but the common people, who had not asked for war.

Then they found Melissa, stretched out behind the stone defence wall the workers had abandoned for that day. Anthony saw her first, and caught his companion's arm. He watched Lascaris go over to her and turned wordlessly, leaving them. Such things happened swiftly in war. It was possible that they, and he also, would be killed by the next volley of stones.

Melissa felt herself lifted in the strange man's arms. In the weariness that had come she felt no surprise that he addressed her in Turkish. Later they alternated with Greek, stiffly answering one another; he was foreign, she decided, though where he had come from, and why he was here, she did not know. He carried her to a more sheltered place and there set her down and, keeping hold of her, told her gently that her father's death had been swift. "There is nothing left of the house," he said. "I know it," she heard herself replying.

She had begun to weep for old Paul, who had always been kind to her. Presently the young man began to comfort her, using gestures of increasing certainty as he stroked her limbs and body. The pleasure his caresses brought Melissa made her shiver a little, as if with guilt; how could she stay here with her father newly dead, and let a strange man stroke and comfort her? Yet this usage was what they had led her, in the years at Mehedia, to expect from a man; the young soldier who was to have been her bridegroom in Constantinople would have acted so.

"What is your name?" she asked him timidly.

"Philip Lascaris. And yours is Melissa, Gulbehar, Flower of Spring. You were intended for me from the beginning."

"Ah ..."

A strange thought took her, while she contemplated the strangeness of their finding one another, here where almost everyone was dead. In Islam they had taught her that the body was for pleasure; but the Christian Church said one must mortify the flesh. Perhaps she was of Islam. His caresses gave her pleasure. That he should be Philip Lascaris, for whom she had looked so often!

The whining noise of gunfire had started up afresh; she had difficulty in hearing him as he spoke, rapidly and with urgency. "Melissa, I asked your father lately for your hand. He refused me. Do you also refuse? I would not take you unwillingly."

"No. I do not refuse." He smiled delightedly, and their mouths met. Later, he would kiss her all over. But she was timid, as a girl should be, and this pleased him. Their marriage-night might not take place in a bed; it would not matter.

Smashing of newly-built walls, and flares of sudden fire came as timber caught among the remaining buildings. Could anyone live through this night? She clung to him in fear; and heard him laugh. For the first time, in the firelit dark, she saw the white gleam of his teeth, and looked at his face. He was handsome, she thought; not like the fat eunuchs in the Serai, or the few young men she had met since coming home.

He seemed able to follow her thoughts. "Tomorrow we'll find a priest in the town, if he still lives," he promised her.

"Afterwards, after this war, the Grand Master has reserved me a command in Naples, possibly later in Spain. Will you come with me?"

Spain; Naples. The names held fascination. His voice had been wistful, holding uncertainty for the first time. "He is a stranger here," she thought, "and so am I. Neither of us will ever be quite the same as those who know of only one side, only one faith. It is good that we should be together."

"I will come," she said, and he kissed her again. She let him lead her by the hand away from the ruins. Tomorrow they would go to the priest, if they lived as long as he. For tonight, it did not signify if they lay together. It was for this that she had been born. It mattered less now if she died soon; she would have fulfilled her destiny.

When the time came, she opened herself to her bridegroom, and to love, as naturally as a flower opens its petals. The Turk fired his final salvo and retired for the night; and darkness deepened over ruined Birgù.

Thirty-two

Night after night, in the hope that he would return, Fiammetta had gone back to the house Graham had taken. But he did not come. Whether he was still angry with her, or whether his duties about the Grand Master occupied him, she had no means of knowing. In any case she did not expect word to be sent while the battle raged about the walls. He owed her nothing.

Once the Turks exploded a great mine under the town. A shower of smoke and flame, shooting upwards, had heralded a great breach in the toppling wall, and instantly the enemy hordes had rushed in, finding themselves in the streets unopposed. But the opposition had formed itself at once, with the Grand Master himself leading the foray clad only in light armour. "This way, my lads, this way!" she had heard him shouting. They had driven the yelling Turks back, as in every other encounter. The Grand Master's courage was beyond any; she had often seen him stand out in front above the posts of action, shown up clearly by the rising flames; it was as if he knew the sight of him standing there would make the men fight twice as bravely, and accordingly risked his life.

But there was no sign, no word, of Anthony. He must be either unhurt or dead; day by day, without avail, she had searched the faces lying in the hospital. She must accustom herself to having lost him; after all his first love was the Order.

A knock sounded at the door and she went down, flinging a robe about her. The thought that perhaps he had come, after all, to her in the dawn made her heart beat fast and gladly. This time, she would not deny him, even though it might be the only time they had together, these few hours remaining between darkness and light. She could never be more to him than a casual mistress; she must snatch the moment when it came, then set him free.

But it was Philip Lascaris who stood in the doorway, carrying a flushed bright-eyed Melissa wrapped in his cloak. "Anthony said we might come here," they told her. They said that they were married, had found a priest from St. Lawrence hurrying from dispensing the Last Sacraments to the sick, and made him marry them. Fiammetta let them go upstairs to the warm bed. Disappointment ate at her like a sickness as she sat huddled below, waiting for morning. Could Anthony not have sent some word to her with the pair? Now she must stay on here till dawn broke, trying not to hear the love-sounds from upstairs.

It was unendurable; she unlatched the door and went out into the grey light. The disordered streets were still and quiet, great stones hurled across the way which must be stepped round. She picked her way, following the almost unrecognisable track down to the shore. Mustapha's gun-sites no longer covered the cave. It was safe enough for her to come home.

The cave was still, dark and private. She lay down on the rock where so often sleep had come to her and gazed out at the night sky. A single planet, pear-shaped and bright, hung still above the horizon. She recalled how at Mehedia they had taught her the planets and that this was Venus, Melissa's now and not her own. She shrugged a little. Anger and even longing had left her; she felt empty. Was it of importance? To have hung the planets in their places, to have made the world turn about the sun, all those matters which the Arabs knew of before the West, was a greater thing; one which showed how unimportant lives and loves were, how little this would matter in a hundred years, even ten. Men and women who would never hear of the Great Siege of Malta would be born, live and die forgotten like the ancient nameless race of men who had lived on this land while it was still attached to Africa.

Change; summer, winter, age. Soon she herself would be an old woman. Must she live to be old? She and Toni, and Anthony, all unharmed by fire and steel, seemed fated so. But Anthony would live wrapped in the great cloak of the Order of St. John, and she—

She turned her thoughts elsewhere; to the hurt remembrance of Yaya crying for her maidenhead, the body of Hafiza buried in the nearby shallow grave. She was more fortunate than they, perhaps; God knew, as He knew all things.

She said her prayers and slept, and did not dream.

A dazzle of sunlight woke her, or perhaps it was the dark figure of a man seen against the cave's mouth. Even on waking she recalled the first time when Toni had come here, and had found her Anthony's clothes. But this was only a Maltese she did not know. "They are looking for you," he said gently. "There is an errand for you by boat, over on the west shore. Will you come now? It is arranged with the fishermen."

She followed him; everything was indeed arranged, as with any order of the Grand Master's; guides to take one overland, boatmen to meet one at the further coast. "You are to go to Gozo, to bring back the healing fungus from the rock," they told her. "Bring as much as you can, for His Highness's wound and for others."

She set out across the western water by noon, hair concealed in a napkin. She had no wish to attract the attention of Mustapha's patrols; this time, though she still wore Barbarossa's jewel, her reception by the enemy would be less kindly.

The fungus rock had a curious formation she would remember, and the sight of the thick lichen growing against the background of stone and sea. She culled it with a knife into a flat basket. Here in Gozo the sounds of war were far distant, only the constant booming of guns sounding like faint thunder from the larger island.

Yet they had had their share of war here. Still within living memory was the black year when every soul on Gozo had been killed or taken into slavery. The tall thin parsimonious Gozitans, different in colouring and temper from the open-handed Maltese, were rare now; some had migrated in time to Malta to return here in old age, so that there were still towns, churches, a convent, tilled fields. Fiammetta bit gladly into the fruit they were able to buy, at a price, from a farmer near the rock. It was long since anyone had eaten fresh fruit on Malta.

They loaded up the boat, she and the fisherman who had rowed her over, and made ready to return. Looking back over the narrow water she watched Gozo to the last; it could be a refuge, had in fact been so lately for those the Grand Master had not sent across to Sicily or up to Mdina when the siege began.

It seemed to her also that she saw the tall shapes of ships, two or more, against the horizon. But within moments they were gone; it might have been cloud.

The journey back down the coast was uneventful; they went by night in order to evade snipers. Fiammetta asked the second guide who met and helped her with her load if there was news. Yes, he told her, there had been an attempted attack against Mdina, but the cavalry had beaten it off; and the Chevalier de Robles had been killed at Birgù. Fiammetta felt tears rise; the brave Knight who had led her with the Little Relief down this very coast had been a tower of strength in the siege, defending his own post nobly and suggesting many stratagems to defeat the wily Turk. "How many will be left alive or whole when all this is done?" she asked aloud. The man answered swiftly.

"Few, and those not the bravest, for they are dead. When the Turk goes he will leave an island black with bodies, his own and ours."

"When he goes?" She turned a look of surprise on him. "Do they speak yet of his going?"

"Yes, he is tiring. His losses have been heavier than ours, and worse than that he has made the Grand Turk look foolish. Before the storms come in autumn, he will go; may it be forever."

Thirty-three

Many people thought the Grand Master mistaken when he did not withdraw all his troops from Birgù and Senglea into the protection of Fort St. Angelo. But he said "How can I abandon all the loyal Maltese?" and again, "There is not enough water in St. Angelo for us all". Then he was silent; but his shrewd eyes held many things, among them the knowledge that once inside the great Fort, with its curtains and cavalier, its batteries rising tier upon tier, the target he would present to the Turk would be one that could be surrounded in days; the Turk would starve it out before autumn. Neither he himself, nor his entourage, he said, would leave Birgù. As at the beginning of the siege he had made a speech to the people in the market square, now he did another thing to reassure them; he blew up the bridge between fort and town, to prove to all comers that he would stay in Birgù.

Battles raged daily; stormed breaches, counter-attacks, defences each with an epic history, great names felled in every charge. Still daily, between his duty-tours of the besieged ramparts, the Grand Master would go to the church of St. Lawrence to pray. There, watched over by the Hand of St. John which he had not removed to safety, he asked God to save the Religion in Malta. And surely as the summer ended it began to seem as though this might be. The Turkish ammunition, which they had wantonly spent, ran short, and the murmuring in the lines increased; it could be heard constantly on the lips of Janissary and corsair, Spahi and Iyalar and, at last, the command.

"We have done what we may," they said. "It has all been to no avail; we might have saved our ammunition and our men. It is not the will of Allah that we should take Malta. How otherwise could so pitiful a force, with so few provisions, have held out against us?"

And, chiding one another like old women, they demanded to be sent home.

Fiammetta had tried to learn of the progress of the siege during her few days' absence, but it was impossible; the town when she returned hardly existed, all being in ruins except that house where the Grand Master had made his headquarters above a shop in what had been the main square. "They have tried again to persuade him to withdraw to the Fort, but he will not go," the Donat who took her load from her at the door told her. "He seems to have a charmed life, and that is our salvation; but his knee hurts him. He will be glad of the healing moss."

She left him and made her way straight to the hospital, anxious for Anthony. Constant gunfire and splintering stones still made it needful to shelter on the way.

The hospital was full. Wounded men, and some women, lay about the floors and three or four to each bed, which had no vacant places for long. The smell of festering flesh made the air foul; there were not enough helpers to tend each man. Fiammetta caught sight of Melissa Lascaris, her own hand bandaged, limping round with linen strips among the patients by the door who could walk. Her face brightened when she saw Fiammetta.

"We have been fearful for you," she said. "Philip is up now at the Post of Robles, and is well and unhurt. This? Oh, a splinter caught me when the house was destroyed; it is only a little bone broken." She moved off about her tasks, and Fiammetta spared time to marvel at the strengthening effect love and marriage had had on the girl who had used not to be able to endure more than an hour in the hospital. For Melissa to have had an injured hand a month ago would have meant that she took to her bed. Now she seemed no longer a prey to her old sickness and childish fears; but everyone was in a state of chronic ill-health, puffy with undernourishment and carrying wounds which in ordinary times would have been crippling. Now one ignored a burned hand, a sprained limb, a simple fracture; there was too much to be done for those who were worse off than oneself.

Among these she found Anthony.

He had a four days' growth of beard; she scarcely knew him, so thin and wasted had he grown. He lay untended on the bare

floor and at first she thought he must be dead, for there seemed
no wound on him. She knelt down, and took his wrist; the blood
still beat there thinly, and as she touched him he moved his head
a little, and murmured something. She leant her own head down
close to him to hear what it might be. It was her own name.

"Fiammetta."

He could not know her, could surely not even sense that she
was there with him. She held him, trying to give him some of
her own warmth; his flesh was chill. A Sister of St. John passed
by; how calm they always seemed, these sisters, with the great
cross on their robes!

"He was brought in thus yesterday," the nun said. "A stone
struck his head during the firing. Sometimes since then he has
called out confused speech; at other times, he is silent." She
knelt down and gently prised open one of Anthony's eyelids; the
pupil of the eye did not focus to light. She rose and stood and
looking down on him.

"Do what you may," she said, and looked at Fiammetta.
"Only you can do aught, for he has been calling your name."

For many hours she stayed there, holding him; her own
weariness, the fact that she had eaten nothing since return,
forgotten. He seemed at last to know or feel her presence and at
one time, like a child, turned his head so that his face lay buried
between her breasts, and remained there. If they could die so,
she thought, how gladly she would die! As long as he needed her
she would hold him thus, asking neither food nor rest.
Presently, the bombardment began again, great stones crashing
across the roof of the hospital itself; she tried to keep the sounds
from him, cradling his head against her with her hands over his
ears. After what seemed an endless time his breathing changed,
becoming more like that of sleep, steady and even. When the
nun next passed by night had fallen and she brought a lamp, its
yellow light falling against the folds of her smooth habit. She
looked down at the two of them, and smiled.

"He will live now," she said, and then "There is a message
for you from the Grand Master which I have delayed giving
you. He desires to see you when you can go to him."

Fiammetta laid down Anthony's head gently, not to disturb
his sleep. Now that he would live her task, she knew, was done:

but it wrenched at her heart to leave him. How much she had wanted to be with him when he should waken, opening his eyes at last on lamplight or the light of dawn! Would he ever know that she had knelt there holding him, or that he himself had called her name?

La Valette was seated by his table, fully clad but with his injured leg propped up. His face was drawn and old and she remembered that a Spaniard named Aiguilar, who had been high in the Grand Master's confidence about fortifications, had deserted recently, causing him much grief. "If his trust is abused, that is the worst thing of all," she thought. "He stakes the progress of this war, and his own life, on those he loves and who he thinks love him." Yet was love too strong a word for one who seemed to have so little humanity? They said that when his nephew had been killed he had looked down at the boy's dead face and had said "The death of others grieves me as greatly".

But now, seeing her enter, he smiled. "I have to thank you for your journey for the moss, Fiammetta," he said. "Nothing else has relieved the stiffness in my wound; but soon now, I hope, I shall be about again with all those whose hurts are slight."

He bade her come forward. "They tell me you are a good nurse," he said. "My lad who changes the linen for me has gone to relieve them in Birgù. Will you dress it in his place?"

"Gladly, Monseigneur," she said. She knelt down and began to unwind his bandages. The wound itself was still angry and discharging, and she knew that he made light of it.

"Monseigneur must try to move it a little, every so often, though it will be painful," she told him. "Otherwise it may stiffen in healing."

She applied herself to anointing and changing the linen on the wound, not noticing his silence except to ascribe it to pain. But when she looked up with her task completed, he was frowning.

"How is it that the ring was returned to you?" he asked, and his voice was harsh.

Inadvertently, her free hand crept over to hide the jewel. She had hardly taken it off in all that time since the Little Relief, when Anthony had slid it on her finger under cover of his cloak.

It might soon be the only memory she would have of him; it had grown to be a part of her, and now—

"You do not answer me," said La Valette.

He reached forward and took her hand, examining the engraved signs of the Koran on the ring. Contrary to the fear she had, he did not remove it. He said in an idle voice, leaving go of her, "I gave it to you on your return: but before that it was in the possession of Monsieur de Graham, as I think. As he has asked to become a Knight of the Order, I ask you again how you came by it once more."

Pride flamed in her; he might, she thought, have been addressing a servant. "I can give you my word that I will not hinder his joining, if join he may." That should be as Anthony willed, not this old man. In any event, had word come yet from the Pope? It might be that Anthony's parents' handfast marriage would be forever a bar to his acceptance into the Order.

Aloud she said, as La Valette did not answer, "There is a hindrance, I believe, to his being admitted meantime owing to some doubt as to his legitimacy".

"That is so, and it is not yet resolved. There have been some few matters intervening. But he is a young man I should like to see among us, after this war."

The voice was even, but on meeting his gaze she found it dark with dislike. To such a man, she knew, any obstacle had no personal value. He had just shown himself grateful to her; but that would mean less than nothing if she interfered with his ordered plans. And Anthony's disposal had been a part of those, was still so. She spoke aloud, fighting a little.

"Monseigneur, does not war change many things? Might it not cause a change of heart in a young man, who until then had known of only one goal on which to set his heart? If he should still want, more than anything in the world, to join the Order, I would not stand in his way, nor would any honest woman. I swear to you that he has broken no vow nor conducted himself in an unseemly way."

"That may mean much or little," he said drily. "Where is Monsieur de Graham now?"

"In the hospital, with a head injury. He is not conscious and may not be for some time. Monseigneur, do not punish him for what he has not done nor even perhaps thought of. There has been nothing, I say it again, between us, no deed that takes two to fulfil."

"And the house in Birgù?" he said expressionlessly.

He had dismissed her, leaving her without satisfaction as to what was to be done with Anthony. But she had reason to hope, in his evident interest, that Anthony would not be denied admission provided the letter came from Rome. The Pope, as always, would have the last word; every despatch coming by way of Sicily might bear it. Meantime, the war must be fought; but she herself would fight no longer.

"You have done well," he told her, as a valediction: and then, as if to rescind his last words to her, a woman, "You must not see Monsieur de Graham again. I shall expect you to withdraw from Birgù."

As she went out a guide accosted her. He was to take her to Mdina, he said. Fiammetta admitted, with irony, that Grand Master La Valette was thorough.

Mdina was thronged with refugees, sheltering in houses, churches, the Governor's residence, the streets. Among familiar sights there was an ancient lady, veiled, huge, and blind: she was Gajn Siva, nurse of the Sultan's daughter Mihrmah, captured many years since and never ransomed. After a time Fiammetta went to her and tried to persuade her to speak in the tongue they both knew; what tales she must have of Constantinople, of Suleiman the Magnificent and his wife Roxellane, of the secret world behind the lattices! But the old woman by now was imbecile and dumb; she no longer knew what went on about her or why she was here, seated day after day in the sun as she was, doing nothing. Fiammetta's aching mind could not be consoled with stories.

One day they all, even Gajn Siva, were addressed by the Governor. "A Turkish attack is riding towards Mdina. It is perhaps their last hope. We must patrol the walls, women as well as men; the infidel must think we have plenty of troops in the town." He provided breastplates and morions, placed them, armoured, all in line, made them fill the spaces behind the ramparts with double-file, then cross quickly, as Mustapha's spies rode round the curve to the north face, and establish themselves there to be seen. All day they marched and counter-marched; by sundown word ran round, in a tired whisper, "They have gone back, thank God and His saints". Mustapha had been deceived, and now thought Mdina better fortified and protected than even St. Elmo had been. And he would not risk such a siege again.

Afterwards, Mdina returned to her silence.

Fiammetta remained in Mdina for the rest of the war, which had almost run its course. She made herself think neither of past nor future; when news came by way of Toni Bajada she listened, and said nothing.

But without being asked, he told her Anthony Graham was safe. Two days after she had left the hospital he had been sent back to his battery, for every man who could stand must fight. "He does not know where you are," said Toni.

"Do not tell him." Her fingers clenched on Dragut's ring till it bit into the flesh. The temptation to hurry down into Birgù was torment. She must not allow herself to remain in a place where that could happen. For the first time, she thought of her own fate after this war. She saw nothing; it was all dark, and she turned her thoughts back to events in Mdina.

But Toni had more news. The two ships Fiammetta had seen, ghostly as cloud, had been Don Garcia's. That cautious commander had in fact embarked three times before at last permitting his troops to land on Malta; and they would have only one final battle to whet their swords. To thank Don Garcia for his tardy gift of four thousand men must have taxed the Grand Master's courtesy, Fiammetta thought; yet that would not falter on such an occasion. Perhaps he had spared some pity for the Viceroy; his son, the young Federigo who had shown so much promise, had been killed at last in the relief of Senglea. Yaya's ravisher Juan de La Cerda, too, had redeemed himself on release from prison; having tried, as they said, in every action to lose his life, he had done so at last before St. Michael's, bravely enough to wipe out forever the stain of cowardice which had clung to his name ever since the hysterically delivered report on conditions in St. Elmo.

Fiammetta had the task of telling Yaya of La Cerda's death.

She occupied herself with small errands, little things, nowadays. Yaya only said, "Then my children will have had a brave father". The Spiteri, the twins, were to be born in the autumn.

But that was to be after the Turkish fleet had departed, with a full bellying of sail; the gongs were silent. At once the stream of refugees made their way downhill to what was left of Birgù. Fiammetta did not go with them. If anyone had asked, she would have said, "I must stay with Yaya, for the birth". But no one asked. She mattered nothing now; the rebuilding of shattered homes, the gathering of wounded menfolk, mattered more.

The autumn sun made the scarred roads golden; the green shade of cactus leaves dulled everywhere. Sometimes Fiammetta and Yaya would walk in the courtyard of the Casa Inguanez, sometimes again about the walls of Mdina which had not been called upon after all to resist siege. The city had withdrawn again into its ageless proud retreat, shutting newcomers out. Only the shadow of a priest's hat against the sun in the narrow ways broke the pattern of wall against wall, golden roof and unbroken tower, that had always been Mdina. "One thing is different," said Yaya joyfully in a whisper one day. She smiled, as if the new life she carried were a symbol of hope now and not despair and shame. "The Count is reconciled to the marriage of Toni and Bianca. She told me yesterday. She is very happy." The title of mistress and maid had long been dropped between Yaya and Bianca; the two were friends.

"That is good news indeed," said Fiammetta, and almost felt the ache in her own heart dispelled. "I wish them happy."

Yaya was chattering on. "His new livery in the Maltese Guard is so splendid, it persuaded the Count that he is now someone of importance. And, of course, everyone is still talking of Toni's bravery in the war. The things he did were miraculous, as though he could make himself invisible, like a *djinn*." Yaya pressed her hand to her side. "I have a shortness of breath, Fiammetta," she said. "Do you think we could go home?"

The marriage of Bianca and Toni brought rejoicing to Mdina, even though it was quietly celebrated because of the bride's health. Four days later, Yaya's labour began; it was long and

not easy, and it took all of Fiammetta's coaxing to persuade her
to keep her eyes on the Birth Rose which Bianca had placed by
her bed, saying that as the petals unfolded, so would the
birth-pangs ease. But after it was all over Yaya was content,
and slept with a brown baby boy lying swaddled on each side of
her.

I must go now, Fiammetta told herself. She could not endure
the sight of the happiness of Toni and Bianca, or that of Yaya
feeding her babies with sweet milk drawn by the small greedy
mouths from each breast. They all had someone now to care for,
to be cared for by; but she had no one. She had learned to
accustom herself to loneliness, knowing that it was the will of
God. There would never be marriage for her with any man, and
the cloister would not satisfy her. She lacked the singleminded-
ness, the patient calm of the nun. Whatever fate held in store for
her she must go out to meet it alone.

Some days after the birth of Yaya's twins she set out, leaving
no direction. Toni Bajada's light eyes had dwelt on her for an
instant when she said goodbye to him where he sat with his
wife. He understood, she thought. She made her way out of
town and down to the further coast, carrying her few belongings
in a kerchief.

Anthony Graham had confronted the Grand Master on the day
after Don Garcia de Toledo, Viceroy of Sicily, had been
entertained to a great feast at Birgù. The mockery of its
remembrance still haunted the Grand Master's smile. So low
had their provisions been, eked out by gifts of fresh fruit from
Gozo and with their last few barrels of wine, poured out like
heart's blood in silver flagons for the man who had helped them
too late. But behind his courtly, meaningless phrases could be
read his grief for his dead son. So decimated were their
numbers, only La Valette himself, Sir Oliver and a handful of
the rest robed and cloaked to greet the Viceroy and sip the
welcome wine. Out in the streets was the roystering noise of the
four thousand troops Don Garcia had brought; how joyfully
they would have been received a month since!

But now Don Garcia left, leaving letters behind him, in some
doubt as to his master King Philip's anger. Had Malta fallen,
Don Philip would have praised his economy in not sending men

or ships; but with news of the great victory resounding, bells rung in cities everywhere, the Pope sending offers of a cardinal's hat to La Valette, and even Protestant Elizabeth Tudor giving open thanks in England's churches, it would be taken as a disgrace to Spanish arms and Spanish pride that her only fighters for the Faith had been volunteers and those members of the Order who had reached the island in time. King Philip had hastily ordered a jewelled sword to be made, and presented with all despatch to the Grand Master. Meantime, Don Garcia could expect to be deprived of his Viceroyalty; the most merciful fate for him thereafter would be a life lived in obscurity.

Anthony Graham read all this in the Grand Master's smile. A dish of pears, left over from the Gozitan gift, lay by him and Sir Oliver in an earthenware bowl. The young man fixed his eyes on it, comforted by its simplicity, avoiding the sight of the darkly cloaked Knights with their lined faces, the blandness of the shining eight-pointed crosses they wore.

He knelt before La Valette, who bade him rise. "I think you know the news which came for you by way of the Sicilian ships, and that it was good," he heard the Grand Master say. A feeling which was the ghost of regret troubled Anthony. How much he would once have given to be accepted forever into the shelter of that warm, formally phrased approval from the Pope! As for La Valette, he had saved Christendom; it would be an honour second to none to serve him for life. "But not I," thought Anthony. He could remember, dimly, calling for Fiammetta and that she had come; to put himself forever beyond her, turn his back on her, was not possible now. If it took the rest of his life he would search for her.

He began to speak, stammering at first and then gaining courage when the worst part, the telling of it, was over, and the Grand Master's welcoming smile had changed to cold doubt and then to incredulity. It was not given to La Valette to understand how any man, young, Catholic, and free, accepted as eligible to join the Order, should want to withdraw for such a reason as a woman. These desires passed with youth, if one had ever had them; they went the way of love for one's native country, of liberty to follow one's will. He spoke of it to Graham, gently as one might reprove an erring son.

"You know well that when we give thought to join the Order we put away all such things," he said. "I myself have never revisited Provence, though in my youth I loved her well. Other love I have put away from me in the service of Our Lord, Who suffices me. Do I now appear to you as a man who wants the things he may not have?"

"No, Monseigneur; but I—"

"The love of Our Saviour sustains me always, has done all through this bitter war; I am His servant, and it is given to me to know His orders; in that pursuit all lesser matters vanish. I have never desired children, wife or home; it is nothing to me that when I die this shell will be all that remains of Jean Parisot de La Valette. I have lived to serve in the greatest brotherhood ever made by man for God. That same service I now offer you; do you decline, and for such a reason?"

"Monseigneur, I decline. I love a woman of great courage and beauty, who also loves me. Through all this war I have come to know her worth. Lacking her now I am nothing, not even fit to serve in so great a brotherhood as yours has been."

"Has been?" La Valette leaned, forward, brows knotted. "Our day is not yet done. You speak as the Turk thought when he sailed to these shores. You are blinded with visions of Eve in Paradise, as much as any Turk. I had thought better of you, but have it as you will; we need not fear for our numbers now, when the siege is won."

"As Monseigneur says." The young man withdrew, flushed and near tears. A certainty had come to him that the Order had indeed lived through its greatest day, that everything which pertained, from now onwards, to the Knights Hospitallers would be as the glory of the sunset reflecting on a changing sea. Never again would there be such bravery as had seen shown in this barren island which forever, now that the battle was fought and won, would eclipse the memory of Rhodes, perhaps even Jerusalem. From this time on memory would become tradition, tradition harden in its gilding until what had been a fighting man's armour became embroidery, enamel, tapestry, tombs, a fanfare of remembrance held year after year where the blood had spilled scarlet on the ground and in the sea.

But that was not why he had declined to join. He chafed for Fiammetta.

"Monseiur de Graham will not be one of us," said La Valette aloud to Sir Oliver, and turned to his old friend as if the matter were no more to him than the loss of a hawk or a dog. For instants, the petulance of a disappointed old man showed in the drooping of the mouth above the whitening beard; then he was comforted, as though with the promise of the summers to come, the prospect of riding out, a while yet, with his hawk at his wrist, his hound at heel. So it would be; and he bade farewell to Anthony Graham in cool friendship, as to one who had fought well, before he turned to other matters and forgot him.

As for Anthony, he set out alone to search for Fiammetta. The task was like one in a dream, so greatly had everything changed; not least himself. It was a land where dead bodies still lay thick, many whose names would never be known now; and though many had seen Fiammetta when she bound up their wounds or helped them, no one knew which way she had gone. After a few days' weary search, he went to Mdina; Toni Bajada would surely know where she was. He had not heard of Toni's marriage, and came upon him with his wife by him, Bianca sewing an embroidered sleeve. The straight light gaze of the Maltese met Graham's. "She was here, but she has gone," said Toni Bajada. "I do not think that you will find her."

"Not find her? Did she leave no direction, speak of no plans?"

"Her plans are ended. What was there in the future for her? She would have been welcome to stay on here till you came, as you have come. That she did not do so means that she would not stand in the way of such fortune as God had sent you. She has no home of her own, and she would not become a nun. There is no place left in the world for such a one, and we did not delay her going, as it was what she wished."

"In the name of God, which way did she go?"

"Towards the sea."

He went, and searched every shore, asked everyone he met to spread word. Had she so doubted him? He feared that it was true; he had been sullen, churlish, lecherous once, unconscious for the rest; only now he knew he loved her. If there was no future in the world for her, what of him, lacking her? The Grand Master had plans to build a new capital; he would not wait to see it, with its streets at right angles, running straight, from Mount Sciberras where the Turkish guns had once sited themselves to flay St. Elmo. He would not wait, if Fiammetta's bones were soon to become bleached coral, drifting with the sea. He had his own land, his own Queen to return to; it was probable that Mary Stuart needed a sword-arm. In the end, for lack of better fortune, he would go; and divide his life between the bare house which had belonged to those of his name, the wildfowl in the marshes, the hares on the hills. That would only be for a little space, for there was trouble in Scotland; in three years' time Anthony Graham would lay down his life for Queen Mary at Langside, and his soul be free.

Fiammetta had found a boat and had rowed herself out by night beyond the Gozo strait. When she was far enough out to sea she would take to the water and swim, knowing that help was too far away to save her, knowing that even she could not master the leagues of sea. The night had stars and no moon, the kind of night they had been used to take for freeing prisoners from the galleys. The velvet of the dark encompassed her round, caressing her as the water would soon do; sky and sea were her familiars.

Was she a sinner? The priests would say it was sinful to take life, even one's own. Her own mother had disdained to take her life. But for what purpose should she herself live? She had accomplished what she had set out to do, avenged her mother and father, and had found love and denied it; it would not come again. Anthony must be made safe in the Order, governed so that to his life was added lustre and distinction; he could not live it out with her as his mistress without soiling himself and her, and he had never spoken to her of marriage. Yet she had loved him so greatly that lacking him now she lacked everything; except this, the caress of the dark and the water. She shipped the oars, let the boat glide and began, swiftly, to divest herself of her clothes. She had come naked to the island, and naked would leave it. When it came to the ring on her finger, though, she would not take it off; it was all she had of memory. For instants she took leave of the world of the senses; hearing the slap of water against the boat's sides, the faint sounds of movement and life on the island's shores. If there were to be punishment for this sin of hers, surely it could take no worse form than to live, and to hear nothing any more. And Anthony? Would they meet again?

She stood poised and naked in the boat, a slip of white flesh against the sky and water; then she dived, the silken coolness greeting her thankfully, as though it were a bed.

Next day, the boat was found on Gozo, and lying within it Fiammetta's clothes and her cloak.

Thirty-four

The roses at Belland bloomed and died, and each day Isabella Bainbridge would go out with a flat wicker basket to cut the dead heads with gardening-scissors. Sometimes Fiona watched her grandmother's gloved hands at work; she herself was possessed of a curious lassitude, not even grieving for the roses. Sometimes Isabella would take her to the great kitchen with its scrubbed deal table and newly-blacked range, and let her watch the petals being packed and dried in salt. Soon they would be ready to make up into sachets to freshen the linen-cupboard or scent the air from a repoussé silver box in the great drawing-room. But Fiona was seldom in the drawing-room, and never when callers came; then, she was taken back into the care of Lily Soames and left to amuse herself with the crayons and drawing-blocks which had been sent on by Juliana. She did not try to portray Belland with its ridiculous tower; instead she once tried to draw Mdina, the walled city with towers and flat roofs golden in the sun, and beneath it pumpkins ripening on the farmhouses, green and striped and orange. She remembered these clearly, but other things were vague; coming to her in voices, as in dreams.

She could remember some of the voices, telling her Toni and Bianca had a fine son; that Yaya's babies were grown into mischievous boys who never left their mother in peace a moment of the day, and who would climb the tree in the courtyard and try to shake its blossom to the ground. She could see the tree dark against the wall, and the fallen blossom lying on the stone; but could not draw it. Other things she remembered could not be put down; Lily Soames watched always, and Fiona began to feel that she herself was a prisoner, watched and hustled out of sight. Where was Chuli? Chuli never came to see her. And that other ...

Once she had news of his death. She could see him lying on a steep hill, among other dead men in armour. That day she had hammered on the door and called his name.

"Anthony! Anthony! Anthony!"

Lily Soames had come forward and had laid her hand over Fiona's mouth. Fiona struggled, and bit it. After that Lily wore a bandage over her hand, and was careful not to touch Fiona. She hates me, the girl thought; she is glad of whatever is going to happen.

For she knew that her body was changing, that nowadays she could not have it laced tightly, that her waist was thick and her steps heavy. When she went out of doors they put a cloak on her; this was welcome, as it was growing cold.

"If it happens again it might be heard by anyone," said Isabella to her husband. Juliana's brave lie about the man on the Green, perhaps only half believed, had been shattered by Fiona's crying of her lover's name. "The servants ... it must not become a matter of gossip. She had best go to this Irish house Agnes spoke of; there it will not matter."

Timothy was silent. He was loath to believe the truth about Anton Muntz. Agnes never came to Belland to see her daughter; it was being left, all of it, to Isabella and himself. He looked at his wife with affection and anxiety; the strain of the girl's condition was beginning to tell on Isabella, who was fragile and must not be given additional burdens. He would speak to Julius about the passage to Ireland, and the women could make arrangements for Fiona's stay there. Lily Soames must make the journey across and then return to her mother. It was probable that Fiona need not come back; Juliana now, understandably, did not see her, and no one else cared; certainly not the girl's mother. Timothy thrust away the thought he had that Agnes had become a cold and selfish woman, and said, "She must not be left with you longer. The *Queen* can take her across." Anton had helped design the new paddle-ferry, which made revolutionary speed. It was fitting that his mistress should embark on it to bear her child far away from Belland.

Then he told himself that he was growing bitter and vengeful; the young man had not been able to lead a satisfactory married life with Juliana since her miscarriage.

Fiona knew that they were taking her on a journey. She

watched Lily Soames, her hand still clumsy, pack her things; the brass-bound trunk which contained her gowns was locked and bolted, and the coachman and one of the gardeners came to carry it away.

Fear took her, she who had never been afraid. What was to happen to her? Where was Anthony? She remembered that, this time, he had been her lover; she had not denied herself to him again. But that was long ago, and now they would not let her see him. She had no defence against them; they had brought her into this house, away from him. Now—

The parting came. The carriage was brought and she and Lily put into it; Timothy would accompany them to the ferry. He took his place, grave in his tall hat and overcoat, a thin old man, the fire in him subdued. Fiona looked at him, remembering how he had taken her on his arm to show her the paintings and there had come that terrible recognition of the St. Elmo bodies floating across the bay to Birgù. She had been ill after that, she thought; everything had changed. Now her grandmother put up her face to kiss her farewell, blue eyes anxious and sad. Her lips were moving; of what use when she herself could hear nothing of any farewell?

The horses took off, and Belland with its tower, and the rose-gardens, was soon out of sight. They were to take the long journey up to town to embark on the Irish ferry. Country sights, fields and cows and grey stone cottages, gave place to grim warehouses and terraced streets. The sky was grey; it would rain, perhaps, on the crossing. She saw Timothy make courteous talk with Lily Soames, who sat by her like a wardress. Her own eyes sought Timothy's as if for help; but he would not look at her.

Terror took her. They were sending her somewhere which was not Chuli's house, nor the house she had lived in before with Mama and the rest. They were taking her somewhere far away, removing her from Anthony.

Where was he? Why had he not come to her again? They had lain close so often these past months that she must surely be a part of him as he was of her. The thought that she might never see him again came, and terrified her. Surely God, her fair-haired mother's God Who had died to save men, could not be so cruel?

Then she saw Anton. He was standing among the small

crowd on the pier that admitted passengers to the great new paddle-ferry. Bright with fresh paint and slender lines she stood, her promised speed due to the new alloy that would permit steam to rush through the pipes faster than ever before. Anton was more now than a part of Bainbridge's; he, not Julius, was its heir now Timothy grew old. Had he come to see the new ferry take off? Had he come to say goodbye to her, Fiona? Chuli was on his arm. She was wrapped warmly against the cold winds. She was smaller than Anton, just reaching his shoulder.

Lily escorted Fiona on board. She had not been allowed to go near Anton and Chuli. A press of people was about them, and one could sense the excitement that accompanies a ship about to get up speed. A throbbing came from the engines. Fiona felt it, though she could not hear it. The men began to unloop the coils of cable from the derricks on the pier.

The ship began to move; the great paddles heaved, then gained momentum. Left behind, on Chuli's arm, Anton removed his tall hat, leaving his dark hair to be ruffled by the breeze. He knew, then, that she was going away, and had done nothing. Chuli lifted her small gloved hand, and waved. That was all. They were gone from her. Anton belonged to Chuli. There was no one for her, Fiona, in all the world.

She felt the ship pulling out into the river. Presently the water changed from brackish grey, as it had been near the pier, to a cool colour, as it had been ... when? As it had been on a myriad days and nights when she had slipped into it as a welcoming element, like coming home.

She drew away from Lily Soames and made her way over to where the new paddles whirled, sending jets of water back between their sharp blades. She stood for a time, staring down at the ruffled water as the ferry made her way out to sea. Anton had made this ship which was carrying her away. What was it that told her so, when she knew nothing of that part of his life?

And it had happened before. Once long ago, as now, she had known that she could not have Anthony for her own, must not spoil his life and what he wished to make of it without her. It had happened again, that was all. She would choose a moment when no one watched, not even Lily, and then ...

The moment came. Lily was busied with finding the baggage. No one watched Fiona, no one eyed her as she slipped over the rail to where swift death waited in the flailing paddles below. When Lily turned, it had happened. Fiona had gone; the water received her, as it had done before. Passengers screamed. The ferry ploughed on, then stopped, and her paddles backed with all the tensile strength of Anton's alloy. But it was too late.

Thirty-five

"You must not blame yourself," said Juliana. "Thank God it was quickly over. The paddles—"

She shuddered, almost putting herself on a par with the white-faced man in the chair. He had flung himself down on their return home, not eating, for a long time not speaking to her. Now, he answered.

"How can I do otherwise than blame myself? But for me, she would be here, well, happy enough, troubling nobody. Now there is scandal and pain and death. Indeed, I blame myself; I am her murderer."

"No, Anton; I am."

"You?"

"It was I who persuaded you to come to see her off, thinking that to be forever among strange faces, poor Fiona, might be less bitter if we had waved her farewell. And I—I wanted her to know that I did not hate her." The last was said in a small voice, like that of a child. Anton raised his face from his hands, and looked at her with the expression of a man awakened from sleep. How many men had wives who, in this situation, would be as understanding as Juliana? Some women would have forgiven, it was true, as she had done; but would never have understood.

He remembered the mangled body they had brought down the gangway at last under a canvas cloth; the blood seeped through the canvas, staining it, and the dripping of sea-water had not ceased from her clothes. He had not looked upon her face, had not dared do so. Now she was buried, with all the trappings of funerals. His life could go on outwardly as it had done, working successfully at the yards, designing his ships and ferries, becoming an acknowledged authority on certain alloys, certain formulae. A machine might do as much: he could become one. But within himself he knew that he would always have this sense of dread, this last failure of all.

"Will you not eat something?" said Juliana gently. "I can have them bring up a tray of light supper, a little cold chicken, some wine. You must not be ill, Anton. If you live as you are doing you will become ill indeed, and it would break my heart."

"Your heart is too good for such as I am."

"Anton! There has been misfortune; others have it, perhaps not in such a form. Never think I do not know the trial it must have been to—to have Fiona in the house, when I—That was stupid of me, perhaps; I should have left her with Papa and Mama. But she was so lonely, and no one cared for her."

"You loved her, Julie. You were always kind to her. Never reproach yourself; reproach me, if you must."

He got up and began to turn about the room. She watched him, uncertain whether or not to order the light food she had suggested. His face was haggard, like a much older man's; he had lost the tautness his movements ordinarily possessed, as though a coiled spring were behind the power: now the spring was broken. If I knew what would restore him, she thought, I would bring it; anything, even a woman from the streets. She loved him enough for that, she knew; nothing would grieve her or shock her again, if it would make him well.

She said "I had perhaps best reproach myself, for it was I brought you to this disaster."

"No. It was decided long before you were born, or I. It is a thing of fate. You know I told you of it before. No matter what I do that will follow me always; twice I failed her and caused her to take her own life. What am I? No name is too bad, no slander too black for me. They will be talking now, perhaps, at the yards. It will not have gone unremarked that she lived in my house, then left it. Tongues will not be idle. Your father knows; I can tell it in his manner. As for the Old Man, I have not been alone with him since it happened. I do not know if I can ever be alone with him again."

"Would you be happier if we left here, went back perhaps to Germany?" she said softly. "Or there is America, where we were happy and made friends. We are young, Anton. In time perhaps I can bear you children. There is no need to stay where you imagine you are—talked of. With your skills, we need not beg for a living." She smiled a little; her lips were stiff, as if they had not smiled for long. She smoothed her black dress nervously. Would he respond to the suggestion that they go away? But he was shaking his head, silently. "It will make no difference," he said presently. "I am what I am, and have been."

"Anton—" She did not take time to think whether or not she was relieved not to have to travel to a far country, away from her kindred, her friends. "I am stupid," she said, "but I have always thought that when a bad thing happens, it is of ño use to hide it away in one's mind. It is better—you know how we have talked—to bring it out into the light, and face it; then sometimes it turns out to be other than we have feared, perhaps even a blessing. Oh, I do not explain myself well, for I never could. But if you feel that you must go back to the beginning, to the place you were in the last time, where you knew her—to go back—"

He looked at her, and something that had been dead in his eyes returned to life. He stood up and went to the bookcase, where a long dark atlas lay on the shelves. He came to the table and spread it out, opening it at the index, running his finger down the lines. She was glad for him; to see him occupied, no matter with what, might relieve the blackness of despair in him, might restore him partly to himself. Presently he spoke. "I am looking for a name," he said.

"Malta?" She could not tell how she knew; perhaps he had spoken of it.

"Valetta. That is what they called the new capital city. The old was shot to ruins."

"And you will go there, Anton?"

He did not answer directly, or look at her. "Will you come?"

She was wise. "No. You must go alone, and—and find out what to do next and where to go. It may be that you will not want me as part of your life any more. You are free to do as you wish."

"Juliana—"

"Do not say anything now, till you have decided. Make your travelling-plans, find out when you may leave. Tell Grandfather you are taking a holiday; you have had none this year. You are—" she made herself smile—"a director; surely you may please yourself?"

After he had gone she would succumb to her own private agony. There was no one to whom she could talk, and unburden herself; it would not be believed, such a tale, and they would only think her deluded by him when she knew it was the truth. ... And friends outside the family must not know, and within the circle was no comfort. The tale of the man on the Green had been tacitly accepted as a suitable explanation of Fiona's pregnancy; no alternative would be entertained. Julius had forbidden mention of Fiona's name in his house, that had once so grudgingly sheltered her. What he, or any of them, would think of Anton's departure Juliana did not know; she must think of the right answers when they questioned her.

Would he ever come back? Had she lost him forever? What would become of her own life if he never re-entered it? But to have him imprisoned here by a possessive wife, forging chains of family, friends, reputation, would not have kept him hers. She would wait, for as long as it was necessary, perhaps for all her days; but she would wait.

He stood on the place where, three centuries ago, guns had been sited to fire on St. Elmo.

He saw the rebuilt, star-shaped Fort, as he had seen many other things which had changed very little with time; the crowding *faldettas* in the market-places and churches, and one thing which was new to him; the great Co-Cathedral of St. John where he had gone down to the crypt which held La Valette's tomb.

"Leave me for a little while," he had said to the guide, who left his lantern. Anton was left alone with the silence and the memorials to those two lifelong friends and allies; La Valette with his carved effigy on the tomb, and a plain slab, nearby on the floor, commemorating Sir Oliver Starkey. The friends had been close in life and were so in death.

But there was no message for him here. He took the lantern and mounted the steps again, to be accosted by a beggar woman. "Sir, I am very poor ... "

He gave her a coin, and allowed himself to be taken through the great church with its baroque memorials to later Grand Masters, its statues and busts in marble and bronze. Outside, the streets of La Valette's precisely planned capital were thronged with careless happy people. He went out into the sunlight among them. It was as he remembered, shadows contrasting sharply on surfaces of soft yellow stone. But he knew no one here.

He travelled to the uplands of the island, and saw crops growing in the earth which had been unloaded by Nelson's navy to spread on the bare rock. But cactus-plant was everywhere, as he remembered well; and thin ragged sheep.

He was assailed by a sense of deep personal loss. Nowhere, neither here nor anywhere in the world now, was there anything to remind him of Fiammetta. She had gone, as Fiona had gone, into the depths of the tideless sea; a sea older than history, a sea called Tethys, which had once covered half the world.

He went down to the shore, staring at Gozo across the strait. This was—he remembered it—where she had gone out by boat, and had not come back. He would not go across to Gozo to ask questions that were futile after so long. It was here, on Malta, that he and she had fought and disputed and loved, and failed one another; now, there was nothing for him, neither word nor sign.

He went to the sea's edge and observed the crisping of little shells along the water's rim. He bent and picked one up; so fragile, yet able to withstand the wildest storms. He let it lie in his hand, seeing the pink and mauve colours in it. Once a living creature had inhabited it. Once the sea had contained all those who lived and ruled before man came; great snails, whorled and drifting shapes, unknown now.

An object lay in the sand; out of curiosity he stooped and picked it up. Suddenly a great sensation of shock, of joy, went through him. It was green with age, eaten by sea-salt, brought back to him on the drifting of the waters year after year, so that now, in this instant, he possessed it. She had sent it to him at this moment: he had no doubt of that.

He rubbed at it with his finger; presently the Jewel of Barbarossa shone again, clear fire in the day. The engravings on the ring were half obliterated. He stood there, oblivious of the water creaming about his feet.

He slid the ring on his finger. Did she see him do so,

wherever she was? Had she meant to free him, as Juliana had done, left him to his own choice of a life?

For love set the beloved free.

He made his way back to his hotel, which was not too clean and troubled by flies. He sat down at the marble-topped table in his room and took a pen in his hand. He knew what to say. He addressed it to Juliana at their own home, so far away, across sea and land. She would hardly receive it before he himself joined her. He had made his choice. He gazed at the shining Jewel on his finger and clearly, calmly wrote the words he would say to his wife.

My dear,
I am coming home.